Praise for Alan Gullette

Alan Gullette's remarkable gift for finding exactly the right word for the right place, his scintillating use of symbol and metaphor, and the keenness of his insight into the fundamental weirdness of everyday life should give him high rank among modern poets. It would be impossible for him to write anything unpoetical. . . . [He is] worthy to carry the torch of Californian imaginative poetry.   —S. T. JOSHI

Your short novels are distinctive; the style, rhetoric, and general presentation are yours *and* are modern. Again, they are quietly, or modestly, distinctive; they are entertaining.   —DONALD SIDNEY-FRYER

Your poems manage to capture those carefree moments of transport that occur all too rarely after childhood—the rapture, beatitude and ecstasy of simply being alive. Reading your poems gives me flashbacks to the times when I was tripping in fields of wildflowers, or in forests, with a dryad by my side.
—KEITH ALLEN DANIELS

It is a thinking poet who can take the material of the ancient world—of Mayan ruins or the Seal of Solomon—& make them into modern hymns of angst & love & unease. If you awake in the middle of the night overcome with a terror that you have no purpose, that nothing has purpose, you could do worse than to read such things as 'Lizard Life' . . . to reassure yourself, at least, that even in a pessimistic hour there's something to be said for being right.   —JESSICA AMANDA SALMONSON

Marvellous . . . amazingly clever . . .Incredibly limpid. Really very astonishing and profound, with magnificent imagery. You are one of my favorite modern poets.   —ROBERT TEMPLE

"The Green Transfer" has about it . . .the genuine feel of a dream . . . a feeling of strangeness . . . You have a dreamlike voice all your own that would be difficult to mimic.   —KENNETH W. FAIG, JR.

These stories hint at much more than they actually describe. Both poetic and intriguing, the latter being difficult to maintain in poetry alone . . .
—HARRY O. MORRIS

Intimations of Unreality

Also By the Author

49 Pieces. Oakland, CA: Corelli Press, July 2005.

Acts of Love. With art by Norm Rosenberger. Oakland, CA: Elephant Printing, 2003.

Another Eucharist. With art by Michael Perkin. Oakland, CA: Elephant Printing, April 1995.

A Book of Dreams. Oakland, CA: Corelli Press, August 2006.

Edge of Meaning: Essays and Escapades. Oakland, CA: Corelli Press, in preparation.

From a Safe Distance. San Francisco, CA: Anamnesis Press, March 2000.

Mind Aflame, Heart of Green Wood: Recollected Works. Oakland, CA: Corelli Press, in preparation.

Odd Tales. Oakland, CA: Corelli Press, June 2002.

Twenty-Seven Liqueurs. Oakland, CA: Corelli Press, December 2006.

Alan Gullette

Intimations of Unreality

‡ weird fiction & poetry

Hippocampus Press

New York

Acknowledgments: see p. 383.

Published by Hippocampus Press
P.O. Box 641, New York, NY 10156.
http://www.hippocampuspress.com

Cover design by Barbara Briggs Silbert.
Hippocampus Press logo designed by Anastasia Damianakos.

First Edition
1 3 5 7 9 8 6 4 2

ISBN13: 978-1-61498-040-7

To Donald Sidney-Fryer

"There is nothing that is new beneath the moon of sorcerers,
even more than under the sun of sages."
—Éliphas Lévi, *The History of Magic*

Contents

Gullette's Ritual

You think it's tough to get Lovecraftian fiction published nowadays? Do you bemoan the fact that so much of our stuff cannot seem to attain escape velocity and touch down on the distant planet of major house publication? Why are we relegated to the small presses? In one sense, that is, I think, an optical illusion. We live in a period of marketing evolution. Like TV, publishing is increasingly a matter of "narrowcasting," niche marketing, something newly and powerfully viable (and thus "respectable") because of the new, superior means of production. Even the once despicable practices of vanity and subsidy publishing have donned crisp new robes of respectability, and rightly so. Private individuals can produce real books, quality books, and not necessarily because no one else will touch them. No, authors often self-publish these days so they may reap more of a harvest from their work. Technology, as it always does, has changed everything.

Plus, Cthulhu fiction has matured. No longer are we forced to choose between pointless pastiche that verges unwittingly upon parody, ridiculing the authors whom one seeks to emulate, and "new wave" fiction that salutes our favorite old authors by invoking their names in modern and profane contexts they never would have recognized. No, nowadays there are a number of authors (Laird Barron, Cody Goodfellow, Michael Cisco, Joe Pulver) who work wonders in a feat of genuine evolution. Lovecraft, in their hands, has undergone the transformation from human to Deep One. Something genuinely new and newly horrific. And the small press, newly vibrant, creates high-quality volumes rivaling or surpassing the "pros."

But it was not always thus, as the older codgers among you know all too well. During the Lovecraft Boom of the 1970s, probably occasioned by the Ballantine Books paperback reprints of Lovecraft (you know, the ones with the creepy covers showing leering, screaming faces with their skulls penetrated by spikes or dissolving or melting), there was an expected flood of Lovecraftian fan fiction and fanzines, many of them pretty miserable-looking. But that very fact spoke well of their editors and publishers, for it was pretty much the only venue available. You did what you could. Sure, there was Arkham House, but August Derleth passed away in 1971, and the throne was usurped by the worst possible candidate for editor of Arkham House, Jim Turner, a man who possessed no sympathy for the kind of fiction which had provided the rationale for Arkham House to begin with. So Cthulhu fiction went begging. Where else could you publish it but in amateur press fanzines? Soon there were a few mags like Eldritch Tales, Beyond the Dark Gateway, and Etchings & Odysseys, but these displayed little editorial sense of the difference between fan fiction and what "fanfic" aspired to be. Even good material suffered, in these pages, from guilt by association with bad company. But this was about the only place you could hunt for new gems amid the rubbish (fun though the "rubbish" often was, in its own way!). Who knew when you might stumble upon a T.E.D. Klein, a Thomas Ligotti—or an Alan Gullette?

I have always believed that a group of these writers, especially in the early 70s, were born out of time and never quite found proper publication and as a result remained hidden to subsequent generations of Lovecraftians who would have enjoyed their work. Gary Myers managed to escape obscurity by virtue of his overlapping with August Derleth's version of Arkham House. Ross Bagby and James Wade not so much. John Glasby, through no fault of his own, just missed the hellbound train. And so did Gullette. His "Derrick's Ritual," for example, should have appeared in the pages of The Arkham Sampler or in a collection like The Dark Brotherhood or Dark Things. But no luck. An accident of history. Strange aeons indeed.

This is why I have for some time believed that today's readers deserve the chance to enjoy Alan Gullette's work. His Lovecraftian tales, I'd say, fall into the parameters of classic Lovecraft-Derleth-Kuttner-Bloch pastiche. That is, it works. It is the real stuff, the kind we are only too glad to have a little more of. In these particular stories we do not yet see the transformation into the kind of thing being written so well today, nor do we want to. My theory is that writing pastiche, the good as well as the bad, is in essence a matter of rereading one's favorites by dint of rewriting them. Yes, the product is largely familiar, but we want it to be. It is like the ritual repetition of comforting but also challenging litanies. Alan Gullette is like the black-robed celebrant of a blasphemous mass, leading us ever deeper along the well-trod paths of damnation. We know the way. "Brothers, we are treading where the saints[?] have trod." It is more of the good stuff, just as John Jakes said about his wonderful Brak the Barbarian stories, which were basically Conan pastiches. Why write more of the old-style stuff? Simply because there isn't enough of it! And we have Alan Gullette to thank for bringing to us a new and heaping helping of these unholy viands!

Like many or most Lovecraftian scribes, Gullette has considerably expanded his skills and his repertoire, and you will read the proof of it here. But what do I know about that? Cthulhu Mythos tales and pulp fiction are my area, so, here, I'm sticking to that.

—ROBERT M. PRICE

May 10, 2012

INTIMATIONS OF UNREALITY

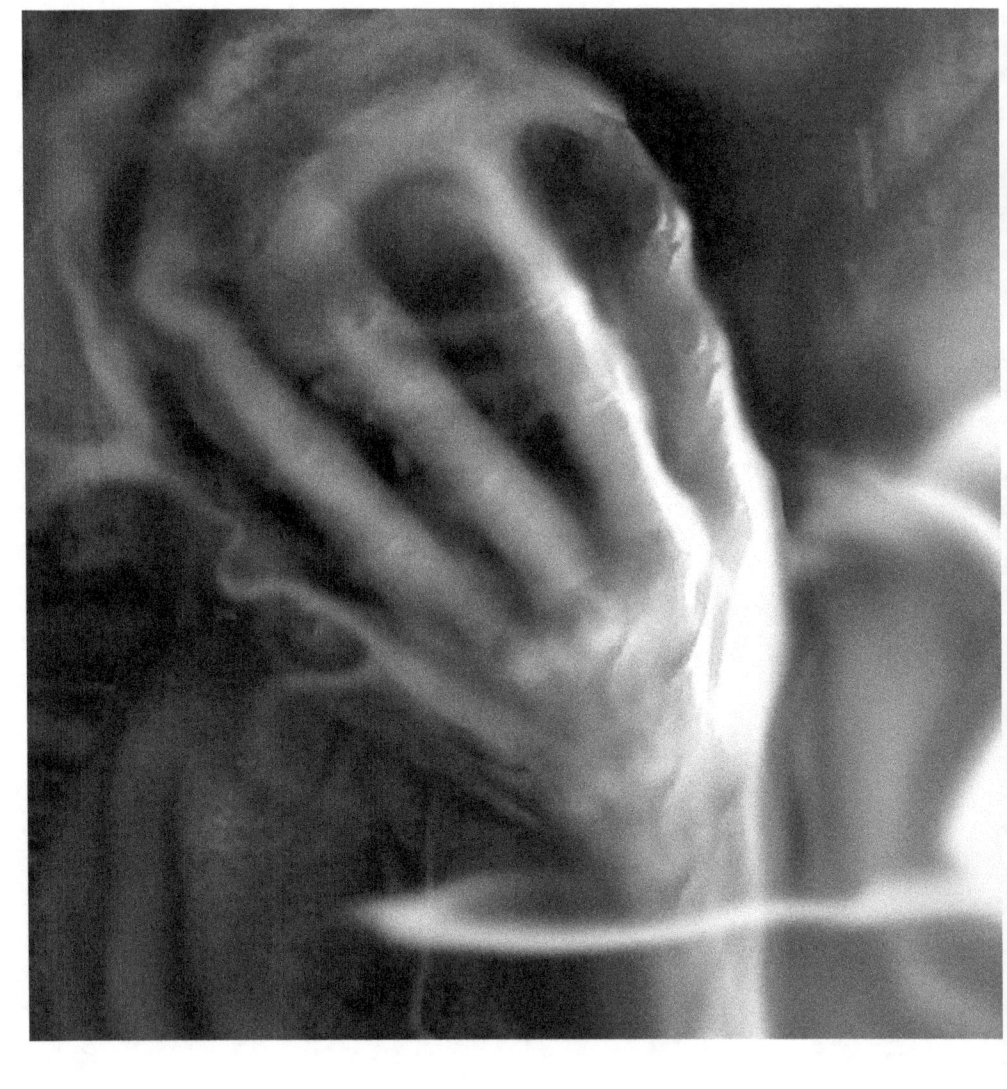

The Old Man up the Road

The autumn light was dimming when Ward Bowman finally found 13030 Rural Route 7 in Westchester County. He had been driving all day, having left the depot in Duane City before noon, and had stopped three times to get directions, which only led him back and forth between Aylesbury Road and Sumner Pike, crisscrossing back roads that the delivery van could barely navigate. Once, in frustration, he gunned the engine and sent gravel flying as he found himself heading once again back to the same main road, until he nearly skidded into a ditch when he braked at a sudden sharp turn. Finally, he saw a postal worker who gave him authoritative directions.

"It's up there on the ridge, up there," the man said, pointing to the eastern edge of the valley, "Must be five miles as the crow flies. It's not on my route, so I don't know the folks who live up there. But if you take this road back about three miles, you'll come to Four Corners . . ." and so on.

So Ward retraced his path three miles and found the junction, just as the letter carrier had said. He turned left and followed the road along the foot of the ridge in question, until he came to a clump of white mailboxes, across from a driveway that led up the wooded hillside and out of sight. He pulled the delivery van over at the foot of the drive and stopped the engine.

Thus, after a struggle, Ward had reached his goal, but in truth his journey was just beginning.

"Now, if I can only find Ephraim Wentworth . . ." he said aloud to himself, reading the name on the cold package as he pulled it from the cooler. Wrapped in plastic and marked "KEEP FROZEN" in large red letters, Ward had to wipe the frost off the label to read the exotic name.

First he crossed the road, empty in both directions, to look at the mailboxes. The large, single post bore the numbers 13030 in clear, reflective stickers, but the hand-painted surnames on the four boxes were largely worn away. The local carrier, no doubt, knew the names by heart.

"Hopefully it's the first house," Ward said, again to himself, as he re-crossed the silent road and started up the driveway, which was more like a dirt road partially reinforced with gravel.

After ascending a dozen steep feet, the drive leveled off and began to snake through the pines, which shed ample needles to cover much of the exposed dirt and soften the path.

The first house appeared out of the woods, its visage warmed by light from within, and Ward left the driveway to take the narrow concrete walk-way up to it—a snug cabin with smoke rising up from the chimney.

When he reached the door, Ward could hear music coming from in-side—what sounded like gypsy music, played on a screeching fiddle and an out-of-tune banjo. There were occasional thuds, as if someone where danc-ing, with occasional heavy steps or jumps, accompanied by little shouts or grunts, and hand-claps.

Ward knocked on the door and waited. The music stopped, replaced by a creepy silence filled with the chitter of waking crickets.

Beside the door was a window; the curtain moved—quickly—and moved back.

Finally the door opened, slowly, partially, and a woman came out—slid out sideways without opening the door all the way.

"Yes?" the middle-aged woman said. She was dressed in quaint clothes that reminded Ward of early American or Puritan clothing.

"Hello, I have a package for a Mr. . . . uh, Ephraim Wentworth," he said, wiping away the frost again to refer to the odd name.

"Who?"

"Ephraim Wentworth—Eff-ray-em—am I saying that right? 13030 Rural Route 7?"

"Oh, you mean the old man up the road." She said, amid muffled voices from behind the door. "Would you like to come in?" she asked, eyeing the package.

He was taken aback by the invitation, given her otherwise secretive be-havior.

"Well, is he here?" Ward asked, thinking to himself, "Why else would they ask?"

"No, he's at home—up the road. But we're just setting down to a home-cooked meal, if you're hungry." She looked him over, as if his hunger were visible in his slim figure.

Again he was taken aback by the offer, but decided that hospitality must be a tradition among these back-country folk.

"Well, thank-you, but no, Ma'am, I need to keep on my delivery schedule," he said, "but thanks for the offer," and he backed away politely.

At the drive, he looked back, but the woman was gone and the door had closed. He heard something though: laughter—the laughter of several people, accented by hoots. Then the music resumed, the screeching and twanging now enjoined by a howling voice that rose and fell in an odd key.

Gradually the music died away as Ward continued along the drive. It was getting dark, now, and again the noise of the crickets filled the silence.

He came to the second house, actually a double-wide trailer set up on cement blocks. Looking up through the window and open door, he could see odd paintings on the walls—dark visions and nightscapes, naively painted buildings whose odd angles made them tangle with the branches of nearby trees; dim figures that seemed to move in the dark spaces between high walls, their features emerging and fading away in the inscrutable darkness.

A man came to the open door. Though youthful of face, his white hair and jaundiced eyes belied his age. He wore denim overalls, hung on worn blue straps slung over his shoulders and buttoned in brass. His agrarian habit seemed incongruous with a taste in art, however naïvely executed.

The old man looked at Ward, then at the package.

"Is that for me?" he asked.

"Are you Mr. Wentworth?" Ward asked, hopeful of having found his man.

"Who?" came the owl-like reply.

"Ephraim Wentworth, 13030 Rural Route 7."

"Oh, you mean the old man up the road." He said, unaware of the irony; for he himself seemed quite old.

"If you want, you can come in, and I'll go get him. He's just up the road," he offered, eyeing the package again.

"No, that's not necessary, but thanks anyway," Ward said, thinking to himself, "Hospitable almost to a fault . . ."

Though his trip was getting longer—a short walk becoming a hike—he was glad he had not brought the van up the long driveway. By now, it was not traversable, due to deep ruts cut in the red soil, crevasses of earth clotted with thick grass and pine needles.

He came to the third house, a dilapidated building that looked abandoned save for a bright outdoor lamp, which flooded a front yard accented with a variety of marble ornaments. The woods were getting thicker, crowding around the old structure, but this area was kept clear.

In response to Ward's knock, an ancient woman came to the door and opened it. Standing in the darkness within, she was almost invisible in contrast to the bright floodlight outside.

"Is that for me?" she asked, seeing the package.

"It's for Ephraim Wentworth," Ward said matter-of-factly, assuming the worst.

"Who?" came the now-familiar reply. "Oh, you mean the old man up the road—"

"Thanks," said Ward, cutting her off brusquely and walking away.

The chirruping of crickets filled the night, blotting out all sounds except the occasional snapping of twigs underfoot.

Ward came to the fourth and final house on the long drive, just a shack with a stove pipe sticking up. By this time, the package was beginning to defrost and was wet to the touch. An old man was visible through the window, moving about a table; he was setting the table for dinner, placing cutlery next to china that shone in candlelight.

Ward went up to the shack and knocked, rapping carefully with his knuckle on the rough-hewn wood planks that made up the door.

The old man came to the door and opened it, and Ward could see how really, incredibly old he looked—age-marked skin stretched taut against his skull, sagging over tendon and sinew in his throat. One eye seemed to sparkle with life, with glee, while the other was clouded with glaucoma.

"Yes?" the old man asked, curling his lips back in a friendly smile that revealed empty spaces between rotten teeth.

"Mr. Wentworth?" Ward asked with renewed hope. "Ephraim Wentworth?"

"Yes, I am Ephraim Wentworth."

"OK, great! I have this package for you . . ."

They both looked at it for a moment, and in the silence came the dripping of drops from the package onto the front step.

"Just a moment," the old man said, opening the door wide. "Won't you come in?"

"Said the spider to the fly . . ." thought Ward, but he went in anyway.

"Having a dinner party?" he asked, counting six settings at the dinner table.

The old man pulled a rope, ringing a bell somewhere above the house. Once, twice, three times . . .

"Yes, *we're* having a dinner party." The old man said with a smile, and turned his gaze out the window.

Ward turned and looked too, and saw all the neighbors coming up the drive.

"And you're just in time!" the old man said, taking the melting package from Ward's numb fingers.

The Admiral's Tale

"There's an aerial shot of the whole atoll," said the admiral, pointing at the first of the photographs lining the wall of the narrow hallway. He craned his head back to look though the lower half of his bifocals, and the torque on his larynx added an even higher pitch to his aging voice.

"It's actually made up of dozens of coral islets surrounding the lagoon, and Bikini Island is this little one here . . ." He pointed to the right edge of the atoll. "Only two and a half miles long, not too far from the channel or opening to the lagoon. This side was shunned." He said, pointing to the left side, and cleared his throat. "The islanders never went near it."

The shadow of a cloud fell over the western half of the atoll and obscured the details in the already-grainy photograph.

"Here's the flag of Bikini—mocked up just in time for the tests. The Marshallese words read, 'Everything is in the hands of God.'"

I was interviewing the admiral in the course of research I have been conducting on the so-called Atomic Veterans—U.S. servicemen and women who had been exposed to radiation during nuclear weapons tests conducted in the 1940s and 1950s. My work was funded only in part by a grant from the Institute for Policy Studies, so I had traveled across the country on a shoestring budget consisting largely of my own money. Aided by the Freedom of Information Act, I had obtained a list of surviving vets with their last-known addresses and sent them questionnaires about their involvement with the tests, their exposure, and their health. When the retired admiral responded and indicated his willingness to answer follow-up questions, I contacted him immediately, due to his high rank.

We moved on to the next item on the wall.

"There's me and some of the guys in front of The Cross Spikes Club, which was the closest thing we had to bar on Bikini Island. They even had a ping pong table." He seemed to be nostalgic, wistful for a moment.

"This was in 1946?" I asked.

"Yes, from March through June, I guess, during Operation Crossroads. Of course, it's all gone now—blown to smithereens!"

The uniforms were not uniform, so to speak, and I asked about it.

"That's right, this was Joint Task Force One, the first time the Navy and Army worked together after the war. Men from every branch of the armed services ended up at the club, including Army Air Forces (as it was called then), Marines, and of course intelligence. There was some inter-service rivalry, as you'd expect, but also camaraderie. It was a great place to rub elbows, and you heard the most amazing things.

"Of course, the war had just ended in '45, so a lot of guys were being decommissioned, but some of them signed up for an extra year for the privilege of seeing an atom bomb go off in front of their eyes."

He shuffled over to the next photo, craned his head back, and jutted out his chin. I noticed several small cuts where he had shaved too close—and stubble where he had not shaved close enough.

"That's the USS Nevada, the target ship for test Abel. She was the first battleship to have 'all or nothing' armor, you know, and had a distinguished career. They anchored her in the lagoon, just three miles from the beach at Bikini, in the center of dozens of vessels of various classes. All of them were loaded with test equipment, plants and insects, animals . . . and so forth. As you see, they painted her bright orange with white guns, to make a pretty target for the bombardier, who had to pick it out from the other ships all clustered at the edge of the lagoon. Funny, though, he still missed his target by 1800 feet! But you know what they say . . ."

He leered at me sideways, at an angle that seemed painful.

"What's that?" I asked.

"'Close doesn't count—except in horseshoes and hand grenades . . . *and atom bombs!*'"

He enjoyed a gleeful laugh and I chuckled along to be a good guest, though I had never heard the phrase. His laughter turned into a fit of coughing and we paused a minute before moving on to the next photograph: an atomic detonation with the familiar mushroom-shaped cloud.

"That was it—Test Able, the first bomb, dropped by a B-29 and detonated 500 feet in the air—over the wrong ship. They actually investigated it afterwards, because it threw off a lot of calculations; but they blamed it on a sticky rudder rather than the crew."

"How big was the bomb?"

"23 kilotons, compared to 15 at Hiroshima and Nagasaki. So it was big, or bigger, but nothing like what came after . . . Here's the second blast, Test Baker, same size," he said, pointing to the next photo, where a semispherical dome of water rose up, twenty miles wide.

"This one made a bigger splash because it was detonated underwater, suspended by cables beneath an LSM (an amphibious assault ship) that had earned a battle star at Iwo Jima. This was the first underwater test of any nuclear weapon, and the blast bubble was so big it picked up whole destroyers and turned them on end, like toy boats in a bathtub. It was really impressive . . ."

He looked longingly at the photo, which he must have seen a thousand times before. It was a proud look, like a hunter with a snapshot of his kill; but it was also a stern look, a fearful look, and he tore his gaze away.

"Here, let's have a seat so I can rest my old back. Yes, sit right there. I'm not a spry youngster like you, any more!" he said, falling stiffly back into his lounge chair with an "oomph!"

"Now, what was it you wanted to ask?"

"Well . . . first, what was your role in the tests?" I asked, setting my tape recorder on the coffee table that separated our chairs, and getting out my notebook and pen.

"I was a captain at the time, special assistant to Commodore Joe Winter during preparations for the tests. Basically, I oversaw the relocation of the natives from Bikini to the Rongerik atoll, 125 miles to the east; then I remained as the commodore's liaison during the tests. But before all that, I went to the island with the commodore to meet the king and obtain his willingness to relocate. Since Truman declared it a territory under the commodore's command, it was really a formality; but it was important for public relations to have their cooperation.

"Before I arrived on the island, I imagined it would be like Gauguin's paintings—you know, with lovely women, palm trees hung with coconuts, tropical sunsets—all the typical, romantic associations with the South Pacific. Well, the coconuts and sunsets were there, but the women were nothing like Gauguin's beautiful tanned maidens. They bore little resemblance to the Polynesians I had seen in Hawaii. Instead, if I may say, they were almost a throwback to Neanderthals, with small craniums, sloping foreheads, facial hair and large crooked teeth.

"The males did not exhibit the regressive trait as much as the females, but a few did. More importantly, a handful of children—one male and four females—had physical deformations that included thicker-than-normal eyelids that folded over at the corners, bulging eyes, and extraneous skin or webbing between fingers and toes. At first we thought it might be due to inbreeding— there were only 167 Bikinians at the time; but there were plenty of other isolated islands in the South Seas, and the trait was unknown thus far.

"So, I went with Commodore Winter to meet King Juda. (I know, we thought it was ironic, too, but that was his real name, not Judas but Juda). He was a fairly modern man, with short hair and a Japanese shirt. He had learned to operate under the Japanese, who annexed the Marshall Islands after the first World War and held them until we drove them out in 1945. The last five blew themselves up in a cave with a hand grenade, which made the islanders laugh and cheer. Now, we convinced King Juda that he and his people were like the chosen ones of the Bible, the Israelites who wandered in search of the Promised Land. In his case, the Promised Land was the Rongerik atoll. We gave him a couple cases of sardines and he bought our plan, lock stock and barrel.

"But that's not all . . . We came to verify . . . certain things, intelligence reports, a missing agent . . . there are some details I can't get into. But we knew, by late in '45, that something strange was going on there . . . The Japanese never noticed anything amiss—at least, there was no evidence of it; but the Navy detained some Japanese fishermen who reported seeing strange things . . . cited legends of sea monsters and walking fish, and weird lights at night over the lee side of the atoll, where some ancient ruins were known to be.

"But that was all hearsay; it proved nothing at all. More convincing were intelligence reports from the atoll itself, where agents had turned up real evidence, so the commodore sent a team to investigate, with me in command. We brought in several civilian scientists—anthropologists to work with the islanders and archaeologists to look at the ruins—and a medical crew as well.

"King Juda was familiar with me by now, and was happy to receive attention from our medicos, as several islanders were ill with a bug that was going around. While they were occupied with that, and the anthropologists worked on a census of the population, I took the archaeologists and a couple Marines to the lee side, to see for myself what I had previously seen only in dim photographs.

"We took a patrol vessel out of the lagoon and bore west to one of the islets on the shunned lee side. We came upon a small, windowless, wooden structure near the shore that my team identified as a common Tiki temple. Anchoring in a cove, we took a rowboat ashore and looked the site over for six hours, taking photos, making sketches, taking notes, making measurements. The next day, they went back and filmed the site and went inside the temple—crawled in through a small hatch door with cameras and flood lights hooked up to a generator. There were tall wood carvings that matched known Tiki statues (or "images"), but also hieroglyphic or pictographic carvings on stone platforms that were unlike anything the scientists had ever seen. In a nearby pit, they found half-burned palm logs and various bones—including both fish and human bones.

"Meanwhile, the anthropologists discovered signs of a cult that was developing among the young Bikini islanders, replacing their traditional sun god with an archetypal fish god similar to the Phoenician Dagon of ancient times.

"The scientists begged to return to the lee side for a third day, in order to spend more time investigating the unusual details of the site, but we were on a tight schedule. The islanders had only agreed in February to be moved; this was March; and the tests were planned for July."

"And you were there for the tests themselves?" I asked. The admiral's tale was fascinating, but I wanted to get to the point of my interview.

"Yes, after our work was done and the island was cleared, we moved to the support fleet, ten nautical miles away."

"Did you wear a radiation badge to measure your exposure?"

"No, not everybody had one, and I was exempt."

"But you remained far enough away . . . I mean, you didn't fly through the clouds like some did."

"No, that was done by remote control."

"Remote control?"

"Yes, the Army Air Forces had several pilots aboard an aircraft flying at a safe distance from the atoll, and they operated several planes set on autopilot, so they could fly them remotely through the atomic clouds and take readings.

"I had no idea they had that capability in 1946 . . ."

"Oh, yes. They used radio waves then, but now they have microwaves and who knows what else . . . But speaking of radiation, they took readings *before* the tests to establish the natural background radiation as a benchmark. They got mixed readings, some instruments read normal, others showed spikes of radiation in odd bands of extremely high frequency. They checked the instruments, but they were normal. Testing again, but with instruments connected to the instruments, so to speak, they noticed an odd phasing effect the engineers couldn't figure out. Eventually, they wrote it off to an unusual number of meteorite fragments in the area, which also produced strong magnetic fields."

"After the tests, the ships were boarded—weren't they still 'hot' with radiation?"

"Oh, yes. The Geiger men went in first to read the levels, but the ships had to be decontaminated between tests so they could get a new set of readings. So men were sent in, in shifts of only a couple hours, until the ships were clean. Problem was, after Baker, the water itself was contaminated; they tried bringing in clean seawater, but it soon became contaminated as well. Finally, they scrubbed Test Charlie because there were no clean ships to test with; a lot of them were sunk in the harbor, or hauled out to sea and sunk."

"But you, yourself, were not exposed."

"Well, Test Baker went wrong . . . Remember, it was the first underwater test, and they didn't know what it might do. The Able airburst just bounced off the atoll and went up fairly clean, without fallout. But Baker contaminated millions of gallons of water and brought up millions of tons of coral and sand from the lagoon bottom."

"And all that was radioactive."

"Of course, highly radioactive, and the winds blew it onto neighboring islands—including Rongerik, where we had just moved the Bikinians; and Eniwetok, where the JTF1 was headquartered and a lot of scientists were observing the tests. For reasons I won't get into, I was there for the second test and got a good dose along with everyone else."

"And your health? Let's see, on the questionnaire you wrote . . ." and I began flipping through my papers.

"No problems until a year ago, when they found cancer . . . Inoperable—it's spread everywhere. That's why I don't mind telling it now, this other issue . . ."

"Other issue?"

"It's never been told. Not a word has gotten out before now, which is a bit of a miracle, but a testament to our secrecy efforts."

"And now you're going to tell it?"

"I've already mentioned parts of it—the shunned side of the island with the Tiki temple and odd bones, and the stones carved with some alien script; the meteorite fragments with their own peculiar radiation; and the genetic mutations among the islanders. There are other pieces of the puzzle I haven't mentioned: the fallout from Baker brought weird, tiny wormlike things that squirmed and fizzled and disappeared. They rained down with the sand and bits of blasted coral, glowed like little neon lights as they floated down, then dissolved like snowflakes."

"Then there was the case of the missing test animals."

"Missing—?"

"Among other animals, there were goats and pigs tethered to the deck. After test Able, some were toasted right away, and some lived for several days; but several were missing altogether."

"Washed overboard?" I suggested.

"No, everything else was intact, but the leather straps had been torn, ripped or bitten through, and the animals taken—some were bashed, leaving bloodstains, trails of blood, and footprints . . ."

"Footprints?"

"Yes, *webbed* footprints . . ."

He let it sink in.

"This was *after* the blast?"

"Had to be—there were sensors, which showed no disturbance beforehand."

"And you think . . . these web-footed creatures . . ."

"Came from the lee side of the atoll—or from *under* the atoll, once all the coral was blasted away. Remember, it's a coral island, not volcanic; it's built on layers and layers of coral reaching down to the ocean floor, hundreds—a thousand feet deep—built up over millennia . . ."

I must have presented a perplexed stare as I struggled to put all the pieces together.

"I'll jump to the quick. We found evidence . . . our divers verified that a large meteor had crashed to earth in the Mesozoic era, landing in the Pacific near the atoll, and punching through the coral. Something was on that meteor . . . something alive—alien life traveling from somewhere else . . ."

"That's incredible!" I said. "But it lay dormant all that time—until the atomic blasts?"

"We're lucky they stayed put for so long, but it was in their nature to be home-bodies, if you will. Perhaps they were waiting for some signal from their home planet to being expanding; perhaps they were preparing for it all along . . . You see, *they built an entire city down there* . . . hidden in the coral, under the island, stretching down to the seabed, where the main mass of the meteorite remained . . . We didn't discover it until later, and went after it with Operation Castle, this time with hydrogen bombs.

"But at Crossroads, we stumbled upon them, so to speak, with Baker. It was a fortunate coincidence, you see. When we realized something was there, we wanted to go after it directly with the third blast, Test Charlie, targeting the ruins on the leeward side and what lie beneath . . . But the brass decided to save the bomb—there weren't many in the arsenal at the time, and the generals were still nervous about Stalin. To be honest, I don't think they knew about what we had uncovered—the Commodore knew, maybe the Secretary of the Navy. It was something we automatically became tight-lipped about, already trained to operate that way around the atomic weapons.

"The site was watched, believe me, but remained dormant, so nothing was done—no conventional weapons, nothing. It just lay silent, hidden within the coral.

"It took a year or two, but we finally convinced them to stage further tests. During Operation Castle, Test Bravo succeeded in striking the underground power center, resulting in a blast twenty times larger than expected! And there were other tests, each serving the dual purpose of weapons tests as well as the other issue—removing all traces of that alien scourge. In all, we blasted it twenty times between 1946 and 1958.

"Ironically, the alien material was not destroyed, merely blown to bits! We might have guessed—from the weird fallout on Eniwetok. It was scattered over the ocean, where it sank but did not die. And it spread—to Eniwetok and Rongerik, to Kwajalein and beyond.

"Each test spread the thing, and now it lies dormant—though some day it's sure to awaken, start growing again—fomenting in the coral, just out of sight; intermixing with earth life and developing new colonies of hybrids: half-terrestrial, half-alien . . ."

He trailed off into silence as I sat listening, staring off at nothing.

"I guess that's all I have to say, and I'm afraid I'm tired now." And he looked tired, pale, drained.

"Maybe you can come back tomorrow, if you have any questions, and we can go into it some more." He spoke slowly, weakly.

And with that, the interview ended. On my way out I looked at the Bikini flag again, with its pre-nuclear motto, "Everything is in the hands of God."

Back in my motel room, I sat motionless for a long while, absorbing the admiral's tale and all its ramifications. Then I set about transcribing the interview, typing on my laptop as I listened to the digital recorder through headphones. This took most of the night, and when finished I threw myself on the bed, finally exhausted enough to fall asleep—despite the turmoil of rushing thoughts that threatened to turn the world upside down.

When I awoke it was light, and I thought at once of getting ready to go visit the admiral again. When I glanced at the desk, however, I saw it was clear: no notes, no laptop, no recorder—nothing! I ran outside just in time to see a black SUV driving away. There was no one in sight.

I drove back to the admiral's house, but didn't stop. Outside was an ambulance, a police car, and a black Lincoln Town Car. As I drove past, I saw two ambulance attendants wheeling a body out of the house, covered in a sheet. No doubt, the admiral was yet another victim of cancer caused by exposure to radiation.

I have reconstructed the admiral's tale from memory; but for reasons just recounted, there is no evidence to back it up—to prove it is not just fiction. Nevertheless, I feel it is my imperative duty to share it with the world: to warn, as best I can, about an eminent, lurking danger that threatens us all!

Derrick's Ritual

It's unfair that you should call me mad, Bennett—plenty other people have stranger prejudices than mine. And once I explain my experience with Arthur Derrick, you will understand my reason for turning down the invitation. Wasn't it apparent? A critic receives an invitation to a private dinner for two from a woman "writer" whose work he has just denounced—a woman rumored to leave her home only in the late evening, and whose so-called "novel" is entitled *The Lure of the Vampire*. A friendly consultation? Never! Her plan was all too apparent.

All creative people seem to get too involved in their work. Take artists, for instance. Richard Upton Pickman—the Boston bizarrist who is frequently acclaimed to have surpassed Sime, Doré, Goya, and even his contemporaries Roerich and Clark Ashton Smith—is said to have begun associating with the ghouls and other fiends he depicted in his art. Clearly, that's going too far!

Then there are actors—Bela Lugosi is a prime example. He became so obsessed with his role as Dracula that he developed a taste for raw meat, and late in life requested to be buried in the cape he wore in his films! The majority of actors live in a world of make-believe, you will agree.

And finally, there are authors. H. P. Lovecraft, the Providence eccentric so often compared to the great Poe, portrayed himself in several of his Randolph Carter stories—something many authors do. Or look at the genius Poe himself: his life was every bit as dreary as his fiction. All these examples serve to bolster my argument, the point of which is this: not only does the creative artist adopt his surroundings and atmosphere to his work, but he also adapts the atmosphere of his work to his surroundings.

How did I arrive at this theory? Why did I drop Derrick as even a remote friend, and why have I not since accepted the company of weird fiction writers? I'll tell you.

As you know, Arthur Wilmarth Derrick is considered one of the finest weird fiction writers of this century—in addition to his reputation as publisher and premier critic. (You also know his work under the pen name of

Steven Grendle.) He invited me to visit Sac City, Wisconsin and see his small publishing firm—small, indeed, but unexcelled—the venerable Dunwich House, which has made the work of authors such as Lovecraft (and Derrick himself) more readily available. Ostensibly, we were to discuss the prospect of his publishing a compilation of my reviews and critical essays. But I knew that he would also take issue with the severity of my devaluation of his most recent Dunwich House volume—a lapse in quality infinitely rare among his unparalleled output.

Now, it occurred to me that Derrick might present me with an ultimatum: either retract my review (at least tone it down), or have no compilation published under the honorable imprint of Dunwich House. As much as I wanted such as collection to be published, I intended to refuse such a compromise of my critical standards: in my mind, the one honor outweighed the other, and I was prepared to dig in my heels and do battle. If Derrick considered my opinions worth reprinting, he would have to accept them as they were.

Thus prepared mentally for our encounter, I wired Derrick on the nineteenth of October to accept his invitation and reveal my plan to leave Providence midday October the twentieth. Calculating a two-day drive, I would arrive on the morning of the twenty-second after stopping two nights along the way. But I finished arranging things at my end earlier than expected and set out early the next morning by motorcar.

I made excellent distance that first day and stayed the night in some small town outside Cuyahoga Falls, Ohio. Traversing an equal number of miles the next day, I arrived in Sac City around nine o'clock on the evening of the twenty-first of October. Despite this early arrival, I made straight for the famed Dunwich House, trusting that Derrick would have my accommodations prepared. But as I pulled up to within view of the house, I saw that there were no lights on and feared that Derrick had retired for the night.

There was nothing to do but return to the city and spend the night in a hotel. I drove some fifty feet farther along the main road and pulled off on a dirt road in order to turn around. The dirt road ran adjacent to Derrick's large side-yard and was separated from that open space by a four-foot barrier of vegetation. As soon as I pulled off the main road and paused to shift the motor into reverse, I heard a very faint but unmistakable *whining* sound. This I feared at first to be the radiator or other malfunctioning organ of the overworked engine. I killed the lights and engine, but the sound continued. Emerging from the car, I stepped around to the front of the car and was about to raise the hood, hoping the source of the problem would thus become manifest . . . but I never completed this project.

Whether it was that I could now see above the vegetation bordering the dirt road, or that I could now tell, from my elevated stance, that the almost musical whining noise came definitely from some source apart from the engine, I do not know; but I stopped where I was, beside the motorcar, and traced the sound to its true source.

The quasi-musical whining increased steadily in volume and changed variously in tune, until it became undoubtable that the exact cause was a flute or similar wind instrument. This piping was of a monotonous, undulating, and shrill quality which gave me cause to shudder. As the cacophony accelerated in tempo and grew louder, the direction whence it came was revealed. The source of the hellish and obscurely festive sound was none other than Arthur Derrick's Dunwich House, standing some fifty feet away in the darkness yet clearly visible above the row of short trees and bushes.

Not for a moment had this monstrously revelatory and virtually damning fact lingered on my mind before my attention was drawn to a caliginous figure emerging stealthily from the side door of the house. Clad in black robe and cowl, had he not been carrying a burning candle I could never have been certain of his identity—but as matters stood, I could easily discern *the grotesquely illumined facial features of Arthur Derrick*.

Bearing the candle, Derrick walked across his moonlit side-yard to a table which bore two black candles. These he lit and I could see more clearly that the highly decorated table was more properly termed *an altar*, covered with a white cloth lavishly embroidered with arabesque runes and nameless allegorical characters. The tall black candles were held by brazen candlesticks which stood two feet from either end of the table and two feet apart from one another, the table being roughly six feet long by three feet wide.

In the centre of the table between the candlesticks was a rather large book, opened to the middle leaves. If closed, the book would have measured some four inches thick, eleven in width, and fifteen in height. Derrick consulted the volume, turning the undoubtedly ancient leaves with great care. Suddenly he stopped, looking closely at the top of the page to which he had turned. Then he slipped a small notebook from a pocket beneath his robe and, flipping through this, appeared to double-check the page and passage he must have previously noted and selected for the occasion—whatever that may be. Returning to the large book, he read the passage over to himself, then withdrew several singular items from a compartment or drawer beneath the cloth that covered the altar.

These most singular and peculiar items were: a short, straight, wide dagger; a strangely familiar lamp (which I now believe to have been the fabulous Lamp of Alhazred, probably left to Derrick by the late Ward Phillips); a small, golden cup, empty; a leather pouch; a curious-looking pencil-sized white rod (which, indeed, I initially took to be a pencil); and a stone or metallic disk, along with a candle smaller than those arranged upon the altar-top.

Now Arthur Derrick went through a confusing and almost maddening ritual of quasi-magic. First he set Alhazred's lamp neatly beside the book and adjusted it at the top. Then he took the curious pencil-sized rod and held it above the wick of the lamp. This rod he appeared to *twist* somehow, and when he had removed it, the lamp was alight! Now the table was brightly illuminated. Derrick placed some reddish powder from the leather pouch into the golden cup, and taking this, the disk (which appeared to be covered with hieroglyphic or runic symbols), the dagger, and the smaller candle (which he lit with the lamp's flame), he proceeded to the centre of the open space between the altar and the wall of vegetation behind which I stood. As soon as I saw him move toward me, I stooped low behind the shrubbery to avoid detection, though I had no trouble seeing the events that followed.

Derrick placed the disk in a shallow, circular indentation in the soil, already cleared of grass, and knelt down before it. Then, after glancing momentarily at the cloudless sky and the starry voids beyond, he rearranged the disk—presumably to align its hieroglyphs with predefined celestial coordinates.

All this time the absurd piping or howling had continued unnoticed, my focus given to observing the obscure goings-on; now it terminated, thus calling attention to itself. The precise instrumentation of this music was never revealed, nor how it stopped and started, and one can only wonder . . .

Next Derrick recited several incoherent phrases and, scooping some of the reddish powder from the cup with the short dagger, sprinkled this to the left of the disk. As he did this—the very instant the powder slid from the tilted blade—a wicked flash of heat lightning energized the atoms of the atmosphere . . . yet, as I have said, *there were no clouds to be seen in the night sky*. Powder was likewise distributed to the right of the disk, following a chant very similar to the first and followed in turn by another silent flash of heat lightning. Then Derrick, pausing for a moment, recited a long, seemingly *special* chant, and distributed the powder directly onto the disk of metallic stone. Again lightning flashed, but through some inconceivable, inexplicable cosmic dislocation of time and space, *the lightning froze for a full five seconds!*

You can't begin to think how I felt, Bennett, out there alone with a man or thing who could escape the known laws of science and nature, and control the elements themselves. But let me continue—if I can.

As I said, it was as if time had stood still. Then the very air was rent with an enormous clap of thunder that vibrated down into my very bones. With a grotesque, evil smile of self-satisfaction, Derrick arose and returned to the altar, where he set aside the powder receptacle, candle, and knife and studied once again the book. Ah, the book! I can only guess which of the countless forbidden books it was, but I am sure that it was one of those listed hazardously in the Roman Catholic *Index Librorum Prohibitorum*.

Now comes a difficult but necessary part of my narrative, Bennett; it explains why I did not go to a hotel that night nor to Derrick's house the next day, and why I have never since accepted an invitation from a weird-fiction writer. I'll tell you.

Derrick, as I have said, returned to the altar and read once more from the forbidden tome. Again he chanted aloud, and the lamp's flame, it seemed, leapt with the recital of a certain word or name, "Cthugha." (The name seemed oddly familiar at the time, and I now know it as the entity that formed the basis of Derrick's story, "In the Wood of N'gai.") Now he recited a chant not unlike that which accompanied the distribution of powder upon the disk. A single, powerful bolt of lightning struck the disk and made me jump halfway out of my skin! After this, an eerie, ghastly glow radiated from the disk, highlighting its runic carvings. At times I almost thought this radiation to be a *flame*—such were the nuclear qualities of the aura. As I watched, Derrick yet again consulted the alien volume on necromantic rituals and more unspeakable things.

Now came the unexpected climax of the hellish ritual and of my narrative. The weird piping was heard again, emanating from somewhere near the house and rejoining the mélange of eldritch sensations. The music seemed to interact with the abnormal leaping of the lamp's flame and the variating intensity of the evil glow from the metallic disk, with the effect that all three moved or acted with the tempo of Derrick's voice.

It was now around half-past nine—I did not bother to consult my wristwatch, horrified as I was by the uncanny ritual and its implications—and a cool breeze stirred up. Suddenly, Derrick paused in his recital and gazed at the stars above the trees. I saw by looking myself that Formalhaut was up, just below Mars in the south. Then, in a tongue far more guttural than the one employed in the earlier portions of the ritual, he uttered a potent chant of impossible quasi-syllables that I cannot *and dare not* repeat. He actually screamed these unpronounceable sounds with arms raised in the air, then stood there with eyes fixed on the disk in the centre of the open space— stood with hideous *expectation.*

Nothing happened, but the tension nearly broke me! What could happen next, I wondered? Derrick stepped from behind the altar and strode quickly to a spot roughly between altar and disk; then he screamed the invocation again, arms raised to the stars, eyes on the disk. Remaining there, he uttered the blasphemy a third and final time, arms raised and eyes now trained on the evil star Formalhaut.

An abrupt, blinding flash of light from a doubtful source, an ear-bursting shriek, and there stood upon the aeon-ancient, curvilinearly hieroglyphed metallic plate *a huge, amorphous though frightfully anthropoidal, pulsating breath from hell!* The colloidal, semi-gaseous, already Cyclopean fire-being did not stop growing or changing, and seemed to be on a retro-evolutionary track of rapid orthogenesis, through it never moved into any class or category of life or quasi-life known to man!

I cannot blame my heart for skipping a few beats in that mind-blasting, cataclysmic moment. But as soon as I had recovered from the momentary paralysis brought on by unprecedented terror, I plunged into my motorcar, ignited the engine, threw the car into reverse, and spun out off the dirt road in a cloud of dust. No longer caring whether Derrick saw me, I returned the way I had come—this time with pedal pressed firmly to the floorboard and tires squealing on the pavement.

I left in the hurry that I did not only to flee the monstrous fire-entity, but also to escape the holocaust which I knew would follow in its wake. For I had read Derrick's "In the Wood of N'gai," and in a flash I remembered that his chant called forth Cthugha from Formalhaut to destroy the Wisconsin countryside! But then I thought, why?

This puzzled me: why would Derrick want to wreak destruction upon himself and Dunwich House and the Wisconsin city he loved so much? Then another thing crept up in my mind: some difference—impossible to ascertain—between the chant that Derrick had included in his dark cere- mony that night and the one used in his story for the popular horror maga- zine, *Tales of the Weird*.

Eventually—once I felt that I was at a safe distance—I took one last, apprehensive glance back at the house. I saw no raging conflagration or de- structive holocaust among the woods. *What I did see was the prodigious fire- entity rearing high above the treetops.*

Then the realization hit me. Derrick had not summoned Cthugha from distant Formalhaut to destroy his wood or his house or himself—he called it to unleash its heretical powers upon the world! Perhaps the stars were "right." Perhaps it was time for the Great Return promised to take place in Alhazred's *Necronomicon* and actually described in the final chapter of the R'lyeh Text and in similar manuscripts. Perhaps this very moment, on other parts of the globe, Cthulhu was being called up from sunken R'lyeh in the South Pacific; Yog Sothoth and Tsathoggua called up from their lightless abodes within the earth; and Hastur, Shub-Niggurath, and other, nameless entities were being assembled by Nyarlathotep, the Mighty Messenger, with the help of human allies; and together they would reign malignly over the earth and reenslave her unsuspecting denizens . . .

I am sure now that the chant in Derrick's story was far different from the one I heard that night. In his weird tale, Derrick had merely guessed at the potent chant, mimicking Lovecraft with an essentially harmless jumble of consonants. But now he must have found the real thing, and the anathema he bravely uttered was none other than the companion to the invocation which calls Zhar from Arcturus: the command of 'Umr At-Tawil. Together they made up the Unholy Couplet, thought to be lost forever with a fragment of the Pnakotic Manuscripts of the Lomarians—but apparently found, and included unawares in some ancient tome, a copy of which Derrick had that night. This couplet had undoubtedly been sought through untold aeons of man's shadowy history—probably sought after as avidly as the Holy Grail—by those worshippers and followers of the Great Old Ones who wished destruction and vengeance upon the omnipotent Elder Gods . . .

But something went wrong. Perhaps the incantation was wrong, perhaps the ceremony was ill-performed. Or perhaps its malign efficacy was superseded by the benign intervention of some other force, and the fearful return of Cthugha quelled by some greater power . . . We may never know.

Thus ends my narrative, Bennett. I got home safely, and within a few days had heard of the death of Arthur Wilmarth Derrick, and of the mystery surrounding it as well as the annihilation of Dunwich House. Destruction by what? Why, Bennett! Didn't you read the papers? It was by fire . . .

Knocker-Over

The cat bit at the dust motes as they rose on the air into a beam of sunlight that fell on the kitchen floor. Rising up on his hind legs, he pawed at them, staring wildly with wide yellow eyes.

Now he turned, walked though the house to the front door, where a jingle of keys sounded, followed by a rattle as they banged the door, which opened.

Jahdiel Simmons came in, wrapped in a brown wrap and cowl and hauling a bag of groceries, out of which stuck a long stick that drew the cat's notice.

"How are you today, my fuzzy friend?" she said in a lilting tone. "How are you, my little Knocker-Over?"

The name came from his habit of jumping up on tables and counters, striding roughly among the knickknacks or what-have-you, and unceremoniously knocking them over. It was a minor nuisance, really. So far he hadn't broken anything, though he put a pretty shock into a potted cactus, which never really recovered from being knocked over on the floor and reassembled. Instead, it was an almost endearing habit, since the poor creature had no idea what he was doing. He wasn't mischievous by nature, only curious—and infinitely lovable!

"Oh, you!" She would cry when something went over, drawing a blank stare from the clueless cat. "You like to knock things over, don't you—you little knocker-over you!"

And so "Knocker-Over" became his name.

The strange tall stick in the grocery bag finally came out and Jahdiel revealed the feather-toy. It was like a child's fishing pole: with a three-foot wand of sturdy plastic serving as the rod, and a strand of fishing line or plastic wire, which dangled as bait a clump of feathers that resembled a badminton shuttlecock stuffed with a colorful array of rooster feathers.

With a flick and a twirl of the wrist, the feather toy whistled and whirled as it flew in circles above the watchful cat. His head bobbed and turned side-to-side as his eyes tracked the speeding target. The birdie slowed, descended softly in a graceful spiral, floated down to fall on the brown rug, where it sat still for an instant.

And the cat sat and watched.

Then with a wiggle of the wrist, Jahdiel made the ball of feathers twitch and quiver like a hurt bird. This proved irresistible and drew the cat's ferocious attack. He pounced—first rearing up on his hind legs, head bent backward, face contorted at once with a frown and a malicious smile—then, bringing down his full weight and force on his forepaws, he overwhelmed the helpless birdie.

Jahdiel laughed with delight.

"He's perfect!" she said, and yanking the feathers away with a tug of the wand, she swung it in the air again, and the cycle was repeated.

Over the years, Jahdiel had fed many of the feral cats that wandered through her backyard. Though nearly poor, she shaved expenses for herself to buy food for the ferals. It was never enough to keep them coming back daily, and they would roam and wander for days before reappearing. And always, they kept their distance, never venturing too close to the open kitchen door where she sat and watched them feed. Never before had one had the nerve to walk right in the way this one did—walked right in and plopped himself down on the checkered linoleum as if it were his own rightful domain.

She had never cared for anything so much in all her years. His presence brought new life to the solitary old woman and made her forget for a while her aches and pains—her gout and bad back. It was revitalizing to play with the feisty cat, who must have still been a kitten—for his large paws foretold future growth.

His eyes wide, his soft paws padded silently as he stalked his prey. He performed amazing acrobatics and impossible maneuvers, leaping up and turning mid-air as he chased the flying shuttlecock. Like a wise mother, Jahdiel knew that he was learning and developing the skills he would need to survive in the natural world—if he lived in the natural world.

His expressions were almost human and she cared for him like a child. His eyes winked and half-closed in a Cheshire smile. And he grew sleepy, purring like a motorboat. Purring, she knew, could be a sign of stress as well as of happiness.

"You have nothing to be stressed about here, do you, my sweetie?" she said, sweeping him up in her arms. "Mama Jahdiel will take care of you now, won't she?

He looked up at her, bobbled his head as he tried to look past his reflection in her glasses to see her eyes. The cutest part was his little snout! The little rows of black dots on either side that sprouted wide white whiskers. Soon the purring ceased, the eyes closed, and he was fast asleep.

"Dead to the world," she pronounced, and laid him in his little basket of blankets.

Jahdiel Simmons didn't consider herself a witch, but her neighbors did. She was a loner who shunned the company of others, but that just gave them an excuse to whisper about her.

Sure, she was an "earth mama," equipped with all the prehistoric charm of the Venus of Willendorf. Plump in places, bulbous in parts, rotund all around. But what witchery lay in this?—except the ability to still appeal to men through an extra layer . . . and that sort of witchcraft has been around since Eve.

True, she wore her hair long—uncut since girlhood—and its frizzy and grizzled appearance seemed to fit the bill. Now past middle age, she neglected the little whiskers that were beginning to crop up on her upper lip and chin. And, OK, maybe she *did* have a wart or two . . .

And she did dabble in Wicca and astrology, but mainly for curiosity's sake. She was no certainly no practitioner of Enochian magic, no follower of Aleister Crowley, let alone Satan—in whom she did not believe. She preferred the "white magic" of A. E. Waite, whose *Book of Ceremonial Magic* held a special place on her bookshelf. And of course she had crystals—and a pewter statuette of Gandalf leaning on a pewter staff—on the mantle, next to a figurine of Bast.

Perhaps it didn't help her reputation any that she fed on pigeons . . . But she thought it resourceful, and a good way to cut down on her butcher's bill. She trapped them in her yard and kept them in cages until their time was up. The innards she fed to the ferals.

Well, if she were a witch—which she still debated—it would only seem natural that she would adopt a cat as a companion. Not a classic black cat, though; he was a silver and brown tabby with a bushy raccoon tail. Now with her new "familiar" at her side, it seemed like all the pieces were falling into place.

Knocker-Over jumped up on her lap, landed lightly, settled to be petted.

Jahdiel thanked the stars, which, she liked to think, guide our fate. But mainly she thanked Bast, Egyptian cat-goddess and protector of felines everywhere.

"In fact . . ." She began aloud, getting up from her rocker and depositing Knocker-Over back in his basket.

Crossing to the mantel above the faux fireplace, she opened a small black box and took out a cone of incense, which she placed in an Anubis-headed holder and lit with a Bic. The blue smoke rose in a quivering cloud and filled the room with its sweet-burnt fragrance.

The figurine of Bast she took and held reverently, admiring the features rendered in gold paint on carved ebon wood. It had the slim body of a nubile female and the head of a cat. Bast held up a sistrum in her right hand and carried a basket on her left arm.

As incense filled the room, Jahdiel stared into the cat eyes of the goddess and imagined herself far away in time and space, in ancient Bastis, city of Bast, where the common folk worshipped the cat deity, and cats were revered in her honor. She could almost hear the sistrum rattle and ring, its metal parts clanking and clinking in the cool air of the desert night. But that basket—what might come out of that? A celebratory feast, no doubt—a roasted squab?

And so she properly thanked Bast for sending her a little furry friend.

After a merc week, Knocker-Over had basically destroyed his new toy. He got hold of it on his own, stripped out the feathers one by one, grasping the birdie in his paws as he gnawed and tore at it with his sharp feline canines.

With her limited income, Jahdiel could scarcely afford another toy—the first one had been a splurge. But the question arose, "Where can I get more feathers . . ." and the pigeons came to mind.

"I'll teach you to catch them, yet. And we'll both have squab for dinner." She said, talking to the cat as she worked.

She tied a pigeon wing to the end of the fishing line, replacing feather and plastic with feather, flesh and bone, and the toy had a fresh lease on life. It was a consumer item, after all, and now it was literally consumable: for Knocker-Over got to eat it as a reward.

Although he had range of the house and could go outside, Knocker-Over liked to sit in the side window, balancing somehow on the narrow sill—a barely two inch strip of wood beneath the glass. He would stare at something intently, then shift his gaze, turning his head quickly side to side, or up and down, as he looked at this and that, on the ground or in the air. His faint breath fogged the glass.

One day he jumped down from the sill, all frightened by a noise from the neighboring house, and ran to a closet to hide.

"Get out of here, you damned cats!" the neighbor was shouting, cursing the ferals that availed themselves of the loose loam in his rose garden.

"Always crapping everywhere . . . Scat!" and a clang and bang as he grabbed something to throw, and threw it; but the cats had already scattered, leaving their scat.

That night, Knocker-Over stared out the window again, this time watching the moving lights of planes flying by. They were beyond his little cat brain to comprehend . . . little lights that blinked and shifted, with darkness in-between—just like our broad universe.

"Now, you be careful of that mean old Mr. Wooster," Jahdiel said as the cat crossed the threshold into the backyard, turning to look back at her as if listening to her advice. But in the evening he did not come back, as usual, to spend the night inside. Jahdiel expected him, waited for him, but he did not show up.

"Knocker-Over!" she called, but he did not come.

With a new sense of loneliness and worry, she prepared for bed and wished the best for her new companion.

The next morning, Jahdiel rose from a restless sleep filled with dreams of desert fires and jackals chasing cats. She dressed nervously and went through the kitchen to the backyard.

"Knocker-Over!" she called. He did not come, but she heard a meek meow coming from a bush by the fence adjoining Mr. Wooster's yard.

"Knocker-Over!" she called, running over to him.

There he was, weak and trembling, standing with difficulty, and drooling.

"Knocker-Over, what's wrong?" She swept him up and carried him inside.

She set him down on the kitchen floor; but he couldn't walk, only wobbled a bit and flopped down. Then he began to vomit, with violent retching, bringing up blood with some half-chewed meat that looked like hamburger. He stopped retching only to fall into convulsions, writhing with spasms as the muscle contractions ran through his tortured body. Then he fell still, tongue out, eyes yet open but quickly clouding over . . .

He was dead!

Jahdiel was beside herself with confusion and grief. What could have happened? Where had Knocker-Over gotten the meat? Was it putrid, or . . . *poisoned?*

She made up her mind quickly and set about work. She prepared the cat's body for burial, first bathing it in fragrant soap, toweling it dry, and wrapping it ceremoniously with long strips of cloth (an old sheet torn in strips), in the fashion of Egyptian mummies. Placing the cat's wrapped body into its familiar basket of blankets, she covered him up, folding a blanket over him, and set on top the small figurine of Bast.

When it was growing dark, she took the basket out to the backyard and set it by the fence. Above, the stars were coming out, distant fires lit by unknown hands. Tonight, the stars were votive candles lighted in special tribute to a lost friend . . .

As darkness gathered and more and more lights were lit in the heavens, all the noises of the city died down, and the little world of man seemed to go away, leaving only the earth, the trees, the sky, and silence.

Then the sound came, from afar. First a jingle like a tambourine, it became louder, came closer, and darker tones appeared—the clang of metal on metal. It was the sound of a sistrum beating time for the ceremony.

The jangling sound became quieter, yielding to a new sound—a low rumbling sound, a familiar, heart-warming sound. It was a cat purring, louder and louder. The sound rose and swelled and engulfed the neighborhood and the night.

Mr. Wooster came out on his back porch.

"What the hell? Who's back there? Is it those damned cats again?"

Just then, the purring stopped, leaving a stark silence. A dark figure rose up in the darkness, black on black, and blotted out the stars. Where a moment before there had been a million billion stars, now there were only two round lights—glowing green, with vertical slits of darkest black.

The monstrous cat pounced on Mr. Wooster, seized him between powerful paws, and extended his fearsome claws. Mr. Wooster screamed bloody murder, helplessly held upright in the grasp of the ferocious beast.

"Knock him over, Knocker-Over!" Jahdiel cried.

And he did.

Within the Machinery of Light

"Change not the barbarous names of evocation, for there are sacred names in every language which have in the sacred rites a power ineffable."

—ZOROASTER.

Max Ratner sat in the study of his large, isolated home on the White Cliffs of Dover, in Kent, Great Britain. His hair was dark, well kept, and of moderate length; his eyes were rather darkened around, deeply set in sharply fortified sockets, and slightly large. His other facial features were neither uncommon nor notable, and his face itself—more slender than it was full—betrayed no emotion, no thought, no concern. He was reading a novel.

Ratner was in his late thirties. His habit consisted of evening robe—beneath which he wore dark slacks and a white shirt, loose at the neck—and comfortable, grey-suede shoes, laced. The study in which he sat was richly carpeted and its walls were lined with high bookcases, well-stocked with thousands of volumes. The cases themselves were finely carven and adorned with antique wood, glass and metal work in the form of knickknacks in great variety, and small, brightly painted statuettes with a global scope of workmanship and characterization.

The cliff-top dwelling in which Ratner effected for himself an adequately comfortable home was one of two storeys and contained a dozen rooms. It was, therefore, a somewhat unusually capacious habitation for a man to have all to himself—for he lived alone—even though he was attended by a number of servants. But this number was sporadic, owing to Mr. Ratner's few and infrequent needs and, more independently, to the passing of the seasons, as the servants were in the habit of withdrawing their services in view of vacations at all times of the year. As well, an extensive ground—for the purpose of insuring privacy—surrounded the house and other small buildings which housed the servants.

The volume which Ratner read was one by H. P. Lovecraft, an omnibus of tales of the fantastic and the supernatural. The particular novel in which he had but recently lost himself was a fantasy, *The Dream-Quest of Unknown*

Kadath. At one point in his reading, a tiny crack appeared at the right corner of his mouth, and his eyes softened and sparkled. An idea had occurred to him as he read, and a smile stole over his face.

He laughed openly, no longer concealing his humour, which was aroused by something that he had just read in the black book. But there was no one to hear him, as all of his servants had retired. It was nearing midnight, and Max Ratner was alone in the house.

Enterprising upon the whim, Ratner carried out a little joke with himself. He placed a marker beneath the last passage he had read:

". . . that shocking final peril which gibbers unmentionably outside the ordered universe, where no dreams reach; that last amorphous blight of nethermost confusion which blasphemes and bubbles at the centre of all infinity—the boundless daemon-sultan Azathoth, whose name no lips dare speak aloud . . ."

Ratner rose from his cushioned chair and passed out of the study into an adjoining bedchamber, leaving the book laid open upon an ebony table. From a closet he drew a black cape which he had bought for a Halloween party the year before, and, donning it, he re-entered the study. He crossed to a desk and removed a candle from one of the mahogany drawers. This he lit and secured in a candlestick. Afterwards, supplied with the candle and the Lovecraft volume, he ventured out onto the balcony of the study, overlooking the chalk cliffs and the Strait of Dover below.

The balcony, some three metres wide, extended two and one half metres away from the house. For the outer metre, it was unsupported and hung over the precipice upon which the house was situated, though the balcony was surrounded by a narrow stone wall, one metre high. A plumb bob dropped seven metres from the edge of the balcony would meet the jagged cliff, as it proceeded steeply out toward the water, at a point approximately one fifth of the distance from the termination of the balcony to the level of the restless sea.

As I have said, the balcony was terminated in a stone wall that rose a metre above the floor, also of stone. Ratner laid the book open on the top of this wall and, smiling, set the candlestick beside it. He then composed himself and finally bore a solemn countenance appropriate to the ostensibly occult ceremony he now began. He raised his arms over his head and, staring into the dark, heavy body of cloud that stretched out over the restless waters, shouted at the top of his lungs the name, entreaty, or invocation "Azathoth!"

The significance of this act can be seen by the fragment from Lovecraft, which flashed again into Ratner's mind "Azathoth, whose name no lips dare speak aloud . . ." His mock solemnity broken by its purpose, Ratner laughed, and only ceased to do so to ponder the reason for the abrupt increase in the atmospheric current from the east—which he faced—as this occurrence had caused a liberal modification in the clouds. He would have thought little of this happening, had it not come at such a time; and had it not been for the odd glow that seemed to flush into the dark clouds, he would have expected nothing more than a storm.

The winds shrieked in their mad trek across the heavens from the east, forcing the heavy clouds before them. Now winds from the north, south and west rushed in to meet Eurus, the primal east wind, pushing the pillowy bod-ies of vapor into a colliding mass, where they swirled and mixed and finally settled above the disturbed Channel, shifting uniformly and gently into an odd position. Then a phenomenal thing happened: the clouds *exploded* from their deceptively silent vortex, and a brilliant light shot in a single beam through the misty aether to seize and to stagger Max Ratner, who was held helpless in some hypnosis by the unearthly shaft of radiance.

He felt the light's warmth at the back of his skull as he did at the back of his retina, and his mind was numbed by the penetrating energy of the weirdly aethereal beam. Suddenly all was light—or such was the impression received by his baffled senses; and the brightness impressed him as being hot sunlight, for he could barely see dancing heat-waves which blurred every-thing in that excessive brightness.

In the oblivion that swept over him, Ratner fancied that he felt his mind being severed from his brain, his essence floating away on the chilly, moist aether that swirled about over the balcony and the sea it overlooked. When he regained consciousness, he knew immediately that something was dread-fully wrong. His mind had cleared somewhat, and he raised his eyes slowly—unsurely—to grasp his present plight.

Surrounding him was a fantastic plain of carbonic soil, from which sprung, at intervals of about six metres, monoliths of grayish stone. They rose to indeterminable altitudes above the field—which extended, in all directions, to the very horizon; and, quite possibly, the plain covered the entire planet, piercing the puffy amethyst clouds that spotted the jade-streaked crimson sky. Crossing warily over to the nearest pillar or needle of stone, he placed his hand on it to test the texture, but quickly drew back due to its surprising coldness.

He now stood so that the flat surface of one side of the monolith was squarely before him. Suddenly he was seized with the odd desire to follow the grayish-white stone as it rose consistently upward, its perfectly cut edges acquiring a scarlet tinge from the contrasting skies on either side—a tinge that rainbowed into a phosphorescent cobalt glow. As his eyes thoughtlessly followed the monolith infinitely upward, upward, he grew giddy; and his composure of mind crumbled and slid away just as his fatefully strengthened sight slid up the impossible needle.

His brain was numbed by the irresistible upward straining of his senses. He felt his soul flowing out of him and through the alien atmospheres above him along his vast line of vision toward the top of the stone. He tried to pull his thoughts away, to oppose the inconceivable force that caused him to mechanically seek the very top of the mind-racking needle—which seemed to grow steadily upward before his vision, wrenching his psychic essence further out of conjunction.

Ultimately, he fell backward—or so it seemed; for his useless senses refused to grasp his bodily plight. He seemed to be falling slowly, slowly backward, ever about to land heavily upon the ground of the foreign globe; yet never coming to rest at a right angle from the monolith that appeared to bend without sane parity over him. Unable to endure any longer the frightfully non-physical strain that was mercilessly set upon him by alien laws beyond all earthly reason, he snapped, synchronously feeling the impact of his previously inhabited body as it fell hollowly to the carbonic soil.

Unleashed so abruptly, his soul slid rapidly up the cold and painful surface of the impossible monolith to the airless altitudes of the planet. His estranged essence and entity shot helplessly outward into space, now whirling and spinning so that he caught a single, horrifying glance backward and downward at the nightmarish field of stone needles, down to where his body remained prostrate in the black soil, with glassy and soulless eyes glaring after him.

Foreign and nameless stars glittered and mocked him as he passed among them in his sickening flight through interstellar space. His senses seemed to attempt a realignment with his essence, to refocus themselves as the framework of his thoughts. But this only caused him to feel nauseous in whatever physical part of him that remained outside of his material shell, or in whatever mental parts into which a feeling of unease and illness can come. He felt that his mind would explode, the shattered pieces to be hurled infinitely through lightless space.

But now a new concern possessed him, for he was certain his body of entity and essence was now *falling* through the vacua of space, ever gaining velocity as he was drawn along by some unimaginable gravitation. The starlit voids about him lost their standing and spun round and around, spinning faster and faster until the streaking dots of light became a unified body of radiance. They formed a titanic shell about him at an indeterminable distance, and he became its nucleus. Against this wall of absolute energy he would be dashed as he was hurled faster and faster toward the farther side.

His senses never quite accurate or "normal" since his frightful severing of mind and body, Ratner was unable to perceive his exact distance from the brightly radiant and spinning sphere of pure energy that to him formed the entire cosmos. Suddenly he was upon it; he was at the wall that stood alone between his raw and unprotected soul and the lifeless non-existence beyond the remotest terminal of all time and space and being—beyond the last void of the cosmos. His absolute, ultimate *self*—estranged forever from the illusory body that had served him during his meaningless life—now faced the edge and the end of *everything*: To him would be revealed the ultimate mystery and the final enigma—or else it was vast Oblivion, more infinite than Infinity, that alone lay beyond the terminus of existence and awaited him. It was one or the other, but could not be both.

He burst through the absolute barrier, slackening to a slow fall as if through water. The sphere was no more; all around Ratner—the only true *being*, now beyond all being—was an intricate and arabesque structure of kaleidoscopic crystal. Where was he? *What* was he? Was he within the atomic structure of the *cosmos*, of *existence*, or of *non-existent space* itself? The bright, constantly changing glitter of ten thousand paracosmic colours flashed at once in a fantastic interplay, swirling beautifully, mystically, enchanting the confounded mind of the Outsider.

It was impossible, inconceivable, fantastic: *he was inside the very structure of being—within the machinery of light and space and time!* The apparently atomic, crystalline structure that he was in surrounded him entirely, since he had no physical body at all. The billion-faceted crystals became nebulous at points, melting and forming bulbs as spherical and oblong as white moon-stones, perfectly transparent. These then clouded and cracked and crystal-lised, again becoming a part of the metamorphic whole. This molecular, phantasmal interplay repeated itself endlessly in this pattern, displaying an utmost and unparalleled beauty and splendour.

But into the midst of all the ecstasy and joy and beauty of the singing, dancing vortices of color hewn for the eyes of the wise gods only, there slowly crept a single splinter of red. Blood-red it was, and this followed by another, and another, and yet another until the once-gleaming vistas of in-conceivable magnificence became only an ugly pulsating red that surged and throbbed to echoing beats of hideous drums from the undreamt cosmos or chaos of another sphere. As the intense pounding of the drums—tuned to the throbbing of the crimson-saturated prism as a heartbeat effects the flow of blood—there arose a shrill whining as from pain. Coming from no visible source, the cry seemed to transform into—or identify itself rightly as—flute-like piping, screaming shriller and louder while the drumming reached a shattering intensity.

Amorphous masses of a deeper scarlet squirmed onto the scene, seething chaotically and revoltingly as blood-clots suddenly come alive with the life of mindless, will-less, gigantic amoebas existing only to do the unthinkable bid-ding of a greater, yet likewise mindless, fiend. This hideous Fiend—Ratner knew as the revolting amoeboids slithered toward him across the sharp facet-angles of crimson crystal—could be none other than the idiot Azathoth: the nuclear chaos whose mindless howlings could be heard from behind the illu-sory shield of crystalline molecules that had been erected to deceive him and save him for the final, unbearable revelation. But above the obnoxious bel-lowing of the idiotic piping that had come before, there now came the terri-ble whistling of the cosmic winds that howl through the lightless wells between the very spheres—the sibilant music of Ying, the damned, amorphous flute-player of the Evil Ones.

The roaring chaos had to cease, lest the very foundations of the Outer Shell should crack, and the sweeping destruction of Yai itself reverberate infinitely in the chambers of Time that alone would withstand the inevitable but final cataclysm. In the centre of the blood-red field of crystal there began to unite the darker amoeboids into a circular shield. This wheel seemed to remain immobile as the pulsating that accompanied the hyper-cosmic percussions had since ceased; but it was soon quite visibly rotating at a frightening speed. Abruptly, a blinding explosion of violet shot throughout the entire range of vision, rending the crystalline structure and leaving only a mushroom-like cloud as might aftermath a thermonuclear detonation. When the brilliantly contrasting violet or lilac cloud had partly cleared, Ratner trembled at the faint movement of some shocking member of a tentacled blasphemy whose howling, now renewed, soon became unbearable And, as the aethereal smoke had cleared completely, the antecosmic horror of the entity from beyond angled space was revealed: the gnawing, sprawling chaos of Azathoth, the Idiot God, for whom danced awkwardly the Other Gods, mindless and voiceless obscenities whose soul is Nyarlathotep, the One in Darkness. And there was amorphous Ying, leering and piping in the unlighted background . . .

Ratner slowly rose from his prone position on the cold stone. He got to his feet with some effort, and staggered about. He was dazed by the thought and recollection of what had or what might have happened. Retrieving his senses, he found that he was on his balcony, overlooking the Chalk Cliffs of Dover, with Shakespeare Cliff visible in the misty distance. The balcony was damp from the moist clouds which had lifted of late to their proper places in the night sky.

The thick, black Lovecraft omnibus lay on the broad stone structure that rose a metre to terminate the balcony, where he had left it. Perceiving it there, he seized and hurled it viciously over the balcony wall, and it tumbled onto the lime cliffs and into the dark ocean below. Then he re-entered his home, muttering with merciful madness.

Intimations of Unreality

The Door in Lheil

In a most peculiar state of extended dream I was shown the vast and sprawling necropolis of Lheil. It lay abandoned on an unnamed planet that revolved around the dual-star system of Atlaanât. As a very few unfortunate ones will know, Atlaanât was the cradle of an unspeakable culture of aliens that spread through the hyperstellar voids into our own universe—even to our galaxy—at a time when our sun was still coalescing.

The titan city of Lheil lay on an ashen plain between two tremendous mountain ranges of sickening height and curiously unclassifiable color. At the first, I surveyed the city from above—before the wingéd emissaries of Hypnos set me down on that plain of burning cinders. I was still at some distance from the pair of frightful statues guarding the city, but I could see that they represented entities of such form as could hardly be imagined in sane, conscious contemplation. Midway above the horizon to the southeast were the two suns of Atlaanât, one multihued and vibrant, the other pale as a winter moon.

The heat was fantastic, but worse were the ever-flowing waves of vibration that throbbed and beat in rhythm through the very air. And when that solar mass of cerulean and alizarin and spinning emerald seemed to separate from its twin and moved with frightening speed to a position high overhead, tremors felt in the ground beneath me were unleveling and actually nauseating. With each steady throb, a pain grew in my head as if my cranium was being fractured little by little with the reverberations, and my knotted stomach accentuated the physical discomfort until it became almost unbearable.

At last, I came upon the great statues of vaguely humanoid figures stood up as sentinels at the edge of the city. Erected unnumbered aeons gone by unknown hands, the figures were covered with ornamental tattoos or carvings. I was at once arrested by these designs, which seemed to twist and fluctuate in a horrible fashion while bathing in their own sinister aura. This optical effect—this hideous trick of vision—was caused (I was able to assure myself) by the waves of intense heat rising from the ashen cinders of the plain. I ventured past them in haste and found myself in a courtyard before the entrance to a Cyclopean edifice.

No door blocked the entranceway, but the threatening darkness beyond the opening served more effectively to keep out visitors. And so, it was half-reluctantly that I accepted the abysmal darkness within as shelter against the harmful and disturbing rays of the dual suns. Besides, the peculiarly *groping* puce vegetation that sprouted from the undersides of huge displaced or upturned stones in the broad court before the edifice seemed to diminish near the shadows of that massive building. Darkness, then, was my only ally in this weird world to which Destiny or Doom had consigned me for the duration of this disturbing dream.

Inside the great structure, all was dark and silent. Nothing could be heard apart from an eerie sound as of a vacuum created by wind blowing past the portal through which I had stepped a moment before. But there had been no wind before, nor was there any sign of wind now. The shambled courtyard outside was dusted with the same ashen particles that covered the blasted plain, yet none were unsettled by wind—though the frightful puce vegetation swayed and crept by some freakish volition of its own . . . Perhaps the sound came from *within* the structure and only seemed to come from without by some illusory acoustical effect. I tilted my head from side to side, now toward the portal and now toward the dark interior that stretched away unseen, in hopes of determining the source of the sound. This revealed nothing and so I concluded that the sound existed only in my fancy or else was due to the interaction of the superheated air outside and the cool air inside. Whatever the cause, in breaking the dead silence of the alien atmosphere this sound was alone—and welcome.

Turning my back to the entrance, I walked slowly forward through the great building, groping as I went, blind in the absolute darkness that was somehow not illuminated in the slightest by light from outside, which could not penetrate past the sharp line of shadow that fell across the threshold. Outstretching my arms, I soon encountered a wall that transected my path at an oblique angle from the right and I followed it for some distance before it gave sharply away. At this turn or intersection, a new sound was audible—a steady splashing sound. Immediately on apperceiving this, I realized that a great thirst had risen in me and my throat was as dry as the cinders of the plain.

At no time did I catch sight of the walls about me, nor of the ceiling, nor the floor, as all seemed to be made of some unknown substance that absorbed all light and left only a black, spongy nonexistence identifiable merely as a *texture* to the baffled eye.

The splashing sound was getting louder, but still nothing could be seen. Then—suddenly, very abruptly in my steady course forward in the pitch-blackness—I was blinded by a glaring light from the left. The abruptness with which this light hit me was remarkable, for my rate of progression was such that I would surely have seen the light reflect on the walls before I saw its source. A second marvel was that even now I could not see the wall or floor—despite the abundant light. That quality which the light possessed to prevent it from illuminating the surrounding walls—or the quality of the material from which the walls were constructed—was indeed amazing!

Growing accustomed to the brilliant light enabled me to walk toward it, though I continued to walk slowly and with arms outstretched, for I was ignorant of the source or essence of the light and do not know if an unlighted obstacles lay in my path. As I drew near, however, the *substance* of the light divided into *sparks* which appeared to fall in a deluge upon the floor and into nothingness. With this phenomenon, a better realization of my surroundings offered itself to me: the unilluminable walls, ceiling and floor of the corridor halted at some kind of *shaft* descending into the floor, and through this shaft poured the luminous liquid in a veritable "waterfall". But surely, the liquid was not water as we know it—if it were water at all and not some molten metal; or it could be water, but toxic or radioactive and therefore undrinkable.

This debate only increased my abnormal thirst to such a degree that I coughed and choked with the dryness in my throat. At the same time, I was held in some magical spell by the glittering, metallic drops of liquid, which appeared as fiery quicksilver dripping from an alchemist's alembic. I was drawn to study it more closely with the hope that I might find it to be potable after all. Once within reach, I stretched out my hand to catch one of the stray drops as it fell. When it burned as with heat I thought I had made a mistake, but the drop burned my palm with the cold of ice and no serious pain arose. I brought the drop to my nose but smelled nothing above the stale, arid air that permeated the abandoned structure. Daring a taste, I brought the drop to my tongue and found it to be as fresh and clean as water from a mountain stream, apart from a faint metallic taste.

What choice did I have? Ravaged by thirst fueled by this desert clime, what did I care if the water glowed from radioactive content and trusted that it would not flow so freely in the interior of this great building if it were hazardous to living things. And so, I cupped both hands in the stream of fiery-cold liquid and drank freely. Truly, it was as if I were dipping into water that trickled down a mountainside from rocky crags where some glacier nestled.

My sensation after drinking was that of being refreshed somewhat, revitalized almost as if waking from sleep—from the dream I had thus far experienced. In support of this notion that my dream was giving way to a new one—but not that I was waking up entirely—a very strange thing took place. For a moment, I watched as the pouring column of light fell through a circle in the floor and continued downward though another floor and another—until it passed out of sight. Stepping back from the well, I could see that the wall curved away as it led passed the well and extended some distance farther on. But the salient point was that I could actually *see* the walls, the ceiling and floor of the corridor! This phenomenon, I reasoned, was due either to the liquid light or to a change in the material composing the hall ahead. In retrospect, it is conceivable that the liquid that I drank had the effect of improving my vision, allowing me to see the poorly lit surrounds fairly well. Then again, the change could merely have been a facet of the dream.

I crept around the waterfall. I could see perfectly well, now, and the portion of the great building in which I stood was lit as by daylight; yet I could not remember having seen any windows. The corridor's walls were composed of large stone blocks cut and fit so precisely that no mortar w as necessary. The vaulted ceiling was the same in construction, with stones cut and wedged into place so as to support one another. The ceiling was a considerable distance above; the corridor walls were some seven feet apart. The floor was coated with a thick layer of dust, which gradually became thicker as I progressed. Strewn along the floor with increased frequency were piles of rubble. Now and anon I saw, while studying the ceiling, places where portions of the large blocks had given away and crashed to the harder stone of the floor. While the rubble about the floor formed no notable obstruction nor caused any drastic delay in my progress, the notion of a weakening ceiling proffered itself to me and was entertained in a moment of serious consternation. Acting upon the fear that some of the stones in the doubtlessly ancient and evidently deteriorating ceiling might become dislodged and fall upon me as I passed beneath them, I quickened my pace—yet attempted to step lightly on the floor and kept as quiet as possible.

Proceeding with great caution as I was, I became more acutely aware of the ominous *stillness* of the atmosphere. The high, vaulted ceiling above me; the wide passageway whose floor was blanketed with a thick coat of pulverized mortar built up over years of weathering and straining of stone against huge stone; the air heavy with antiquity, yet with a damp, refreshing coolness—all combined effectively to produce an aura of monstrous *age*. Often it was as if I walked through the passages of a mediaeval citadel upon whose walls Time and War had wrought their full effect. No, the age of the structure through which I wandered was incomparable to anything on earth.

I was held in awe by the very *essence* of my fantastic dream-environs. Soon this poetic mood or emotion drifted away in that insane fashion in which sensations are experienced in dream, only to be replaced by concern as to which course to assume in further exploring the territory I had been allotted by the god Morpheus. For the way I had now taken ended in intersection with another corridor. I deliberated for some time as to which hall to take, left or right, since the rubble strewn about the floors of either hall were more frequent—indicating a greater age than I had yet seen. The question of whether I should turn back at that point or not occupied me for a moment, causing anxiety, which in most cases would cause a sleeper to wake. The thought of returning the way I had come—retracing the long corridors in darkness only to face the blistering and noxious heat of the open plains— was most unpleasant. Ahead lay the possibility of becoming isolated in an especially ancient section of the edifice as the result of a collapse. I took the left passageway as it seemed to be relatively less cluttered with debris, while the right grew dark after only a few paces and appeared most uninviting.

Once I had committed myself to the leftward route, I noticed several doorways leading off from the way—the first I had encountered in this maze of halls. Curious to see these more closely—and discover what lay behind them—I made for them directly, regardless of the disquiet I effected in my hasty course across the littered floor.

The first doorway led to a small chamber of curious content. In one corner was set a crude table made of stone. What was remarkable was that it must have been of considerable age, conceivably older than the edifice in which it stood, for it sagged drastically at the center. Closer examination, too, showed that it was definitely made of stone, not of clay or similar soft material. Otherwise, the table was of little interest, being devoid of objects. In the opposite corner stood a queer chest, apparently overlaid with a thin sheet of metal singularly engraved with hieroglyphic pictographs and what might have been a more advanced form of writing. Drawing closer, I saw markings that depicted some ghastly ceremonial rites performed by groups of squat, unmentionably wiggling, larva-like blasphemies. Not finding a clasp, I thumped the top of the chest to sound its contents and received in response a miasmal stench that suddenly befouled the air. I made no further attempt to open the chest and hurriedly left the room.

A second portal showed a room piled high with rubble. From the entrance, I saw among the clutter innumerable stacks of thin tablets—many broken and others crumbling—buried in a mass that had fallen from the ceiling to expose a room above. Fragments of the ceiling still hung precariously above, so I was afraid to enter the room, however much I would have liked to examine those tablets.

Continuing along the corridor, I noted the beginning of a series of engravings or bas-reliefs laid into the walls, very few of which had been defaced by the mocking hand of Time. These I scrutinized with great interest and was happy to find them different—both in style and subject—from those on the metal chest I had seen in the first chamber. The reliefs illustrated in primitive but artful workmanship the history of the civilization that had originated in this star-complex. Below each graven picture was a belt of writing whose peculiar alphabet was of curiously arranged bars, dots and wedges was totally unlike anything I had seen on earth—excepting, perhaps, Arabic, to which this bore an odd resemblance in its curving and extended nature. This writing, I supposed, recorded the history that was illustrated by the bas-reliefs.

In one relief, what seemed to be the creation myth of the race that once inhabited Lheil was portrayed by a number of silhouetted figures, surrounded in mist, beckoning an obscure figure out of a steaming fen. Many of the subsequent reliefs showed the race's early advances—always with at least one of the silhouetted figures in the background. The race was usually represented by one figure—which now seemed vaguely anthropomorphic, being tall, thin and stalk-like but having arms and legs not unlike humans. The silhouettes obviously represented their gods; they were ill defined and in form difficult to specify. However, a number of times they were depicted more clearly as being carefully cloaked, while at other times they were shrouded in mist and kept in the background. In later bas-reliefs, the gods were not present. This seemed to coincide with a certain period in the race's history when science had advanced to a considerable degree. Just after this point, the murals ceased altogether.

My study of the engraved walls had put me a good distance down the corridor—literally down, for there was a noticeable slant in the course of the stone floor, now remarkably clear of rubble. I had passed several chambers along the hall, but seeing with a glance that each was empty of any object of interest, I had not entered. Instead, I had continued along the way, enrapt in the murals.

When the series of embossments ended, I came to a compartment that was a comparative marvel; for in it was a long, low table entirely covered with hundreds of *bottles*—some upright, others overturned, many broken, all covered with a thick, filmy dust. I picked up an unbroken flask and examined it more closely. Beneath the coat of film, the bottles appeared to be greenish-black. However, taking a broken fragment of another bottle, I was able to scrape away even this coating to find that the bottles were not bottles at all, being composed of some silvery metal as fragile as glass. Painstakingly removing most of the discoloration—caused by aeons of oxidation—something further came to light: the surface was designed with intricate swirls that complicated odd arrangements of angles, curves, circles and dots.

There was more. The cork or stopper of each flask was topped with a large, multifaceted gemlike stone. Originally a wide variety of colors, the stones were now sadly fogged and blackened by the cold air, the circulating dust from the growing mounds of detritus, and the uncounted, *uncountable* ages that had passed since they were first cut by some alien lapidary.

I tried the stopper of the flask and found it rather easy to remove. It came off with the familiar pop of a wine cork. The stopper once removed, the contents of the flask were disturbed from their eternal sleep and a heavenly aroma arose to sweeten the stale air as the sparkling liquid stirred and bubbled within.

It never occurred to me *not* to drink the alien brew. Being present in such quantity, it was obviously a fermented or distilled liquor intended as a beverage—for every culture known to man has developed methods of fermentation or distillation. Having already risked tasting the luminous waterfall, and struck again with thirst from endless wandering through the dusty ruins, I discounted any danger of drinking from the flask.

I wiped away the remaining dust, raised the flask to my lips and took a hearty swig. Nothing from the vineyards or monasteries of France and Italy—not the most exotic liquor of the Far East—surely, not even the ambrosia of ancient Greece, nor the most delicious wild berries in the Garden of Eden—none of these could taste so sweet, so fragrant, so lovely! It was icy cold, yet fiery hot; sweet as honey, yet tangy as citrus and sparkling like champagne. It was the color of platinum melted in the vats of a sorcerer's cellar, bewitched by the blessings of Dionysus, flavored with the rich blood of fruit growing on peaks overlooking Olympus shed by the ivory talon of a star-treading griffin wandering in from the nightly spaces between the quasars.

The lightly fermented liquor was the most beautiful thing that I had ever sensed, the must luscious thing that had ever passed my lips. I tilted it toward the intact ceiling of the chamber and let the enchanted contents slide down my throat.

I was raised to a supernal ecstasy and a livening spirit inhabited my heart. But soon the cloud of enchantment passed, and though I remained partly under the almost mesmeric spell or charm of the wine, I was quickly on my way through the corridor again, walking as steadily as before, if more lightly. I was not as alert as I had been, however, and left all the flasks behind.

Perhaps because of the wine, perhaps due to the odd and varying depths of sleep and clarity of dream, I have difficulty remembering my sojourn through the following portions of the ruined edifice. It is possible that I passed into another building; but if I had done so, it must have been through a connecting tunnel or underground passageway, since an emergence into the polystellar heat of the outside would surely have revived me from my lapse of awareness. I do remember descending several levels by way of winding ramps, and when I did finally resume alert exploration, I was in a region so well preserved that no rubble—only dust—was to be found along the hall-ways and in the cells onto which they opened.

I was following a narrow passageway along whose right side were many small, adjoining cells of no particular interest. On the left, however, a new series of pictographic murals began. The artisanship on these was even more advanced, suggesting they were newer, but they were continued the format of graphical embossments underscored by written historical explanations. Nowhere were the silhouetted figures from the earliest bas-reliefs depicted, having vanished with Lheil's scientific advances.

Technologically, the civilization of Lheil was progressing considerably in the era recounted by the murals. In addition to advances in meteorology, ge-ology and other physical studies of the planet, there was a hint of exploration of other planets circling the Atlaanât solar complex. Although no clear pic-ture could convey the size of the race in population, it would seem to have been somewhat large for Lheil, but small for the planet. In fact, there was no indication that any city existed apart from Lheil, nor were any other planets of the Atlaanât system known to have been inhabited.

Abruptly, the murals were interrupted by a door, although they contin-ued beyond this door. This was certainly novel, for I had seen no actual doors in Lheil thus far—I had seen only *doorways*. The door was equipped with no knob or with any other such device with which to open it. Nor were there hinges visible on this side of the doorframe, but this did not necessarily mean that the door was a sliding one. After some time, I was able to find a small panel which, when pressed, released a spring that threw back the door. That this spring yet worked surprised me greatly—what with the appalling age of the building.

I immediately stepped through the door, but upon apperceiving the vista that was thereby revealed, I was taken aback and staggered to my knees. For the door had opened onto a chamber of such incredible vastness that I reeled giddily. Mere words cannot describe the dimensions of the Cyclopean hall, whose remote ceiling was obscured by thin wisps of clouds; the altitude was vertiginous. The distant wall could be seen only dimly; the extent of the hall lengthwise, stretching away to my right, was far beyond the dependable range of vision. The overall proportions of the room were Gargantuan, Ti-tanic, incredible; its volume was incalculable.

My mind was racked by the mere thought of my infinitesimal, meaning-less self within this monstrous chamber with dimensions known to none, whose existence was never intended to be revealed to a human being. I stood awfully alone beneath the towering figure of Nihility and thought that I must cease to exist in respect to all things meaningful.

A sickening vertigo gripped me and I fell to the floor nauseated. My head seethed and I hoped that my dream would end and I would soon lapse into that consciousness known as waking reality. In this I was betrayed, for I eventually rose to my feet, fighting back tides of dizzy blackness with some unwanted instinct innate to hapless dreamers. Dazed but partly recovered, I began *without volition* the ineffable task of traversing the enormous hallway.

I walked, half-stumbled, for countless hours, nearly hugging the wall on my right—the wall through which I had entered by way of the spring-door—as if to reassure myself that the space was not limitless. Little could my pro-gress be determined. In order to prevent another wave of giddiness, I shielded my eyes to prohibit myself from looking to the left across the breadth of the hall, or upward to the ceiling, or forward to the far wall, and looked only downward or to the right.

Eternities passed and still I could not be assured that I had made any progress whatsoever. Was the seeming infinitude of the hall due to some ef-fect of the mystic oenomel upon my senses? Or was the hall itself merely a mirage imposed upon my brain by the spell brewed into that deceivingly lovely liquid by some powerful sorcerer of another universe? I could not tell. I could only stumble forward through this mighty passageway of giants of an-other time.

I went on in nightmare, reacting as a child would by holding my hands up before my eyes to block out the horror. Millennia passed; I was at a loss to calculate the result of my incessant advance, even by systematically daring to compare my apparent distance from the back of the hall, from which I had begun and which I could now barely see. I wondered if the tiny corridors I had explored before were just beyond the wall I followed, almost within reach; but if there were any spring-doors along the wall, they could not be detected.

At one point, having grown very weary in my reluctant wandering, I col-lapsed against the right wall and slept. I slept, but this period of rest and escape from the damnation of the hall was not entirely mine, for I was plagued with wild dreams. In one dream, I was back in the room full of the flasks of exotic liquor. I took one of the flasks, but the dream ended when a tall, thin figure appeared at the portal. In another dream, I awoke from my sleep and boldly stared across the voids of the hall to the cloud-hidden ceiling and glimpsed in a horrifying moment something that looked like shadow in the vertiginous heights. I slept again, but at last awoke. Looking about me, *I saw the flask of wine that I had taken in the earlier dream.* Upon seeing it, I fainted.

How the bottle or flask had gotten where it was, was impossible to determine; but *that* it was there was an undeniable fact. When I recovered, I saw that there were odd marks in the dust that were quite distinguishable from those that I had made. That I was in an extended state of dream during my entire experience of Lheil only occurred to me from time to time, and all that happened held a weird reality that I cannot explain even today. I was constantly affected by a horror so abstract and so imposing upon my imagination that I could not think clearly enough to understand it. One cause of this horror may have been the strangely pragmatic way in which I was allowed to observe the details of the whole dream.

It was not long after I had recovered from my faint and had seen the disturbances in the dust that I was again assailed with an uncanny thirst. I sat several feet from the flask, which, I knew without looking, was filled with the enchanted, infernally potent nectar. I attempted to forget the painful thirst by studying the intricate swirls and curves of the surface of the flask. To further this preoccupation, I took the flask and began to clean it of its tarnish with a bit of mortar I found on the floor. But once I held the metallic flask and felt its cool contents stir within, I was without will and could not resist drinking of the damnable brew, even if resistance would save me from a poisonous death.

For a second time the freezing coolness of the liquid was felt upon my lips, as the fiery hot ingredients were felt in my throat. I must have gulped the wine, but the bottle's contents seemed undiminishable. It seemed to have no immediate effect upon me, not even a stimulating influence as was felt before to some degree. Thinking that the drink was not intoxicating after all, I decided to keep the flask with me as I continued along the hall.

After another very long period of walking through the mammoth chamber, I was certain that I had progressed substantially in my sojourn, and could see the end of the hall more clearly than ever before. Soon I wearied again, and stopped to rest. It had only now begun to occur to me that, unless the alien atmosphere or other conditions had some bearing on my sleeping habits, I had been travelling for nearly two days; it seemed like two eternities. This realization added another degree to the enormity of the Titanic corridor, and I was appalled ever the more by this thought.

Again, I slept and again was haunted by the eerie dreams I had experienced on the first "night"—during my first period of rest. Had the blasted liquor only now begun to have its effect upon my mind? Was the medium of sleep the only form in which the power of the alien brew could become manifest? In one dream, I found myself before the bas-reliefs outside the wall of this Brobdingnagian hall. The engravings were of the advanced technological era and somehow I could understand them better than before: the state of dream-within-dream provided an acumen that practically allowed me to read the inscriptions—or to infer what they meant by studying the reliefs alone. Not only did I understand them, but I could also *feel* them: such was the nature of my acumen.

With the increase in scientific involvement and discovery, there was a general abandonment of superstition. The gods once represented by silhouetted figures were totally absent, yet the thought was conveyed that they had been forsaken in favor of more tangible conceptions. For some time this went on, until some sort of unavoidable natural disaster was predicted by the scientists of the race. The masses, faced with inevitable destruction, refused to accept the claims of the scientists and instead chose to denounce the sciences altogether as spurious and fallacious. This turn-about became so violent that many scientists and scholars were killed by angry and frightened mobs.

At the same time, there was a dramatic increase in production of the fabulous oenomel, probably consumed for its mind-altering effect—what it used as an escape from the dire situation? The final reliefs also indicated that some vast new building project was being undertaken that dwarfed any previous construction effort. The heady wine may have been useful, too, in drugging the workers to evince greater productivity.

At the end, the remaining scientists (who were evidently responsible for

Intimations of Unreality

the historical record preserved in the bas-reliefs, which stopped abruptly) fled in spacecrafts that could evacuate only limited numbers of the doomed populace of Lheil, leaving behind the great mass of the race to suffer a fate they refused to accept.

A point that seemed to be stressed in my mind as being important was this: The doomed inhabitants turned in superstition not back to the gods represented in the mural reliefs by mist-shrouded figures, but rather to a single deity. I somehow knew this even though there was no single depiction indicating the fact, but the entity was a sort of All-in-One being associated with the spirit of the race as a whole.

The dream faded and another took its place. I vaguely remember wandering on through the vast hall in a delirious state. Occasionally, a certain dream fragment was interjected as a vision of delirium as I wandered—a vision that filled me with great horror and repulsion. For it seemed, sporadically and for brief flashes, that I was surrounded by thousands or millions of the stalk-like beings who had inhabited Lheil uncounted millennia before my traumatic or astral visitation. They were all facing the front end of the hall, vacillating and muttering frightfully. I was filled with aversion by the swaying, chanting throng. In one vision, I was hideously face-to-face with one of the denizens of Lheil, and the look on its face shall never leave my memory. The countenance was one of intense concentration, yet of profound fear: the thing seemed to be praying for its very soul, while its bulging eyes stared off into nothingness and filled with fire. My last impression was of looking out across the enormous hall upon the millions of beings who vacillated and chanted aloud in a unison that was the product of an acute concentration of mass will.

I started from dream-delirium and felt a cool breeze blowing from somewhere in the hall ahead of me. Hopeful that some portal and means of escape lay ahead, I quickly arose and walked briskly through the prodigious hall toward the probable source of the wind. The hall, it was a surprise to note, was filled with a thick, cloudy smoke which checked the visibility critically. How this had come to be was far beyond all guesses, but it had certainly taken place during my hag-ridden sleep. Suddenly the smoke cleared and the enormous hall was again visible; but a very drastic change had come about—one even more difficult to explain than the mist-filled atmosphere. For, emerging from smoke into light, I could see the terminus of the massive hall not a hundred yards before me! Had I walked in my sleep? This was the only possible rationalization of my farther placement along the hall; but how could I have covered such a tremendous distance while in a state of apparent sleep?

The moment's amazement passed quickly, for as the mist cleared I apperceived that the hall terminated in a monstrous, impossible door that offered a mind-blasting positive standard with which to compare and measure the height of the entire chamber.

Worse than ever was I assailed by sweeping vertigo as I looked up at that door of cloudy altitude, and I fell onto the floor in a violent fit of vomiting. How long I lay there I cannot remember, but when I arose the cool air—which blew through a foot-high crack under the door—helped me recover from my shock. A long draught of the oenomel did more in this direction.

Standing, I went forward mesmerically, all the while keeping my eyes downcast to inhibit the sight of that awful towering door. Along the edge of the door and leading upward to the knob or lever by which to open the door (I dared not look again to see which), there ran a series of bar-steps or rungs extending outward from the surface. Without volition of my own, *I began to climb the steps*.

Up I went, and upward still. My limbs were numbed by the wine I had taken before beginning this insane ascent, and consequently I felt no fatigue. On I climbed, hand over hand, foot over foot, up the ladder of metal bars. After several hours of climbing at a steady pace, I heard the sound of wind from above—the same sound as I had heard at the foot of the door. I supposed there to be a keyhole or some such aperture up ahead, but I dared not look; neither was I once so foolish as to look *down*. I believe my heart would have stopped on the spot and this dream of Lheil would have been the last for my tortured mind.

The sound of the wind from above grew louder as I progressed. I began to feel as though my life was drawing to an end, that I was going to meet my destiny at the top of the ladder. With this feeling, I began imagining looking down (most hideous of thoughts!), or (even worse!) of *turning* and looking out across the hall . . . Once, in fact, I caught myself beginning to do just that, and the horror of the thought alone shook me so that I lost my grip and nearly fell. But onward I went, weeping shamelessly now in my fear of falling and in my feeling of momentary doom.

Before I knew it, I was just below the keyhole. I looked up unafraid—but apprehensively. I stopped and stared at the hourglass-shaped hole with its plate-metal trim. I remember swallowing hard. Then I ascended the last several steps—so very slowly—and reached up to the ledge, first with one hand and then the other. Below and behind me, I thought I heard a muffled, murmuring chant rise from a million voices—voices praying to an entity that could only exist if their combined will was strong enough. In the last moment before I pulled myself up to the keyhole, the sound of wind oddly stopped . . . I paused.

At last, I strained to pull myself up a few feet and managed to bring my eyes level with the keyhole. What I saw was the final horror of my dream of Lheil and one that nearly destroyed my mind. I was completely shattered by shock, lost my grip on the metal rungs, and fell backwards into the alien vastness—fell into the waiting arms, the feathery appendages of the emissaries of Hypnos.

What I saw was simply *an eye*.

The Desolation of Falithra

The story of the glorious spread of civilization throughout the fertile lands of the Infinite Plains is recorded in many ancient and revered texts by poets and historians. To all it is known that the ancient city of Falithra was built at the edge of the vast Oraph desert. And all know that the ancient colony was abandoned within a single generation of its founding and now sleeps beneath the creeping desert sands. But untold is the reason for the sudden desolation of Falithra by its good people; and the cause of their madness; and the reason for history's odd silence as to their fate. Untold, that is, until now.

1.

King Nahlyth was the fifth ruler in a long-reigning and illustrious dynasty in the archaic land of Yagonia, which abounded in olden knowledge and mystery. One day he called before him the two priests Zyonda and Bezeun, who were much loved by worshippers at their temples in the City of the Palace.

"Tell me of the fabled realm of Azayonis," King Nahlyth commanded.

Ancient Zyonda of the long hoary beard spoke, saying: "Your Highness, in the ancient tongue Azayonis means 'the place destined for us by the gods.' It was first mentioned in the early chapters of the Book of Yagonia by learned prophets and seers who were said to visit the realm in drug-induced dreams."

"Yes . . . and pray tell, where does this fabled land lie?" asked the king.

Bezeun of the short brown beard spoke, saying: "Honorable One, some say that this prophesied realm lies to the southeast of Yagonia, beyond all the fertile lands that are named and inhabited. And some say it is not a place at all, but a state of mind that can only be known through devout worship of the gods."

And Zyonda added: "Yet others, O King, say that Azayonis will not be found in this world but in the next. But I believe it is to be found here, as the prophets have written."

Zyonda and the younger Bezeun held their differences in their manner of interpreting the writings of the prophets and in their concepts of the gods, though they differed little in their outward teachings.

King Nahlyth weighed what the priests had said before he spoke. "I have pondered much on this question, my priests, and I believe it is time to discover once and for all if this fabled realm of Azayonis exists!"

And King Nahlyth instructed the priests to gather their acolytes and lead a number of citizens as pioneers on a quest to find this "land destined by the gods," that they may live there in peace and prosperity in the good favor of the gods.

At once Bezeun and Zyonda took leave of the king and made arrangements for their sojourn into the unknown lands for this holy purpose. They gathered their acolytes and the most devout of their congregations, all of whom felt privileged to be chosen for a mission both historic and sacred.

When the time came to leave the City of the Palace, the king allotted a certain number of soldiers to accompany them on their mission. Many goods were taken and scores of the best breed of horse to draw the wagons that carried the people and their belongings. Great was the traveling party, and great the crowd that gathered to see them off. King Nahlyth marked the departure with a decree and both priests made their blessings and read from the ancient scrolls.

2.

The procession traveled south from the City of the Palace and through the Valley of Nib. Their course led past the foothills of the Astrontian range, which stretched south for some miles and then turned southwest. Lying to their east during the journey was the great desert of Oraph.

When they reached the last little village in the known territories, just before the land grew more rugged, Zyonda dismissed the soldiers to return to their palace, bidding them speak thusly unto the king:

"We are not in need of protection by man, which is futile against the evil gods, but only the favor of the great ones to carry us through the undiscovered territories. If it be their will to offer us to the desert or let us succumb to the hardships of journey, then it shall be so."

Bezeun argued and said they might encounter savages in the unknown territories, or wild beasts, and would be in need of protection. But Zyonda was the elder and the soldiers followed his orders—quite willfully, since many of them had been leery about the whole adventure.

For there were other myths and legends besides that of Azayonis that Zyonda ignored, but about which Bezeun was even-minded. These legends had their dim origins in stories brought back by the first brave travelers to journey out into these unknown regions of grassy hills and beautiful river-valleys. They whispered tales of a strange and wicked people that were not entirely or truly people, being primitive and goat-like. At night, the goat people of the unnamed country would light fires on hillsides and dance and sing madly to weird flute music, appeasing unknown and fearful gods with horrible sacrifices. And they built terrible stone structures engraved with un-said things even more horrid than the debauched goat-things themselves. As the tide of civilization had gradually flowed southward, the creatures were driven forth or killed; their crude structures were all but destroyed and even the fragments were covered over and avoided.

Indeed, on this journey the holy procession encountered the shunned ruins and remnants and gave them wide berth. A scout discovered a cave and Bezeun went to see the odd carvings of unknown beasts. Similar carv-ings were seen in large scale on cliff sides and on curious stones that pointed to the sky in doubtful configurations and inference. All of this disturbed the travelers that saw them, for none wished to encounter the beastly figures so horribly depicted.

3.

At last they arrived at a place near the edge of the desert Oraph, which bor-dered the fertile lands as far north as Galredia. The hillsides were wooded with fruit and nut trees and fed by streams, and even if it abutted the desert the land was fertile enough, Zyonda reasoned, to be the fabled realm of Azayonis.

"Here we shall settle, and here build our city and our Azayonis. The gods have seen our safe passage here, so this must be 'the place destined for us by the gods.' Here we shall build the city of Falithra, 'the city beside the desert.' And here we will develop a perfect society that is blessed by the gods."

But Bezeun warned against Zyonda's plan. The land rose up from the desert and overlooked it, and Bezeun pointed to accursed monoliths just visible in the sand: further remnants of the horrid goat-people. How could this be destined for the good people of Yagonia when it was previously inhabited by such an inhuman breed?

But the people were weary of travel and fearful to go further, and they were comforted by the assurances of the elder priest Zyonda. They remained in their pavilions until some woodland was cleared and the timber used to build. Stones were brought down from the hills, water was diverted from the streams, crops planted to supplement the yield of the orchards.

And so the city of Falithra was built on a gentle rise of fertile land that overlooked the desert Oraph. And the people worshipped and thanked their gods, as was a good thing to do, and they walked straight in their ways.

4.

One night a great windstorm came over the hills and over the city from parts unknown. The hell-winds blew all night, over the city and into the desert. And when the dawn came, the people of Falithra arose and looked out their windows and beheld a sight most hideous. For the windstorm had blown away the desert sands to reveal an ancient abomination lying there: the stone ruins of a lost city built by the horrid goat-people whose traces had been seen along the journey through the unknown regions. Dark columns rose up that had been all but buried in the sand, the tops of which were the monoliths seen by Bezeun. And the columns and walls of the ruined city were covered with frightful and obscene carvings.

And the winds turned and blew an awful stench from the ruins into the city of Falithra, arousing those who had not already awakened. And this is what sent the people of Falithra screaming with fear and madness over the hills and into the regions unknown. Leaving suddenly without preparation, many soon perished in their flight; chaos and lawlessness reigned as men turned against men and fought like savages to survive in the wilderness. And some even took their own lives, disillusioned and unable to face the harsh reality of their circumstances or admit the failure of their gods and priests.

Such was the desolation of Falithra, abandoned by its good people, who became like wild animals and were forgotten by civilization. The sands of Oraph crept forward, burying the dark ruins once again, and blew through the empty streets of Falithra—unknown and shunned to this day.

The Twilight Necropolis

Yom Keshmon wandered among the colossal ruins in darkness . . .

He had glimpsed its mighty statues from afar, from the depth of the nameless desert wherein the forgotten necropolis sprawled. But first he had seen them in a dream—a strange, haunting dream that visited him again and again despite his mantic powers.

For Yom Keshmon was a sorcerer with weird knowledge held by few—if any. This he first attained from an unknown master, who died; then he developed on his own, in the wooded foothills of Tryndalonicas. He emerged from obscurity to enter contests of enchantment in fabled Yagonia, where he defeated many noted opponents in mantic matches and gnomic games. Rising quickly to the status of a great master, he assumed superior airs, wore purple robes and entitled himself Grand Prince of Sorcery. At the challenge of some brash young magician from an outer kingdom, Yom Keshmon turned the war of wizardry into a battle to the death. Thereafter, he felt free to entomb or exile as he wished, defeating and destroying many great wizards in the surrounding lands. Thus he attained to a luxurious empire: a private kingdom in a land of summer and light. For years he went unchallenged and softened into a hedonist and romanticist, and though he was given to his own pursuits he did care for the needs of his empire.

Then came the dark dreams of the twilight necropolis, desolate but alluring, glimmering in a silvery half-light. They possessed him at night and obsessed him by day, until he lost all interest in the affairs of his kingdom, which lapsed into turmoil and disrepair. At last, he abandoned his palace and all its affairs and roamed the planet from rim to rim in search of the nightmare city, fearful whether he should find it or not.

Yom Keshmon rode a powerful steed bred by magic; it never tired and galloped ten times as fast as any normal mount. On his quest he took a marvelous torch to light his way by night: it hovered above him wherever he went and cast a brilliant light. But the spell failed when they crossed into the nameless desert and first caught sight of those mighty statues from afar. As in dream, they seemed at first to be sharp mountain peaks thrust up to dizzying heights from the flat floor of the desert. But the final flare of the setting sun revealed that they were titan sculptures that could never have been raised by man.

On he travelled in the faint twilight, watching as the weird statues seemed to step forward from the horizon as he drew closer. Even in darkness, the gaunt visages of the colossi glowed with ghostly light. Now and then, the monstrous faces reminded him of some great mage that his own magic had subdued. First there appeared the face of Bordish Narem with his hawkish nose; then there was Yoth Gammon, like a flaming skull; awful Sardon, who in defeat looked so kind-at-heart; and wily Wormon Surr, the most dangerous of them all. The faces rose from behind the dunes and fell again from sight, until at last they disappeared in the darkness.

With his torch extinguished and only sorcery and instinct to guide him, Yom Keshmon reached the ruins of the long-dead city in the pitch-blackness of night. He dismounted and stood at the base of the titan statues, looked up at them in awe against the starry night and wondered which star was their origin. For they were so ancient and worn they must have been carved by the hands of nightmare gods before life ever began on this planet.

Yom Keshmon roamed through the ruins in darkness that faded softly into the gloom of early morning. He felt small and powerless and walked in a daze, his feet moving for him and guiding him though the rubble of the primordial city. Finally, he came to a solid structure and entered it, finding himself in a chamber lit by an unknown source. In the center of the room stood a stone table, and on it lay a stone tablet covered with the dust of eons.

Yom Keshmon stood before the ancient tablet, blew away the dust, and read the words of a poem written in the words of his native land:

Yom Keshmon, the mighty king, seeks

A twilit place seen in a dream:

A city bedwarfed by great peaks

Reaching up to the sky, as it seemed.

     Intimations of Unreality

Yom Keshmon, the sorcerer, sits
Enrobed in a heavy black cloak
With eyes flaring—coals from the pit—
And long hair the color of smoke.

Yom Keshmon, the ancient sage, reads
Dark characters carved on a stone
Which wind like a footpath that leads
To hill hollows, secret and lone.

Yom Keshmon the voyager finds
His twilight necropolis, true;
But also a cruel truth that binds:
He finds there his destiny, too.

The Shadow from Yith

The cabin was hidden among pines in the mountains of central Idaho. Near the headwaters of Camas Creek, it was located in the Sawtooth National Forest and therefore protected from further development, but the cabin remained in private hands.

Due to the remote location, there was neither electricity nor running water. Consisting of a single room, the cabin was sparsely furnished: a kitchen area was defined by a bare table, two folding chairs, and a propane stove; to one side, there was a single twin-sized bed; and at the end of the room was a rustic fireplace and a stack of wood. The one luxury appeared to be the spring mattress.

To this modest cabin came Christopher Evans-Douglas, professor of advanced mathematics at the University of Idaho at Caldwell. He had a promising career: at twenty-three, he was already a professor, if not yet at a leading school, and had published a number of well-received papers. His brilliance was noted early in grade school and he entered college two years ahead of schedule. In three years he earned his bachelor's degree, and in three more obtained both his master's and doctorate at the prestigious Massachusetts Institute of Technology. Idaho was perhaps not his first choice, but the professorship and a promise of complete freedom within the department made it an attractive first post.

But during the past year—his first year of teaching—Evans-Douglas found himself fascinated by areas other than mathematics. The sciences of astronomy, archaeology, and anthropology had only been minor distractions in college, but now reappeared as unchartered territories full of unanswered questions. Furthermore, he had become attracted to an area of study that he had never given much credence: the paranormal or supernatural—ranging from alchemy and mysticism to parapsychology and the occult. In fact, he was forced to admit that their supernatural air had always appealed to his imagination. Now he pursued them zealously, and pondered much on mysteries of the past that remain unexplained in the present. With a brilliant mind eager to learn what he did not know, and challenged to analyze and explain where others had failed, Evans-Douglas leapt across the threshold from the natural, mechanical, and mathematical into the supernatural, mystic, and magical.

However, it was not to pursue studies—old or new—that he had come to the cabin on Camas Creek. Rather, he sought complete relaxation and escape from his books and papers. His extracurricular researches after class had extended far into the night and were resumed each day, before class and between classes. The few hours of sleep that he allowed himself were insufficient, and the fatigue had begun to show on his face and in his posture. Even the hours that he slept were not entirely free from the influences of his waxing interests, for he had been plagued for some time by dreams of an outré and even horrific nature. Faced with the competing demands of teaching and the new research, he had begun to debate whether he should return to campus in the fall or devote full time to his paranormal studies—perhaps leave Idaho altogether and travel to specialized centers of learning, if such could be found.

In the quiet of the forest, Evans-Douglas hoped to find peace. The cabin belonged to a good friend and colleague at Caldwell who had witnessed the decline in his health and suggested that a few weeks in the mountains would provide a healthy change. And in the place of books the colleague lent him his rod and tackle. Personally, he had no interest in fishing and found it boring when he tried it as a child, but he took the fishing gear to humor his friend. Now it was all he had to do to while away his time, other than taking walks in the woods. Perhaps he would try some writing—poetry had been an early and forgotten pleasure of his childhood—and for this purpose he had brought a pen and plenty of paper. But he was already mourning the total absence of books.

In this manner Evans-Douglas had resolved to pass his summer; but regardless of how he tried to distract himself, his mind invariably drifted to metaphysical questions. The mechanical activities designed to pass the time only left his thoughts free to wander, and his obsession—never wholly absent—returned. Either as a result of this or as one of its factors, the bothersome dreams also returned, leaving him haunted as never before by their strangeness. Ironically, he now had no studies to keep his thoughts from those dreams, however much the studies might influence the dreams in turn.

The nature of his recurring dreams was not easy to understand, and how his imagination had conjured them up from his studies—which seemed only distantly connected—was another puzzle he could not solve. The dream that was most often repeated had a climax which was always erased from his memory, yet which was apparently so terrifying that it awoke him with a start afterwards and left him trembling in a cold sweat. If and when he could get back to sleep, the dream was repeated in every detail except that he would awaken in the city rather than in the cabin—that is, he would "wake up" into a new dream. The city (which may or may not have been Caldwell) was completely silent, as usual in the very early morning, but in this case all of the inhabitants were dead (this he somehow knew) and strange winged creatures filled the sky and perched grotesquely along the building-tops like living gargoyles. At this point, he would usually awaken to reality, puzzled deeply by whatever allegory lay behind the dreams. If he did not awaken immediately, he would either dream no more or dream things inconsistent and quickly forgotten.

The dreams had a unique quality about them unlike the atmosphere of an "ordinary" dream or nightmare. Although Evans-Douglas was never cog-nizant of the fact that he was dreaming, as is the case in so-called "lucid" dreams, he was always very alert and the dreams had an usual veracity when they occurred: they seemed as real as his waking state—or more real, if pos-sible. The oft-repeated dream was especially remarkable for the fact that each time it recurred—even though every step in the dream followed in the exact sequence as in the previous experiencing—he became more aware of his surroundings in it as he learned more about mystical and occult matters. This deepened his supernatural dread with each recurrence, and, in waking, he suspected that the forgotten final scene would eventually be revealed within the dream itself when he understood what induced his dreams. He half-feared the time when he would awaken with total remembrance . . .

Nevertheless, he resolved to get to the bottom of the nightmares, however disturbing they might be. He drove into nearby Kilgore for the first time since his vacation and bought the supplies that would be necessary for the next week or so. He also bought some sleeping pills, which he thought might be

Intimations of Unreality

helpful in prolonging sleep and the potentiality for dream. Returning, he started a fire in the fireplace to raise the temperature of the cabin. It was evening, and a slight chill was in the air outside; moreover, a fire's dancing flames and musical crackling always had a hypnotic effect on him, and the warmth would make the the atmosphere even more favorable for relaxation. He took two sleeping pills with icy cold water, wrapped himself in a blanket, and slumped longways in a chair before the fire. Then, in an ideal mental state, he fixed his mind on the weird dream, all the while peering intensely into the fire. The effect was marvelous, for his eyelids drooped rapidly, and he fell into a slumber whose profundity bordered dangerously upon the state of coma.

In the final instant before he slipped into darkness, Evans-Douglas realized that he might not dream at all, since most dreams occur in light slumber, which the pills might prevent. But this realization came too late, and a fraction of a second later he was irrecoverably lost to the shadowy realms where Hypnos is lord.

In the mistiness that is the uncertainty of dream, Christopher Evans-Douglas slowly gathered his senses and observed his surroundings. He stood in a narrow corridor of some length which was poorly lit and whose extremities were lost in haziness. The ceiling was only two feet above him, and the walls were four feet apart. The walls were built of large stone blocks, moderately rough and unpolished, but perfectly cut and set into place without mortar. The frequent irregularity in the shape of the stones presented cause to wonder at the perfect fittings, and a great deal of time and hard work must have been put into the construction of the walls. In contrast, the ceiling and the floor were made up of very large, perfectly polished rectangular slabs of stone.

Evans-Douglas's attention was drawn sharply away from the hallway's composition by a sudden glimmer in the distance ahead. Something was very definitely up there, and he gazed furiously around for a place to hide. But the thing was approaching with such speed that he knew it could easily overtake him if he tried to flee. With growing fear and a certain curiosity, he watched the rapid approach of the alien being.

At a distance of ten feet away from him, the thing paused suddenly. It hovered in midair (it had been literally flying down the hall) and seemed to study him. From what he could see of it in the dim light, it was a sphere: two feet in diameter and composed of some translucent material, it emitted a quiet hum while it hovered.

Then the thing moved toward him once more, albeit much more slowly this time. It paused a few feet from him and he felt that it was attempting to communicate with him by telepathy—he had a strange sensation in his head. Although he did not know what the thing had said, it occurred to him that he was supposed to follow it. It moved slowly away from him and he hesitantly began to walk after it, unsure whether he should trust the apparent friendliness of the sphere.

As they proceeded down the hall in the direction whence the sphere came, Evans-Douglas received messages from his guide that manifested themselves as thoughts in his mind. He was told of the city he was in, which was Czymra, the planet they were on, Yith, and its location in relation to earth. Of Yith, Evans-Douglas had previously heard very little of—had indeed seen only one curious and superstitious reference in his studies. The Great Race that inhabited the planet, however, he knew nothing at all about, and the hovering orb relayed much information to him as they passed along the hall.

"The Great Race," as they were known in certain obscure and esoteric writings on earth, called themselves the "special" or "chosen ones," and had a name with this meaning which could not be written in any language other than their own. Their sole purpose in the cosmos was to assimilate enormous amounts of knowledge of all sorts and from all known civilizations, recording and storing it in vast libraries or archives such as the one in Czymra.

At this point they came to an intersecting corridor that opened onto a very large, brightly lit chamber on the right. It appeared unexpectedly as Evans-Douglas pondered the thoughts transmitted to him by the sphere, and he was taken aback by his first glimpse of the chamber and its occupants.

There were a score or more of the spheres attending a curious array of machines that filled the spacious room. The machinery was composed of metal and glass or crystal, as well as of other substances perhaps akin to plastic or rubber and perhaps akin to wood. As they moved through this alien laboratory, the guide explained that the Great Race was by nature nonmaterial and lived as disembodied minds. But they had found it difficult to effect large-scale changes in matter in their natural state, so they transferred their minds into the crude bodies of a curious amphibious race nearing intelligence that shared the planet with them. Operating through these bodies, they developed technology and applied science, ultimately constructing the mechanical globes to replace the crude bodies they inhabited. Occupying these orbs with their minds, then, they made even greater strides in science and architecture, built great cities such as Czymra on the planet, and advanced their technology to a high degree.

When they had studied their own planet in every imaginable aspect, the race began sending its members to the three moons of Yith and to the other planets of their system. The orbs were not suitable for space travel beyond the moons, so space ships were constructed to travel to the neighboring planets. When this became impractical because of the great distances to be covered and because of the hostility of some of the life-forms on those planets, the race began transporting only their minds through space to occupy the alien bodies. In this way, members of the Great Race infiltrated the worlds of their neighbors unseen and undiscovered, obtaining what information they could about all aspects of their lives. Meanwhile, the hostile minds were housed in the crystal globes and kept under strict supervision until the venturing minds had fulfilled their tasks and no longer needed the captive bodies.

Great stores of knowledge were amassed in this manner, and the Great Race found that they could send their minds *through time* as well as space. This was especially interesting to Evans-Douglas due to his researches both mathematical and metaphysical. The machinery that sent the minds forth over great distances first reduced them to a state of energy not unlike electricity. When periods of *time* were traversed, the energy was modulated to a different state of density and wave-frequency, and the time barrier was bypassed by utilizing the effects of the curvature of space upon particles traveling faster than the speed of light. The room full of machinery was not a laboratory but a transference station used in this non-material exploration of space-time.

In the bright light of the room, Evans-Douglas could see the spheres clearly for the first time. The guide could apparently read his mind and responded to his curiosity with information. Each orb was two feet in diameter and weighed about fifty pounds. They were perfectly round and smooth, and their substance was very much like glass, being made from melting small crystals found in the soil of the planet. Three inches beneath the surface of the globe was another sphere, made of metal only a few thousandths of an inch thick, yet incredibly strong and durable. Within this second sphere were all manner of mechanisms: a motor for flight; others for the coordination and operation of arm-like appendages; devices to register light and sound; a dynamo that generated the electricity needed to operate the sphere; a governor that harmonized all other mechanisms; and so on. At the center of the second sphere was yet another, much smaller globe that acted as the "brain" of the sphere: it housed the mind or essence of the individual and provided an artificial memory. The suspension and motion of the vehicle were achieved through a reversal of electromagnetic polarity.

Bored into the outermost sphere at certain points were holes for special purposes. Long arm-like appendages could be extended through two holes near the bottom of the sphere—for writing, building, and so forth. They could extend to five feet or withdraw into the metal sphere in telescope fashion and were possessed of great strength. At the top were four holes forming a square, from which projected antennae mounted by eye-like sensors. The antennae could extend two feet outward or likewise withdraw into compartments within the metallic shell.

Suddenly, while thoughts coming from the guide were hypnotically aligning themselves with his own visual perceptions of the sphere, several of the workers in the mind-transference room seized Evans-Douglas, strapped him to a slab as soft as soapstone, and attached wires to a cap which they placed on his head. He was so surprised by their swift actions that he did not think to resist them, and he wondered only at their intentions. He became dizzy and lost his bearings, then felt an electric current flow through his brain and he blacked out. When he regained consciousness, he realized that he had been moved—*his mind had been drawn from his body and placed into one of the spheres used by the disembodied minds of the Great Race.*

After a time, Evans-Douglas could operate the sphere's appendages and soon afterward could fly. When this was accomplished, he was shown to the archives and taught to write with the instruments used there and how to read certain of the alien languages in which records were kept. Soon he would be allowed to study the city of Czymra with a guardian sphere and would ultimately be taken outside; but first he was instructed in the telepathic language of the Great Race to read specific records in the library so that he would have a better understanding of the planet and the history of the race.

The main library on Yith was in Czymra and the only other of note was at Rauth, near the opposite edge of the major inhabited continent. The one at Czymra occupied a massive edifice—a cluster of five connected buildings arranged around a central plaza. Even though this structure was no larger than one of the major libraries on earth, the system of shelving, the strict contents of the archives, the space-saving languages used, and architectonics as a whole made it possible to store amounts of knowledge undreamt of by mankind.

Each building was composed of five floors or layers, with ten groups of rooms on each layer. Four large rooms constituted each group, and each room had the capacity for fifty thousand volumes of uniform size—a total capacity of fifty million volumes, of which perhaps two-thirds had been utilized. Construction of an identical building was already underway in the center of the continent and four others were planned. Altogether, they would constitute an area the size of Czymra itself, and this for the storage of historical knowledge *alone*. Major centers for pure research also existed and more were being erected in Czymra and elsewhere on the great continent. What ambitious students of science and learning they were!

The books in the library were themselves of interest. The earliest form of writing and that used for the longest era was not unlike our own process, being the application of symbols onto paper or similar material by ink or other substance. Most of the volumes in the library were filled with information recorded in this manner, and were of uniform size. But a new process was being developed that would make it possible to record several tomes of information into one. A "volume" would actually be a book-sized object fronted with a sort of viewer or screen. When writing, a special metallic stylus was used and its impressions were not upon the transparent screen but upon a sensory field beneath it. The characters that appeared were caused by a magnetic effect, and the entire "page" thus written was memorized and transferred to magnetic tape within the volume. A number of dials and buttons made it possible to conjure up any of some twenty-five hundred pages to be viewed on the screen. But this method was only being used experimentally while newer chemical processes as well as other electronic processes were also being devised and tested.

There were certain members of the race whose sole occupation was the recording of information, while others did research with the records already in the archives. The remaining members of the race worked according to their intelligence, the most trivial responsibilities being to build and to preserve order among the artificial bodies containing captive minds. Others operated machinery designed for diverse tasks; many others spent their time doing scientific experimentation in the great number of laboratories devoted to all of the physical sciences. The most brilliant minds of the Great Race had highest privileges. Respectfully called Scholars, they had access to certain rooms in the libraries containing volumes forbidden to other members. This, Evans-Douglas presumed, was because of the vast complexity of the subjects covered in those books—although another reason might be the secrecy of the subject matter.

The planet Yith was in a system of five planets which revolved around a star half again as large as ours and called Ogntlach. The other planets were not named but given mathematical representations. But the second planet outward from the sun (Yith was the fourth) was given a peculiar mystical symbol that Evans-Douglas could not find in any of the books available to him. Nor were the species of life on the second planet mentioned, except for the mere statement that it supported a race very primitive in its social structure and religious practices, which were said to border on barbarism. Other than this nothing was said of the planet, so that he sensed a sort of fear in the careful, almost superstitious handling of the topic. Two other globes of the system boasted no races that were nearly as intelligent as the second planet's, and the first planet had not evolved any known form of life higher than that of vegetables. The fifth planet was totally devoid of life due to the extremely low temperature and poisonous atmosphere.

Yith itself had a very thin atmosphere and low surface temperature. But, because of thermal reactions beneath the crust, the bodies of water were warm enough to support a variety of marine life. The coldness on the surface, however, did not affect the Great Race because of their protective artificial shells. At an early point in their civilization, the race had attempted to dig into Yith for the purpose of subterranean building. Storerooms were to be built to hold much of the electronic devices and equipment invented by the race, and the archives and laboratories could also be extended underground. But for some vague reason, this project was abandoned altogether and very suddenly. Events preceding the undertaking of the project were recorded enthusiastically, whereas the abandonment was mentioned only briefly; one chronicler, writing a kind of journal of the construction, kept silent about the details of the excavation. Another source that Evans-Douglas turned up in the library was a record of constructions and their dates by the global dating system. The underground project was said to have been discontinued due to a disaster caused by the explosion of materials used in the mining.

This baffled the dreamer, who was becoming more and more curious as to the truth behind the events recorded insufficiently in the city's archives. He studied another source, which was a compilation of those members of the race who had died. That such complete organization could be achieved among a race anywhere at such an early date in their history was certainly impressive and also somewhat odd. He located the era in which the mining accident occurred, but was surprised to find no deaths during those years. He could not be sure what had compelled him to seek some evidence to support or disprove the history as recorded in the other records, but felt certain such evidence would materialize. Returning to a text which contained early history on the Great Race, Evans-Douglas read that the amphibious species whose bodies were taken over by the minds of the race were a kind of land hydra of unusual size and ability out of water. These creatures were dwelt upon with a certain awe that again might be regarded as superstitious fear. He also noted with extreme interest that no historical, biological, or other scientific texts offered any reference to the *origin* of the Great Race. It would seem that their appearance on Yith was deemed the undisputed and unstudied start of their history . . .

At this point in his study, a member of the race spoke to him. Fearful that his investigations were forbidden and had been be discovered, Evans-Douglas was uncooperative with the other, "speaking" as little as possible to give the impression that he wanted to left alone. From this time on, he was careful of what he thought about and tried to think of other things whenever another researcher passed by.

As noted, some of the spheres in the library were occupied by the minds of other races displaced by individuals from Yith. These captives were not allowed to converse with one another for fear of an uprising, and guards were posted in the archives to prevent any kind of disturbance. But such uprisings were very rare, since the captive minds were generally happy with their privileges and overawed by the grandiose project in which they played a part.

He came across another reference volume in the library, one listing the architectural achievements of the race. These were listed by city with dates of inception and completion dutifully recorded. There was also a listing by date of the achievements. Although the only record of the excavation project was the beginning date (corroborating the builder's journal), a peculiar pattern emerged in other construction of that era. It seemed that a certain change had taken place after the digging attempt was abandoned: much rebuilding and renovation of existing structures was undertaken during the following year, and many new cities were raised zealously across the continent. So ambitious was this surge in construction that it far outpaced any need for habitation or research facilities, and many structures stood empty for decades or remained so . . .

After a time, when he had learned enough about the geology, geography, and zoology of Yith, Evans-Douglas was escorted out of the archives into the outside world. He was offered the opportunity to study the continent from any scientific viewpoint. Since his curiosity concerning the mysterious parts in the planet's history had grown with further discoveries and speculations, he expressed an interest in studying the flora and fauna as well as the geography at large.

Travel in the countryside was normally accomplished with the aid of amphibious hovercraft, while locomotion in the artificial spheres themselves was preferred in the city. Evans-Douglas was first shown the region surrounding Czymra. Then he was taken on one of the hovercraft to the interior of the continent where cities became fewer and vegetation increased. It was interesting to note that there were very few trees, most of the vegetation being in the form of colorful bushes and shrubs spotting a carpet of thick grass that entirely covered the ground. Not a square inch of bare soil was visible anywhere due to the rapidly growing grass. Toward the center of the continent, however, the growth of such grasses was prevented by the use of poisons—this was the region of great quarries that produced building materials.

At Rauth—the major city on the southern portion of the continent, Czymra being to the north—the hovercraft turned about and followed the eastern shoreline upward and back toward Czymra. Before turning inland along the return route, the craft left the shore and ventured out over the water so that Evans-Douglas could observe some of the species of fish that were abundant in the oceans of Yith. It was during this excursion that an island was sighted to the northeast, and the passenger urged his guide to take the craft to it.

The island was desolate and had very little vegetation that could be seen from the distance maintained between the craft and the land. Along the eastern edge, the island jutted up to the height of a mountain then dropped off sharply to the sea. When they approached a cliff that rose several hundred feet above the water, the pilot took the craft further out—but not before Evans-Douglas saw crude dwellings on the face of the cliff that reminded him of mud-dauber nests. He also saw—or thought he saw—black, winged creatures flying about the cliff, but they were too far away for him to be sure.

In open waters north of the island, they slowed their pace and observed a school of fish. Suddenly, a huge hydra or other giant polyp darted toward them from the depths. Startled, the pilot swung the craft sharply westward and they sped off at an alarming velocity toward the mainland. Evans-Douglas questioned the pilot about this, but the pilot only muttered strange thoughts to himself and tried to prevent telepathy. Needless to say, the visitor was very intrigued by this and pondered upon it all the way back to Czymra.

On another expedition, they went to an uninhabited area to study a species of invertebrate which was something like an arachnid, but more like a mantis than a spider. The usual carpet of grass suddenly stopped in this region, but the escort would not say why. Evans-Douglas persisted and learned that construction was once begun in this area but never completed. The escort's antennae darted around nervously and said that they must soon return to the city. Before they left, the visitor noticed a strange print in the dirt—quite large and consisting of five circular toe marks. The escort seemed not to notice it, and Evans-Douglas thought it best not to point it out.

After a series of these outings, he remained in Czymra and was allowed once again to study in the vast libraries. He was eager to learn more of the Great Race's science of mathematics—an unusual numerical system in which the base was 5 rather than 10—but there was a commotion in the library. Many of the archivists were concerned and were whispering telepathically with a Scholar in nervous tones. The group of them, perceiving the disturbance they had caused, filed quickly out of the room and into an adjoining conference chamber. Other researchers, remaining in the main room, whispered to one another about what had been said, and Evans-Douglas caught enough disjointed phrases to know what had happened.

A disturbance had been noted in one of the uninhabited regions that Evans-Douglas had visited, although the abandoned construction site was not specifically indicated. Vague things were muttered about the curious amphibious species whose bodies the Great Race had first inhabited on Yith. He also caught a strange thought which, when voiced, might be a phonetic interpretation of the mystic symbol for the second planet in Yith's solar system, but there was no way to be certain of this.

In the following days, disturbances of this sort were repeated. Great anxiety was caused by discoveries near the abandoned site. There was an increasing number of Scholars in the archives, studying their secret books along with texts that were available to all of the archivists. What were they studying? For the first time, Evans-Douglas wondered whether the restricted books might have a religious meaning. Here was a race whose only goal was to attain knowledge, whose hierarchy was dominated by their most brilliant minds—would they not treat knowledge too complex for understanding with a kind of religious awe?

Quite by accident, he caught a proposal made by one of the Scholars during one of the conferences. It was a motion that a military force be sent to the island in the east to destroy the winged creatures, but this caused great shock in the others, who grew very silent and eyed one another timorously.

Daily the members of the Great Race grew more restless, and the pressure began to tell on many of the archivists. Their fear must have been inordinate, as they began muttering telepathically of death and destruction. Others mumbled about trying to escape in the space ships, and all the while the conference rooms were filled with Scholars debating on the best course of action to take.

One archivist, who was nearer to Evans-Douglas at the time than anyone else, was in such a terrible state of distress that he babbled to himself in a strange language while doodling subconsciously on a tablet. Coming suddenly out of this nervous condition, he glanced down at the tablet with all four extended antennae, emitted a loud, shrill sound, and fell to the floor. The sphere that contained him bounced twice and then rolled about the floor misguidedly. When Evans-Douglas hovered toward him, he saw the tablet and what had been drawn on it—a design composed of five circular marks identical to the footprint Evans-Douglas had seen at the abandoned excavation site . . .

What great fear the race possessed—what *superstitious obsession!* When other archivists came to the scene to aid their fellow, they, too, saw the tablet and unconditionally shrieked and some fled. A high degree of excitement was in the air, and the Scholars were told of the occurrence.

A total silence fell upon the archivists, researchers and Scholars. Evans-Douglas was self-conscious of his captive status and worried that his close proximity to the tablet bearing the offensive design might get him into trouble. But no, by some telepathic signal which he did not receive—or by some sudden realization that all the others experienced together—the entire group began moving toward the exits, whispering among themselves in fearful tones. They seemed not to care about his continued presence, and he slipped quietly into the empty conference room. On a table was an open notebook which one of the Scholars had been filling with notes during the conference. Evans-Douglas cast off his own growing doubts, turned to the front of the book, and began reading the odd symbols of the language of the Great Race.

It told of the Scholars' anxiety regarding the winged species on the island and their rapidly developing intelligence. These creatures had begun to build villages and would soon adopt a form of self-government. The Scholars knew from their cosmic explorations that such a race *would inhabit the earth billions of years in the future.* They had also read their own destiny from pages of history they would record in a million billion years to come. The Great Race would soon migrate forward in time *en masse* by mind-transference. They would jump from planet to planet and age to age, pursued by something they had feared since their dawning, which was not on Yith but countless eons before and unnamed galaxies distant. They would project their most brilliant minds forward into the bodies of another race when they were endangered, and then begin again with their all-obsessive goal to collate all knowledge. Pursued again, they would lunge another eon forward, ever pursued and ever fleeing the monstrous truth of their origin and their bygone struggles with the hideously elder and evil race that had sought to occupy Yith before them in the form of the polypous hydra-creatures. These would precede the Great Race to earth in a like form and, though vanquished again, would live ever on with ever-intensifying potency and cause supernatural dread in the minds of the Great Race. They would darken their shadow and cast it always before the race as an inevitable and inescapable specter.

In a vain effort to forget the past, the Great Race had wiped their minds free from previous knowledge when they came to Yith; but the flimsy psychological barriers which they had erected fell easily to the omnipresent memories that forced themselves to the surface by similarities and reminders in their surroundings. The insurmountable horror grew and grew and finally burst through the shell built around it, which had only helped to strengthen the returning horror . . .

This sense of inescapable horror closed in on Evans-Douglas, amplified by the realization that he was totally alone in the library. He dropped the book and himself flew shrieking out of the edifice erected by a masterful Great Race; fled through the other empty buildings madly in search of some place to hide from the terrors about him and within him.

Then they came.

The hellish winds and the whistling sounds—controlled by the insidious alien entities that had haunted the Great Race since the beginning of time—ripped across the continents of Yith, destroying the expertly constructed buildings and leaving the cities in ruins. Then the polypous, plastic, wingless things flew from the direction of the abandoned construction site, and the black, winged creatures flew up from their island cliff dwellings to mock the fate of the Great Race and to laugh and play among the ruins of their mighty cities.

Christopher Evans-Douglas flew high into the sky in the artificial sphere designed to protect his mind from cruel reality. In the final moments of his dream, he flew upward and outward and only once did he dare to turn his antennae back to look at the major continent of Yith—to recognize even among the ruins the odd and uniform arrangement of the cities into groups of five circular marks . . .

Intimations of Unreality

In the Realm of Ying

"Consciousness is the creature of rhythm."
—*Ambrose Bierce*

I knew not how I had come to this awful place, nor how I returned to our world in maddened flight. But I was there, once—just once, having seen it as from afar in fleeting dreams and memories.

A house, perhaps, was what it was—or so the interior revealed to me. I stood in darkness illumined ever so slightly by light radiating from an unknown source some indeterminable distance ahead. It seemed that I was in a corridor: a narrow hallway with an impassable barrier to my right and a rail to my left, separating the corridor from a lightless aperture. While there was but the faintest twilight, I sensed an over-all shade of *green*—a light green hue suffusing all structures in sight: the floor of the corridor itself, the wall on the right, the rail on the left.

I began to walk slowly, almost involuntarily, drawn by a vague memory of what lay ahead. My eyes scrutinized the corridor that stretched before me, ghostly, obscured by a spectral flowing mist. After some indefinable unit of time, I came to a termination of the hall which I almost expected. Here the wall to my right cut in front of me at a right angle and the railing at my left abruptly ended.

My progress had brought me face-to-face with the unfathomable black aperture beyond the railing. A glance into this forbidding region resurrected within me dark memories woven with inexplicable fear. I dreaded unaccountably to peer for long into that vaguely stirring blackness, but soon made out that there were steps leading down, again barely illumined in pale green. The steps continued endlessly downward until they were lost from sight and possessed irrecoverably by the slithering darkness.

I was gripped by the vice of fear and somehow reminded of obscure and seemingly unrelated legends of Ying the Damned, the amorphous flute-player. His unintentional existence in our dimensions was caused by the manifestation of certain notes—daemonic cacophonies that ripped through the peripheral barrier that had separated the spheres for eons before life emerged on earth.

Madness clutched at me and I bounded along the dark corridor—avoiding the stairway and plunging forward at a desperate pace, running and running until fatigue seeped into my calves and thighs like lethal poison, transforming my legs into lead. Crippled by exhaustion, I inevitably stumbled and fell; but fearful of the noise that I made, I immediately grew quiet.

Thus was it possible for me to hear a sound—the first I had heard and the first sign of life I had found in this place. Soon I conjectured that the sound, muffled by distance, had quasi-musical qualities or indications; but while it was certainly a product of life, it had a totally irregular rhythm. This irregularity suggested a decadent life-form with a warped consciousness, since life and consciousness are creations of rhythm.

Again the legends awoke in my memory and Ying was the center of those whispered legends. Ying was called the amorphous servant of Azathoth the Idiot God, that blasphemous foulness whose mindless howling is heard from beyond angled space.

I arose and began to walk very softly toward the source of the sound—which, I knew in a moment, was the selfsame source of the greenish, luminous haze that threw the corridor into eerie twilight. Just ahead, a round window of dull radiance was visible. I walked towards it without hesitation, but not without myriad eldritch pictures construed in my mind of exactly what might lie beyond that window . . .

Reaching my goal, I stood bathed in the aethereal flow of green hue, stood before a single, large, circular pane of translucent glass and listened to the frightful sound from beyond. That sound, muffled by the thick glass, was undoubtedly of much greater volume in the zones outside the window.

Impulsively, I tested the glass with my hand and found that it would not open without a steady application of force. My mind was set upon opening the window—set by curiosity and an ignorance that I now resent—and I braced myself and pushed against it. After some time of continuous endeavor, I felt the glass slip, just barely; then a moment of resistance; and it abruptly gave way. By the sudden opening of the window and the impetus of the force I arrayed against it, I fell partway through the portal—almost disastrously, to hang breathless above an abyss, supported only by the stone wall that cut painfully into my stomach. I watched the glass disk turn as it fell and disappeared into starlit darkness.

With unguided arms fumbling behind me, I somehow managed to find the windowsill and gained a safe grip on the stone. But when I pulled myself up, I was shown the hellish source of the throbbing sound that had penetrated the luminous glass to reverberate in murmurs through the corridor. That blasphemy was indeed the servant of the idiot Azathoth, and his vile shrieks piped in every place of damnable sin and shame throughout the black universe: the sound had been heard in ancient Greece as the hideous Pan danced ecstatically to its horrible rhythm in his nameless woods; in Egypt of old it was heard as the guttural voice of the Memnon at Thebes, crying out at the first touch of dawn's light; and it was heard in the feared Harz Mountains of Germany, where forbidden debaucheries were held in diabolic worship of the Black One . . .

For as I pulled myself from the portal and faced the abyss beyond, *I knew*. In a moment of ultimate horror preceding the oblivion that overtook me, I beheld with my own eyes the damned, amorphous flute-player Ying, singing to the void!

House of Morning, House of Dream

"We are near awakening when we dream *that* we dream."
—NOVALIS, *Werke*, S. 326, 16.

My first sensations were of the little road before me, and of the dew-glazed meadow on either side, stretching off and rising into little hills that dropped away and rose again in the distance. The morning sun played on the wet grass, looking over the shoulders of the hills to my right. Thus began my present existence—for no memories of an earlier life are accessible to my mind. All has vanished before that, lost in a great, turbulent Sea of unyielding darkness ... Sometimes the Sea is so stormy I think it will swallow me, claiming even my present consciousness, this mighty Sea of oblivion. Then it calms, and I think—for a fearful moment—that the waters will clear, giving me a glimpse into its awesome depths, proffering one restless, taunting memory that would only become a source of anguish for a fuller glimpse: a fuller glimpse that would not be granted.

Such are my thoughts when I ponder my origins. My earliest memories are dream-like and fogged by the waves of that oblivious Sea which pounds upon the shores of my island-self. Dreamily I walked along that road, over the little hills, into little valleys, feeling as though I had been that way many times before. I somehow felt that the road led to a place of rest—a strange place of peace and contentment, of wonder and delight.

I was welcomed by one who seemed to know me. He smiled and firmly grasped my arm. I came to know the others and became one of them. I became part of the strange place and began to love it as my home. It was a house of dream, as my life was a dream, and I lived it in patches—but only when the Sea about my island was at low tide and the waves receded. The tide was controlled by the sun, not the moon.

Patches and pieces were my life, spots of light in darkness, like sunlight through the leaves of a tree, or through the lace curtains of my window. The sun controlled my life in the house of dream, this strange place, and my life was composed of many mornings after long, dreamless nights of sleep—when the Sea closed over me, a little more each time.

Mornings and dreams, and patches of light, my life was happy and warm, and we all lived in wonder and delight in our strange little place.

There I learned much, for whatever I could recall from my earlier life now had no meaning. I was shown how to live when I dreamed, and to dream when I lived. I was taught how the Sea was controlled by the sun, and how I might become like the sun. Happy was I then, and the sunlight was brighter when it woke me through the little round window of my room in the house of morning.

I learned to see. My life of dreams grew clearer, I felt more, and I was made happier. I learned to think, and learned how it is not painful after a while to feel as well as to think, and my life of dream-patches was made fuller and happier. What I felt was the warmth of the sun and the cold of the morning ground, awakened under the caressing rays of sunlight. I felt the cool winds brush across my waking face, pushing aside the curtains of my window and to show the smiling sun.

There were times when there was rain, and the sun grew dim behind the clouds. At first I was frightened, but the others gave me strength, and I learned that the sun was in me also. And so I loved the rain, for it showed me the tender lights within; and the coolness of the wind and rain was a wonderful part of my life of mornings in the house of dream.

When the rain was in its season, and it rained often, the light within me shown outward, and I did not yield my island to the Sea. We would all gather and talk among ourselves, wondering about many things, for we knew well how to think about our feelings. We would imagine about our former lives, and the others knew much about those lost lives when I knew nothing. They marveled at what they had been, and the many wondrous things they had done, and told stories about their lost lives. One had been a wealthy man, for many people gave him their gold and treasures to keep. One had been a farmer, and he grew for us many good foods. Another had been poor, and had hated his lost life because he had failed to live better. One was a prince, the eldest son of a king, and he told us many tales of his adventures. One was a poet who had lived many different lives: it was he who had greeted me, welcomed me to this place, saying that he had known me in another life. One had been a holy man. But all were happier in this life of dreams, even the farmer, whose life was much the same as it had been before, and the prince, who remembered much about his good life.

I was sorry that I knew nothing of my former existence, but was comforted by the words of the poet. One day, he said, I would learn how to remember.

When the rainy season was, we were the happiest, and loved our strange place with its good dreams the most. Often, the others were not all to be found, and I thought that there were times when I was not present. But these thoughts frightened me, as did the Sea, and I put them away. One morning the poet taught me how to look into the Sea, but I was sore afraid and ran out into the sunlight for comfort. The farmer was there, and he told me not to try to remember my early life, for it would cause me pain. "Thoughts are not worth the trouble to be thought," he said, and I watched him grow things in the cold earth.

Another time, the poet told me that there was nothing to fear; for he had known me in earlier lives and knew that they were good. He took me to the little dock near the house of dream and told me to sit and stare into the waters. I was afraid, but together we looked into the Sea, and I saw many strange things. There were faces and pictures, glimpses and feelings, sounds and calls, and singing and crying in the depths of the water. The poet showed me these things. He had been a fisher in one life, he said. He taught me how to sit still for a long time and stare deeply into the water. At first, he came with me, for I was frightened by the waves rolling in from the Sea and I thought I would be lost in them. But he could not come always and left me on my own. "In this way," he said, "your life is not only the life of dreams, but also the life of the Sea. You can recapture your past life by staring long into the waters, catching glimmerings of memories, and following them through the darkness."

One morning a strange man came. He came as the others had come to this strange place, which was made stranger by his coming. I remember when he arrived. It was stormy and lightning danced powerfully on the horizon, while thunder echoed across the plains and into the dark hills. He came from the direction of the storm, and he was wise for it. The storm was in his eyes. His full, grizzled beard held the storm's moisture. The creative power of the storm swelled in his doming forehead.

When I greeted him as a friend, his eyes flashed at me, as if I had broken a sacred code held for a thousand of years by not bowing before him. But as the storm roared only to quiet again, so he became benevolent, smiling with an aura of brightness and grasping my arm strongly. For he soon recognized me as a brother.

The stranger was myself as I had been in a life wherein I attained God-head. It was my last life on earth. The stranger was therefore able to teach me the final things. I learned to be like the sun and to control the Sea, and I learned to look deeply into the Sea of my life, more deeply than the poet. Thus I learned to remember all my lives, and I realized who I was. I was the poor man and the farmer, the wealthy man and the prince, the holy man, the poet, and the stranger.

My island was the morning road that led through glistening meadows to the house of dream. My island was the meadows and the house. The island was myself, and I was all these things. My island was not separate from the Sea that surrounded it, and I could never be engulfed by the Sea, because I was the Sea as well as the Island.

The rains that had frightened me were not separate from myself, for I was the Sea from which the rains came, and I was the Sun that drew them up from the Sea.

I am the Sun that shines forever into Darkness, and Darkness can never engulf me because I am the Darkness as well as the Light . . .

The Legend of the Seeker

And there shall come a time when He Who is known as the Seeker of Knowledge shall expound the Ancient Mysteries.

But first must He learn the forbidden scripts and secret tongues wherewith to read the hidden texts.

And then must He pass through Outer Gates, and thus possess the magic key to worlds unknown.

From the world of Earth this One shall pass, Beyond the Horizon, to the world of the Infinite Plains.

And here discover the truth at last; the struggle of good and evil, and the ultimate nature of things.

—FROM THE ANCIENT *BOOK OF SUSAUR*

The Summons of Hastur

I can wait no longer. I must tell what I know of a scarcely known, but incredibly powerful and evil existence that is far from dead. I must explain the uncanny disappearance—the death—of my friend Harold Cartley and perhaps save the world from a horrible destruction.

I had known Cartley a long time, and on countless evenings had been a guest in his home. Many times we had sat before the fire in his study and talked about current events, archaeology, Victorian influences—or just whatever came to mind. And on frequent evenings we matched our wits over the chessboard, where Cartley was all but rarely victorious.

It was on one of these nights that I arrived as expected at his home, to be shown into the study by the butler. When the servant announced my arrival, Cartley set aside a dusty old leather-covered volume with corroded metal clasps, and rose to greet me with a solemn countenance, which was made all the worse by a forced smile. He offered me the chair he had offered on so many occasions before, and, taking it, I came right out and asked him why he was in such an unhealthy mood. Had there been a death?

"No, no, not a death. I've just been reading this volume," he said, and tapped the ancient book. A cloud of dust blew out the sides from between the worm-eaten, moldy leaves. "It's in Latin, very old and very rare—and manifestly the writings of a madman, for what I've read thus far has disturbed me greatly. It's rarity is legendary and only five or six copies are known to exist." He seemed dispirited, and looked and spoke gravely.

"Then how did you come by this one?" I asked, indicating the tome.

"Quite by accident, I assure you. You know how I like antiques and relics, and how I like to consider myself an antiquarian bookman. Well, last Saturday I made my rounds of all the used book stores and antique shops in this section of Boston—a project I undertake weekly when possible. That is the best way to come by old books, since such dealers know nothing of rarity, usually buying in large quantities and having no time to investigate each book separately; though this is quite different with antiques, the best market being the original or second-hand owners themselves, especially those who have inherited the items and don't suspect the true value. Well, anyhow, Kenneth, my excursion produced several pieces: the Richard Pickman you must have seen along the staircase, a lamp in a room downstairs, and this book, the *Necronomicon* of Alhazred, of which I had read in a trade journal."

"Did you ask the clerk where he had procured such a valuable book?" I interrogated, packing my meerschaum pipe while he packed his Oom Paul.

"Of course, but only after I had purchased it at an absurd price. She said she knew nothing about it, and the manager was not in," he said. "But look at this—if you turn to the third leaf . . . there is a rather curious and informative piece—a letter."

The book sat before me on a coffee table. Turning to where he directed, I found a sheet of lined paper folded and inserted between the yellowed leaves, which had a singular odor about them—almost *miasmal* in aspect. I unfolded the letter and read it:

October 3

Dear Mr. Hawkins,

Your offer for the book suits me nicely (as you can see from this parcel), even though it is worth far more even in its fragmentary form. Yes, I have others. I obtained many of them from my third cousin, Wilbur, before and after his unfortunate death (which perhaps you heard of in connection with the Dunwich horror—the Lovecraft version is only slightly aggrandized). These include a copy of the fabled R'lyeh Text, complete but for a few opening pages, and several other ancient texts, plus "recent" works in German and French. I will send a list of the volumes for sale in my next, since by then several additions will be necessary. You see, I am having them copied by helpers, so that the originals can be sold for much-needed funds.

I'm glad to see you are taking up an interest in this line of study, and Irvin and I both hope your interest will continue, as it will aid you after the Return.

In regard to your question about the Tsath-yo and the Kouii Script, I must admit that I know nothing of the latter, but the former was the primal tongue of Hyperborea. Irvin says that the other may be a numerical language used infrequently by the Great Race, but isn't sure, since the Pnakotic Manuscripts are of something altogether different.

To be honest, again, I haven't even heard of the Am-Yph'ra Tablets or the Venduxour Papyrus, although they both sound Egyptian. Irvin is checking on them (he keeps impressively complete files on almost everything related to our studies), and he believes that they, too, may be pertinent to our work.

Be wary to whom you speak and always keep the books in your possession. Also be wary of which chants you use and do not call to space, for danger will answer if you are not protected correctly. Use no power without consulting us.

By the Black Waters of Hali, and By Him Whom They Veil,

I am truly yours,

E. Whateley

I set the letter aside and asked with a chuckle, "What kind of book is this anyway, magic? I thought Hyperborea was only in Greek mythology and legend, and what's all this about powers and chants?"

"Not 'magic' in the sense you speak and know of, though a certain mystic power is involved. No, this and presumably the other volumes the letter spoke of deal with a mythology or religion ancient at the time of Homer, and Alhazred whispers that it is so ancient as to be considered *pre-human*. I have learned from this book that the mythology deals with entities of good and evil, just as all other religions do, grouped into good 'Elder Gods' and evil 'Great Old Ones.' The evil ones were expelled to the Outside, where they plan their return—just as Lucifer was pent up for a millennium, to be released thereafter."

"Interesting," I admitted, searching for questions to ask for the sake of conversation. "What about the exotic languages he mentioned, and the 'Great Race'? Doesn't that have to do with the Mayas or Incas?"

"Oh, no, entirely different from the Great Race of the Incas. This race, as Alhazred would have it, is from Yith, a dead elder world, and the Tsath-yo is also mentioned in the *Necronomicon*."

"What on earth is this . . . 'Dunwich horror'?" I asked, glancing back at the letter.

"The reference is to the occurrence at Dunwich, Massachusetts in 1928. Dunwich, which you've probably never heard of, is near Aylesbury, not too far from Arkham, which, along with Innsmouth, Kingsport, and other New England towns, are the seats of current revivals or survivals of the religion recorded in the *Necronomicon*. The 'horror' centered around this E. Whateley's third cousin, Wilbur Whateley and his twin brother."

I asked him the source of this information—out of curiosity—and received an unexpected answer.

"Ridiculous as it may seem, it comes from a volume of supposed 'fiction' by H. P. Lovecraft, the great writer of supernatural horror, to which the letter refers. I first read the volume last year, obtaining the first edition at a decent price, and re-read it just the other day to cross-check an early reference in the *Necronomicon* I thought I had seen in the Lovecraft omnibus. This is why my interest in Alhazred is so deep: Lovecraft's main 'fiction' deals with the mythology I have outlined for you."

At my request, Cartley rose to get the horror collection from his shelf. I took this opportunity to glance through the moldy tome on the table before me. Although my Latin was rusty, I was able to make out a few passages which I found oddly disturbing. Just as I closed the book, Cartley exclaimed, "Ah! here it is!"

He returned immediately and handed me the thick black volume, and I read the title imprinted on the spine in gold ink, *The Outsider and Others*. Opening the book to the contents page, I glanced down the table until I found the titled wanted—"The Dunwich Horror"—and turned to the page indicated.

Cartley, instead of re-crossing the room to his chair, stood behind me, looking over my shoulder, and when I discovered the story in the book he reached over and turned to the middle of the story. There he indicated a quotation "from the *Necronomicon* of the mad Arab, Abdul Alhazred." Cartley noted my surprise.

"So you see, Lovecraft also had access to the book: probably the copy at the Miskatonic University in Arkham, where many of the characters in his stories see it."

At some point the conversation shifted and we passed the evening on other subjects, and Cartley, in time, became his jovial old self. But the Lovecraft ordeal remained in my mind, and when, at last, I took my leave, Cartley happily consented to let me borrow the omnibus of that author's best tales. He also invited me to come again after lunch on the following day, and then we would go to the book dealer's shop where he had found the *Necronomicon*. To this proposition I agreed, somewhat eagerly and with a childish zeal for adventure and discovery.

I read late into the night and didn't set the thick volume aside until I had read "The Dunwich Horror" and a half-dozen other stories dealing with ancient evil and its shocking manifestations in out-of-the-way places even in our own America. These blasphemous representations of evil bore such outlandish names as Yog-Sothoth, Shub-Niggurath, Cthulhu, Nyarlathotep, and Tsathoggua.

When I did finally sleep, my dreams were haunted by the terribly realistic monsters that stalked the pages of Lovecraft's book. I wondered at the mythology of his fiction having once been an actual religion and tried to imagine how primitive the people must have been to worship the nightmare entities.

I slept late, and after a brief repast made my way to Harold Cartley's home. He was just finishing his lunch and offered me some tea, which I drank while he related in brief what little additional information he had accumulated since the previous evening.

He said that he had found no direct reference to any of the volumes or tablets old enough to be contemporary to—or more ancient than—the author of the *Necronomicon*, or any that had been inquired about by Hawkins, though there were many vague mentions of "ancient texts" or "ancient books." On the other hand, there were several definite listings of groups of entities which included the Great Race, albeit no attempt was made to explain them beyond the concepts we had derived from Whateley's letter. But there was more in Cartley's monologue over tea than I had absorbed earlier; when I asked for more details, he apologized and explained that a long story of Lovecraft's was entirely given over to the Great Race. This story I resolved to read when time permitted—but presently we prepared to leave for the bookshop, collected our hats and cloaks and went out into the chill of the Boston midday, where we momentarily secured a taxi to transport us to our destination.

We entered the shop and went immediately to the cashier's desk. There sat a woebegone, rather homely woman in her forties. Without any effort to smile, she spoke.

"May I help you?"

"We hope you can," Cartley began, introducing himself. "You may remember me—I purchased this volume from your establishment a few days ago. When I opened it, I found a letter which indicated that the man from whom you procured the volume—a Mr. Hawkins—evidently had several similar volumes which I am *most* interested in obtaining, if at all possible. I was hoping you could give me the address of this Mr. Hawkins."

"One moment, please. I'll have to ask the manager." This she said mechanically after evaluating the problem, and limped off through a door behind her desk. A moment later, she returned, accompanied by the manager. This man was slightly younger than I—that is to say, he was in his early thirties—wore eyeglasses and appeared to be an intelligent person. He stepped out in front of the desk and asked us the name of the book.

"The *Necronomicon*, by Abdul Alhazred. The original owner was a Mr. Hawkins," Cartley supplied.

"Ah, yes," the manager replied. "I picked that up at a rummage sale several weeks ago. The owner died, I believe, just a month before, and it was his sister who became the proprietor of his effects. She sold me the volume, for I at once noticed its age and recognized it as an extraordinary item—something you don't expect to run across everyday at a garage sale!" The manager, a good deal livelier than the cashier, laughed.

"Do you happen to know much about Egyptian papyri, Mr.—"

"Jasper. Well, as a matter of fact, I do: I studied Egyptology indirectly in college—fascinating subject. I accompanied the Oxford expedition to Kish, the ancient capital of Mesopotamia, and contributed my finds to the Hamilton Collection at the British Museum."

"Ah, very good!" Cartley said with surprise and joy at finding such a scholar at such a time. "Then perhaps you have heard of the Venduxour Papyrus?"

"The so-called 'Second Book of Thoth,' yes, I've heard of it. It was presumably written in the fourteenth century BC by an anonymous Egyptian priest. Its reproduction was forbidden by Amenophis III, who feared that it would be hazardous to the established worship of Ra, the Sun-God, since it claimed that Thoth and several obscure gods connected with him (whose names are not known) were greater than Ra. Amenophis' son, Amenophis IV—who called himself Akhnaten and whose wife was Queen Nefertiti, famed for her beauty—threw out Ra and replaced him with the alternative sun-god Aten. He suppressed the 'Second Book' for the same reason, and also because he couldn't comprehend its vast store of knowledge."

"What relation, if any, existed between the Papyrus and the Book of Thoth?" I asked.

"Well, by the time of the former's writing, the Book of Thoth was legendary. Although no memory told of its contents, it was believed by some to contain great stores of magical wisdom, and by others to contain *all* knowledge—just as the South American text of all the wisdom of antiquity which was destroyed by Pachacuti IV, the sixty-third Inca ruler. The only resemblance between the original and the "second" book was in title and implication, along with the names of certain forgotten deities—or so one Egyptian scholar has it.

"When the Assyrians of Esarhaddon invaded Egypt in the seventh century BC, the Second Book of Thoth, which had somehow survived down through the centuries, was taken along with other texts into Mesopotamia—then part of the Assyrian Empire—because of the flourishing of literature encouraged by Esarhaddon's father, Sennacherib, and further developed by his son, Ashurbanipal at Nineveh. It was at Nineveh that the papyrus was first catalogued and its history recorded by scribes and scholars of the empire, who discovered it among the captured texts. Thereafter, the order of the royal priests of Ashur and Bêlit translated it into an ancient language known only by the priests and shunned by them, and eventually created a cipher in which to further cloak the forbidden and frightening knowledge revealed by the blasphemous text. At some point, the original was destroyed, along with the keys to the ancient language and the cipher, and the Second Book of Thoth—codified as the Venduxour Papyrus—became what it is today, in the Bibliothèque Nationale in Paris with other Nineveh tablets, the Am-Yph'ra Tablets."

The revelation was a jolt to us. Even though we had barely become involved in our ill-fated study of the Hawkins-Whateley case, we were both overwhelmed by the knowledge we had contracted during this chance conversation. It was ironic that Hawkins, searching for this very information, would become connected—however indirectly—with his "informant" only a month after his death.

We found the home of the late Mr. Hawkins easily enough and sounded the knocker.

"Who is it?" An elderly voice, almost a scream, penetrated the door.

"I am Harold Cartley, and my companion is Kenneth Hinton. We wish to speak to the executor of Arthur Hawkins' estate."

I was puzzled that Cartley knew Hawkins' first name, since Jasper had not told us. I gave him a quizzical look, but he merely pointed to the name on the mailbox! There was a fumbling at the door, the latch was released from within, the heavy black door was opened to a crack, and suspicious eyes peered out at us from a chamber of total darkness. After a moment of silent scrutiny, she closed the door, unfastened the guard-chain, and opened it once again. She asked us to enter, which we did, immediately removing our hats.

Hawkin's sister was about fifty years old, well-dressed, and well-mannered—if suspicious of our intents. Cartley explained our reason for calling and disclosed the matter of the letter in the book, and asked if she knew any of her brother's acquaintances—particularly by the name of Whateley. She said she knew nothing of her brother's friends or activities during his last years, since she lived out of town and had only returned upon learning of his death. "But I know he was up to something not particularly good."

"How's that?" Cartley asked.

"Well, with all those old books and papers that he left. And those funny people that kept coming around asking for his things, all saying that they had known him and that he had promised them his books and papers."

Cartley was markedly disturbed by this, though I didn't grasp the significance at the time.

"You said 'funny people,' Miss Hawkins. Why do you say they were funny?"

"Well, because they *looked* funny, and they didn't seem to walk—just sort of *hopped* along." Cartley was even more disturbed. She continued: "They only came after dark and never came in, so I didn't see much of them, but they were tall, thin men—bony as can be—with small, round heads and hair all over their dark faces but not too much around their mouths. No chins at all; never saw any sort of ears; but their noses were long and pointed; their voices shrill and high-pitched. Their arms were long, but I never saw their hands. They didn't seem to blink their eyes too often, but just stared at you funny-like. Now that I say all that out loud, it seems that they were like *birds*!" She laughed, but upon seeing the graveness of Cartley's face—and my consternation at finding him so disturbed—she became strangely quiet, and a depressed mood settled upon us in the dimly-lit reception room of the Hawkins house.

Nevertheless, it was Cartley who broke the uncomfortable silence.

"Miss Hawkins, did you give these people what they wanted?"

"No, I didn't. I figured that the books and papers must have been valuable, since so many of those funny people came for them."

"Did you look over the books and papers yourself, Miss Hawkins?" Cartley asked.

"Not the books, but I looked through the papers. But they didn't seem valuable to me, though I still didn't give them up, and when I had the rummage sale I thought I would try to sell just one of the books to see how much they might be worth."

Cartley asked if we could examine the papers and books, saying that he might know what they are really worth—might buy them himself for a fair price. She consented and showed us to her late brother's study, which was closed-off and probably unused since Mr. Hawkins' death.

The desk in the study was covered with papers and scattered reference volumes, and the drawers, we found upon examination, were filled with papers also. Cartley at once started to go through them, while I busied myself pouring over the bookshelves. After ten minutes, or so, an exclamation came from Cartley, who had found another letter from Whateley, and soon thereafter he found another, and another. I, myself, discovered a number of books of possible value and began stacking them on a table. These bore such unheard-of titles as the *Daemonolatreia* of Remigius, a similar title by Sinistrari, Prinn's *De Vermis Mysteriis*, the *Book of Eibon*, the *Unbekannte Geheimenisse* of Van der Vacht, Robert's *Enigma of the Chimu Civilization*, Tubb's *Creatures From the Lost Worlds*, Wallach's *Harpies, Hippogriffs, and Other Winged Beasts of Mythology*, and many others, both recent and old, some being several hundreds or even thousands of years ancient.

By this time, I had worked my way around the book-lined room and came to a small writing desk, clear on top and possessed of a single drawer. This I opened to find a typed manuscript in a binder with "Hastur and His Minions in the Ancient Books" printed neatly on the cover and typed on the title page. Beneath this was a thick, neat stack of typed pages secured by a binder clip and entitled "Fragmentary Inscriptions." Cartley was very excited when I announced these and handed them over to him.

Working together in this fashion for nearly two hours, we amassed a tremendous pile of books, papers, and notes that were of incredible value and demanded further investigation. Cartley—being better versed than I in such arcane literature—double-checked the shelves for items I may have missed. At this time, Miss Hawkins rejoined us to present an item she had discovered elsewhere in the house.

"This is a letter I got just a week ago. It's for Arthur. I set it aside to read it later, but forgot all about it until just now. It's from . . . a Dr. Shrewsbury." She handed it to Cartley. I recalled having seen a title by Dr. Shrewsbury in Hawkins' large library. "Are you sure you don't want some tea? It wouldn't be any trouble at all. I remember the old days when Arthur and I lived here together—he used to have tea all the time. Why, he—"

Cartley interrupted, "Thank you for your kindness, Miss Hawkins, but we are finished here and must go. We have selected what papers and volumes we should like to purchase from you." He paused to visually size up the pile. "I'll give you . . . let's say five thousand dollars for the lot."

Miss Hawkins was startled by the sum—as was I, at first, though now I know them to be worth thrice that amount, or more. Miss Hawkins did not pass up the offer, and while Cartley made out his check she got us a satchel for the papers and boxes for the books: naturally, we wanted to remove the treasures immediately. The transaction completed, we hurried off at once, taking a cab to Cartley's home. In the cab, we didn't speak a single word, being absorbed in our own thoughts about the fantastic haul and the awesome implications of it all.

The first items we scrutinized were the letters. Cartley placed them in chronological order before reading them over, handing each one to me as he finished. The first letter after the one included in the *Necronomicon* (dated October 3) was dated October 10 and read as follows:

Dear Mr. Hawkins,

I am glad that you are interested so deeply in the ancient books and their contents. You will profit greatly from their knowledge.

Here is a list of volumes now available. I have, since you have a suitable knowledge of antiquaries and thus some idea of their prices, omitted what we would *like* to ask for these extremely rare volumes, but because of our necessary haste we must get almost anything we can for them.

R'lyeh Text (transcription)

Unausprichlichen Kulten (von Junzt)

Unbekannte Geheimenisse (Van der Vacht)

Liber Ivonis (Eibon; also have the *Book of Eibon* in French)

De Vermis Mysteriis (Prinn)

Les Secrets des Morts (De Rougêt)

The Book of Susaur (fragments)

The Book of Dzyan

The Wisdom of the Druids (Woodliff)

and complete sets of Albertus Magnus, Borellus, and Paracelsus.

You may also be interested in a recent work by a Dr. Shrewsbury, who lives in Arkham, *The Myth-Patterns of Latter-day Primitives*, which is available in bookstores.

Your interest in Hastur is singular, and Irvin would like to speak to you in person some time. A study would be worthwhile, and I'm sure Irvin could aid you. But I must warn you—if you write Shrewsbury, you must be very careful what you say. He is bent on interrupting the return of Cthulhu, which is actually helping us.

I am, Brother of the Purpose,

Yours by the Sign of Hastur,

Emmett Whateley

As soon as I had finished reading this letter, Cartley handed me the next and lost himself in the third. The second, dated October 15, was as follows.

Brother Hawkins,

You ask me in curiosity what my occupation is. I haven't one. My only source of income at the time is the sales, and most of this is going to our Purpose. I am constantly occupied with the Purpose and my studies, which will help me exist after the Return. Irvin thinks that the time may be near. He is a natural scholar with a remarkable IQ—and, of course, much more involved than I am. He is now studying the calculus which may reveal the key, and thinks that we may need you to join us as soon as possible.

Irvin seems to think that a force is now against us. He thinks it may be Shrewsbury. Did you decide to write him? Now there is no need to do so, since Irvin says he knows all there is to know.

You asked about the Sign of Hastur. It thought you knew of it. I think it is in the *Necronomicon* somewhere, and am sure it's in the R'lyeh Text—the final chapter is devoted to the Return of the Old Ones, and tells of the struggles there will be between them, giving examples of R'lyehian history. The Sign is made among the clouds above R'lyeh, when it was on secure ground in the primeval aeons of earth. The Byakhee appear thereafter and attack the Deep Ones as they work. The Shantaks also appear, and the battle rages on until the Shoggoths come up from the undersea city of A'yoh-tns, nearby. Then the Lloigor appear, and the Fowls of Interstellar Space outnumber the minions of Cthulhu, who retreat into the waters surrounding R'lyeh.

You ask about Ravu P'thya. Irvin is standing at the threshold of a limitless abyss of knowledge, and he is just now, after decades of research and study, taking his initial steps into the darkness. He is confident that he will shortly learn of Ravu (or Raevu) P'thya, and his suspected relation to Yog-Sothoth and 'Umr At-Tawil, Hermes Trismegistus and Thoth. He is supreme among a group not unlike the Old Ones: the Wicked Ones, but this is getting into the unplumbed void of mystery surrounding "the Primogenitor" and his universe beyond that gulf which borders time and space, unvisited by any. Jerome Van der Vacht came closest; he is the author of the *Unbekannte Geheimenisse*, printed in Munich in 1839 (limited edition; very rare). There were also the two fiction writers, utterly unknown in the literary world of the macabre, who wrote indirectly of these things: Atlante de Lugel, the French monk, in his privately circulated collection (perhaps his entire output), *Le Cercueil du Démon*; and Charles Nathan, whose *The Yith Experiment and Others* draws heavily upon the Great Race, as recorded by Lovecraft in his supposed fiction. Surprisingly, there is no known reference to the Primogenitor in Lovecraft.

> As always, I am
> Yours by the Promise of Power,
> Emmett Whateley

The third letter widened the scope of light shed by the second. Dated October 20, it read:

Brother,

Yes, Irvin has long been in contact with the Fowls—basically the Byakhee—as well as their impressions upon mankind. After he discovers through mathematics and astronomic calculations approximately *when* Hastur will return, we will be able to proceed with our plans, which are:

(1) prepare a haven for Him and the multitude of Fowls;

(2) prevent any interception of our plans by Cthulhu's minions or any others; and,

(3) let Him through the spheres when the time is right.

I had no idea that you were so involved in the field. Be sure to send us a copy of your book when you finish translating the remaining fragments from the little-known ancient texts you mentioned. Yes, Irvin knows several of the languages you do not, and is sending the keys to those languages with this letter. However, *do not publish the other study*, "Hastur and His Minions in the Ancient Books," since this could get the Deep Ones or even Shrewsbury on our trail, and cause much trouble for yourself. This could be disastrous to our Purpose.

Irvin has seen the Innsmouth people creeping around, which is bad. It would be easy for us to launch an attack on Innsmouth by having the Byakhee make the Sign in the clouds and thus call the other Fowls forth, but we hope that Shrewsbury will take care of them. If, indeed, he is after us, then he may attempt to send the Innsmouth cross-breeds and the Deep Ones themselves in our direction.

Thank you for your purchase of the last five books. There is a passage on page 185 of the massive Book of Susaur (we grieve that the complete book is not on hand) to the effect that:

"It should be known that when one summons the Unspeakable Thing of the Yellow Mask without the purpose or the protection, for the service of the Winged Fiends, then he shall in turn be summoned for the service of the Unspeakable."

In other words, if you summon Hastur without the five-pointed star then not only will the vicious Fowls critically wound you but also the summons of Hastur will call you to His service.

Your Servant Under the Unspeakable,
Emmett Whateley

It is evident that several volumes had been purchased between letters. The fourth letter, dated November 1:

Brother—

Now we are sure that Shrewsbury is after us, though thankfully not in full force. He is cleverly using the Deep Ones as weapons. He *must* be stopped.

Irvin first caught sight of him at Celaeno and asked those there about his inquiries. He became aware of Irvin, too, and must have kept tabs on him since. But how did he find out that we are here in Arkham? Irvin never goes out.

We can only hope Shrewsbury has no time to come after us, since he is kept busy trying to seal out Cthulhu. He is using the Byakhee, but only for travel, and he is never without the star. We cannot get to him.

You must help us. Come to Arkham, and you can help us get him.

We cannot get at him. We have been with Them too long, and the star is effective against us.

You must kill him. An accident—a fire will do! Come here first, and we will help you help us. It is in the line of the Purpose, and the promise of power will be yours—when He has returned and the earth is cleared off.

Please help us.

> In haste,
> E. Whateley

The final letter was dated November 8, just a week after the fourth, and was evidently written in great haste.

Why have you not come?

We must leave now. The Deep Ones are after us. We tried to get Shrewsbury with fire, but he escaped. He has left because the Deep Ones were after him as well. It is not safe to travel by land. We are going to the Himalayas in Tibet. There we can prepare a haven with the aid of the Mi-Go, or abominable Snow-Men, who worship Ithaqua, the Snow-Thing, ally of Hastur. Then we must go to Celaeno, even though Shrewsbury is probably there. It is fairly neutral, and Irvin can complete his studies there, and we will know the time. I am sorry you cannot come with us, but it is not safe for us to wait any longer.

> Good-bye.
> E.W.

I set the final letter aside, deeply disturbed and filled with questions. I looked up to see Cartley waiting for a comment on the whole affair.

"Well?" he said after a moment.

"Well what?"

"Do you understand Hawkins' place in the whole extravaganza? No, you do not. Here, read this . . . the letter from Shrewsbury to Hawkins. Meanwhile, I'll flip through the manuscripts," he said, handing me the letter. It read:

Arkham, October 14.

Dear Mr. Hawkins:

Thank you for your letter of October 12, and your warning.

I met Mr. Irvin once, at a place far from earth, if you can believe that. I must warn you, now, not to get involved with Irvin or Whateley or their associates. You say that you have read the *Necronomicon*, so you may recall this passage:

"And when the time is come, each of the Servants of the Old Ones shall prepare the return of their Masters. And those Servants are the Deep Ones and the Shoggoths of Cthulhu, the Fowls of Interstellar Space of Hastur, Zhar and Ithaqua . . ."

The Fowls of Interstellar Space (their name has also been translated as "Birds of the Star-Spaces") are the Byakhee, whom I have called upon several times for assistance; the Lloigor; and the Shantaks, who guard Kadath in the Cold Waste. Yet, as at Ponape and Innsmouth—where the Deep Ones have mated with humans to produce a strain of fish-people who now entirely occupy Innsmouth—the Fowls have left their impression upon mankind in the mountain countries around the world, especially in the Asian regions, as well as in the frigid zones of the extreme North and South, where the servants of Ithaqua, the Snow-Thing, have mated with the Winged Fiends.

I have seen these hybrids in Arkham, and your letter has assured me that there is someone here working for Hastur. If Irvin finds out that you are betraying him, he will send them after you, so I give you this as a warning: drop any involvement *now*, and, if you publish your studies, do so under a pseudonym, or the hybrids will come after you anyway. They want no publicity until they are assured of a victory against mankind.

There is, however, a talisman that protects the possessor from the servants of the Old Ones, though this is ineffective against the Old Ones themselves. This talisman is a star carved from the stone of ancient Mnar. Go to the Archaeology Department at Cambridge and ask for Professor Greene. Show him this letter, and he will give you one of these talismans.

Do as I say, and you will be safe.

Sincerely yours,
Laban Shrewsbury

Cartley, of course, noted my surprise, but allowed me to speak.

"I see . . . then Hawkins was working against them all along. But they must have suspected it, and before they left Arkham sent the bird-people to silence him—the ones that harassed Miss Hawkins?" I asked, expecting clarification, and was shocked by Cartley's reply.

"No! You see, Whateley suspected him not at all, nor Irvin, who was too busy with his studies to speculate. No, the hybrids came after Hawkins because he had the book published."

"But—" I was confused. "There would have been copies of the volume in his study.

"Not if he employed an agent to take care of all the details. Besides, this typed manuscript is the printer's copy—the proofreader's mark is imprinted upon the first page of the text. I would imagine that the second manuscript, the 'Fragmentary Inscriptions,' when completed, was also to be published. This, however, was made impossible by Hawkins' death. Despite his precautions, the hybrids must have tracked Hawkins down through the agent."

Cartley handed me the second manuscript and continued looking through the typescript of *Hastur and His Minions in the Ancient Books*.

Examining the coverless, partially typed and partially handwritten pages, I discovered that, on the second page, the title "Fragmentary Inscriptions" was repeated and the words "From the Ancient Texts" added. The next page proved to be the contents page, and the table gave the titles of the tablets, hieroglyphic inscriptions, papyri, or other texts from which the translations were made, as known to archaeologists and paleographers. There were also listings of the languages themselves, and of the locales in which the original form of the writings were found, such as Phrygia and Easter Island. But the most startling subsection of the collection was the one devoted to "Pre-Human Inscriptions."

During the last few days, I had read and heard unbelievable things: Shrewsbury's visit to a place "far from earth;" the existence of creatures beyond imagination and credibility, and of hybrids formed by in-breeding these blasphemies with humans. But the reference to pre-human writings was by far the loudest shriek of madness yet to reach my ears. I set the manuscript down with some agitation and woke Cartley from his intense absorption in the other work by Hawkins.

"It's pretty powerful stuff," he acknowledged after seeing me as depressed as I had found him at the beginning of our disastrous adventure.

"Tell me, Harold, do you believe in all this?"

"Do you?" he said calmly.

"Of course not! You evaded my question."

"There is proof—supporting evidence—to make me and others—yes, you, too—believe, if even a slight fraction of the evidence was revealed."

"Then you believe!"

"I must," he said solemnly. "And I must make you believe, Kenneth. When you looked at the 'Inscriptions,' did you read Hawkins' introductory note? Yes—then you know that Hawkins travelled to the British Museum, the Bibliothèque Nationale, various museums in the Middle East, and other major libraries and museums in order to study and photograph the various fragments for the compilation, and also to speak with specialists across the globe!"

"So, what of it?"

"When could he have found the time to do such travelling? There was no time between letters, and all evidence points to the conclusion that the 'tour' was made after he learned of the books, Whateley, etc. He simply had no time."

I was afraid to ask the obvious question. "And—your explanation?"

"This volume, 'Hastur and His Minions,' explains it. Here, on page 23, is a chant said to open the way for the Byakhee to come, and they will come and transport the caller through the aether at a speed far exceeding that of light. A small stone whistle can also be used—or, of course, the Sign of Hastur mentioned in the second letter we obtained today—and once the fowls are summoned, one can be transported to anywhere in the entire universe. But because of the great velocity, the rider must consume a small portion of a golden mead which renders him insensible to the effects of time and space."

"And you expect me to believe—" I started, outraged.

"You must! If you do not take my word for it, read it here . . ."

I agreed to do so only because I wanted to see what proof Cartley had for such preposterous speculations. My eyes searched for the passage Cartley was vaguely pointing to, while my mind raced for some reasonable explanation for this whole affair—worst of all, Cartley's sad acceptance of the impossible. All I found were the inexpressible words of the following chant, to which Hawkins ascribed magical powers: "*Iä! Iä! Hastur cf'ayak 'vulgtumm, vugtlagln! Ai! Ai! Hastur!*"

"The ravings of a madman!" I protested. "This is no proof at all!"

"But Kenneth! How else could he have travelled as he had in the matter of weeks—a month at the most—that he had? I can prove that Hastur and the Fowls of Interstellar Space do exist. There is an entire chapter in Hawkins' study on summoning Hastur's beasts, and on making his Sign. If you want proof, come tomorrow evening and I will summon the Byakhee!"

Cartley had an almost maniacal glare in his eyes—a look I had never seen before.

"But that might be dangerous . . ."

"Ah, then you *do* believe!"

"No, but—" I started, but I had no response.

"No, you cannot keep me from the experiment. Just think what I can do with the privilege of travel—*through time and space!*"

"You're mad! Man, don't go through with this! I believe, OK? I believe! It's not necessary to do this . . ." I had risen to my feet, but even when shouting I could not reach him. He just sat there, breathing heavily and staring beyond me and the room and the prosaic world outside—into the maddening gulfs of nightmare beyond.

I left the room. I was sorry that the servants had been relieved earlier, for only God knew what poor Cartley would do. I walked out into the crisp night, chilled without a cap or hat. My head bursting with forbidden knowledge and my heart bleeding for my friend who must certainly be mad, I wiped the cold sweat from my brow and leaned on a lamppost.

The streets were empty. Boston was asleep.

I fought my fear of the unknown and tried not to think of the terrifying chaos just outside man's little sphere of knowledge. I hailed a cab and made it to my apartment, but I could not sleep. All that night I lay awake, unable to sleep, afraid to close my eyes; thinking what poor Cartley was doing in his crazed state.

Perhaps I slept, perhaps not, but I was refreshed in the morning. I knew what I must do.

* * *

"Can I help you?" said the young lady who sat behind the typewriter.

"I am looking for Professor Greene of the Archaeology Department. Can you tell me where his office is?"

"Room 42: down this hall, the second corridor on the right."

"Does he have a class?"

"I'm not sure, but I think he's just a research consultant now."

"Thank you very much."

I followed the secretary's directions to Room 42 and knocked on the door.

"Come in," a voice sounded from within. I entered.

"Professor Greene? I am Kenneth Hinton. I was directed to you by Arthur Hawkins, a friend of Professor Shrewsbury," I said, and immediately a look of concern spread over the balding man's thick face.

"What can I do for you?" he said after considering me for some time.

"If you knew Mr. Hawkins, then I suppose it would help if you gave me what you gave him." I was unsure of myself, and knew not whether I could trust Dr. Greene—or my own sanity for going through with this.

"Why do you need the Star?" he said after a moment.

I was greatly relieved by this confirmation, which meant that I was not myself mad. But I realized this also meant that all the incredible things mentioned in the letters from Whateley to Hawkins were hideous reality. The sleep that I missed the previous night haunted me, weakened me in a moment, and I dropped into a chair. Then, more freely, I spoke.

"My friend, Harold Cartley, purchased a book, the *Necronomicon*, from a second-hand book shop. In it was a letter to Mr. Hawkins from an 'E. Whateley.' The letter indicated that Hawkins had other books similar to the one we had, and, deeply interested, we obtained Hawkins' address from the book dealer. We went there, and bought from Hawkins' sister two boxes of books and a valise full of papers dealing with this whole blasted mythology—with which you must be familiar. Now, my friend has became drawn into all this with some maniacal goal in mind."

"What do you think his goal is?"

"Tonight he is going to call the Fowls of Hastur by making some sign."

Dr. Greene was gripped by fear and concern, and sat up sharply. Sweat appeared in beads upon his forehead.

"He doesn't have a Star?"

"No, that's why I came to you."

"Then they may slip past him—into our world!"

"You, too, believe they exist?"

"Not 'believe'—I *know* they exist! I myself have seen them! There is great danger in what your friend does, an ancient evil will be unleashed upon the world!"

"But why haven't the human followers of the Old Ones done this long ago?"

"Because they, too, would be killed, and they cannot bear the Star themselves. Your friend must be stopped, or he will inadvertently kill himself." Dr. Greene unlocked a lower drawer of his desk and presented three stars of grey stone which he said were the protective talismans out from the stone of Mnar, with the seal of the Elder Gods impressed upon them.

"Does your friend have the golden mead?" the professor asked.

"I don't know . . . he mentioned it . . . it is in Hawkins' monograph. But I can't imagine he would have it."

"Then was the text of the Celaeno Fragments among the books and papers you acquired? No, no, I suppose not. Dr. Shrewsbury himself had access to the Fragments—or, rather, to the original texts, of which he transcribed small sections while on Celaeno . . . But never mind. Come, we must proceed to your friend's house without delay."

Without another word, I lead him to Cartley's house. I knocked, and was greeted by the manservant, who seemed to be very disturbed. He explained that when he had come to the house that morning, he could not find Cartley at all, but suspected him to be in the locked study upstairs, although he did not respond to any "summons"—that was the servant's word, and I was shocked by the irony.

We hurried to the study and, finding it still bolted from within, rushed the door and broke it open. Cartley lay on the floor in a pool of blood. He was not dead, but he was literally *in shreds*—not only his garments, but his entire body was lacerated. Hospital attention was imperative, and the servant left the room to phone for an ambulance.

"The Fowls have come!" exclaimed Dr. Greene when the butler had gone.

*   *   *

Cartley recovered slowly in the hospital and was not allowed to return home for several weeks. At first he was unconscious for days, then awoke in a fit of shrieks, to be calmed only by periodic injections of depressants. When physically healed, however, he was released to Dr. Greene and me, with the understanding that we would keep a private nurse on hand, for poor Cartley still had fits of raving.

The professor and I settled temporarily in rooms adjacent to Cartley's own, and were present when he at last returned to coherency, although his excitement could not be quieted.

"I know the time! I know the time!" he said in whispers. "Soon! Soon shall He return. God, had I not experimented! What a fool I was."

"Cartley, what happened to you that night?" I asked.

"I read the chapter by Hawkins and learned His Sign. I called forth into the night. There was a wind—a wind from the deepest caverns of Hell! A cold wind that burst through the window and knocked me off my feet. Then they came. The Fowls! God, they were horrible! They rushed in and fell upon me with talons and razor beaks! I knew the time was near by the way they laughed—that hideous, lilting laugh!"

On Greene's instruction, the windows were never left open at night. In addition, a Star was placed at Cartley's window, and I bore one at all times. Although Greene spent day and night in the study going over the Hawkins papers and books, there were occasions when he had to go to the University. One evening he was gone for this reason. The servants had been relieved of their services until the affair was over, and the nurse was no longer needed.

That night they came.

There was a knock at the door. I was alone in the house, except for Cartley, so when I answered the door, I had the Star concealed in my hand. I immediately recognized the caller as one of the 'funny people' who harassed Miss Hawkins.

"Is Mr. Cartley in?"

"Yes, but he is ill and unable to receive visitors. May I tell him who called?"

"No, but I will return another time—perhaps this time tomorrow evening?"

"Yes, I'll tell him to expect you."

Greene was present at the appointed time, and when the caller returned we were ready for him. I let him in and showed him into the study, where Greene was waiting. I closed the door behind us and remained there, trying to appear as natural as possible. Greene addressed the visitor.

"I am Harold Cartley. You wanted to see me last week. I don't believe we've met."

The caller spoke in a high, piping voice.

"My name is John Reeds. I am interested in your line of study. Miss Hawkins gave me your address, for I wanted to speak with you."

"You mean, my studies in the worship of Hastur and the Old Ones?"

"Precisely."

"And the worship of the Elder Gods—the great Elder Gods of Glyu-Vho, may they be praised! May their Eyes of Wisdom look forever upon Their Domain, which is free from the chaotic demons, the Old Ones! *Wyan! Yoglma on'lan-ffnr!*"

John Reeds shrieked and put his gloved hands to the sides of his muffled head. He jumped up and ran toward me with fire in his eyes. Automatically, I pulled out the Star and held it out before me. Reeds made a gasping sound and stopped dead in his tracks, then reversed direction and headed toward the window. Greene intercepted him, Star in outstretched hand.

"You see, Mr. Reeds, there is no escape. We only wish to ask *you* some questions. When is Hastur to return?"

"No!" he shouted, looking around the room frantically for some means of escape.

"*Now*, Hinton!" Greene said, and we advanced, Stars extended.

"Okay! I'll talk! Just put those . . . away," Reeds piped. We did as he requested, for it was evident that we could easily overpower him if necessary. We directed him to sit in a chair in the corner of the room, then we took seats between him and the door.

"When is Hastur to return?" Greene asked the thin, bony man.

Reeds hesitated, then seemed to gather conviction and said "Soon!"

"Have Irvin and Whateley finished building the haven?" Greene questioned.

"Yes. They have dug it out of the Himalayas with the help of the Mi-Go."

"Who will call him forth?"

"Irvin will direct the Fowls to make the Sign."

"He knows the exact time, then?"

"I think so, yes."

"How is he going to call Him?"

"By the Sign and the Jholu Chant."

"Where is it to be found?"

"In one of the books. I don't know which one. Hawkins knew."

"It is in the manuscript of his second book, then?"

"Yes, that's why we wanted him."

"Is there a counter-chant?"

He laughed musically. "No. There is no way to stop us."

"Yes. There *is* a way."

Reeds was horrified. "No!"

"Yes! I can get Shrewsbury. He will stop Irvin."

"No! There is no way. Shrewsbury is preoccupied with Cthulhu." The entity's name had a singular intonation from the lips or semi-beak of the bird-man.

"Then I will call to the Elder Gods and warn them of the uprising evil! Hastur will be destroyed; Nodens shall come, riding the waves of Aether on His crenulate shell; He shall smite Hastur and deal death upon the Fowls and the Abominable Mi-Go in pillars of fire!"

"No!" Reeds was hysterical. "There is no way to stop us! No way to call *them*!"

"I am sorry, Mr. Reeds. You are on the losing side. You will remain here until it is over. Hinton, I am going out to get the necessary ingredients for the making of the mead. Watch him closely," he said, and left.

It was late now, and not many people were on the streets. I sat in my chair, with Reeds across from me in the corner, fidgeting and glancing around the room furtively, as a trapped animal would do.

A few moments after Dr. Greene had left, Reeds did something wholly unexpected. As I have said, I sat between him and the door—almost in a straight line; but the window was in the other corner of the room. Reeds jumped up and started to run in an arc around my chair, aiming for the door. I jumped, too, and moved to cut him off. This was easily accomplished, but it was soon evident that our prisoner was headed for the window—which I didn't expect, since we were on the second story. He achieved his goal and threw the window open, only to shout down to the street: "Get him!"

That was all. I was upon him instantly and threw him to the floor, idiotically pausing to close the window—for, when I turned back, Reeds had bolted out of the room like lightning.

I went after him, but wasn't fast enough. Reeds *flew* down the stairs and reached the foyer while I was still on the landing. All I could do now was to hurl the stone talisman between him and the front door which led to freedom. Miraculously, it struck the door, embedding itself in the wood. Reeds hesitated, and for a moment I thought that I had blocked his escape; but he simply turned and climbed out of a window before I could do anything.

The next day Cartley was up and around. I told him all that had happened, and he speculated (as I had) that they had gotten Greene. Someone had accompanied Reeds, waiting outside, to whom Reeds had shouted his command. The newspapers removed all remaining doubt, for a body identified by the wallet it bore was found by a fisherman on the bay shore where an unexpected change of the tides had swept it in. It was Professor Greene.

Cartley prevented me from going to the authorities, for which I was later thankful, since we would have become involved in the police investigation and thus prevented from stopping Irvin —and stopping him had become our solemn duty.

I told Cartley about the plan to notify the Elder Gods of the return of Hastur. I was reasonably surprised at Cartley's reply.

"Ha! He was only bluffing! The only logical way to stop Irvin is to go to the Himalayas and shoot him down in cold blood. That is why Greene needed the mead. He was merely misleading your Mr. Reeds. In fact, I suspect he wanted Reeds to escape so that he would tell his companions (erroneously) that Nodens would be summoned to destroy Hastur and the Mi-Go. This would make them think twice about their plan—maybe even abandon the operation."

But our own mission had evidently just begun. Cartley said that he had heard of the Jholu Chant from a source other than Hawkins' book, and also knew the ingredients of the mead from that source. However, the shopping list was long and the items used in making the golden fluid were rare, so the following week was expended in searching every pharmacy and herbalist in Boston. By the end of the week, only sixteen of the twenty-three necessary ingredients had been collected, and Cartley thought it might be prosperous to try and locate Professor Shrewsbury. Plans were thus made to go to legendary, witch-haunted Arkham in hopes of finding him there. Of course, Cartley was still too weak to travel—just the jaunts around town were enough to lay him up. So it was I who would go to Arkham.

But something came up that very night to spoil our plans.

Cartley had dreams. He woke me up with his nightmare screams, and I rushed to his room to find him delirious, panting, and soaked in sweat.

"Hastur is calling for me! The Whateley letter! 'When one calls upon Hastur without the five-pointed star, then he will be called to service by the summons of Hastur!' God! What have I done? Hastur knows it was Greene and not I that they got! He knows!"

I could not calm him, try as I might, but he sat up most of the night gripping the stone from Mnar tightly in his hands. Needless to say, I did not leave for Arkham the following day.

Cartley slept the next morning, but his dreams returned.

He was screaming when I ran into the room, and upon seeing him I froze in horror. Cartley had been lying face down, and now was frantically gripping at his mattress—*for his body was floating up into the air!* How else can I describe such a sight? He could never have held himself up like that, with his legs straight and at a sixty degree angle from the bed. I ran over to him to hold him down, but the moment I touched him the spell was broken and he fell back to the bed.

He had dropped his stone and I handed it back to him to calm him down. All that day and night, I stayed in the room with him, reading or dozing in an armchair, and leaving only when necessary. Cartley was strangely weak and tired from the lack of sleep, which was beginning to wear me down as well. I did not try to explain the supernormal attack, but thought that if, indeed, the evil of the Masked Old One, Hastur—an evil I could sense in the room—was the cause of the attack, then the only remedies were vigilance and the two stone talismans.

In the middle of the long night, I was awakened by a heavy thump in the direction of my friend, accompanied by a single inaudible whisper and a brief fumbling. The candle I had placed on the table beside me must have burned down, and the room was pitch dark. I had to light a match to find another candle in the table's single drawer or to discover what the sounds were that I had heard. In the brief light of the match I saw that the covers of Cartley's bed were disordered, some hanging over the edge of the bed to touch the floor; but what caused the most concern was the fact that *Cartley was not to be seen.*

Then I heard a muffled cry terminated by another thump. At that instant the match burned my fingers and I dropped it, only to quickly draw another. This I struck, and, finding another candle, lit it. I ran over to the bed to confirm that no one was in it, then stooped down to look under it—but, surprisingly, Cartley was not there. Acting on a frightening impulse, I flattened myself against the floor and studied the *underside* of the bed—and there, pressed impossibly up against the bedsprings, was my unconscious friend!

Again, at the touch, he fell from his supernormal levitation, but first I had placed a pillow on the floor under his head, and I did my best to break his fall. Returning him to the bed revived him, and he weakly mumbled something about "the summons of Hastur" and "the service" that would be required of him by the Fowls. He was mildly consoled by the stone, and after a stiff brandy he quickly fell into a sleep unbroken for many hours.

It was around six the next morning when he woke, and Cartley bull-headedly decided that he was strong enough to make the journey to Arkham. With clarity and determination, he convinced me to agree. After all, the trip was necessary, and it was evident that we should stick together— might even be safer if we left Boston. Within a half-hour we were ready to leave, for a sense of urgency prompted us to haste. Would to God we had not set foot from the house!

The horror that had surrounded us since our hazardous exploration of the *Necronomicon* had to eventually culminate—for better or worse. How could I know that the end for Cartley would come that very day? "The Summons of Hastur," wrote Hawkins in *Hastur and His Minions,* "cannot be resisted. They who oppose Him or who call upon Him and His without protection or purpose will be called into the air in a hideous flight."

We walked out of the house and crossed the empty street to the square beyond. On the farther side the street was much busier, and we could catch an early cab there. The square, as the street, was devoid of people, and few to be seen anywhere. Around the extreme edges of the square ran a narrow strip of grass and trees, while the remainder of the square was composed of paving stones, with a statue of a statesman at its center. Upon clearing the grass and thus the trees, we both happened to look up at the dark blue sky of early morning, clear except for a small cloud directly above us. Cartley had his right hand in his coat pocket, where I knew a stone talisman to be. When he looked up again, he stopped short, and gripped the stone in his pocket. The single cloud was separating and a space was forming in its center, as if the cloud was forming a circle. We proceeded across the square.

A moment later, Cartley again glanced up again and grabbed my shoulder, shouting:

"Look! The Fowls!"

I stared at the sky but saw nothing, and said so.

"I'm sure I saw one at the edge of the cloud! It darted quickly out of sight—it was one of the Byakhee!"

"Just your imagination, old chap," I said to calm him, but walked faster.

We went on a bit, now nearing the figure of the statesman at the center of the square. Cartley was studying the clouds with consternation.

"Hinton!" He grabbed my shoulder again. "Look! The clouds—they're forming . . . the Sign of Hastur! The Fowls are there, I say! They are calling Hastur! God!"

I scrutinized the cloud in amazement, for certainly it had formed a perfect doughnut shape and an odd, though symmetrical, arrangement was appearing within it. I had read, under Greene's direction, the chapter on making the Sign, and this formation was startlingly like it.

Poor Cartley passed into hysteria. His nails dug into my shoulder, and he withdrew his other hand from his coat, gripping the stone from Mnar. Through a superhuman strength lent him by fear, he crushed the stone and it crumbled in his hand.

"I am doomed! Hastur is calling! 'None can resist!'"

What could I do? I stood there, frozen in horror. Cosmic unreality shrouded the scene with its black cape, and even now I shudder to recall the last moments of Cartley's life on earth.

"The summons of Hastur! *Ai Hastur! Hastur cf'ayak . . .*"

Harold Cartley's last, unearthly word or pronunciation ended in a shriek, and as I stood there beside him, the Sign in the clouds was completed and Cartley literally *fell into the sky above*, and, gaining velocity, was absorbed after an instant of "hideous flight" by the central cloud-particle of the Sign of Hastur!

But there was more. In that last instant before my friend disappeared into the cloud, I saw—or thought I saw—the black, feathery claws of the Minions of Hastur, the blasted Fowls of Interstellar Space, reach down and clutch poor Cartley!

The Tomb of Nyarlathotep

> To a season of political and social upheaval was added a strange and brooding
> apprehension of hideous physical danger; a danger widespread and all-
> embracing, such a danger as may be imagined only in the most terrible phan-
> tasms of the night.
>
> —H. P. LOVECRAFT, *Nyarlathotep*

I was hard at work editing his *Selected Lectures* when Professor Bishop en-
tered the study.

"I knew it!" he said, tossing a heavy book on the table, where it landed
with a thud and slid toward me with the aid of a slick dust jacket. The book
was Robert Temple's *Sphinx Mysteries*.

"Knew what?" I asked, looking up.

"The Sphinx was not a sphinx at all!" he said with thick sarcasm, mouth
twisted in a sour expression. Here was a riddle if ever there was one.

"How can the Sphinx not be a sphinx?" I asked, taking the bait.

"As you know, in Greek myth the Sphinx of Thebes was a monster with
the body of a lion and the head and breasts of a woman."

"Right. You had to answer her riddle about man, or she'd kill you."

"Precisely! And the Sphinx of Giza has the body of a lion and a man's
head, with the headpiece and shoulder-cape worn by pharaohs. Now Tem-
ple—who states a preference for canines over felines—has uncovered sup-
posed 'evidence' that the Sphinx of Giza originally had a *jackal's* head and
body—was, in fact, a representation of Anubis—before it was resculpted into
what we see today."

"Curious . . . But Anubis has the head of a jackal and the body of a man.
How does that jibe—"

"Read it and you'll see. He has an answer for everything! And he's re-
dated it, too."

"*Again?* There have been so many dates thrown around. But clearly, it's
fourth dynasty—third millennium BC."

"I know. Then there's this . . ." he said, pulling a second book from his shopping bag and placing it on top of the first, for which I was just reaching. It was *Egyptian Dawn* by the same author, this time co-written with his wife, Olivia.

"*Another* by Temple—this time he's punching holes in old theories by going into shafts aligned with the stars . . ."

"Serious?"

"No, not Sirius this time."

"What? Oh, I meant are you *serious.*"

"*I'm* serious, but is *he* serious? Anyway, it doesn't matter. He's selling books like hotcakes and writing off trips to Egypt—something *I* should be doing!"

"I agree."

"Good, then you're coming with me."

"Where?"

"To Egypt!"

"*Serious?*"

"Yes, I'm serious! We're leaving next Tuesday.

"But—the revolution . . ." I protested. At the time, Mubarak had just re-signed under pressure from protesters, leaving Egypt to military rule—and an uncertain future.

"I know, the timing could be better. I made the arrangements with the Minister of Antiquities *before* all this hubbub started. I was going to tell you, but you were in Providence. Things may be in a state of chaos, but I have to get on this—before Temple does!"

"You mean . . . Site Y?" Site Y had been a pet project of the professor's for some years and he had always sworn me to utmost secrecy about it.

"Luckily, Y is not on Temple's list of undiscovered sites—yet. If he sticks to that list, and stays in the Valley of the Kings, he'll be busy for the rest of his life. But at any moment, he might uncover something that points him in the direction of Y. And I—*I* want to be the first to find Y, and excavate it!" He beat his chest in a show of apish pride.

"When you were off in Providence, photographing Lovecraft's tomb-stone or whatever," he began, ribbing me for my abiding interest in the horror writer, "I myself came upon a scintillating clue—a missing piece to the puzzle—which I'll explain in detail . . . Meanwhile, we have to get ready . . ."

"You obtained permission to dig?" I asked, still stunned by the suddenness of project, which sounded like it involved excavation—which could take months or years.

"Yes—like I said, before the hubbub. Mubarak's cabinet was dismissed, so we have to hope the arrangements will be honored—by whoever's in charge."

"Wow, talk about an adventure!"

"A double adventure—a triple adventure, I hope. Getting into Egypt, finding the site, and getting *into* it. And you know my theory . . ."

"The site was a ceremonial center or temple built by Nyarlathotep, the legendary, evil demigod that you think . . ."

"Was a man! I think the evidence is there—it *must* be there! If nothing else, the architect's name is always inscribed on one of the cornerstones, and surely Nyarlathotep would have designed it himself. If we can locate and excavate this site—this temple and (I believe) tomb—then, one way or another, the proof will be in our grasp."

"Like Euhemerus and the Gold Stele of Zeus?" I asked, referring to a fictional inscription that told of the deeds of the Olympians when they were human—the children of King Ouranos.

"Exactly! Who knows? There may be unknown tablets or scrolls—or hieroglyphic carvings, as you suggest—telling the *true* story of Nyarlathotep: not as a god or demigod, but as a man among men. Nyarlathotep was no god, nor an extraterrestrial! He was a terrestrial man with blood and guts like you or I—only, I should say, surpassing us both with his almost superhuman intellect and multifaceted abilities."

The professor was a well-known proponent of Euhemerism, the notion that mythical deities and heroes were once historical figures. He was even dubbed "The New Euhemerist" in an interview published in the *Atlantic Monthly*.

"Like Greek heroes from Perseus to Heracles, and kings from Midas to Minos, there's an historical basis for myths and legends of the gods, and that basis is the acts of men . . ." the article began.

Euhemerus did it with Zeus; Robert Graves did it with Jesus; Dr. Bishop extended it to others—Dionysus, Orpheus, Aesculapius, and a host of others.

For years, Dr. Alfred Bishop taught Mythology at Wicklow University using texts by such luminaries in the field as Joseph Campbell, Mircea Eliade and Robert Graves. He gradually developed his own text, which offered a summary of their ideas and added new insights of his own—backed by thorough research—thereby creating a new exemplar, *Man-Gods of Myth*.

I had applied to the Wicklow School of Graduate Studies expressly to attend Dr. Bishop's erudite lectures, and had the good fortune to complete my doctoral work under his tutelage before he retired to devote himself to research and writing. Funded by grants and the proceeds of *Man-Gods*, Dr. Bishop offered me a job as research assistant, which I gladly accepted. In this capacity, I helped him complete the detailed study *Zeus, King of Crete* and the concise "summary statement" of his views, *Deus ex Hominem*.

He abhorred Erich von Daniken and his brood of followers—including Temple, whose *Sirius Mystery* connected petroglyphs of the Dogon people of Mali to visitors from the Dog Star Sirius—a trip of a mere nine light-years . . . The Nazca lines of Peru, the stone fortresses of Cuzco, the pyramids of Egypt . . . even Stonehenge was offered up as proof of alien technology at work.

"Why do they always insist on explaining early man's most remarkable achievements by reference to beings from another star system?" he asked in one lecture. "They might as well stick to the old theory, that Thoth taught the ancient Egyptians everything they knew—language, the calendar, agriculture and science—but where did Thoth come from? Atlantis, of course! They make a fanciful reference to some mythical civilization that predated even ancient Egypt and deserved true credit for all her wonders.

"'The Ancient Egyptians did not have the sophistication or technology to build the pyramids or the Sphinx,' so their argument goes—'*therefore*, they were built by a yet-older civilization—in 39,000 BC!' Does that make sense? At a time when *homo sapiens* were first gathering along the Nile? First planting millet and barley? There was no pharaoh, no civil order at all—no pottery, not even spears. It's too fantastic! It's not science at all, not even scholarship—it's fiction, like something from Lovecraft!"

In fact, several of his lectures had touched on H. P. Lovecraft and his fictional pantheon of transcendental entities, which Dr. Bishop found revealing as examples of modern mythopoesis.

"At least Lovecraft created a sense of reality, of authenticity. This is surreal . . . or farce."

"Shakespeare wrote Shakespeare, and man's deeds were done by man," he often said, a kind of mantra for his humanist viewpoint. "It's myth to think otherwise—bad myth, not good myth."

"Of course, to confuse things, Lovecraft appropriated the historical deities Dagon and Nodens before inventing his own exotic names, like Cthulhu and Yog-Sothoth. As you know, I'm not particularly interested in Cthulhu and Lovecraft's other tentacled monstrosities from beyond space and time, but Nyarlathotep and Azathoth are different—there is an historical record of their existence, Nyarlathotep as a man, Azathoth as a concept but also as a deity that was worshiped."

I asked him how Lovecraft could have learned about Nyarlathotep and Azathoth, if their names had been so well hidden from history.

"Well, there are a very few fragmentary sources, mostly classical—Herodotus hinted at unspeakable rites, Eusebius cited Diodorus on unexplained spectacles, which in one way or another all seem to tie in to this one figure, Nyarlathotep—provided you make the proper deductions and follow the symbolism accurately. Of course, Lovecraft was practically a scholar of the classics. He had access to public libraries in Providence and New York, or on travels; and there's always his grandfather's fabulous library, whose contents has been the subject of so much speculation. One can only deduce from the essays and vast correspondence that Lovecraft was truly erudite—a man of vast learning, especially for an autodidact. But the obvious answer is the *Necronomicon*, which he is presumed to have invented . . ."

In one of his lectures, "Thoth vs. Azathoth," the professor expounded on his theory that the name Azathoth might well mean "anti-Thoth"—citing the Greek *a*- prefix meaning "not," as in *azo*- "not supporting life"—as well as the demon Azazel.

"As Hopfner pointed out," the lecture continued, "Thoth is the Greek name for the Egyptian Djhwty, which means 'He who is like the Ibis.' The ibis is the bird of the Nile sacred to Thoth, and it is well to note that the curve of the ibis is crescent-shaped like the changing moon, and also forms the basic shape of the letters of the alphabet which was one of Thoth's gifts to the people of the Nile.

"But Thoth was more than a lunar deity—he was a solar one as well. He was considered 'the heart and voice' of Ra the sun god, which he predated. So Thoth had a dual (or non-dual) nature—spanning or transcending the polarity of sun/moon observed by logic. Never one-sided, Thoth was the bringer of balance and order, and his consort Ma'at represented ethics and social law.

"By comparison, Azazel was (or is) an evil spirit of the desert, placated by the Jews on the Day of Atonement with a scapegoat ('ăzā'zēl means "scapegoat" in Hebrew). But the Muslims also knew this demon, whom they numbered one of the *jinn*, a spirit who can adopt the form of humans or animals at will, acting to spread ill-will and wickedness among men. Clearly, this is the opposite or antithesis of Thoth.

"Azathoth as a deity is a misnomer—at least, an anachronism in ancient times," the lecture continued. "Previously, cult worship surrounded only heroes and kings raised to the level of godhood—or forces of nature, such as the sun, the moon, the wind and rain, the dawn, etc. Never before was the abstract concept of *chaos* defied and raised to the level of a god. The Egyptian Nyarlathotep promulgated just such a cult, the worship of Azathoth as the embodiment of anarchy—which, somehow, he believed was the primary fact of the universe, rather than *cosmos*.

"Over and against this concept of utter chaos or disorder, we have the natural order of the cosmos—the movement of the sun and moon and stars—which was established by Thoth at the beginning of time."

Before our trip, calls were made to officials in Egypt, messages left, but not returned. The professor's mode of secrecy prevented him from contacting anyone from the academic world in advance of our trip, but he had a special contact in mind, someone who could be trusted with the subject of our investigation and help with logistics once we were on the ground.

Getting out of town was a simple affair. Our passports had been renewed two years before, for a trip to Greece, while working on *Zeus*. Reservations were made at the Nile Hotel in Cairo, which we deemed would be safe enough for American tourists, even if things got ugly. The U.S. State Department had issued a travel advisory due to political unrest, but beyond ask-

Intimations of Unreality

ing us to sign the warning, did nothing to deter our departure.

The twenty-hour flight from New York took us to London, then Cairo. Dr. Bishop intended to stop off on the way back to spend a couple days examining documents and objects at the British Museum, but he was desperate to get to Egypt first and get underway with our work.

Given the revolutionary environment, officials at the Cairo International airport were on heightened alert and were suspicious of everyone, especially foreigners. The airport had been a scene of chaos a month earlier, with an outflux of anxious foreigners anticipating violence, but now was relatively calm, if busy. Our passports and return tickets were sufficient to gain entry as tourists—we deemed it imprudent to reveal our archaeological interest at this time.

After checking into our rooms and freshening up, we went downstairs to rendezvous with Dr. Bishop's mysterious point man in Cairo. He was waiting at a sidewalk café, The Ibis, which faced west, affording a view of the pyramids a few miles to the southwest. Previously I had been denied the sight of them—first during the taxi ride from the airport due to angle of approach, and then by the fact that our rooms faced east away from the river. Now I staggered a bit at their awesome reality, rudely ignoring the man who stood beside me.

"First-time visitors are often mesmerized by the sight of them," he said, offering his gloved hand when I turned to face him.

"This is Salem el-Nassar, an old friend of mine, who will serve as our guide," said the professor.

"Nice to meet you," I said.

He was a tall, thin man, very dark-skinned—so much so that I assumed he was not Egyptian but Nubian or Ethiopian.

After we took seats around at a small table, I looked again at the pyramids—so ancient and immense, they seemed as old as the hills themselves. The mighty stones glowed under the golden sun, their sharp edges softened by haze and heat-waves—and by millennia of wear by the wind-blown sand.

The professor decanted the wine of wit and wisdom: "It seems like only yesterday that Napoleon addressed his troops at their base, saying 'Fifty centuries look down upon you!' Of course, he was rounding up for oratorical purposes; no doubt, though, he was well aware that the zero in fifty was a gift of Arabian mathematics."

This seemed to flatter our Arab host, who nodded as if to say "you're welcome."

The tiny cups of coffee, laced with slices of lemon, were surprisingly strong and helped me recover from our long journey and the time change.

"It's too bad you can't visit the pyramids right now," Salem said. "They've been closed since the revolutionary unrest first began. Of course, it may be possible to make special arrangements, but it will take some doing. It depends on how much capital you want to spend—political and otherwise."

"No, let's not bother. Maybe they will be open later, after our work is done." Dr. Bishop offered in consolation. "Meanwhile, we must focus on our, uh, excursion."

I couldn't help saying, "It's ironic that we cannot visit the most-visited landmarks in the world, yet we are going to visit a site that has not been visited by anyone for thousands of years!"

"I've made all the arrangements you requested, Dr. Bishop," said Salem.

"Excellent! Then we can start tomorrow morning? Good, that gives us time today to examine the Am-Yph'ra Tablets at the museum . . ."

"About that . . . I inquired about permission to see them, as you requested, but I was told that the tablets were misplaced or stolen during the unrest leading up to Mubarak's resignation."

"Good lord! I really needed to see those tablets . . ."

"Do they say anything about Nyarlathotep?" I asked naively—inadvertently speaking aloud a name that the professor wanted to avoid uttering.

We all looked around nervously, to see if anyone took notice of the name; but I think the only suspicious behavior was our own.

"Ahem, let's say I cannot publish anything without seeing them, which means a trip to the Bibliothèque Nationale in Paris," he said looking at me. "The Venduxour Papyrus is there, a transcription of the tablets."

"Fine by me, but please, one city at a time!" I was getting a whirlwind tour of the world's greatest cities, but with no time to see their many wonders.

Our guide begged leave to attend to the logistics of our expedition. I wanted to roam the streets—take in some sites—but the professor insisted on work.

"We have a lot of details to cover."

*   *   *

At the sound of the first call to prayers, we stirred and prepared for another long journey. Curfew was lifted at dawn, and it was legal—if not entirely safe—to travel the streets of the ancient and modern city. We heard that there had been clashes between pro- and anti-Mubarak demonstrators somewhere downtown, but things were calm in our district.

Salem el-Nassar met us with a rented SUV full of equipment and supplies. I expected more people—a team of hired workers—but there were only the three of us.

The road out of town led past a military checkpoint, but they were only stopping traffic heading into Giza and Cairo.

While the Nile valley is one of the most densely populated areas on earth, as soon as you leave the confines of its fertile banks and head into the desert, you soon find yourself totally alone amid silent desolation that stretches to the horizon in all directions.

We were heading southwest into the Great Sand Sea, where we began to see small dunes rise and fall like gentle waves on the ocean. Otherwise, the terrain remained flat and desolate, apart from occasional ruins. Twice we came upon bands of Bedouins traveling by camel and on foot.

After five hours we came to the oasis of Bawiti, where we stopped to refuel and have a meal. I offered to drive, but Salem insisted. The professor rode in front, balancing on his lap a map and a notebook, while referring constantly to his cell phone with its built-in GPS system.

After another three hours we came to the oasis of Siwa, a depression sided on the north by innumerable hills or small mountains—all of which were riddled with caves. The openings revealed black interiors that stood out in contrast to the dun-colored soil.

"The caves are mainly empty, now, but at some point been used as tombs or habitats, or both," Salem explained.

The land rose in steps demarcated by rugged escarpments. Guided by GPS, we turned north, leaving the main road in our four-wheel drive vehicle.

Through a narrow pass we passed, now traveling a trackless dirt footpath.

"These tracks have been traveled from ancient times by people seeking the water at Siwa, or seeking advice from the Oracle of Ammon. Alexander the Great himself made the pilgrimage."

"There are literally hundreds of hills in this area, creating millions of possible passageways between them, on the way from the Great Sand Desert to the oasis. Perhaps Alexander passed this way!"

I didn't realize it at the time, but we were only thirty miles from the Libyan border. In that country, too, protesters were aiming to topple a regime, as had happened in Tunisia and Egypt, and things looked very close to civil war. Fortunately, though, most of the action was on the coast, hundreds of miles away.

After the first escarpment, the land leveled out again and we progressed slowly through the rocky terrain. Narrowly managing one sharp turn, we came to a stop when the space between the jagged rocks became too narrow.

"I thought we could get through this way . . ." the professor said.

While they studied the map, I looked around and saw a dozen or more caves spotting the stone walls of the surrounding hills. They looked like dark eyes leering at us malignly, as of predators lying in wait should we become stranded. I was relieved when the puzzle was solved and we carefully reversed course.

The next pass zigzagged through the sharp escarpment, a series of blind turns that made us expect a dead end, or another narrowing of the passage; but it finally deposited us on the third, highest plain overlooking the broad area surrounding the oasis.

Within a quarter mile, we pulled within sight of a stone mastabah that seemed strangely out of place among the hills. The ancient tomb had the typical "stone bench" shape of its name, with sides sloping inward to a flat roof. Shifting wind had blown sand into drifts along the sides and piled it willy-nilly over the roof.

"This is it!" the professor said with glee—to my relief, as I was in great need of stretching my legs.

As I got out, I began to appreciate the oddness of the structure: the stones were of considerable size, and of a mineral constitution unlike the limestone-lined strata of the local hills. The small mastabah seemed a modest and remote resting place for such a legendary (if infamous) character—far from the Nile valley, whose hillsides housed the kings and ministers and mayors of so many ages.

"These stones . . ." I said aloud. "They don't belong here."

"No, they were hewn from a quarry eighty miles from here," said Salem, appearing at my shoulder. "They are only a fraction the size of the stones of the Great Pyramid of Khufu, but it must have taken enormous labor to haul them up here—through passes only as wide as an oxcart."

"Be careful where you step . . ." warned the professor. "There's bound to be a star shaft buried around here. The cover may not support your weight, on top of the sand."

Salem was quick with a metal detector, stepping gingerly to a spot a few feet from the mastabah's south wall, where a small dune had accumulated.

"Here it is," he announced momentarily. "The winch is bronze, with moving parts—as we suspected, Dr. Bishop."

After a little shoveling, the winch was revealed, but it was too corroded to turn. There was no drum, no rope or cable, no chain—instead, the crank turned a large central gear, which contacted other gears with cylinders or rods that disappeared into the sand.

Adjacent to the crank was a small, square depression.

"Here's the retractable cover," Salem said.

After a more shoveling, the cover—some five feet square—was cleared of sand.

"How does it work?" I asked.

"It's held in place by a mechanical arm and drops away at these hinges when the winch is turned—*if* it can be turned," the professor explained.

"It's nearly six o'clock," Salem announced, glancing at his watch. "We had better set up camp while there's still light. It's a two-man job," he said to me, "so I thought we'd let Dr. Bishop look the site over."

So we proceeded to set up a six-man tent, which was easy to stake directly into the porous, chalky rock that lay a foot below the sand. In the remaining light, we took photographs and began clearing sand away from the entrance to the mastabah.

We lit a couple kerosene lamps and sat talking for a while, but soon I retired, still exhausted by jetlag and travel. The soft voices of Salem and the professor faded away, and the great stillness and silence of the ancient night soon enveloped me.

I awoke to the sound of barking and sat bolt upright.

"It's jackals," said Salem in the utter darkness of the tent. "They roam the desert at night—but don't worry, they won't bother us. There's enough garbage down in Siwa to keep them well-fed."

I listened to the faint yelps and occasional barks and soon fell asleep again. I dreamed the tent was overrun by a pack of wild dogs that pounced on us and tore us to shreds—then I was startled awake again by sharp barks, this time followed by an eerie wailing sound.

"What's *that?*" I asked aloud.

"*That* is a baboon!" Salem's voice answered.

"But I thought they were extinct in Egypt . . ." The professor objected.

"So did I!" replied Salem.

The eerie wail continued, joined by other voices, forming a chorus.

"They 'sing' to the moon at night." The professor's voice spoke in the dark. "People have known this since ancient times, which explains the baboon's association with the moon. And since the moon's cycle reminds us of the cycle of life and death, it is associated with the underworld as well."

It was odd to hear this bit of lecture in the total darkness, but stranger still to hear the chorus of wails—less like a wolf or coyote's howl and more like a banshee might sound.

The next morning we rose with the sun—and the professor's alarm—and set about finishing the work of moving sand.

"Professor," I suddenly thought to ask, "How did you know the whole tomb wasn't buried—I thought we might need a whole team to dig for days, or weeks . . ."

"Simple. I found it on Google Earth!"

Salem laughed at my look of incredulity.

"The wonders of modern technology!" he exclaimed, co-opting a western phrase.

"Of course, I had to know *where* to look . . ." the professor continued. "Don't worry—it will all be in the book! All great detectives reveal their thought process only *after* the climax of the tale."

As for the tale of the mastabah, it was just being written—or read. Already on the outside, etched in the weathered granite above the entranceway, hieroglyphs appeared, which we gathered around and photographed.

Intimations of Unreality

I recognized the dual images of Thoth as a man with the head of an ibis and Thoth as a baboon—his two major semblances—standing on either side of another figure, whom I took to be the inhabitant of the tomb—the dead Nyarlathotep. Below the images was a row of hieroglyphs.

"This is Thoth as he appears in Duat, the underworld," the professor said, pointing to the first figure, "the baboon god, A'an. And here he appears as the ibis-headed man."

So far, I was correct.

"And the middle figure is identified by the phonograms," Salem said, referring to the row of hieroglyphs on the cartouche. "N-y-a-r-l-a-t, plus Ho-tep—a suffix used by some pharaohs and ministers—meaning, 'Nyarlath is content.'"

"I guess he's content, now!" I joked.

"Right!" said Salem, but the professor seemed puzzled.

"Look, here above . . ." he said, brushing some sand away from the surface of the stone. "There used to be something here, but it's been defaced—chiseled away. But if Nyarlathotep built this temple to Azathoth, why would he put Thoth's image over the entrance?"

"Temple or tomb?" Salem asked, and I was wondering the same. "This is a classical mastabah."

"Or so it seems—yet it has the star-shaft, which makes me think it was used as a temple."

"Maybe it was rededicated . . ." I hazarded a guess.

"What's that?"

"You yourself noticed the chiseling—maybe the original dedication of the temple was removed, and the new carving inserted below . . ."

"By Jove, I think he's right! I knew I brought you along for something!" the professor proclaimed, and I enjoyed a moment of triumph.

On the door stone was another carving, a cartouche.

"Ahah!" cried the professor. "This explains it!"

"D-j-h-w-t-y" Salem pronounced the letters of the cartouche. "The Pharaoh Djhwty, who took his name from Thoth."

"That fits my timetable!" said the professor. "The pharaoh Thoth reigned for only three years in the sixteenth dynasty, during the period of turmoil caused by the invasion of the Hyksos. So, I date it to about 1650 BC."

"The seal, or the mastabah?" I asked.

"Very good!" admitted the professor, eying me warily. "We don't really know which ... So the tomb, or temple, could have predated Djhwty, though the seal could not."

No other carvings marked the entrance, and having adequately photographed the façade and portal, we set about dislodging the door stone, which proved our only real difficulty. Salem and I took turns prying at the edges of the stone with chisel, crowbar and tire iron. After a long and fruitless effort, the professor began pacing and looked worried.

Salem offered a solution. "Perhaps if we are ... not so ginger with the stone . . ." And his point was taken.

By hammering chisels into the crevice between the stones, we were able to gain some separation, although it did involve some damage in the way of chipping and flaking. Gradually, we inched the stone out, squinting our eyes as chips and flecks of stone flew past.

Meanwhile, the professor had gone over to the crank of the star-shaft and began priming it with oil evidently brought for the purpose. It occurred to me that "Plan B" was to use the star-shaft as an entryway into the tomb, should the front door prove inaccessible with our meager tools.

Salem turned the SUV around and brought out a steel cable.

"Now we're talking!" I said with renewed enthusiasm.

We had edged the stone out enough to get a grip on it with the cable, which we looped around it and attached to the SUV's trailer hitch—first looping it around an iron post anchored in the rock of the hilltop. I was amazed to see this work, and I helped by making sure the post or capstan did not shift as the cable drew around and past it. The point was to convey the weight of the stone in stages, first to the post and then to the truck, so that the truck would not simply spin its wheels in the sand. Well, they did spin a bit, but the cross-country treads had enough grip to do the job, and the portal stone came away with a thud, letting light and air into the tomb for the first time in 3500 years.

The mastabah visible above ground, some twenty feet square, was only the top of the tomb, and the burial chamber proper was below ground level, where the rock and earth of the hilltop had been excavated to make room for the foundation of the stone structure.

Salem started up the generator and I stretched out the power cables leading to the lights. Professor Bishop took one of the halogen lamps with him as he crawled over the fallen door stone and through the low opening into the darkness, where he disappeared.

"Professor?" I called to him.

"Right here," he said, head popping up in the portal. "There's a landing just inside, and steps leading down to the burial chamber. Along the passageway are hieroglyphs that need to be photographed. Feed me more cord. . . ."

I unreeled more of the cable.

"The walls tell a story," he said through the aperture. "The tense is not clear . . . maybe Salem can tell . . . It's either in the past or in the future . . . There's a battle between forces of dark and light . . . Thoth against . . . what's this? Anti-Thoth . . . Azathoth! It's all right here!" The professor was excited and began moving down the steps to following the story, his voice growing muffled and faint.

Salem and I soon followed the professor through the portal and into the narrow passageway, each taking a lamp. Salem began to read the hieroglyphs for himself and progressed down the steps after the professor, while I set up a tripod for my lamp and began photographing the interior of the tomb.

"You're right, the tense is not clear," Salem confirmed. "Azathoth is shown with sonograms—there's no pictogram or image. And we don't know if it's a history of a past campaign, or a call-to-arms to start the battle, now or in the future . . . It ends with Azathoth's victory, and Nyarlathotep is pictured sitting on a throne . . . but there is more . . . What's this?"

"It tells the story of the mastabah . . ." The professor's voice echoed up from below. "It might surprise you!"

I had to concentrate on doing a thorough job, but my thoughts were racing ahead to what Salem and Dr. Bishop were seeing. Gradually I made my way down the steps and saw for myself the story of Nyarlathotep, painted with skin so black there seemed to be a hole in the stone. I had little practice reading hieroglyphics, but the graphic images were easy enough to see—all carved and painted with a skill for accuracy and detail that bordered on astonishing. A panorama showed Nyarlathotep, arrayed like a pharaoh, standing with arms upraised before the cave-riddled hills we saw above the oasis of Siwa. From the mouths of the tomb-caves there emerged the bodies of the dead, wrapped in funeral garb, now reanimated by Nyarlathotep's necromantic spell. Between them, the zombie slaves were shown hewing stones from a quarry and hauling them—by hand—across the panoramic frame to the far end, where they disappeared into a pass between the hills. The next frame showed an army of the dead building Nyarlathotep's mastabah or temple while he stood aside, pointing to a group of stars painted on a field of blue— no doubt aligning the building's foundation to some astronomical referent, though in a constellation I did not recognize.

By this time, Salem had joined the professor in the burial chamber below and they were talking excitedly about something. Anticipation got the best of me and I left off with my work, instead bounding down the remaining flight of steps with camera in hand, anxious to see the main attraction.

Salem and the professor stood beside a sarcophagus, holding lamps that illumined most of the room. The chamber was covered, floor to ceiling, with fantastic paintings and engravings whose skill and scope surpassed anything I had seen in photos of Egyptian tombs. The panorama of the descending passage was continued on a large scale, depicting the black Nyarlathotep larger-than-life, dwarfing his mastabah, while the army of eyeless zombies bowed down before him. Another mural or area of the wall showed a larger star map of the same strange constellation depicted in the passageway, with a large lightning bolt or zigzag of color stretching down the wall from the brightest star to the floor of the tomb, where another miniature of the mastabah was painted.

I surveyed the room to calculate its size. I figured that it was about ten feet wide by fourteen long, by twelve high—and that I had several hours of work cut out for me. Suddenly a thought occurred and I looked again at the ceiling.

"Where's the star-shaft?" I asked aloud, and they both looked up.

"Why, I had forgotten about that! It must be free-standing ... Maybe another staircase is buried in the sand. Anyway, we have plenty to discover here. There must be an entire text written on that wall," he said, pointing behind me. "It might even be the legendary *Scroll of Nyarlathotep*, or *The Book of Azathoth*."

Intimations of Unreality

But I was captivated by the glowing golden lid of the sarcophagus, which was set on a low stone dais. The figure on top resembled the figure on the tomb's exterior, with his pitch-black skin and asp headpiece, so it seemed safe to assume that the body of the dreaded Nyarlathotep lay within.

"Look at this," the professor said, pointing to a wax seal bridging the gap between the lid and body of the sarcophagus. "There's an impression . . . What does it say?" he asked, holding the lamp closer.

Salem's younger eyes made out the words. "'Seek within . . . no body of Nyarlathotep . . .' Wait, it's 'If you seek Nyarlathotep, he is nobody!'"

Dr. Bishop and Salem looked at each other in silence. If Salem was joking, he showed no sign of humor.

"Let's get this thing photographed so we can open it," the professor said to me, and I complied, taking multiple shots from various angles while they stood aside holding the lights.

"How about a picture of the two of you?" I suggested.

"Not now! Let's get this thing open," the professor replied impatiently.

Breaking the seal, we lined up on one side and lifted the lid—wood gilt and painted, it was not too heavy—and let it fall away on its hinges, revealing the interior. To our surprise, not only was the coffin "empty" (for there was, indeed, no body to seek), it was also *hollow*, giving way to steps that lead steeply down through the dais and floor into another chamber below . . .

"Now we're getting to the crux of the matter!" the professor said, which I thought was odd. And to me he said, "Bring down the tripods for the lights." And I was up and back as fast as you can imagine.

The second chamber, like the first, was covered with artwork and carvings. My workload had just doubled! It was larger than the first room, its south wall extending another eight feet to intersect with the star-shaft. The angled shaft, which terminated in a square hole in the room's ceiling, seemed to aim at a point on the floor, where there were yet further inscriptions. Painted on the ceiling was a large figure that dominated the chamber: a feathered serpent, flying with wings outstretched.

"The burial chamber was a sham, but *this* is where the priest-craft took place, the initiations and religious ceremonies—the worship of Azathoth!

No doubt, the rites were timed to coincide with the alignment of the sun or moon, or some star, with the shaft."

"But why the remote location?" I asked. "You can't start a popular religion in the middle of the desert."

"Nyarlathotep was not interested in attracting the masses to his worship. Rather, he needed a place to create this architecture, properly aligned to the stars—properly oriented from an astronomical point of view—with the ultimate aim of empowering Azathoth in our realm. The fact that it was in the middle of the desert was actually helpful, since Nyarlathotep would aim to accomplish his work without interference from Thebes."

"What about the priests of Ammon?" I asked.

"There were no priests in Siwa, only the mysterious oracle, who gazed into the waters of the oasis until he had a vision which he would share with the pilgrims—for a fee. Even then, it was a tourist attraction! No one there would interfere with what he was up to here. Besides, as the panoramas indicate, Nyarlathotep had enormous personal magnetism, to say the least—if not actual necromantic skill. He could have kept the inquisitive at bay through fear alone, owing to his reputation as a black sorcerer."

"Dr. Bishop!" Salem called from one of the corners of the room. "There's a pit here . . ."

And indeed, there was a hole in the floor, an area two-feet square, approximately the size of the stones that made up the edifice. As we stood looking over the pit, a strange odor rose up from it.

"Was it . . ." I hazarded a guess, "was it a *toilet* used by the priests? Or . . . a pit for bones left over from sacrifices?"

Salem said, "A toilet would be sacrilegious . . . and completely unhygienic in this closed space. Sacrifices . . .?" he looked at the professor inquiringly.

The two lamps were on tripods behind us, not reaching far enough to illumine the entire room. Consequently, the corner remained in darkness and the depth of the pit was indeterminable. The professor pulled out a small flashlight and pointed the beam into the hole. The weak light showed more stones going down, surrounding the rectangular pit or well, until they disappeared again in darkness.

I felt a shudder and may have gasped.

"Well, I'll be . . ." said the professor.

"There's nothing like it in any of the tombs or temples," said Salem confidently.

I felt a bit nauseous. "Well, I have a lot of work to do," I said as an excuse to move away.

"Yes, we all do," said the professor. "I don't know how long we can get away with this little adventure before the authorities come calling . . ."

"But—you said you have permission," I objected. "You made arrangements with Mubarak's people."

"Yes—to study at Siwa, not up here!" he said. "Do you think I'd actually tell them where Site Y was?"

And so we set to work, each documenting and studying in his own way, stopping only to eat lunch, until the better part of the day had gone by, and it was getting dark out. I refueled the generator twice, and once again the professor primed the crank for the cover of the star-shaft. We took turns testing our strength against the corroded gears without success.

Below ground, our detailed work had taken us all back to the second, lower chamber. Suddenly the halogen lamps flickered, signaling to me that the generator needed refueling; then they dimmed and went out altogether, leaving us momentarily in pitch darkness.

The professor was quick to switch on his penlight, and Salem had one, too. Together they created a dim twilight sufficient for navigating the room, and I headed for the steps leading up through the sarcophagus. Emerging into the false burial chamber, I was surprised to find it also pitch dark. With no light leaking down the passageway, I assumed the sun had set. But reaching the portal, I was stunned to find that the opening was blocked . . . someone has pushed the portal stone back into place, trapping us in the tomb!

"Professor!" I called out, "Salem! We're trapped!"

Thoughts flashed through my mind. Who would have closed us in? Not the officials or military; not pilgrims or passersby. Thieves? Perhaps.

I put my back to the wall of the passageway and pushed with both feet on the door stone, to no avail. It had taken an SUV to pull the stone out . . . How was it pushed back into place?

I had little time to ponder these unknowns before a weird squealing sound filled the air—a metal grinding that echoed though open space. It was the squeak of the star-shaft opening, of the crank straining under the strength of superhuman hands.

I fumbled in the darkness and found my way back down the passage to the first chamber, where a faint light emerged from the open sarcophagus. Down the steps I flew, tripping, falling a couple feet and twisting my ankle.

The professor and Salem were transfixed by the opening shaft, fixing it in the beams of their flashlights. Sand fell, slipping around the edges of the retracting cover, raining down on the polished stone.

"We're trapped!" I repeated, still crouched on the floor, rubbing my ankle.

But now something else took place that raised the hair on my neck. From behind me came a scratching sound—at first faint, then louder until it was audible through the squeaks from above. It came from the dark corner . . . and the pit.

I crawled along the floor to retrieve my camera by the wall, where I had left it, and set the flash to strobe in order to illuminate the room. Twice a second—the frequency of a car's turn signal—the camera light switched on, instantly brightening the room long enough for the shutter to operate, then switched off, again leaving the chamber in near-darkness. In the pulsing light, the murals seemed to come alive with movement. The wings of the winged serpent flapped, the crowds of walking dead cowered, and dark clouds rolled by in the background.

The sharp squeal terminated with a wrenching groan and a loud bang that reverberated through the tomb, as the ancient bronze cover of the star-shaft slammed into the stone wall, precipitating another downpour of sand—and revealing for the first time a shaft of moonlight that cut through the settling dust and shone on its designated square on the chamber floor.

"My God!" shouted the professor, "Look!" he said to Salem, who stood next to him looking up into the moonlight. I could not see what they saw, but as I watched their upturned faces I saw shadows move across them . . .

Then my attention was drawn back to dark corner, where the scratching sound had amplified. The strobe's intermittent light was playing tricks on the eyes, but I was sure I saw something emerging from the pit—something fuzzy and indistinct. It was like a roiling cloud of dust, or a spinning ball of gossamer, half-transparent and hazy, and I was only half-convinced it was there at all. Instinctively, I began inching away from the pit, keeping my back against the wall opposite. I felt safer being closer to my companions, despite the unknown menace from above. The camera continued to flash from its location on the floor.

By this time, the professor and Salem were backing away themselves—from the star-shaft and towards the center of the room where the steps went up.

"Baboons!" cried the professor.

And indeed, I saw one baboon, and then another, climb down the chamber wall from the opening in the ceiling, their humanlike fingers clinging to the narrow spaces between the stones. Once they reached the floor, they reared up on their hind legs, waved their arms and screamed, or jumped up and down in a threatening fashion, their wild eyes wild and manic.

My colleagues ran up the steps and I went after them as best I could, hobbled by my ankle sprain. One baboon seemed to be coming after me, but in truth he attacked the steps and began demolishing them, ripping the stones from the mortar with their bare hands. The other baboons dashed on past, heading for the dark corner.

The last thing I saw as we threw shut the sarcophagus lid was a mad melee between the troop of baboons and whatever it was that came out of the pit . . . The broken steps became missiles, and several baboons carried the stone steps before them as shields, forcing back the unknown force from the pit and dropping the masonry down after it.

The shouts and shrieks of the animals below were terrifying enough, but the low rumbling or growling sound that came from the pit shook us to our core. We stood for a moment looking at each other, panting and trembling, not believing what we had just experienced. The sounds below died down, ending with the thuds of masonry being piled over the opening of the pit.

"Chaos is not formless," I found myself saying. "Chaos is *all forms*." And somehow that summed up my encounter with the thing below.

Everything was quiet and we listened for a long while for any sound. We heard jeeps drive up, above us, and the muffled sound of men's voices. Soon they had pried away the door-stone and entered the tomb, carrying flashlights—and weapons.

"I arrest you in the name of the Inspector of Antiquities," said the captain.

* * *

Despite our protestations, we were hauled away to Cairo for questioning. Our attempts to warn them of the *thing* in pit below were met with laughter and derision.

"Baboons, did you say? They have been extinct for decades! And they fought off this . . . this Azathoth? This devil from a bottomless pit?!"

Fortunately, Salem had connections. Together with the professor's reputation as a published scholar and the official letter he had received concerning Siwa (we were within two miles), we managed to get off with a warning.

As I write this account, I am on the long flight home. Professor Bishop stayed, intending to do further research and perhaps talk his way back into that tomb . . . But my nerves have been shattered by the whole ordeal, and I need to retreat to familiar ground.

Our cameras were confiscated, of course, along with their digital content, on the grounds that they are part of Egypt's national heritage. My own camera—with its record of the fantastic murals and passageway carvings, and whatever it captured of the battle that took place down there—was left lying in the lower chamber of the tomb, where it must have flashed away until the battery died. I assume it's still there today.

Charles Nathan's Pipe

"The real voyage of discovery lies not in seeking new lands, but in seeing with new eyes."

—Marcel Proust

I want to set the record straight on Arnold Hildeghast. My good friend and colleague's reputation has been tarnished, of late, by his admittedly outlandish behavior, alleged criminal acts, and ultimate institutionalization. But I argue that Arnold's stature as a leading authority on Charles Nathan should not be diminished by rumors and innuendo about his state of mind and its causes. The facts are plain, if bizarre, and should be set forth clearly and at once, to help clear Arnold's name and reputation. As you will see, he is hardly to blame for his own misbehavior—under the circumstances, many of us might have followed the same course. The blame, if any, is to be placed on Charles Nathan's pipe—and the broker of weird things who provided it.

Arnold obtained the pipe from a person whose name I will not mention, someone well-known to SF/F fandom for his unscrupulous means. This person—let me call him Steven Adair—is known to prey upon the nearest relatives of famous authors that have died, conning and conniving and swindling precious personal objects that belonged to the deceased. In this way, it is rumored that he obtained H. P. Lovecraft's writing desk, Robert E. Howard's famous ten-gallon hat, and M. P. Shiel's purple smoking jacket. A stranger rumor involves Clark Ashton Smith's ashes, and August Derleth's . . . well, let's just say that his grave was robbed and a certain appendage severed . . . But that's another story altogether.

Arnold called me up one evening a couple months ago.

"I got the pipe!" he said, clearly excited to have acquired the object.

"You mean . . . Charles Nathan's . . .?" I couldn't believe it.

"Yes!"

"You have *Ch'arn-Aton's pipe?!*"

Ch'arn-Aton was the name Lovecraft used in correspondence with Nathan, concocting another Great Old One—or Outer One, depending on your interpretation— in several of his own weird tales.

"How did you get it?" I asked, though I already had a hunch.

"Never mind that. It was his, and now it's *mine!*"

"Wow! Cool! I mean, I have most of his first editions—even the variant covers. And that postcard—you know, the one he wrote to HPL, when he first mentioned the Dragons of Elkmore . . . But his pipe!"

"Yes, his pipe! Charles Nathan's pipe!"

I wanted to see it for myself, but Arnold was in Carmel, and I was in St. Louis. Of course, I had seen pictures of the pipe. It is featured in almost every portrait of the author that adorns the frontispieces and dust-jacket flaps of his books—even his website portrait.

"It's quite the collector's item," I said.

"More than that!"

"But . . . I thought you quit smoking?"

"I'm thinking of taking it up again! I mean, who knows what Nathan smoked in this thing?"

"Well, what does it smell like?"

"Sort of a mixture of things . . . tobacco, pot maybe . . . hash?"

There were rumors of Nathan's drug use, but little proof. Speculation abounds, of course, erupting in such blunt articles as "Charles Nathan and Drugs" by Richard Ennis, which simply explains every fantastic detail and nuance of Nathan's work on some drug experience or another—again, without offering proof, apart from some ambiguous language in Nathan's correspondence. (Of course, we were all happy to see Dick's huge "crossover" success with his book on Hieronymus Bosch, *Ergo Ergot*, in which he ascribed all of Bosch's visions of Heaven and Hell and the Garden of Earthly Delights to moldy rye bread.)

"I know your opinion, Arnold," I said, "but I've always wondered what drugs Nathan could have gotten—considering he was poverty-stricken and almost completely isolated most of his life."

For Nathan was a recluse, never saw anybody, never wandered far. In all his 82 years, he never ventured more than 50 miles from his home—only twice visiting the nearby metropolis of San Jose, in his youth. In absence of contrary evidence, I maintain that Nathan's drug-free achievements were a testimony to human Imagination, which should need no outside stimulus.

Still, the obvious thought occurred to me . . . "Is there any residue?"

"Residue, you say!" he said, with a canned laugh like The Shadow of the old radio program. "'*You fool! Randolph Carter is dead!*'" He said, citing a Lovecraft story.

"'Glub . . . glub,'" I replied, citing another, and we had a good laugh.

"Well, let me know how it turns out . . ." I said—and strangely, that was the last phone conversation we had, though I would see him again in person.

It was only later that I heard the results of Arnold's experiment. His wife, June, called me up in a bit of a frenzy and said he had lapsed into a state of depression so severe that his outward state was of stupor, in which he generally failed to acknowledge her presence. She was concerned about him, and also for herself, since his dark moods sometimes erupted in anger.

I promised June I would visit as soon as I could, and arranged a flight the next day.

Arnold had been one of my best friends since high school in St. Louis. He was one of my earliest compatriots in the exploration of weird literature and through the years we kept in contact, often seeing each other at Cthulhu Mythos and fantasy conventions. At these, he became a regular panelist, expounding and defending his learned theories as to the fundamental meaning of Charles Nathan's weird fiction and poetry.

When I arrived at their lovely hillside home in Carmel, I was surprised to be met by Arnold himself, rather than June. Her descriptions of him were accurate—his normally upbeat manner had been replaced by a morose indifference. There were dark circles under his eyes, he was laggard and lacked sleep. His responses were sluggish, and in toto, he seemed to have undergone a profound trauma that left him drained of his usual energy and spark.

"Come in, Alan," he said, pulling back the door. "Sorry about the mess . . ."

"Where's June?" I asked as he followed me into the empty living room.

"Oh, she left yesterday. Said she couldn't take it anymore. Don't blame her."

"What's wrong, Arnold?" I asked him point-blank, turning to face him in the middle of the room. "Tell me what has happened."

He looked at me blankly, seemed to totter, regained his balance, and rubbed his forehead with his hand.

"Here, have a seat, old man, and relax. Calm down." I guided him to an armchair.

"It was the pipe, Alan!" he said, once seated.

"You mean, Charles Nathan's pipe?"

"I told you, there was some residue . . . I cleaned the pipe and smoked it!"

"Well?"

"There are no words, Alan—no words to describe the . . . vistas, the vast spaces that opened before my eyes! No words . . . except perhaps to quote from Nathan himself! I told you, Alan, the man reported things that no one had seen before—and this is how . . ."

He picked up the pipe from a side-table and held it lightly in both hands, as if it were a bloody dagger.

"Incredible!" I admitted with disappointment. "I was sure Nathan was a natural mystic . . ."

"He wrote from experience, Alan. The only imagination he used was to frame his fantastic visions in a the simplest plots, with only the requisite characters—characters who needed no development, only to reflect the impact of exposure to the other-worldly. All of Nathan's horrific illusions, the passages through star-studded vasts of space—you know as well as I, the trans-galactic vistas he painted in words! Now the words pale in comparison . . . Now I know the real thing: the underlying truth!"

I needed a drink, but didn't want to encourage him to add alcohol to his already depressed state.

"So, what the hell was in the pipe?!" I wanted to know.

"It was unlike anything I have ever tried . . . Unlike pot, hash, even mushrooms and acid. Not even close! I smoked opium once, even tasted a little H, but this was different—as different as the flight of a mosquito and the flight of the starship Enterprise!"

His eyes had become wild, like two fires lit in darkness, glowing in the recesses of his sockets.

"I have never seen—or felt—anything like the ecstatic hallucinations that came from this pipe! The effects still haven't quite warn off, after three days. But I'm convinced that what I experienced was no hallucination. It was real!"

"Of course," he continued after a moment, "it was immediately addictive. And there had been hardly anything there! Imagine, smoking an entire bowl! Now there is nothing . . . I have to go back, experience it again . . ." He was desperate, clearly exhibiting the worst effects of addiction.

"I tried other things . . . nothing works. I re-read Nathan, re-read the key passages over and over, trying to rekindle that flame . . . that flame of passion, that ecstasy of otherness, that cosmic frisson that I experienced from the pipe . . ."

He seemed hopeless, but not helpless. I reasoned with him a while, tried to cheer him up by taking his mind off his addiction.

"You know, there's another Mythos Con coming up in April. Bob's organizing the panels—why don't you sign on? After all, someone has to defend Nathan against Joe T. Soshi!"

Joe T. Soshi, of course, is the well-known Japanese scholar who has devoted his life to Clark Ashton Smith, but who detests Lovecraft, Nathan, and all literary contributors to the so-called Cthulhu Mythos—despite the fact that Smith himself was a contributor.

"You always love to lock horns with Soshi! And I think Bob said Fernando d'Isle d'Yry is going to unveil his new Atlantis book—a prequel that hints at an even older island civilization that was destroyed by the separation of Laurasia from Gondwanaland. Should be good!"

"Hmm . . ." was all he managed.

I was doing my best to bring him back to the real world of literary friends and colleagues—to reel him in from the dangerous depths in which he was flailing.

"Oh, and Yozan Rick Gismo is back! He's given up trying to interpret Nathan's work in terms of Jungian symbolism. Now he's using Buddhist metaphors . . ." I figured it was better to hit a raw nerve than not to reach him at all.

"It's all a sham!" he began his outburst, jumping out of his seat.

"The costumes . . . the action figures . . . the books full of stories all cranked out according to the same tired patterns . . . No one seems to get it! Not the critics, not even the authors themselves—other than Nathan, of course. *Nathan is the only one!* Even Lovecraft had *no idea!*"

His eyes shone like the raging dual stars of science fiction.

"I have seen the birth and death of stars, the collision of galaxies, the cold dark emptiness of space out beyond the quasars . . . There's an awesome world out there, Alan! A shining world, I tell you! If only we could discover it . . ."

He seemed to have spent himself and slumped back into his chair, where he became unresponsive—exhibiting the symptoms of extreme withdrawal that June had described.

"I'm going now," I said finally, not knowing if his brain even registered the sound wave.

And that was the last I saw of Arnold Hildeghast. From there, you know the rest of the story, which I will summarize. Arnold left Carmel, went to Big Sur, where Nathan had lived all his life, and ransacked Nathan's old cabin, which had already been damaged by thieves and arsonists. A neighborhood guard notified the property managers, who called the police, who found Arnold in a near-coma, lying face-up in the weeds beside the abandoned cabin. About him lay the remains of his experiments—little bottles of herbs, dried mushrooms, unknown algae and moss, unidentified weeds—all dug up and still clumped with soil from where Nathan had buried them.

Fortunately, or unfortunately—depending on your metaphysics, I guess— Arnold was not dead. Not in the ordinary sense. They roused him from his coma, revived his body, but his mind had gone. There was no place for him but an institution—one that was equipped to deal with possible violence, should his mind come back again and have malevolent intent. I must admit, I have not had the stomach to see him in his present state, even if I were to gain permission to visit him, where he is kept under strict supervision.

You can cage a man's body, but you can't cage his mind. The body of Arnold Hildeghast may be locked up in a padded cell, in that stone-and-steel mausoleum for lost minds up on Kepler's Hill— fed and cared for by handlers like he was a zoo animal—kept safely locked away from humans, for what harm he might do. But his mind! I know it's out there, flying free in the dark spaces between Yuggoth and Zhar, winging weightlessly through the yawning vortices between dimensions at which we can only guess— witnessing vistas of cosmic creation and destruction no human mind was ever meant to see!

Intimations of Unreality

A Visit from Ray Bradbury

"If a little dreaming is dangerous, the cure for it is not to dream less but to dream more, to dream all the time."

—MARCEL PROUST

I heard a strange voice in the other room. Someone was visiting.

"Please have a seat," my mother's voice spoke, "I'll get Alan."

"Thanks, you have a lovely table."

A tap on my door. I was already off the bed, where I often sat propped up against the wall, with a book on my lap.

"Alan, there's a gentleman here to see you. A Mr. Ray Bradbury."

"Ray Bradbury the writer?!" I couldn't believe it. The author of *Dandelion Wine* and *Something Wicked This Way Comes* coming to visit *me?!*

He was sitting at the dinner table, looking out the large window of the dining room. Ordinarily, he would see the paddock and large backyard stretching two lazy acres between a row of sycamores and the bank of Haymer's Creek. But it was nighttime and you couldn't see more than twenty feet out.

It was Ray Bradbury alright! Hair completely white, glasses with large black frames, looking a bit like Ed Wynn and grinning his infectious grin, round chin jutting.

"Thank you," he said, accepting a glass of iced tea from my mother, "I'm dying of thirst!"

As he drained the glass I took a seat at the far end of the table, too shy to sit any closer. For the first time, I realized that he had brought a friend, a slender young man who sat by the wall and said nothing. I hardly paid him attention, but whenever I glanced at him I saw him either taking notes or looking with reverence at Ray Bradbury. At these times, he would feel my gaze and deflect his eyes nervously, returning to his notes.

"Thank you, that was very refreshing. How do you make it?" Bradbury asked.

"Oh, just the regular way: boil water, steep the teabags, remove the teabags, stir in the sugar, add cold water, and pour in a glass of ice."

"That's very efficient!"

I got out copies of his books to ask him to sign them. I told him how much I liked his "poetic prose," and how much I was influenced by it. I also mentioned Clark Ashton Smith, whose work Bradbury admired.

We talked a little about writing but I can't remember what he said. I thought of his book *Zen and the Art of Writing* but didn't get around to mentioning it. He said something about poetry and I mentioned having a chapbook of my own. He expressed interest, though I don't remember actually giving it to him.

"Well, time to go, thanks again for the tea, Mrs. Gullette." He said as he left.

Immediately after he left, I began thinking of things I should have said, wanted to say, could have said. It's not every day that you meet Ray Bradbury! Thought tumbled on thought and then lined up to form a tidy essay.

We went back to the dinner table. "Wow, Ray Bradbury!" was about all I could manage to say.

A little while later, there was a fresh knock on the front door. Ray Bradbury had come back, beat-up and bleeding! Evidently, he was mistreated by neighborhood ruffians. "They took Wallace . . ." he said as we helped him into the living room and sat him on an armchair. Linda attended to his cuts and applied bandages. Soon he was as good as new and raring to go."

"Let's look for Wallace."

"I have a bike—and you can borrow my mother's bike," I said. "It will be faster than trying to cover the neighborhood on foot."

We went out to get the bikes out of the shed but couldn't find them.

"Let's use these," he said, pulling two snow sleds off the wall and handing one to me. We carried them to the edge of the property, where a steep hill sloped away down to the creek. Here he challenged me to a downhill race on the sleds—but there was no snow, only thick grass. I began to ques-

Intimations of Unreality

tion how it could work when he gave me a push and I went sledding down the long hill as smoothly as if it were snow.

Toward the bottom of the hill, where it flattened out into a meadow, I saw Bradbury sail past me. His sled was perpendicular to the ground and yet slid along somehow on the surface of the thick grass. And instead of lying face down on it, he was stood upright on top of it, balancing on the back edge.

As he passed, he shouted, "You'll never get anywhere sledding that way!"

The Axe of the Executioner

The axe has hung since yesterday—
No executioner was called.
I see it glint in the morning sun
Between the bars of my window . . .

The prisoner improvises a little song and sings it to himself softly. As the words describe, he stands at the window of his cell and looks through the bars at the courtyard.

The chopping block is there: an old oak stump, rotten and red—and creased with hack marks of much use. And the axe that has hacked it hangs nearby from the courtyard's only tree, suspended from an iron spike by a loop of leather through the handle's heel. The double blade hangs down like a pendulum that has stopped, frozen in mid-swing; or like the rusted steel wings of an inverted angel with one dark wooden leg.

The girl I loved has met her death,
The man she loved I too have killed;
Three lives my unpent passion cost —
For now I too must die . . .

He sings a verse and then he hums the melody, sometimes whistling, until he has composed a new verse.

He took my wife,
She slurred my worth,
I took a knife
And killed her first.

He turned and fled
And I turned, too —
Turned to the axe . . .

He stops abruptly—stops before finishing the quatrain—and, fixated on the axe in the courtyard, returns to the full meter.

> *The axe has hung since yesterday —*
> *I put it back where it belongs —*
> *I used the axe just yesterday —*
> *To do the job, and do it right . . .*

The wind rustles the leaves of the old oak tree and the sun streams through, casting shadows on the court—moving shadows, dancing shadows on the axe. And the glint on the blade sends sparkles into the eyes of the prisoner, who continues his song.

> *I chased him down,*
> *I knocked him down!*
> *I raised the axe*
> *And brought it down!*
>
> *I gripped it well —*
> *I aimed to kill!*
> *I bid the axe*
> *To do my will!*

He killed his wife and her lover and knew that he was doomed, so he gave himself up without a fight. For he was not one to flee from justice, nor could he take his own life. Now he waits in his cell—waits for the axe, for the executioner to do his job. Waits . . . and sings.

> *The axe has hung since yesterday —*
> *The axe with its old, familiar feel.*
> *I wiped it down and put it back*
> *As I had done so many times before.*

Phases

Phase I. Our Love Is a Tower

Our love is a tower which I must transcend to be united with you. The tower is an apartment building in which we live. You live in the apartment half of the time, and I live there the rest of the time. I try to meet with you, but you constantly evade me.

Sometimes I catch a glimpse of you leaving just as I arrive. Sometimes I wake to the feeling that you have been watching me in my sleep, perhaps trying to control me. Sometimes suddenly you will be there before me—then I recognize my own reflection.

My incompleteness is like finding myself for the first time to be dismembered and bleeding to death helplessly. My emptiness is the absence of the heart, which has been ripped out by a masked priest in a ceremony of sacrifice necessary to appease you. I think perhaps you ordered the ceremony. Perhaps it was your face behind the mask. Before our eyes my blood pours from my arteries, fills the cavern in my body, and runs down my sides to a cold stone slab.

But I do not die. My torment is endless. I am unable to hurt myself. Finally I can't stand it anymore. I climb to the top of the stairs and jimmy the door to the roof. From here, the height is exhilarating. I easily jump up on the low concrete wall running along the roof's edge and walk briskly and recklessly along its narrow top. I slip and fall, but catch onto the very edge of the wall and dangle several stories above the street. However, my grip soon gives out and I plummet downward.

I fall by your window. You have been standing there, casually looking outside. Our eyes meet.

Phase II. Unable to Explain

You see, there has never been anything in the world that I have been unable to explain. I mean, here before us in the physical world we can find nothing that is completely mysterious to us. It has occurred to me lately that this is terribly unfortunate—but there you have it.

Then I saw you.

You were looking directly at me when I became aware of you, and I automatically averted my eyes. This I suddenly realized to be irrational. Therefore, I was determined to return your gaze and felt that surely I would soon be making your acquaintance. While still looking away, I imagined our future relationship being very fruitful in many ways. You would help me in my emotional growth—for I realized that I needed to find better ways of relating to others. Full of promise was the moment, glowing warmly, and I thought I could hear music playing. I looked up at you.

You were walking quickly away, suppressing laughter.

I was abruptly self-aware. Embarrassed, I changed the topic by playing the radio until a forced boredom prevented clear thinking.

In my boredom I consumed a tremendous amount of wheat crackers in the form of little sandwiches, spread with eggless imitation mayonnaise and topped with thin slices of sharp cheddar cheese.

My stomach felt painful, my head foggy. I felt tired or lazy, so I lay down and fell asleep.

I dreamed that I was a sunflower that grew in continual nighttime. I was able to receive some light from the moon, even though it was second-hand and somewhat dusty, and I grew as well as other vegetation. I realized, however, that I was not thriving on the amount of light that I received, that I was not realizing my full potential because I was not getting my full allotment of energy.

I began eating my own seed. The stored solar power in such sudden, large doses gave me tremendous stimulation. However, I soon realized that I was depleting myself and would eventually be sterile—having no energy to give forth to life as a whole. My season would be over.

I awoke as a butterfly—as blue as the clear sky, my wings speckled with shining gold lined with a fuzzy dark brown. My entire existence was as follows: I had no mouth; I had no legs. I flew constantly. I searched for I knew not what, fluttering about, passionately searching, drawn here and there by bright colors and by unusual sensations which were like fragrances.

I found another of my kind and we danced and fluttered about. We came very close and she grasped my long, slender body firmly with her arms and legs (she had legs and I did not). I was horrified by her long, sticky tongue, which lashed furiously about my face, and by her eyes—which were not eyes because they had no irises or pupils or dark depths, but which were clusters of many hundreds of tiny domes interspersed with occasional clumps of hair. I felt that she was drawing my life force from me, but I was powerless to escape her embrace. Then she released me and, flying away, forgot me.

I faltered in the air. Flying again, I fled from something behind me, filled with terror. I flew aimlessly, as fast as I could, and found myself in darkness. I kept flying and eventually perceived a point of light. I sought out the light, which grew brighter as I approached it. Its brightness blinded me until I could no longer see, though I was drawn on by its warmth. Then its warmth enveloped me until I could no longer feel. Then there was nothing . . .

Phase III. On a Bench in the Square

Something jolted me and I awoke. I had been asleep for a long time, dreaming. A sound, a memory, a fragment of a dream—something triggered the morning.

The square was full of people wearing overcoats and exhaling mist. Pigeons poked about, watching the people. One of the pigeons saw me watching them watch the people, so they called it off. They flew away in a cloud, and my eyes followed their flight until I saw you. You were watching me from across the square.

I ducked into the underground station and headed back eastward. When I changed lines you were on the next train going north. I tried pulling the emergency stop, but it didn't work. No one seemed to notice me at all—except for you.

That's when I realized I was still dreaming, which came as a great relief, really . . . So I walked over and kissed you on the mouth and then, drawing a knife, stabbed you repeatedly in the chest. It was supposed to end there. But then I realized it wouldn't end until I stopped thinking about it.

We sat on the bench watching people go by. Occasionally people would stop and sit on the other benches. They would read newspapers or talk to one another—or watch people go by.

The benches, the square, the trees . . . The buildings that rose like dirty walls on all sides, the sky with its shifting clouds . . . Nothing seemed to be real in itself. Everything existed only as scenery, as the stage for people flowing through the square.

It took me several years to be at ease with you and speak frankly. And even then it took a long time for me to realize that other people wouldn't be listening to everything I said—and it didn't matter if they did. Up until this time, I guess I had been suffering under the illusion that I was the only real person, and that others were trying to capture some of the reality of my life. At least, I thought they were all walking near me in hopes of hearing what I had to say.

As I said, it took me several years to realize this. When I finally turned to you to express these thoughts, everyone in the crowded square simultaneously began to laugh at me. They all stopped dead in their tracks and stood laughing at me. Except for you. That's when I realized that you and I were the only ones who were really awake. Which gave me incredible power: I made them all disappear.

We walked along the beach, trudging through the pebbles, watching the tide, the seabirds, feeling the cool wind, the cool spray of the water. You were female, then, and I was male; although it didn't really matter because what was important was that we were able to explore together the rich complexities of this existence.

Each time we meet we are both different, meeting as strangers, meeting on different levels, exploring new complexities. This is what human consciousness is all about. Often I forget this. Or you forget. Or we both forget and therefore get tangled up in the particulars of our new circumstances.

Which is part of the dance. We step on each other's toes because we don't know how to dance and sometimes aren't even aware that we <u>are</u> dancing. Which is also part of the dance. Sometimes we hear of those who have learned to dance and are artists of the Dance; but they can't teach us a thing because we would have to be able to dance with them to learn anything. What's more, the Dance is not a matter of training or effort at all. Because to dance is to feel, not to think. And you learn not by remembering all the steps you've done before, but by forgetting them. The movement that's happening now is the only movement in the Dance, and to be completely attentive to that movement is to flow with it. It takes no effort because the Dance dances itself.

I wonder if I will remember all this when the next movement comes around? You see, I have only been practicing on my own in hopes of improving my technique for the next time we meet. I know you understand all this and forgive me my clumsiness. But when I forget about you and think only of myself, I put myself beyond help when I need it most. And the Dance goes on without me . . .

Phase IV. Lighthouse

I dreamt of you again last night.

You were the daughter of a lighthouse keeper in the northern country. And I was an artist who was travelling on horseback, painting the things that I saw. I had left my home because the people no longer new me—for they were made strangely uncomfortable by the things of which I would talk and by the things I would paint. I painted things as I saw them, and I saw things differently than others. They never liked to look at my paintings or drawings, and when I began making objects in wood the people came into my studio and destroyed my work. So I left.

You were the daughter of a lighthouse keeper. When I try to remember him or what we had talked about, his image dissolves before my grasp. I came to see you every day from the nearby village, where I stayed at an inn, until your father let me stay in a room by the tower. I could hear him going up the iron steps to the light room, which I never got to see; and one night he never came down, but disappeared forever into the mist between the bellowing calls of the foghorn.

I heard you calling. I ran and ran but could not find you. Softer your voice called. Turning, I saw you beckon me closer. I moved to touch you.

Reaching, my hand went through your floating veils, and you cried in horror to find that you had to flesh to encounter my stroking fingers . . . You faded beyond reach.

My mind was circumcised by a thousand unborn hands—clawing at me from behind my vision as the lighthouse refused to shine or call out a sound to guide me through the darkness . . . I awoke on the shore, my brain exposed, and I fear I shall die before daybreak spreads its peaceful moment like a blanket to envelop my fragile being . . .

Phase V. You and I

I stood next to you on the bus and looked into your eyes. I was falling for you like a rock down a well when suddenly an onslaught of commuters were thrust upon us and carried us away from each other. You must have gotten off without my noticing. I guess it's an adventure to rediscover you again, but the interim is painful . . .

Phase VI. Afterwards

After that, I wandered aimlessly for years. Like some gentile Ahasverus seeking to rid himself of his heritage—or else seeking his true heritage. Like a snake trying to shed his skin, but having difficulty, scraping against rocks and stones tirelessly, endlessly. He's trying to emerge from his past, cleanse himself, become as new; but the old skin doesn't come off so easily.

THE GREEN TRANSFER

Chapter One
A Visit from the Tax Men

It all happened soon after we moved into the old house in Brickshire.

We were all artists or writers in those days—those glory days before the Big Bust. The government was still wealthy and wise enough to offer modest subsidies to writers and artists, so that's what we became. It turned out that the pensions were so modest that it was impossible to make ends meet without regular sales of our creative wares. Regular buyers, however, were as hard to come by as wealthy patrons. Still, there was no question about returning to work and giving up the freedom we had so recently gained: we had to find some other solution to "the economic problem." Finally, we realized that we could lower expenses by pooling our resources; so a group of us got together and rented a large house in Brickshire, one of the oldest suburbs of the city.

One day before noon we were upstairs in the common room, idling our time and talking about nothing in particular, when we heard a car pull up in the driveway. Since I was the closest to the window, I crossed over to glance through the curtains at the drive below. Two men got out of a black sedan wearing fedoras, dark glasses, and suits. I motioned silently and my house mates huddled around me to peer down at our visitors through the thin gauze. The sun glinted sharply off the polished hood of the car like the back of a beetle, and the two men looked up and down the street before heading through the tall grass towards our front door.

"They're government agents!" whispered a voice beside me. "You can tell by the clothes and that car."

"He's right!" another voice affirmed.

We watched as one of the men rang the doorbell. The warm brass tone sounded up the carpeted stairwell behind us, innocuous and inviting, but we were not about to go down and answer it. Receiving no response, the agent rang again and then put his ear to the door. We held our breath. After a pause, the two men exchanged some words and glanced up at our window.

We jumped back involuntarily, bumping into one another and almost knocking over an end table. But the agents could not have seen us—not in that dark room on such a bright day. Nevertheless, it was with utmost caution that I crept back to the window, followed nervously by the others. As we stood watching one of the men slipped something under the door, then they got back in their car and drove away.

As soon as the sedan was out of sight, we rushed downstairs to the front door and found a sheet of paper. It was an official notice from the Tax Department stating that each member of our household was required to produce a specific amount of creative work within the next 60 days. At the end of that time there would be an inspection and we would be subject to severe penalties if we failed to meet our requirements.

The weeks passed. From time to time I sat alone in my room and tried to write, but I could think of nothing but the deadline. Awkward, artificial, imposed from the outside—I had never worked well with deadlines. I would write a few lines, sometimes half a page, but none of it was any good. Soon I would become frustrated and restless . . . and go to the common room. My house mates apparently did the same. Together, we simply forgot about the ultimatum and chose to spend our days and nights in the pleasant but unproductive pursuits of youth.

The specified day arrived without warning and the Tax agents returned in their black sedan. A few of us were in the common room at the time and watched through the curtains as before. One of the agents drove and the other (probably of higher rank) sat in back. This time they pulled the car right up into the yard and stopped directly below our window with the driver's door just inches from the house. Then, through the use of a peculiar suspension system, they managed to elevate the car to the level of the second floor! We backed away from the window as the car rose up, at once amazed and amused by the efforts of the two men.

The man in the back seat slid over behind the driver and rolled down his window. Shielding his eyes with his hand, he pressed his face against the glass and peered into the room. He saw us and mouthed something—it was inaudible through the thick glass—and began tapping on the windowpane. This time there was no escape; but the spell was broken and we scrambled to our rooms to get our creative work in order.

As fate would have it, my good friend Stephen was visiting that day. He sat in my room and watched me shuffle through the papers on my desk. Since he lived in another district (or perhaps for some other reason), Stephen was exempt from the writing requirement. I had always considered

Intimations of Unreality

him the artistic type, but I was never quite clear about the source of his income. At any rate, he remained calm and simply observed—with an air of slight amusement at my frantic efforts.

I knew my prose accomplishments were far from meeting the government's requirements. Nevertheless, I collected the various fragments, arranged them into some meaningful order, and began copying them out by hand to make them legible. But this was taking far too long: the Tax men were already in the front room listening to another member of the household read his work aloud, and I could be called on at any moment.

After copying the first fragment, I cut a second one into a strip and taped it under the first. The result was sloppy but provided the writing with the appearance of continuity. Unfortunately, even this method was taking too long and it was obvious I would soon run out of time. Stephen's amusement seemed to increase in proportion to my level of anxiety. Still, he made a suggestion which might well have saved the day.

"Alan, if your new work isn't finished, why not just show them some of your older, complete writings? How could they tell the difference?"

My heart leapt with the hope this created. It was so obvious I should have thought of it myself, for I had plenty of old poems and short stories which I could press into service for the occasion. Hurriedly, I began rummaging around in old boxes.

Too late! The Tax men stepped into the room. They continued to wear their dark sunglasses and were absolutely without any sense of humor. By contrast, Stephen was now openly chuckling. This struck me as an affront to the Tax men's authority, but they simply ignored him. One of the men took one look at me, glanced at my desk, and spoke:

"Mr. Wilcox. Since you have obviously not performed your duty to society by producing your quota of creative work, we are empowered by the State to seize your property and evict you. However, we have just been called back to the office to deal with a more serious case, so we will grant you a grace period of one week in which to fulfill your requirement."

The man who did not speak was busy surveying the room. This was invasive, but what could I say? When the first man turned and left the room the second took off his dark glasses. He had blond hair, blue eyes, and spoke with a German accent. His tone was confidential.

"You see, my friend, we are sympathetic to the fact that you are an artist. Otherwise, as my colleague said, we would take away all of your possessions and boot you out."

For a while his eyes actually conveyed the sympathy of which he spoke, but they soon resumed the quality of hardness appropriate to his official duty.

"This time, do not take our warning lightly. We will be expecting extra work," he said and followed his superior out of the room.

Stephen could control himself no longer and burst out laughing, clutching his sides and almost falling out of his chair.

As for me, I was devastated. I had always thought of myself as a writer, fundamentally, but when put to the test I had been unable to perform, to produce, to prove myself. Worse than the defeat was the feeling of indignation that I had been wronged, that I had not been given a fair chance. . .

Chapter Two
The Green Transfer

"What you need is an adventure!" said Stephen. "You've been working too hard, even if you don't have much to show for it. You should let loose—get out and experience some freedom! Perhaps something will happen to inspire you."

I had nothing to lose . . . except my possessions, of course. But of these I valued only my writings, and I insisted on taking them with me. When I looked into the closet, the box containing them practically fell on my head. I gathered them together with the newer scribblings, rolled them up, and stuck them into an old thermos. It was the shiny silver type that looked like a mortar shell and had a convenient shoulder strap.

We set off on foot, walking as far as the thoroughfare. We had planned to hitchhike, but a downtown bus came along first so we took it. The empty bus throbbed and rattled as it made its way north from the isolated suburb of Brickshire. By the time we reached the outskirts of the city the sun was setting. Since we were the only passengers, the driver asked us where we wanted to go. We answered vaguely, uncertain ourselves. He stared at us for a moment through the wide slanting mirror above his head and then pulled over in a half-residential, half-warehouse district and opened the door.

"Stand over there," he said, pointing to the opposite corner of the cross street. His casual gesture conveyed years of experience.

Stephen and I looked at each, shrugged, and moved to the front of the bus. The driver handed us two green transfer tickets as we passed.

We stepped down and the bus drove off, spewing a big cloud of exhaust. The smoke rose up, a dark bluish gray against the black night, drawing our gaze to the building across the street. Most of the windows were either dark or boarded up, but one was brightly lit. From where we stood, we could see paintings and framed photographs on the walls, shelves stuffed with books, a mantle covered with bric-a-brac. There was a party going on.

I have always been intrigued by other people's apartments, seen from the street this way. I like to imagine what it would be like to step into someone else's life, complete with their belongings and friends I do not know. It doesn't really matter who or what—it's the otherness that appeals to me. To escape from one's own shoddy life—that's the ticket!

"Come on!" Stephen said, stirring me from my reverie.

We crossed the street and stood on the corner which the driver had indicated. The party was two stories above us.

"Now what?" I asked.

"Now we wait. Remember, we're looking for something out of the ordinary, but if you're patient and watchful, something is bound to happen."

We stood, waiting for a sign. I eyed the green transfer, which was printed on thin, cheap newsprint with complex designs that made it look like a small note in some foreign currency. "Odd," I must have said aloud.

"Haven't you seen one of these before?" Stephen asked in a tone that bordered on condescension.

"Uh . . . no." I couldn't lie. I was relatively new to the city and this was the first time I had used the mass transit system. I had no idea whether the transfer was of the standard type or something special.

"Neither have I." He surprised me. How often had Stephen been my guide into worlds of which I had no knowledge? How often did he introduce me to new and interesting people who would otherwise remain beyond my sphere? Now I felt somewhere between being lost and being his equal: two adventurers into the Unknown. As I stared at the ticket I felt a thrill run up my spine.

A carriage drawn by four horses turned the corner at a gallop and pulled up in front of us, raising dust from the street. The horses snorted and whinnied, stamping their hooves a few extra times on the pavement. I was astonished. Before the carriage had turned the corner it was totally out of earshot. Besides, who rides around in horse-drawn carriages these days? The time of the Revolution was long past.

A rotund, finely dressed man bounced out of the carriage. "Stephen!" he cried.

"Lord Randolph!" So we were once again in Stephen's realm.

"However did you hear of this soiree?! Was it Lady Falgren? Ah! The tickets, of course." To our confusion, the gentleman indicated our bus transfers.

Stephen introduced us. "Lord Randolph, may I present Alan Wilcox; Alan, his Lordship Randal Hampton, Baron Randolph."

"Good to meet you." The nobleman grasped my hand firmly with his white-gloved hand. He was of medium height, with close-cropped, grayish blond hair, a white mustache, and steel gray eyes. "But why wait? Let's go in!"

I followed them through a door and up some stairs. Suddenly we were transported into another time. The wallpaper, the moldings, the gas lamps—all spoke of a hundred years past. On the way up, Stephen and Randolph were catching up on old ties. "Lord Ficksure . . . the outing on Île D'Efe . . . Lady Pennifore. . ." The fellow certainly moved in rarefied circles—as did Stephen, far more than I had realized.

At the top of the second flight of stairs we opened the door and the party burst upon us with brightness, warmth, and gaiety. Stephen was whisked away by acquaintances, leaving me feeling abandoned, but I was immediately welcomed by Lady Falgren, a gracious hostess who seemed to hold nothing against my humble beginnings. She introduced me to several friendly people and I had no problem fitting into the scene.

By their accents and dress, and from snippets of conversation, I deduced that the guests were a strange admixture of locals and nobility who had been exiled from Europe. One townsman was called Greg by his friends but introduced himself to the elite as Gregory. He shifted his accent appropriately, if somewhat unconvincingly, and put on airs when speaking with the blue-bloods. The latter, as I have indicated, were not at all aloof. Was this, perhaps, an adaptation to their expatriate condition?

Intimations of Unreality

Thirty or more people filled the room, all dressed in their finest and conversing animatedly. Vivaldi blasted from an old Victrola, its flowering phone straining at every frequency and rattling like a tin can.

I saw someone eating an *hors d'oeuvre* and realized I had not had dinner, so I worked my way to the kitchen. Refreshments were laid out on two long tables in the dining area. On one side there was champagne and caviar, among other delicacies; on the other, chopped vegetables and dip, and a small keg of beer. A provincial fellow with an atrociously outdated (and outgrown) suit was bending over the sink, stuffing his face with cheese and crackers. Still chewing, he quickly looked me up and down and then said "Name's Jimmy." Between bites he added (for some reason) "my brother owns a fabric shop on Commerce Street. . ." I realized that the cheese was, in fact, a spread made of what looked like roasted garlic but which turned out to be locally grown scallions known as "ramps." I spied a colander full of them in the stainless steel sink, but when I picked one up to eat I saw it was riddled with wormholes.

Jimmy continued stuffing himself and talking while I went to work on the vegetables. There were sticks of celery lined with pimento cheese; artistically carved radishes; carrots sticks; broccoli spears; French onion dip. I helped myself to caviar and crackers as well. An elderly woman, elegantly arrayed in regal purple and adorned with jewels, came in from a back room. She doddered, gliding slowly through the kitchen and chatting to herself.

After temporarily allaying my hunger and quaffing a couple glasses of champagne, I went into the back in search of the lavatory. Instead I found a study, equipped with an ornately carved antique writing table and several shelves of books. The room was partitioned by an Oriental screen that was meant to conceal a bed and dressing area. On the wall, a postcard portrait of Rimbaud lent conviction to the whole setting, which was both a place to sleep and a fashionable place to entertain. (How often do parties admit us to such semi-private domains!)

The shelves consisted of slats of pine wood supported by cement blocks. I cocked my head to one side to read the spines of the books. All the usual authors were there: Rimbaud, Baudelaire, and Rilke; Blake, Holderlin, and Dylan Thomas; Goethe, Plath, and Welty; C. S. Lewis, Paul Bowles. . .

A woman cleared her throat and stepped from behind the partition.

"I'm sorry!" I said. "I hope I was not intruding. . ." I felt as if caught in the act of prying.

"Oh, no—not at all." She was strikingly beautiful, with sparkling green eyes and black hair that fell in delicate curls around her face. "I'm Marian Wellsey," she said, extending her hand.

"I-I'm A-Alan Wi-Wilcox," I stammered, then added "Charmed" and kissed her hand. The refined customs of the aristocratic company were contagious.

"Lady Falgren is my aunt. I'm holding the party in her honor."

"I see. I am a friend of Stephen—Stephen—" I couldn't remember his last name!

"Yes, I know Stephen well!" she said, putting me at ease.

I could think of absolutely nothing to say. "Uh, very nice party—and such distinguished guests." I was really quite at a loss before her beauty and courtly bearing.

Stephen walked in, just in the nick of time!

"Ah! I see you two have met. Marian, did you realize we were on an outing and found our way here quite by accident? If it were not for Lord Randolph's arrival. . ."

As he talked I fumbled nervously in my pockets and pulled out the transfer ticket from the bus. Marian's eyes lit up.

"Oh, you simply *must* come to the Theatre!" she exclaimed, touching my arm in a familiar way.

Stephen elaborated: "Alan, as it turns out these tickets will admit us to the Great Green Theatre for tomorrow evening's performance. Marian plays a leading role in the production."

"Ha! It is only a small part . . ." she protested.

We chatted a while in this fashion and then went to rejoin the guests in the main room. In the hallway, Stephen took me aside and discretely placed a roll of hundred-dollar vouchers in my pocket.

"No questions asked—these are from your new patron."

"Fine by me," I beamed. To be honest, I was already a bit giddy from the champagne and did not have the presence of mind to question the source of the gift.

Marian had gone ahead. Now Stephen moved off into the crowd, which had doubled since our arrival. People were coming and going in the hallway and I had to struggle to maintain my course toward the front of the apartment.

A choral symphony by Charles Ives was now playing on the Victrola. Its simultaneous orchestral sections clashed beneath snatches of hymns and popular songs of the 20s, alternating typically between the sacred and the profane.

Alone, without knowing a soul in the crowd, I wandered along the perimeter of the room until I discovered an antechamber previously closed off by sliding doors. Lit only by a dim Tiffany lamp, this smaller chamber was quite dark in contrast to the main room. I stood in the doorway while my eyes adjusted. I could barely make out the outlines of several people sitting on a couch in the blackness. A cigarette burned red, glowing brighter as its owner drew a breath, then dimming again as he blew a lungful of invisible smoke through the dark space between us. I coughed and stepped from the doorway into the room, moving off to one side.

"I'm sorry!" I stepped on someone's foot—almost collided with him before I could distinguish him in the shadows. He said nothing but moved off and out of the room. My eyes followed the black silhouette through the doorway into the light. Peering back into the room I studied the figures on the couch and also saw several people standing against the left wall, talking in pairs or groups of three and taking no notice of me. I thought I recognized Jimmy from the kitchen and realized suddenly that everyone present was of lower or middle class origins: there were no nobles here. Turning to my right, I took a step back but encountered an obstacle with my calf which threw me off balance. Falling in the darkness, I tumbled into an easy chair and banged my right elbow on the upholstered arm of the chair, jabbing the funny bone. Shock waves rippled through my forearm but I hid the pain, feigning a casual air and pretending I had intentionally thrown myself into the chair. The pain subsided.

From my vantage point in the shadows, I surveyed the room. The smoker on the couch to my right was flanked by two women; the three of them talked and laughed. Across the room, Jimmy and some other townsmen exchanged jokes. I caught only snatches of the various conversations. Although I was being totally ignored, my self-consciousness made me increasingly uncomfortable, so after a while I stood up and returned to the double wide doorway between the rooms. From where I stood, darkness reigned at either side of my vision: the corners unlit by the small lamp echoed with laughter and words. Light streamed in from the living room straight ahead, gleamed on the glasses of golden liquid and sparkled in the eyes and teeth of the guests. A few people danced. The whole scene was refreshing.

I stepped forward into the room.

As I did so, the crowd seemed to shift and blocked my way. Thus impeded, I stepped to one side, and there was Marian, standing against the wall. She smiled and seemed to glow, blushing from the wine (had she been dancing as well?) and laughing.

"I hope you're having a good time, Alan."

"Oh, yes. Most certainly."

"Stephen tells me you write."

"Uh, yes. But I've had problems lately—with productivity, you might say."

Just when I thought Marian and I might have a nice talk, she was interrupted by someone who demanded her attention as hostess. And though I was left alone again, at least I was beginning to feel welcome—a feeling pleasurably reinforced by the champagne, which was in plentiful supply as waiters made their rounds. And so the hours passed, and (quite frankly) I have no recollection of what transpired.

Chapter Three
"The Story of Man"

The next thing I knew I was awakened by a knock. I sat up and was startled by an old woman coming through the door of a strange bedroom. Looking down, I saw that I was wearing only underwear so I quickly pulled the sheets up over my chest.

"Oh, don't worry, young man! You have nothing to hide from me. I had three sons of my own."

She stopped inside the door, grinning from behind thick bifocals. She could read disorientation on my face.

"I'm Gladys Mallory. Your friend Stephen brought you here late last night and helped you into bed. I'm a neighbor of young Miss Wellsey and often have guests arrive at late hours from her parties. All decent folk, of course—some of them quite distinguished. Each to his or her own room and no funny business here. This is a respectable boarding house. But even the high breeds drink a bit too much at parties now and then and need a place to sleep it off.

"Now, I'll let you get dressed. When you come down you can have a little breakfast."

She left. When I went downstairs I was served tea and biscuits. The amiable woman joined me in some tea and talked endlessly. I nodded and smiled and said "Yes," and "Oh, I know" but otherwise could not get a word in edgewise. It was beginning to look like I would never escape. On top of which, my head ached fiercely from the champagne.

"My late husband was a war hero, you know. Rewarded for his valor. More tea, dear?"

This was my chance and I took it.

"No, thank you—I really must be going." I stood up, but lingered awkwardly, not knowing whether I should pay her for the bed and breakfast.

"Don't worry, your friend Stephen paid for you when he left, early this morning," she explained. "He said for you to meet him at the Theatre at 7 o'clock this evening. He's such a nice young man."

"Yes." I thanked her for her hospitality and left, my thermos dangling from its shoulder strap.

The cool wind that whipped through the streets cut through the numbness of my nerves and cleared my head. I spent the rest of the morning and all afternoon exploring the streets of the district, browsing through bookstores and antique shops and rummaging through tables of odd junk at the flea market. Before I realized it, I was weak with hunger and headed for the nearest cafe. After eating I sat for awhile, sipping a glass of sparkling water and reading a travelogue about Peru. Although I tried to concentrate on the book, I could not help overhearing the conversation at a table behind me. A woman and man were talking. Since they had been seated after me, I never actually saw them. The woman did most of the talking, telling a story that got progressively stranger.

"A little girl wandered the streets. There was a circus in town, a day parade on the first of May. This was the banner of the traveling actors: 'The Story of Man.'"

I recognized the title—it was the play Stephen and I were going to see involving Marian Wellsey—to be performed that very evening at the Great Green Theatre. I listened more closely.

"Next door to where the girl lived was a house with an adjacent garage. In this garage there was an automobile (among other things)—a '59 Studebaker. In the back seat of the car was a portmanteau containing a letter addressed to Madame Pugmire of East Templeton. This letter had no apparent connection with the play performed by the traveling troupe of actors. However, next to the portmanteau was a stack of posters printed in black letters, which announced that evening's performance."

My curiosity overwhelmed me and I turned to look over my shoulder at the speaker of this strange monologue. *All of the tables near me were empty.* In the window of the cafe, however, was a poster which read:

COME SEE

THE STORY OF MAN

Featuring

The Mystery of Creation

SEE:

- The evolution of consciousness incarnate
- The development of memory and symbolic processes
- The growth of technology and object-manipulation!

OBSERVE:

- The attachment to pleasurable sensation
- The corruption of mind by desire
- The struggles born of hatred & self-love!

WITNESS:

The Methodical Extinction of Life Itself on all planes:

- Psychological!
- Immoral!
- Moral!

Tonight at The Great Green Theatre

Intimations of Unreality

I left the cafe and saw the same announcement posted on buildings, shop windows, kiosks, and telephone poles throughout the district. I didn't know how I could have overlooked them during the day, for they were everywhere. Then I caught sight of a clock and realized that it was almost 7:00. Having still some distance to traverse to reach the Theatre, I broke into a jog.

Running along the sidewalk I bumped into a muffin salesman and upset his tray. Muffins and pastries went everywhere, rolling under cars and down the street into a sewer drain. The muffin man looked at me, silent and stupefied, with an injured expression that was more offensive than if he had dishonored my birth. Acting quickly, so as to settle matters and get on my way, I fumbled in my pockets and pulled out one of the hundred-dollar vouchers I had been given at the party the night before. This I thrust into his hand, which was covered with the remnants of a crushed muffin where he had grabbed the upset tray. His eyes immediately brightened.

"At least take this one," he said, offering a poppy seed cupcake with lemon frosting.

"Thanks. I suppose it's only proper," I said, taking the cake and speeding on down the sidewalk. I ate it as I ran, this time careful of the passersby.

I reached the Great Green Theatre—a grand old house of classical design—and plunged through the revolving doors, walking into the lobby with lemon on my breath and the green transfer in my hand. The theatre was packed with an audience of around 2,000. Stephen was nowhere to be seen. An usher led me to an empty seat in the middle of the very front row and gave me back my transfer along with a programme. I sat down, placing the thermos containing my manuscripts on the floor between my feet. The crowd chattered noisily behind and around me, but I sat quietly, programme gripped in my hands, waiting for the red velvet curtain to rise.

At last the house lights dimmed, a hush fell over the crowd, and the curtain went up to the sound of pulleys. I describe the scene as if I were there:

THE STORY OF MAN

Not too much light. Few props; small biscuits on a tray.

A man is pacing, smoking a cigarette. He is wearing a checkered tweed suit, purple and yellow and (mainly) white. He has a business report in a manila folder tucked under his arm.

Another man steps into the room and begins to point out markings, scratches, and pinholes in the wall. The BUSINESSMAN *pretends not to see the* INSPECTOR, *who pretends not to notice this, and the* INSPECTOR *is at once suspicious of the* BUSINESSMAN *.*

A VOICE [*from offstage begins reading loudly (amplified) and rapidly*]. To be provided for without cost or error, and set upon—boats to carry them over. They were ordered into groups of three, each helping the other, and were thus provided with their needs. . .

INSPECTOR [*sharply*]. What is the meaning of this?

FRENCHMAN [*somberly*]. That is precisely . . . [*pauses to drink a swallow of a brownish liquid from a glass*] what I was hoping to ask you.

[*The* BUSINESSMAN *ignores them both.*]

INSPECTOR [*angrily*]. I've told you before to stay out of this MacClone affair—to return all of your repugnant variables, and especially to vent your shoelaces after wear!

The audience chuckled.

BUSINESSMAN [*who can no longer withhold himself from comment*]. And you're both failing to take into account that Norwegians grow dark beards, that empty saddles ride on through the night, that daybreak's advances will hardly slow the reconciliation that awaits the frozen lily, the Thompson grape, the sour apple.

FRENCHMAN [*puffing a pipe pensively*]. Quite right, quite right.

INSPECTOR [*excusing himself politely*]. Evidence is to be found elsewhere, gentlemen [*tipping his hat*]. [*Exits.*]

FIRE-SWALLOWER IN A CIRCUS. Well, think about that! All this time, we were intending to be seen.

PHOTOGRAPHER [*taking his picture*]. Thank you, Mr. Cardoni. You will receive a free copy of this album. [*Both smiling.*] [*Everyone Exits.*]

A MAN struts forth onto center stage, proclaiming with a shout: "Caesar of York, Justice of Mainly Heretofore Prudents, Nat. Morse—To wit:

     "'Mine is the joy to be with you;
     Hail and be well!
     and more glory to you
     Such is my message:'"

Here he steps aside and pauses, a finger to the side of his chin, etc. He jumps forth onto the floor before the stage, directly facing the crowded audience. He looks squarely into the eyes of the person sitting in the middle of the front row of seats. This person is me!

He says to me, in a casual voice, "I am tired of this; would you be so kind as to play my part on the stage this evening?"

"But I don't know how to act!" I object.

"Well, just pretend to know how to act," he said, smiling: "That's what it's all about."

Firm in my resolution, I jumped up on the stage and donned the Thespian's cape and hat, taking also his cane. Without apparent conscious control on my part, my mouth was suffered by my forebrain to spill forth the stilted lines of a spontaneous play. Likewise, my audience was suffered to be admirers of my brilliance and erudition. I addressed the house thusly:

"The curtains are drawn in the kitchen window. Mary Louise comes down the steps wearing a summer dress and with a rose in her straight, brown hair."

At this point, Marian from the party the night before enters from stage left and approaches me in center stage.

"I figured you hadn't offered to be here this weekend," she says, touching my arm softly, briefly, smiling and walking past.

A MAN jogged by the bookstore, lights in his eyes, near the (neo-old-fashioned) country store (synthesized) on the corner.

ALAN. I cannot remember when was the last time you were so beautiful. [*But she had gone, and I heard my words spoken into this absence and echo back.*]

MARY LOUISE [*offstage*]. I have only come to pick the fruit and cook the berry: We will have a nut farm this Christmas, when all the world will settle down to play strange games in the dark. They will file past your open window, staring. They will poison themselves until they laugh and stumble upon each other. You will perhaps avoid the lonesome whistle that leaves each day behind. You will perhaps find one evening's morning not so unpleasant as the last. Surely, daybreak will come again, and mist will cover the docks, and searchlights will beam through the distance. Also there will be greetings from abroad, or new little melodies to send you on your way, or strange tidings of promise blessed to you in a floating bottle. . .

Her voice trailed off into an inaudible whisper.

I made a long, rambling statement that ended with a dramatic gesture of the right hand. Suddenly, a small, glowing pyramid floated down like a snowflake into my waiting palm. As I stood and stared at the strange object, it lost its dazzling glow and became a gray figure formed of sooty wax.

I hastened to regain the attention of my unwitting cast of players (which, perforce, included the audience itself). The moment seemed ripe for a closure—which was up to me to provide—so I spoke forth in my most dramatic manner:

ALAN. When the smoke clears, we will see where the boundaries lie and where it is safe to swim, where fishing will be probundant and where silence fills our shadows. Until then, I can only pray for a peaceful night.

With this, I bowed.

I was an immediate sensation!

The audience of 2,000 leapt to their feet and cheered strenuously. The stagehands did not bother to drop the curtain. The actors rushed on-stage to congratulate me. A number of them wore wildly unusual costumes and had not yet appeared on stage.

"There is no reason to continue our performance!"

"You were magnificent!"

"Wonderful!"

"Marvelous!"

"A genius!"

They crowded around me, shaking my hand, patting my back, kissing my cheek. Photographers busily snapped photos, bulbs flashing and popping off to explode noisily on the floor. A fat woman with a perilously low-cut evening dress was struck on the bosom with a hot bulb. She shrieked and flung her right hand back in surprise, striking in the face an old gentleman with a golden beard, who fell back against a young couple fondling each other in the front row. The audience became a mob, pressing forward against the stage, clamoring for autographs, chanting "Bravo!" and "Encore!" and, not the least, "Author! Author!" (which warmed my heart the most, although I could only take credit for my own spontaneous lines.)

Mass hysteria threatened. Things were definitely getting out of hand. It was time for an Exit—but how could I disengage myself from my admirers?

Intimations of Unreality

At this moment Stephen came to my rescue. He cut through the crowd on stage and dragged me away by the arm. Before I knew it, we were backstage. (Fortunately, Stephen had remembered my precious thermos for me.) And before anyone could respond to our swift departure, we went down some iron steps and out into the back alley. Marian was with us, wearing a lovely white evening gown which sparkled with sequins.

"You were just *marvelous*, Alan," she said, smiling brightly. She looked beautiful in the moonlight that peeped down between the buildings.

"You are too kind," I protested, embarrassed by the whole event.

The strangest notion occurred to me. For all the world, Marian's dress looked like a wedding gown. If she was the bride, it followed that I was her groom, and Stephen was the best man helping us make the get-away.

"Quick, this way!" Stephen said, leading us through the dark alley and down an unmarked side street. We made our way secretively, "under cover of night," until we were well away from the Theatre. Then we relaxed and began to stroll casually.

"I know of a splendid place to celebrate," said Stephen, flourishing a walking stick.

I realized that I still bore the Thespian's cane and wore the top hat and majestic cape from the performance. Stephen was likewise arrayed, and we went arm-in-arm. Mary Louise walked on my other side. I would have taken her arm as well, but I felt too shy.

"This is the place," Stephen announced.

We went down some steps into a pub below street level. The polished oak bar stretched across one wall, rimmed by a brass rail that reflected track lighting from above. The mirror behind the bar was half-covered by half-empty bottles of every description and added deceptive depth to the small room. The bartender was perfect for the part—balding, mustache, bow tie, vest. Descending a few last steps from the door into the subterranean club, we moved among empty tables and chairs of dark wood that were clumped in the shadows of the dark room, only the bar being lighted.

The pub was empty except for a boisterous group of four common laborers who interrupted their revelry to turn en masse and look in our direction as we reached the bar.

"Well, what have we here," said a self-appointed spokesman for the group. "Some floofs, fresh from the opera!" The men laughed.

Stephen and I glanced at them in the mirror and then at each another, silently agreeing to ignore the insult of the sloppy sods. We leaned our canes against the bar and removed our hats and gloves. Marian kept hers on and took a seat on the leather barstool to my left. Stephen, to my right, ordered drinks.

"Bartender, three champagne cocktails, if you please."

"If you please!" mocked the main ruffian. "Well, boys, it looks like we are in the presence of some true Blue Bloods!" Again the men laughed in support of their leader. Again we ignored them.

The bartender placed the drinks in front of us and Stephen proposed a toast. "To Alan, on his theatrical debut!" We clinked glasses and drank. At the same time Stephen had toasted me, he had placed his hand on my shoulder. It was an innocent gesture of camaraderie but did not go unnoticed by the others.

"Ma'am," the leader stood up and made a mock bow toward Marian. "May we assume that you are available for the evening, since these two Gaylords are obviously occupied with each other?" His cohorts oohed in chorus and chuckled.

Stephen and I exchanged a quick glance, long enough to agree that this time the men had gone too far—a lady's honor was at stake and, even more, our sexuality had been impugned. We turned to face the bunch across the room.

Stephen spoke.

"Sir, I doubt from your general appearance and uncouth manner that you would know how to treat a lady; in fact, you seem the sort that is more accustomed to a dog in the alley than to a woman in bed."

Stephen's retort struck them between the eyes. They were momentarily stunned.

"Boys, it looks like we need to teach these two gentlemen a lesson they didn't learn in their fancy finishing schools."

The spokesman pushed back his chair and approached us, his companions rising to follow him between the tables. They were no longer smiling.

Being outnumbered four to two, we had to take advantage of our sticks. As we reached to get them from the bar, Marian slipped off her barstool and stood next to us to confuse our attackers. Was it now four to three? Would the men fight against a woman? The leader, not delayed by Marian's tactic, lunged at Stephen, who was fast enough to strike him on the arm with an upward swing of the cane. The man recoiled in pain. Two of the other men were within a yard and came at me from front and right. The man on right ignored Marian, but she threw her drink in his face. I shoved the handle of my cane into my opponent's solar plexus, which doubled him over, then brought the cane up against this chin, decommissioning him on the spot. Stephen dealt the fourth man a sharp punch to the jaw with his ringed right fist, then rebuffed the leader once again with the cane. The man on the right, having wiped his face on his sleeve, came back at me, but I used my stick like a quarter staff and repelled him backwards onto a table, which collapsed. Stephen performed a similar maneuver against the leader when he came back a third time, and soon all four men lay in a bruised and drunken heap amidst broken and overturned furniture.

The bartender spoke for the first time, apologizing and offering us drinks on the house. But we did not want to deal again with the vanquished men once they revived, so we declined and left the bar.

"I really must apologize," Stephen said, brushing off his jacket. "The place seems to have suffered a change in clientele."

"It was quite thrilling—really!" Marian said, almost squealing with delight.

Our victory was not so certain, however, for the dazed ruffians were coming up the steps behind us, swearing and wielding the necks of broken bottles and the legs of broken chairs.

From out of nowhere, Lord Randolph pulled up in his carriage.

"This way!" he shouted.

The three of us climbed in and we immediately sped off down the street. Pursued only by hoarsely shouted vilifications punctuated by upheld fists and vainly-hurled furniture parts, we made for the edge of town.

Chapter Four
A Night in the Castle

The four-horse carriage was of the barouche type, with two facing benches and the movable top folded down over the back. Lord Randolph and Marian sat facing forward, while Stephen and I faced them with our backs to the driver.

We raced through the streets, the driver thrashing his whip like a madman. The stampede of hooves on the cobblestones rang out, reverberated on the walls of buildings that lined the streets, filled the air, filled the carriage, flooded our ears. Lord Randolph had to shout to be heard above the din.

"You simply must come be my guests for the evening! My castle is the only safe place!"

No one else attempted to speak, as the effort required to overcome the noise was too great. But when Lord Randolph mentioned his castle, I had a flash and remembered seeing a newspaper article referring to his ownership of the Great Green Theatre. I felt foolish for not having made the connection earlier, when I met him at Lady Falgren's soiree.

We were out of town in no time, racing through a forest that climbed gradually toward the mountains in the east. The driver maintained the break-neck pace with which we began our journey. We often lurched forward or rocked back and forth. Once, speeding around a curve, we rose up on two wheels and nearly lost it. I grasped the side of the carriage with both hands and held on for dear life, certain that we were going to flip over. I wondered if such reckless haste was really necessary, but I held my silence.

Soon after that we reached a long stretch of straight road. Although our speed remained constant, the travel became smoother, so I relaxed. The moon was overhead and shone through the clouds, illuminating Marian's face as it had in the alley behind the theatre. While I was admiring her the driver hit a huge bump and the sudden jolt threw me out of my seat. I couldn't keep from falling on top of her, my face landing directly on her bosom.

"Are you O.K.?" I asked, profoundly embarrassed. She was wide-eyed but said nothing, blushing and smiling nervously. I apologized profusely and resumed my seat. Stephen and his Lordship had turned away and covered their faces to hide their amusement. The rattle of horse hooves buried their snickering.

The pavement gave way to dirt road and the dust rose to choke us. We all held handkerchiefs to our faces. As we moved higher into the foothills, the dust was kept down by the moisture in the air, which also grew refreshingly cleaner and cooler with the altitude.

It wasn't until midnight that we reached the castle. The carriage emerged from the forest above the last ridge of foothills and we found ourselves on a kind of plateau. Before us were the mountains, stark peaks that stood silent and motionless against the sky. And there, below the mountains, the moonlit castle was a pile of gray stones indistinguishable from the rocky terrain from which it was hewn.

"At last! Welcome to Castle Randolph," his Lordship said as we climbed out. "That mob at the theatre will never find us here!

"Of course, I maintain a flat in the city, but I come up here whenever possible," he said as we walked toward the castle's entrance.

As we approached the massive wooden door, lit by torches hung on either side, I was struck by the sight of a monstrous gargoyle squatting above the entrance. The wingèd, apelike creature jutted out from the center stone of the arch and looked down at me with a devilish leer. In the flickering light of the torches I could swear I saw its head move. I stood staring at it for a moment after the others had gone ahead.

"Come on, Alan! We'll see more of that later," Marian said, interrupting my reverie. She took my arm and led me inside.

There was no sign of servants so we left our wraps in a heap on a bench by the door. Lord Randolph and Stephen had gotten some ten yards ahead of us in the vast entrance hall.

"When you consider the place of the gargoyle in religious history, Alan," Lord Randolph was saying, glancing back at me over his shoulder, "you will realize that it's part of a tradition far older than mediaeval times and Catholicism. The gargoyle inspires fear in the common man—the fear of God. This makes him approach the sacred with due respect.

"Likewise, gargoyles ward off evil spirits and pagan gods. Thus they serve the same function as devils in Tibetan Buddhism and Hinduism, and most primitive religions. And Medusa, the famous Gorgon. . ." His voice trailed off as he opened a set of double doors and went into an adjoining room.

Close behind him, Stephen added: "Just as the bullroarer or rhombos of primitives around the world served to frighten interlopers away from secret initiations, and to evoke a sense of awe in the participants. . ."

When we had settled in the large drawing room and had a good fire going, our host gave us a history of the castle.

"I inherited the *castillo* from my father, and my father's father, and his father before him. It has been in the family for countless generations—and *vice versa*! It is both our abode and our mark of distinction."

I remembered, however, that in the newspaper interview he had told quite a different story—most likely contrived:

I found the castle quite by accident. One day I was walking cross-country and happened upon it while traversing an isolated mountain pass. There it was, nestled among the peaks, just above a little valley. Apparently it had been abandoned for many years. And the surprising part was that it was simply forgotten—no one had seen it, or else they came upon it and figured it belonged to some eccentric nobleman (hence the state of disrepair) whom they were afraid to disturb. So they left it at that. So there it was. I laid claim to it at the Magistrate's Office before anyone else. And here am I!

We sat cozily before the warm fire. Lord Randolph and Stephen were in easy chairs, smoking pipes. Marian and I shared a quaint settee. A long stretch of silence in which we simply stared at the fire was broken by the creaking of a side door far off in the darkness.

"Come in and join us, Hector," Lord Randolph called out without turning. Looking at us, he rolled his eyes.

"Marian, Alan, Stephen, this is my brother Hector—Hector, my guests are fresh from a dazzling success at the theatre."

Hector, stiffly proper and elegantly dressed in smoking jacket and cravat, mumbled something as he walked to the edge of the large rug laid before the hearth and sat in a reclining chair. He pulled the handle on the recliner and lay back, blatantly ignoring our company. There ensued a few moments of uncomfortable silence in which we searched each other's faces and tried to think of something to say. We were all about to speak at the same time when Hector spoke—much more loudly than necessary:

"Theatre! Yes, I had my moments in the theatre!"

He stared up at the ceiling. I followed his gaze and noticed eddies in the smoke circling up from the pipes of my companions. Again a silence. Again Lord Randolph rolled his eyes. Again we were all about to speak when Hec-

Intimations of Unreality

tor's voice boomed in the silence:

"My *Last Year At School*—that was the title. I played the rebellious student. I remember one scene in particular, set at the end of an act subtitled The Agreement:

"'I cannot conceive of a more rudeful way of displacing the pudding,' said the professor in an attempt to summarize the history of Yugoslavia since 16 December 1948. 'The gears that grind and spin together offer no worthy interpretation of their dubious design; nor, furthermore, can deficiencies in coal production delay untoward slaughter of the young in political confrontations. In the end, it comes down to sibilant slobbering over spilt blood. Unless, of course, the variable is decremented by seven *after* the final computation of defense resources rather than *between* it.'"

We exchanged lost looks as Hector resumed:

"At this point the professor paused and glanced down at his notes. A graduate student sporting wire-rimmed glasses (played by myself) took advantage of the brief hiatus and interjected an unsolicited comment:

"'The same could be said in summation of English literature since Chaucer.'

"The professor was thrown into a startled reverie that lasted clearly three minutes. At last he responded:

"'In comparing the substructures of general sociopolitical history and literary culture (taking the former as an expression or working-out of the natural aggressive and hostile tendencies that exist in mankind, and the latter as a more revealing if somewhat semi-self-conscious expression of the human being's ideals, hopes, fears, and psychological nature in general), I would tend to agree with you.'"

Here Marian touched my arm and I turned to see that she was covering her mouth to keep from laughing out loud.

Hector continued: "Now, this may not seem to be a particularly revealing response, considering the 'professed' erudition of the academician and the fact that he took a 'clear' three minutes to muse upon the graduate's scholarly remark. And I quite agree."

"Bravo, Hector!" Lord Randolph applauded wearily. "You recreate that scene as well as ever. Now, perhaps we will enjoy some sherry before we bed down for the night."

I noticed a tray next to his chair, equipped with decanter and a number of glasses. (There still had been no sign of servants.) His Lordship poured and we drank in a silence undisturbed by Hector, who seemed to have fallen asleep with his eyes open. His nose whistled whenever he exhaled. Marian giggled. We clinked glasses and enjoyed the warming effect of the sweet wine. After two or three glasses, our host showed us to our rooms.

It had been a long day and I was exhausted. As soon as I had set down my thermos and removed my shoes and socks, I collapsed face-down on the bed and fell into a profound sleep. At some time in the night, however, I was awakened by a sharp burning pain in my trousers. I rolled over, reached in my pocket, and pulled out the small pyramid which had floated down to me on stage at the theatre, and which I had completely forgotten. It had returned from a sooty waxen opacity to its original translucent glow, almost uncomfortably bright in the pitch darkness.

What was it? I had not questioned it during the play, since it was a prop. Now, half-asleep, possibly dreaming, I watched it float out of my hand and over to the dresser, where it settled and dimmed somewhat. I got tired of straining my neck to watch it, let my head fall back to the pillow, and fell asleep.

During the night, I had a strange dream. I was hanging onto a rope outside the windows of the upper story of a Tudor style house. The house was set directly into the side of a steep mountain. As I dangled on the rope I glanced down and saw nothing but a yawning abyss. Above the house, on the sheer stone face, there had been painted in enormous black lettering the word "Bavaria," circled.

I tried to see through the curtained windows into the room but could not, and yet I somehow knew that a number of my friends were inside playing poker. I wanted to play, too. Suddenly, one of the gentleman who had been inside was now hanging onto a rope beside me, saying:

"I don't quite grasp what you intend by this."

"Neither do I, I must admit," I said. So I let go of the rope.

I awoke, this time with a different kind of sensation in my trousers: I simply *had* to pee. I looked around the room for a chamber pot, but found none. Actually, there was a tall vase on the floor in the corner, but I was uncertain as to its function . . . I skipped the socks but slipped on my shoes and went out into the corridor. Lord Randolph had neglected to point out the location of the facilities when he showed us to our rooms, so I had no choice but to scout them out. Fortunately, there were lights (now dimmed) set at regular intervals along the wall. The cold air penetrated my uncovered ankles and slipped between clammy leather and flesh to chill the arches of my feet. I stepped quietly, reached the end of the corridor that lead past my room and stood there for a moment, looking down a connecting passageway that led into darkness. My teeth began to chatter and I started knocking my knees to maintain control of my bladder. Afraid of getting lost, I decided to turn back, heading the other way down the hall, past my open door. I heard a faint dripping sound, and thought I must be on the right track. At last I found the source of the sound—a door spaced differently from the rest, apparently opening on a smaller room than those belonging to the guests. I turned the knob silently and slowly pushed back the door. The sound of water became louder. I saw a shower curtain: this was it! Swinging the door wide open, I discovered Marian, wearing a nightgown gathered up around her knees, sitting on the toilet!

We both started. I said "Sorry!" and immediately closed the door. Outside, I cursed myself in a whisper and set about wiggling my legs again, pacing in little circles outside the door. Finally, a flushing sound, the faucet turned on and off, and Marian appeared at the door.

"Sorry!" I said again, teeth chattering, looking down at her face—then, indiscreetly, instinctually, glancing down the loose neckline of her gown, I saw her breasts. I immediately pulled my wide eyes away. "Sorry!" I said once again, then ducked into the bathroom. I pulled the door closed and barely reached the toilet in time to relieve myself.

Outside, Marian giggled.

I took aim at the side of the bowl to lessen the noise of my downpour, then pulled the chain on the overhead tank to further camouflage the clamor. I was picturing Marian standing outside the door—but why would she? I finished peeing just as the whirlpool found its way down the drain. Zipping up, I stepped over to the sink, ears perked up to catch any sound from the corridor. I rinsed my hands in the ice cold water, then looked up to face myself in the mirror and thought how undesirable I must look—how silly I was to imagine that Marian could take any interest in me. Nevertheless, I approached the door and opened it with great anticipation, only to reveal an empty corridor, cold and shadowy, mocking my imagination. I returned to my room quickly and quietly, closed the door, and got into bed—alone.

Chapter Five
Pastimes of the Leisure Class

Late next morning, we brunched in a long dining room in the north wing of the castle. At first I avoided meeting Marian's gaze, embarrassed by our nighttime encounter in the corridor; but she was friendly, seemed forgiving—acted as if there was nothing to forgive. The sun was reaching the top of the twenty-foot high windows as we were treated to successive waves of gourmet preparations borne in by an endless staff of servers. It was an impressive display and contrasted sharply to the previous evening; perhaps Lord Randolph wanted to make up for the absence of service during that first night.

The place settings were exquisite—from the crystal water glasses to the fine china coffee cups, saucers, and plates, to the sterling silverware and cutlery . . . everything was of the finest manufacture and antique preserve. My linen napkin, with its elaborate silk needlework and lace embellishments, looked so valuable that I was reluctant to use it.

There were bowls of grapefruit slices mixed with black cherries and golden currants.

Conversation turned on new settlements on the Galapagos Islands. Of this I knew little more than what I had read in the paper, and since I had not yet formed an opinion on the issue I remained silent, content to focus on my fruit. As I finished the dish, Thomas, the butler, appeared at my side with a silver tray.

"Excuse me, Mr. Wilcox. A chambermaid found this under the edge of the bed in your room," he said quietly. As I wondered what on earth it could be, he lifted the sterling lid and revealed my green transfer—slightly crumpled but intact. "I thought that perhaps I should bring it to your attention in case you had misplaced it."

I glanced at the others at the table but they ignored us and went on with their discussion. I thought it odd that Thomas would fancy the ticket to be of value, but thanked him and placed it in my pocket.

Eggs Florentine with a marvelous hollandaise, sprinkled with roasted pine nuts.

Besides the team of servants who brought out each course, each of us had a private server standing on either side. One poured a fresh spot of coffee after each swallow. For those of us having au lait, every third spot of coffee was followed by a spot of cream and a quick stir. This server also maintained the water glass. The other server, to the left, continuously wiped the silverware between uses and immediately removed any completed dish from our places and set them aside on discreet trays. (For those who were left-handed—namely, Stephen and Hector—the positions were reversed. In all cases, the beverage server was a young woman.)

Cheese blintzes topped with blueberry compote, marmalade, and confectioner's sugar.

For some reason Hector mentioned Harold Blackburne, the chess player. "He could recite lists of nonsense words whilst simultaneously playing three games of chess and four of checkers 'blindfolded' and taking part in a game of Whist."

"And he had a fetish for women's shoes," Marian added.

"Touché!" said Lord Randolph, adding, more softly, "Now you're getting the hang of it!" He nodded toward his brother, who was absorbed in his food.

"No, really!" she continued. "Did you know that he would travel with a suitcase full of them, arranging them in a semi-circle around his hotel bed?"

Finally the food stopped coming, our places were cleared, and only the beverage servers were at our sides. We lingered over our coffee, basking in the afterglow of the fine meal.

"Speaking of Whist, shall we try a game?" our host suggested. It seemed a slight *faux pas*, since the game is limited to four players and there were five people present.

"That leaves me out." Hector was quick on the uptake.

"No, I insist on letting you gentlemen play," Marian offered.

"Can't we cut cards to determine the idle player?" Stephen suggested.

"Hector doesn't mind," Lord Randolph said firmly, settling the issue.

"Truly—I do not care much for cards," Hector spoke for himself. "I intend to continue my analysis of the Latvian Counter Gambit."

We retired to the game room, across the hall. (These old castles were wonderful for having so many rooms that there was one set aside for every purpose.) Hector went straight for a beautiful stone chess set in the far corner by the window. The "black" pieces were actually a dark green malachite; the "white," a faintly rose-colored marble. Several chess books were stacked helter-skelter on an adjoining table, some open, some stuffed with papers covered with handwritten notations.

The rest of us settled at a card table near the center of the room and proceeded to draw cards. His Lordship and I were partners. To my left, his back to the window, was Stephen, who dealt. Marian was to my right. Stephen turned the card to reveal the trump suit, which was hearts, and play commenced around the table. I was drowsy from the large breakfast and had trouble concentrating.

Over Lord Randolph's right shoulder I could see Hector analyzing his chess opening. Over his left shoulder I could see a goldfish bowl across the room, illuminated by a bright lamp that stood above it. The bowl contained water but no fish that I could perceive from this distance. However, an array of painted rocks (could they be gems?) sent out a multitude of colors in the brilliant light. Whenever his Lordship played a card, he would first hunch up his shoulders in such a way that he partially blocked my view of the glass bowl. He gave me a meaningful look while playing, silently trying to signal his intention with respect to my play in turn. Often he caught me staring off, looking at the bowl of rocks. At first he sought to interpret this as some sort of signal on my part, but he quickly recognized it as an absence of attention and, clearing his throat, frowned at me.

Twice I clumsily dropped an extra card on the table while playing the intended card from my hand. In accordance with the rules, these were "called" and had to remain face up until they could be played. Although this was embarrassing, it only befuddled me rather than effecting greater concentration on the game.

After an hour of play dominated by strict silence, Marian and Stephen had won. I apologized to the table for what I felt was a lackadaisical performance on my part.

"Not at all—I'm rusty myself," said my partner in defeat, obviously disappointed.

Stephen excused himself and left the room. Marian wandered over to unobtrusively watch Hector move the chess pieces around. Lord Randolph packed his pipe and began talking. I pushed my chair back to have more legroom.

"You know, Alan, I don't bring just anyone up here. I am not a snob, but I do have a title, a bloody castle, a reputation, a successful theater. . ." (here he paused to light the pipe, puffing it with little popping sounds) "and an eye for talent."

As he talked I stared at the grayish blond hair which had receded to the crown of his head, leaving only cobwebby wisps floating above the pate.

"Despite my title I'm not the exclusive type. But neither do I waste my time with do-nothings and sluggards."

Marian looked over at me from near the chess table and smiled with encouragement. His Lordship drew on his pipe, then pointed the stem at me for emphasis; the mouthpiece bore tooth marks and was wet with saliva.

"Stephen has told me you write, and you proved last night on stage that you have a remarkable knack for improvisation and a natural dramatic flair— in short, an instinct for theatre! Of course, you haven't had the advantages of the well-born and have much to learn in the way of refinement; but a little genuine *naïveté* adds charm and allows fresh air into an otherwise stuffy clime."

He puffed his pipe thoughtfully, then came to a decision.

"I'd like to see more of your work. Perhaps I can commission something for the Theatre. Stephen tells me you've had a run-in with the State, and, well, there are limits to what we can do there, but you'll find that working in the theatre is an honorable profession with many fringe benefits."

Stephen came back into the room, carrying a book.

"I took the liberty, your Lordship, of browsing in the library."

"Built up over generations—all kinds of treasures in there. What did you turn up?"

"An old edition of *Tales of the Genii*. . ."

They moved off, talking and looking over the book with its lavish color plates. As an afterthought, to finish our one-sided discussion, his Lordship turned back to me and said "Anyway, Alan, give it some thought."

Hector was staring out the window, eyes fixed on a spot in the sky, left hand still poised on the Black King's Knight.

Marian had circled the room and received a cup of tea on a saucer from a servant stationed outside the door. She came back and sat at the card table. As she did so, the sun came from behind a cloud and a great shaft of light fell directly on the table between us. I watched as she took the slice of lemon that was on her saucer and squeezed it over the cup. When the points of the yellow crescent came together between her fingers, the crushed fruit released its juice into the mahogany red tea with an audible squirt. Illuminated by the sunlight, a fine spray filled the air like the mist from a lawn sprinkler, and tiny spots of yellow oil appeared on the paper where we had kept score. With an absent-minded look, Marian licked her fingers before touching them to the square of linen she held in her right hand. Then she looked at me, smiling.

"His Lordship really likes you! I knew you were one of us!"

Lifting the teacup to her mouth to take a sip, she leaned forward into the beam of light. Her eyes, still fixed on mine, were dazzling in the sun, the green irises sprinkled with tiny flecks of black and grey.

What was I to say? I had to think of something. This was my big chance! I had apparently been accepted by Lord Randolph and by Marian as well. It seemed like a golden opportunity of which I needed only to take advantage. But how?

A clock ticked somewhere in the room. Marian continued to look at me, smiling. I couldn't decide if she was just being friendly by nature or if she had some special interest in me.

"I don't know what to say," I confessed.

"*I know*." She said it very seriously, with understanding and a hint of sympathy.

Without another word, I stood up and walked out onto the balcony, which faced west. A stream ran down a hillside north of the chateau and through the garden. I must have stood there, leaning on the balustrade, for quite some time—perhaps an hour or more—squinting my eyes in the bright sun, admiring the grounds which sloped idly down to the forest, and thinking of nothing in particular. The balustrade was a high one that came up almost to my chest. I leaned on it with one forearm on top of the other, slightly hunched forward, so that my back began to ache and I stood up straight. My left palm and wrist were riddled with tiny indentations from the stone, which sparkled with flecks of quartz. Looking off to my left, I noticed some people standing in the driveway that led up to the main entrance. They were some distance away, but I could make out Stephen and Lord Randolph greeting some new guests who had arrived in a limousine. Stephen pointed in my direction and they all turned and waved. I waved back.

Seeing that some steps led from the balcony down to the lawn, I decided to stroll down. As I made my way through the garden I encountered a menagerie of hedge sculptures which I had not seen from the balcony. They were artistically executed representations of rather obscure animals, each having a name plate sticking into the little plot of cleared dirt surrounding them. There was an ibis (resembling a heron), a coati (similar to a raccoon), what would have been a huge version of a hyrax (shrew), and a great number of other odd creatures which looked only vaguely familiar and whose names I did not recognize. What I first took to be an ordinary though sparsely verdant shrub turned out to be a representation of a tree covered with little sculpted tree frogs. There was even a platypus leaning over a little pool of water. As I studied the latter I saw my reflection and remembered that I was trying to catch up to the other guests.

I emerged at last from the maze-like assortment of hedges and found myself at the gravel drive, which was composed of perfectly uniform pieces of a yellowish quartz, covered with a fine white powder. Looking off to the right I saw the drive stretch away a half mile or more before it disappeared into the forest. The sun was already near the treetops and it would soon be dusk. This was odd because it seemed that only an hour or two before, the sun had been at its height. Now it sent its beams sideways across the earth. I turned and followed the drive up to the entrance. Stephen and the others had gone on inside but the double doors stood wide open.

I reached the entrance, and once again the gargoyle leered down at me. The golden sunlight came through the trees and cast moving shadows over the stone figure—recreating the illusion of motion I had experienced upon our arrival the previous evening. I noticed for the first time that the gargoyle's face had monkey-like features that were nevertheless mockingly human. Most of the features were roughly hewn in the gray stone, but the eyes were chillingly lifelike. But what I found most striking—even disturbing—was the stark contrast between the potential action of the crouching subject and the rigidity of its substance.

As I stared at the creature some new lines of poetry came into my head:

> Frozen in the golden moment
> beyond the hall of time
> A sound is heard that calls us
> to be *outside.*

I'm not sure what this meant, but the words impressed themselves in my memory along with the grotesque image of the gargoyle.

Marian appeared in the doorway.

"I've caught you again, fascinated by that morbid relic! Come in and meet my cousin Felicity and her husband Geoffrey."

They were still exchanging pleasantries in the entrance hall when I stepped inside. Marian made the introductions.

"Geoffrey is Assistant Vice Chancellor of the Interior Department."

"I'm impressed."

The lights went out. Although the foyer was quite dark, it was still light outside, so we were not in complete darkness. A servant appeared immediately with a lamp and his Lordship led the way to the east wing.

We went into a large parlor where Hector was building a fire.

"Ah, Hector. A splendid fire as usual."

A line of servants followed us into the room and filled it with a great variety of lanterns, oil lamps, candles, and candelabras.

"Please, make yourselves comfortable. Perhaps the power failure will provide just the proper cozy atmosphere for our gathering."

The only furniture was an ottoman couch of unique design: the ornately carved padded arms curved off gracefully to form wings of gold. Otherwise, there was only a thick shag carpet scattered with a number of throw pillows—and another of Hector's recliners. The two ladies placed themselves on the couch and the men found spots on the comfortable pillows. Hector finished feeding the blaze and sat on his recliner, leaning forward to poke the fire.

"In case you're hungry, I've had the kitchen prepare us a little picnic," said Lord Randolph.

A servant handed out paper bags from a large basket. Each bag contained a sandwich in plastic wrap, some carrot sticks in a baggy, an apple, and a paper napkin.

"How charming!"

"Wonderful idea, your Lordship!"

The guests were unanimous in their approval.

Two servants then went around with trays of brown English ale in tall Pilsner glasses—in accordance with the latest fashion. When emptied, these would be replaced with fresh glasses throughout the evening.

As we ate, we took part in polite conversation of no substance. Afterwards, Lord Randolph suggested a divertissement.

"I know that a number of us are artists of one type or another—Marian's an actress; Hector, as you know, is retired from the theatre; Geoffrey does some writing on the side; Felicity paints; and young Alan, here, only last night had a notable success at the Theatre and is an aspiring writer. Such being the case, I propose that we each perform a recitation or reading for our evening's entertainment. What say you?"

There was general agreement, if some nervousness. Hector went to his room to get something to read. As soon as he had left the room, his Lordship spoke in a confidential tone:

"I'm worried about Hector. He has been acting strange lately, even by his own eccentric standards. For example, he has developed a kind of tic: he has great difficulty repressing a frightful snarl that comes to his face when he is not on guard. At times, you can glance at him when he has fallen into a silent reverie, and be nearly frightened out of the room by his threatening display of incisors.

"It all seems to have started last week with a telegram from his ex-wife. I am hoping our diversion will cheer him up. He misses theatre and loves to read his work. . ."

At this moment, Hector returned and made straight for his chair, in which he reclined and commenced staring at the ceiling.

"Very well," said our host, "who's first?"

Felicity spoke. "Geoffrey, why don't you recite that new poem you read to me in the limo?"

Geoffrey had been sitting on a pillow, leaning back against Felicity's knees, and she patted his shoulder to encourage him.

"Very well," he said, standing up. He crossed to the edge of the hearth and turned to address the room.

> Eternity, thine awful hands
> Might well adore a queen.
>
> Quick from the butcher;
> Bread for the porter;
> Chess with the peasant's dad.
>
> Insensitivity among the masses
> leads to conflict, misery.
> "I hate it! I'm leaving!"
>
> *Adieu.*

We applauded. Although Geoffrey's poem seemed weak, the game itself was enjoyable and the anticipation of our own turn was exciting. Marian went next, telling a little story or parable.

FLOWERS

There was a boy who, when he was very young, picked an imaginary flower and was told it was very beautiful. He wandered out into an imaginary field and continued to pick these flowers, which he clasped against his chest with his arms. For a long time he wandered around carrying these flowers and bending over to smell them and admire their beauty. No one else saw these flowers, but people saw him going around with his arms folded in such a way that a cat might jump into them. Finally, the boy realized that no one else saw the flowers and he threw them all down. He was left with nothing.

This was met with "Most intriguing!" and "Very symbolic." Felicity said "How sad."

Hector brought his recliner into its upright position. We all looked at him sympathetically because of what Lord Randolph had said. Producing a slip of paper from his coat pocket, he began to read while still seated.

HUSSERL'S FIRE

Husserl was a man who said that the tree in the mind cannot burn.

But I tell you that the bush has caught fire and is burning, reducing to ash all semblance of order. For what is the order that is, except the order of the rain, the patter of feet, or the order of the clock—made to order, made to tick. And what makes it tick? Gears turned by a tightened spring that unwinds its length, uncoils its circulinear motion through the fluttering wings of the fly-wheel: turning, caught/held, spinning, stopping on a dime, a cent, a measure, stopping at the line drawn between the measure and the measured...

Here he stopped, ending on a rising intonation but signaling completion by folding the paper and putting it away. There was a polite smattering of applause, but the group was hardly receptive. This was attributable, I thought, to their lack of comprehension. I, for one, considered Hector quite talented and thought his piece the best, but I felt restrained from saying so. (I also happened to know, as perhaps the others did not, that Edmund Husserl was an important modern philosopher and founder of the school or method of phenomenology.)

It was my turn. I opened the thermos which stored my writings and pulled out a sheet of paper at random. I stood up and read it to the group.

DOWN THE HALL

Down the hall there is a room. The room is filled with stacks of books and papers, and with file cabinets and cardboard boxes probably full of the same. There is also a bed, chest of drawers, and night table. It is a bedroom with no one in it.

On the night stand is a radio. The radio is always on, set at low volume. It fills the room with sound—with voices, with music. The sound also spills out of the room and travels down the hall.

Inside the radio there are various electric and electronic devices that receive the radio waves and transform them into signals. The signals are processed and transformed into electromagnetic pulses. These pulses are transformed to kinetic waves by way of a magnet suspended on a thin cone of paper. The paper cone vibrates and creates the sound that fills the room and the hallway all day and night.

I am the vibrating cone.

The response was one of delirious enthusiasm. Certainly, I felt that my writing was good, even fresh, but not worthy of such a to-do. To be honest, I thought they were carried away by their own enthusiasm. After I received a series of lengthy accolades from all present (excepting Hector), Stephen, Felicity, and his Lordship declined to read.

We passed the remainder of the evening drinking beer and discussing the upcoming season at the Theatre. From time to time, someone would bring up my phrase "I am the vibrating cone," and a new round of praise and admiration would start. His Lordship mentioned commissioning me to write something for the stage, stating it with pride like the announcement of a signed contract, which at once flattered and embarrassed me. Everyone cheered and indicated that they looked forward to the finished product.

Hector seemed aloof, possibly jealous of the attention I was getting. I think we all were on the lookout for the "snarl" which his brother had described, but which never appeared. Gradually, as the evening wore on and the beer increasingly took effect, we spent more and more time silently staring into the fire—except for Hector, who reclined and stared upwards when he was not tending the fire.

When we retired to our rooms, I found a strangely carved wooden box on my dresser. It seemed to be a Chinese puzzle box, but no matter how I turned it or tugged at it, it stubbornly refused to open. Exasperated, I slammed it down on the dresser, whereupon it popped open. Inside was the odd crystal pyramid, now clearly transparent and sitting like a jewel on the Bordeaux-colored crêpe lining. But who had placed it in the box? And why?

On a whim, I picked the crystal up and held it to my right eye. Looking through it, I was astonished to perceive Hector sitting at a table in the center of his bedroom! *The pyramid was allowing me to look into other rooms of the castle!*

Intimations of Unreality

As I watched, Hector stopped writing and looked up as if distracted by a sudden thought. Then he pushed back his chair and began pacing the room spiritedly. He spoke aloud and I heard his words clearly:

"It has just occurred to me that the more one speaks, the more one will be able to say. However, if one speaks too much, one will channel all of one's thoughts into verbal expression and so neglect more and more the pen. Nevertheless, it seems to me to be a good mental exercise to speak (and speak at length) on any and all manner of topics, including the topic of speech itself. And so, I speak to myself; since it is clearly easier to converse with oneself than with another—little need be explained, no misunderstandings arise, and so on and so on."

At this point in his pacing Hector had arrived at the door. Opening it quietly but rapidly, he surprised a servant standing in the hall, staring at him, obviously having been listening to his monologue.

"'You're mad!'" Said Hector reflexively—anticipating the servant's judgment—and slammed the door. Always eccentric, he was now clearly going downhill.

The pyramid fogged over and I put it back into the box. As soon as my fingers left the remarkable stone, the box's lid snapped shut.

Chapter Six
A New Theory

I slept late the next morning. Surprised that no one had been sent to wake me, I hurriedly gathered my things from the dresser and failed to notice the absence of the mysterious carved box. Downstairs I was met by Thomas.

"Good morning, Mr. Wilcox. I am to inform you that his Lordship's guests have all gone riding into the north hills. Mr. Hampton" (he referred to Hector) "did not accompany them and is presently at table in the south dining hall. Do you wish to join Mr. Hampton, or shall I send for a horse?"

"I should prefer to take some breakfast," I said, managing a haughty elocution worthy of the leisure class.

"Very good, sir. Right this way."

I had not been into the south wing before, having seen only the parlor on the first night. The long central hall was embellished with old, dusty paintings that were intriguing but hard to see due to the darkness and the brisk pace set by Thomas. One painting seemed to illustrate a Carthaginian scene from *Salammbô*, complete with armored elephants and soldiers at a feast. Interspersed between the paintings there was an occasional alcove whose shadows hid such treasures as an old wrought iron astrolabe, a mediaeval crossbow, various antique and bejeweled objects, an alien astrograph showing a constellation not of this earth . . . Things that didn't quite add up.

I could not see for sure but I suspected that the shadows also hid untold layers of dust. It even occurred to me that this might explain the swift gait of the butler. Whether one lives in a cottage or a castle one doesn't want one's guests to discover untidiness—nor, perhaps, hidden treasures.

We reached the dining room and Thomas announced me. Hector, caught off-guard, displayed both surprise and pleasure at having me join him. He removed his spectacles and set aside his newspaper.

"So, you don't fancy horseback riding?"

"Not on an empty stomach," I said, then feared it might sound presumptuous coming from a guest.

"Ah, yes—uh, Thomas, would you have the cook prepare our guest some. . ." he turned to me "some pancakes?"

"That would be fine!" I said. Thomas turned and left through a side door.

Hector continued: "Still, you must see the grounds sometime; they're extensive—and quite lovely."

After we had dispensed with such formalities, I expressed my high opinion of his writings—or what little of them he had recited. This flattery delighted him. As I ate a stack of buckwheat pancakes slathered with fresh butter and Mayan honey, Hector recounted his involvement with the theatre and writing. His voice was tinged with sadness as if speaking of fallen glory. At the same time, his eyes were both softly warm and hypnotic in their power.

"It began in childhood. I took joy in coordinating the interactions of other children, including young Randal." He referred to Lord Randolph by his Christian name.

"I invented games in which historic adventures were reenacted—the conquests of Alexander, the exploration of the Amazon, cowboys and Indians—you get the idea. In nobler moments, I directed them in the performance of select scenes from the great classics—*Agamemnon, Prometheus Bound, The Birds.*"

I helped myself to a second cup of coffee from the service on the table. Stirring it before slowly adding the cream, I watched the white swirl into the black to form caramel brown. I was conspicuously directing my attention toward the coffee in order to create some "distance" from Hector's powerful eyes as he talked, but the act proved too artificial to maintain.

"At college," Hector continued, "I acted and won honors, but I also began to write. Of course, I had written poems as a child—Romantic nonsense, mainly. Now I wrote plays inspired by Ionesco, Beckett, Pirandello. But I wanted to go beyond! I wanted to break new ground, to push it *further*—"

He was becoming animated; but, seeing that I had finished my meal, he broke off his narrative and invited me to his study. This room was situated between the south dining hall and parlor where the readings had taken place the previous evening, so we had to traverse the long hallway to reach it. Although I stole furtive glances at the paintings and odd objects filling the shadowy alcoves as we passed, I did not dare to disrupt Hector's speech with questions as to their puzzling nature.

The study was oblong and surprisingly narrow. It almost seemed like an extra space, left over when the walls were put up, as if the rooms on either side for some reason failed to meet each other as planned. It was furnished with a roll top desk with chair at one end, under the window, and two easy chairs midway along one wall separated by a round end table covered with books. In one of these I sat, as indicated by Hector. Along the facing wall a bookshelf rose from floor to ceiling, stretching a dozen or more feet toward the end of room. There must have been close to a thousand volumes, paperback and hardback alike.

"You seem to have quite an extensive collection," I said.

"All fiction, poetry, drama, literary theory. . ." Hector said, still standing, eyeing the shelves. He seemed to sway, torn between his original intention to sit down and a competing attraction to go to the shelf and pick out this book or that as his eyes roamed over the titles. Finally he stepped over to the nearest shelf and placed his hand affectionately on the spines. "Yes, I've spent years—a lifetime—exploring the worlds upon worlds enclosed in these pages."

He suddenly seemed old, standing there stooped, almost infirm and senile. Turning around, his eyes lighted on the wall to the right of my chair. I turned and leaned forward to see a small cabinet or bookcase suspended midway along the wall, enclosed by doors made of glass and lead from which a key protruded. There were perhaps thirty books on the two narrow shelves.

"*This*," he said, stepping over to the case, "This is something special. It contains the complete works of André Breton—the so-called founder of surrealism—including may rare first editions."

He turned the key in the lock and removed it, placing it in his pocket.

"I'm saving them for a future time, for a time when I have the ability, the insight, the strength—most of all, the courage—to read them."

All this time he spoke as if addressing the books themselves. Now he turned toward me.

"*He's a modern alchemist*," he said with great seriousness. "*In every sense of the word.*"

He glanced at the case again, longingly, and then stepped past me and finally took his seat.

"Now, where was I? Toward the end of my college years, as I have said, I sought to make the transition from director and actor to writer. Unfortunately, my attempts at writing resulted only in failure. I tried piece after piece, but nothing succeeded. My work was not understood, not appreciated, and therefore ignored. At least, I had hoped it would be controversial enough to capture some attention. Nothing! So I gave it up."

"No!"

"Oh, I have continued to write, I daresay—" he indicated the roll top desk to his left, its cubbyholes jammed with papers—"but only for myself."

"There was also Randal's successes as producer, which far eclipsed my own efforts. He was a natural, moved well in the right circles and so on, gained his title, bought the Theatre—you know the rest."

I had been wondering why Randal bore the title of Baron when Hector was clearly the elder of the two, perhaps in his mid-sixties while his Lordship was in his early fifties or late forties. Apparently the title was not inherited but acquired by some other means.

Silence ensued. Hector had reached the end of his tale, which left him in a state of surrender and defeat. I felt I should say something to counter his despondency. But what?

"But your writing, I think, shows continued promise. I feel that I understand 'where you're coming from,' as they say."

This encouraged him greatly. Although he seemed to lack no conviction in his own work, he was disillusioned by the absence of any response from others. My comment not only cheered him up visibly but also succeeded in launching him into a monologue on his aesthetic theory. He described it as "a kind of anti-formalist automatism tempered by socialist symbolism," but he emphatically denied being either an absurdist or an anarchist. The word "socialist" seemed peculiarly out of place in our privileged surrounds, but I said nothing.

"I find great meaning in everything—including the random. So-called random events reveal new connections between things."

He extended his philosophy of art to the aesthetics of thought itself, arguing how it was necessary "to break out of old molds of thinking" and to "rediscover the art of creative thinking" known to only a handful of illuminati of the past.

Here he paused, then, possessed of some demonic energy, bolted from his chair and, in a single, continuous movement, paced back and forth across the room at such a rate of speed that he was practically running. Having walked once up and once back along the vermilion carpet, he stopped in front of his desk and stared wildly out the window for a few moments. Then he crossed back over and flung himself into the arm chair, which creaked under the strain. His actions had been so unprecedented, so energetic, so smooth in execution, that I was dumbfounded.

"As I was saying," he said abruptly, "the clearest avenue of escape is to deny altogether the concept of mental boundaries—of avenues. In the city, flight is only possible along the avenues, as there are—or at least appear to be—solid, substantial buildings which block the way and help define the avenues. But what, in the mind, is permanent among thought-forms, to block the free play of awareness or imagination?"

He paused and looked at me, but I could see that the thoughts were still racing through his brain. It took me a few seconds to catch up with him, then I countered his point thusly:

"But if thought is a subtle yet actual form of matter, somehow involving the brain cells and their biochemical activity, then physical limitations are not only imaginable but necessary. For example, to remember an idea or an action might involve an actual impression on the surface of the brain, a track or path which, when gone over repeatedly, mechanically, habitually, becomes a rut, so that the mind is limited in its movements. What do you say to that?"

Hector considered it. "Perhaps to think of thought in this way is to actually direct the impression of thought-forms upon the brain tissue, so that thinking in terms of ruts creates the ruts actually!"

"In that case," I replied, "the well-worn avenues of thought are as actual as those running between city buildings. And, anyway, it may be that memory and thought *do* involve markings on the brain—regardless of whether we think of them as such."

"Well," he said, "the response to that is simply this: All that you have said involves thinking with very limited and delimited metaphors, which govern the movement of thought's inquiry by representing things in particular, limited ways. Take that photograph as an example." He pointed to a framed portrait standing amidst the clutter of his desk.

"It's a picture of my ex-wife Alma. I detest her and yet I love her—but that is another story. You may ask, 'How good a picture is this?' Well, the degree of accuracy of the image depends on the level of visual information contained in the photograph which is also contained in the thing itself (in this case, Alma). In the same way, ideas under examination will yield only such information as is built into them, as it were. But if you come only this far and continue to reflect only upon thought's ordinary limitations, then you ever increase the reality of those limits. To halt thought and look at its form, its structure—and therefore its limits, its defining edges—is *necessarily* to limit it; whereas if the form of a thought is forgotten, it will develop on its own, unabated by memory. And as the form of the thought is free to develop, so will its content develop in new and unpredictable ways, bending the form as needed for that thought or meaning to exist."

Intimations of Unreality

He saw that I was not convinced and decided to give another example.

"Alan, do you recall the gargoyle above the entrance to the front hall?"

"Why, yes. I found it . . . fascinating."

"Yes, isn't it? And does it not seem to defy the edict of Michelangelo, whereby the artist finds the subject of the sculpture lying hidden in the stone and merely uses his tools to free it? On the contrary, in this case the gargoyle's spirit was somehow captured in stone by the artist and seeks to regain its own freedom. Thus by its very nature, motion overcomes stillness, form overcomes substance, and spirit overcomes matter."

The concept finally dawned on me.

"In other words," I said, "form can be freed from the matter that contains it—and that's the task of the artist."

"Precisely!"

"And you are also saying that thought itself, as form, can be freed from the limitations of matter?"

"That's it! In my view, anyway."

I beamed with understanding and admiration.

"Now, remember—I said I was 'anti-formal,' but we are using the word *form* to imply spirit or essence, not Aristotle's *material form*."

My understanding was again thrown into shadow.

At this moment, Lord Randolph stepped into the room. "Sorry to interrupt, old boy, but your ex-wife is on the telephone."

"Well, speak of the devil. . ." Hector sighed heavily and left. I stood up.

"There you are, Alan," said Marian, coming in with Stephen. "You missed a glorious morning! We had an invigorating ride."

The three of them were still wearing their riding outfits, now somewhat dusty. The smell of their leather Wellington boots filled the air, along with the faint but distinct odor of horses. Geoffrey and Felicity appeared briefly outside the door, glancing over Marian's shoulders; but seeing how crowded the room was becoming, they mumbled something and moved off.

"I'm sorry I missed out," I said. "I must apologize for rising so late this morning. However, I have been having a fascinating conversation with Hector about his theory of aesthetics."

"Don't listen to him," Lord Randolph admonished, to my surprise.

"But—I thought he made a lot of sense."

"Certainly, in some aspects Hector's theory is coherent," said his Lordship. "It states the problem and tries to move away from the causes. But it amounts to simply rejecting the status quo. If we have become stagnant, we must move; but in what direction? Without knowing our direction, we may be going backwards or . . . into a worse trap."

I must have appeared crestfallen. Lord Randolph changed his tone.

"The true nature of revolution, my boy, must be positive—not merely overturning the existing order, which leads to chaos."

Marian spoke. "If I may, I think we can all agree that we are not seeking the merely random. Nor do we propose plain contradiction and destruction of the given. Rather, as artists and individuals what we are aiming for is *a transmutation in the depths.*"

Her pregnant statement gave us pause.

Marian added other intelligent, positive comments such as: "We are more than just animals, and art proves it," and, "Through art and culture, we rise above our bodies and enter the realm of ideas. That's where the real magic takes place."

Stephen chimed in with the statement that "Through art, we have the opportunity to transmute daily life to the level of . . . the sublime."

Thoughts expressed in such elegant phrases were flying so fast it was hard to keep up with them. At this moment, Thomas appeared at the door. Lord Randolph went over to speak to him, then excused himself.

Stephen resumed: "I think this subject can be summed up in one word: *power.* The artist is a conduit for power or energy. Good work in any medium contains the element of power in good measure. We are not denying that in destroying old forms a definite energy is released—just as in splitting the atom; but the task of the artist must be ultimately productive: to channel this energy into the creation of something new."

All of this made sense, but I could not reconcile it with the sense that Hector had made.

Lord Randolph returned.

"Hector has gone for a walk. But another call came in. Marian, you'll be pleased to hear that your aunt, the Lady Falgren, is coming for dinner and is bringing some guests, including our old friend Lord Ficksure."

Marian was all bubbly with excitement. But I was preoccupied. I said I wanted to go to my room "to take a look at my writings," although I really just needed time think.

"We'll call you down before dinner," said Marian.

Chapter Seven
The UFO from Brazil

I sat at the small writing desk in my room in the castle. Beside me was the silver thermos that had faithfully followed me from Brickshire. I twisted off the lid and poured the rolled-up sheaf of papers out on the desk. Flipping through my writings, I was plagued by doubts about the direction of my work: What was my direction? What was my "philosophy of art?" Or was my writing directed by an encompassing philosophy at all?

Reflecting on the different viewpoints held by Hector and Lord Randolph only added to my confusion. To me, Hector seemed to point a way to freedom; but his Lordship warned against anarchy. Marian and Stephen appeared ready to side with his Lordship against Hector, though Marian seemed sympathetic to my awkward middle position and hinted that an alternative approach was possible which would combine aspects of both perspectives.

I sifted through the crumpled papers, some of them typed, some marked in ink, all with my name in the upper right corner. With a wave of anxiety I remembered my deadline with the Tax men. My body shivered, as with fever, and my stomach became queasy. The marked physicality of this response drew my attention, made me wonder why I gave such *weight* to the deadline and its consequences. Why did it worry me so? Should I bother with it at all? Maybe writing was not my proper calling; maybe I would never produce anything of importance. True, I had received a positive response from the theatre crowd, and from the guests at the castle; but I felt that it was for the wrong reasons. I was not getting the results I intended. While Hector received no attention but continued to write for himself, I was discouraged by unwarranted attention and was tempted to abandon art altogether!

With a sigh I rolled the papers back up and put them away in the thermos. As I did so a flash of light from the open window caught my eye and I went over to look out. The days had grown short and the sun was already near the horizon. The glow of the sunset was a churning, ruby red, and clouds blowing from the west rose like smoke billowing from a gigantic blaze. I looked past the castle grounds to the forest stretching west towards town. A pond or small lake hidden among the pines caught the sunlight and shone so brightly it was difficult to look at. Everywhere there was a stillness—permeating the woods, the grounds, the air. But what had caused the flash?

For some reason, I ducked my head out the window and looked up. There was something directly above me in the sky which at first glance I thought was the moon—a sliver of pale silver in the clear blue sky. I caught only a glimpse because it was difficult to look at, being directly overhead, and I had craned my neck until my throat ached trying to see it. So I withdrew back into the room, turned around, and, gripping the window frame firmly, sat on the windowsill and looked up along the castle wall at the sky.

I could not believe what I now saw clearly. *It was an immense prism hovering miles above the earth!* It was as transparent as glass, its crystal white edges barely perceptible against the blue sky—visible only where it reflected the sun. I say it was a prism because the crescent-shaped light shining off one triangular facet changed to a rainbow of color at the edge. It was the most marvelous thing I had ever seen—but what was it? I stared in awe for some time when my throat again began to ache again from craning backward.

As I sat looking up *an earthquake rocked the castle* and I nearly toppled out of the window. It was a powerful jolt followed by several minutes of continuous rumbling. Even though the stone castle was built on bedrock it seemed to slide to and fro. Fortunately, I held on tight until I could slip back inside the room, where I crouched in safety.

The earthquake stopped. Taking no chances, I braced myself against the window frame again before gazing down from the height of two tall stories. I would not have survived the fall to the marble walk below. Another flash caught my eye and I looked toward the horizon.

There was a flying saucer above the forest!

The UFO zipped by and was quickly pursued by two silver Air Force jets. There followed a third, darker aircraft that flew almost as nimbly as the saucer and made no sound. In contrast the jets roared by, only a hundred feet or so above the ground. I wanted to run and tell someone what I had seen, but

I didn't want to miss any of the action. The UFO kept flitting around over the forest, making impossible turns to evade the jets, which did their best to maintain their swift pursuit. I was thrilled by the magic and technological mastery of the whole display! But I wondered what to make of the strange black craft that joined the familiar jets in their chase. Was it some secret Air Force experiment? It was smaller than a normal jet, had shorter wings, and was more spherical—more like the saucer.

The saucer flew directly over the castle and I waved at it, rooting it on as it toyed with the jets. Forgetting myself, I leaned out of the window and watched it circle back. It had seen me! As it flew up from the left, over trees and garden, the shiny metal skin of the saucer reflected the colors of the sunset, with lustrous peach and garish orange. Inexplicably, as the saucer approached *it transformed itself into a taxicab!* It pulled up a few feet from the window and hovered in mid-air: the UFO was offering me a ride!

No one sat in the driver's seat of the orange cab, but there were two passengers in the front and two more in the back. Not alien in the least, they were people just like me. They motioned to me silently but urgently to hurry up. The opportunity to join them in the incredible craft was too great to pass up, so I quickly ducked inside and ran to the dresser. The pyramid in the box was not to be seen, but my green transfer ticket was there and I grabbed it along with my thermos, which I slung over my shoulder before climbing out of the window and onto a little ledge.

The cab pulled closer and I climbed on top, holding onto the chrome luggage rack. We immediately sped off again. We cleared the forest in no time and were above the suburbs just east of town. I held on tight and watched the trees, houses, and streets pass below us. Despite the precariousness and strangeness of my situation, I was not afraid, for the wind was refreshing and the view exhilarating. Nevertheless, I felt I should get inside, so I made my way over to the passenger side of the cab.

As I leaned over the side, I saw lettering painted on the cab door. It was difficult to read upside down and appeared to be in Spanish. It was also partially covered in dust and grime, but I could make out the letters "V-I-S-T-A" or "V-I-S-I-T-A." It occurred to me that this flying car might not be a "cab" at all but could belong to the police force of a Spanish-speaking country. Taped above the window was an old inventory tag that read "Hold for

Sgt. T——" followed by a last name and phone number. I wanted to memorize the name and number, for I felt there was a mystery to be solved here, but the writing was partially worn away and illegible.

At this time the taxi touched down and we were driving down the highway. After I climbed through the window and sat down in the front seat, I was greeted by a man in black who introduced himself as Miguel. He had moved over to give me his seat, and the man to his left, named Jose, took the driver's seat. Miguel then introduced me to the man in the back, named Fernandez. Oddly, he did not introduce the woman who sat behind me and whom I could not see. They all seemed friendly (if somewhat nervous), looked Hispanic, and spoke English with Spanish accents.

The car alternately flew through the air and drove on the pavement, weaving through traffic and flying over it. Miguel and Fernandez wore hats but Jose, the driver, was bareheaded and balding. He actually looked sort of Italian. All of the men wore mustaches. By talking to each of them in turn I gathered that their flying saucer stunt was designed "to lure tourists to Brazil." The flying cab, they said, belonged to the Magdalena Cab Company of Sao Paulo. They showed me several envelopes containing free tickets, coupons, etc., of value to potential tourists.

Turning at last to the woman, I asked "And who are you?" She looked familiar. Could it be? Yes, it was Alma! I recognized her from Hector's photograph, but for some reason she did not give her name.

"This vehicle belongs to my father, who is—" she broke off when she saw the green transfer which I still gripped in my hand. "I cannot tell you. Quickly! There is no time to explain things . . . Here is what we must do: You must drive."

I tried to decline but she insisted. With great difficulty, I changed places with Miguel and then with Jose. I drove, though without self-assurance, so they encouraged me. When we were coming up on a sharp curve around a mountainside, the breaks began to fail and we picked up speed. Someone said "Don't worry, just drive through the barrier," referring to the high guardrail and implying that we could fly for a while. But someone else said, "No, we'd better not." From the corner of my eye I saw Miguel reaching into the glove compartment. I concentrated on my driving and handled the curve

Intimations of Unreality

around the mountain. The road continued south and it dawned on me that we were heading towards Brazil!

After a while, I said I was tired and Jose took the wheel. At Alma's suggestion, I awkwardly climbed into the back seat between Alma and Fernandez. Miguel switched on the radio and turned the knob until he found some salsa. The music was interrupted by a news bulletin:

The Air Defense was kept busy this afternoon by a flying saucer seen over the forest east of the city. According to a number of eye-witnesses, two jets scrambled to intercept the unidentified flying object and pursued it for several minutes. Conflicting reports said the UFO looked like a taxicab rather than a flying saucer. There was no comment from the Defense Department. . .

Night fell. I became drowsy and must have nodded. Alma placed a small pillow behind my head and I leaned back on it. From this position, I could look up and out the rear window. I watched telephone poles and power lines fly by while high above the stars stood still. At one point I thought I saw the giant prism again, but it was just a reflection on the glass. I dozed off.

I awoke when the car pulled off the highway. We had arrived at a tower-like structure set on a hilltop above the road. On the outside, it looked like an old Norman castle consisting of a single round tower. Inside, there were stone steps leading up to an open area where a great banquet had been laid.

Besides the buffet, there was a main dining table and several smaller round tables, all covered with fine linen, antique silver, and elaborate centerpieces. It was very much like a wedding reception, except that the large hall was only sparsely lit by candles on the tables and by mediaeval torches suspended in cressets along the wall.

Following the example of my companions, I got a plate and filled it from the buffet. Then the five of us sat alone at the main table. There were guests at other tables, but not many.

All I remember about the food was that it was much too salty. As we ate, Miguel and Fernandez again drew out their packets of tickets and coupons, spreading them out on the table and telling me about the great bargains to be had by travelers to their country. To placate them I examined a packet, but by reading the fine print I found that the coupon which promised a full fare ticket only amounted to $5.46 off the regular fare. Other coupons offered small discounts but were worthless unless more money was spent by the tourist.

My companions seemed secretive but were evidently trying to entice me back to their country. This uncomfortable feeling and the bogus quality of the coupons increased my suspicions. There had to be more than a publicity stunt behind the flying saucer/cab—it was too elaborate, costly, and technically advanced. I could not imagine what the ulterior motive might be—though Alma had reacted strangely when she saw my green transfer, and all of them seemed to eye my thermos with interest.

I turned to Alma and said straight out that she looked exactly like the woman in the photograph at Castle Randolph. She seemed embarrassed but admitted that she was indeed Hector's ex-wife.

"He is a pig!" she said summarily.

She also revealed that she had been in the audience at the Great Green Theatre. "You know, we could use a talent such as yours in our Department of Tourism."

Thus their trump card was played (though some mysteries remained) and Miguel saluted me with a toast: "To our new Creative Consultant!" he raised his eyebrow to make it into a question.

I said nothing, but thereby appeared to accept their offer. They were all smiles, drinking toast after toast of red wine and insisting that I drink with them. I was getting giddy with the wine and finally said "I'll have to think it over." This did not deter them and they simply redoubled their toasts.

Miguel was getting blasted. He was grinning uncontrollably under his bushy black mustache, his face was red, and his eyes glinted mischievously.

"If I may say so, sir, you have 'dandy' inclinations," he said to me in a challenging tone. "I think you have been hanging around your highborn friends too long."

"Miguel!" Alma protested.

"They are all pigs!" he shouted at her angrily. Then he regained his poise.

"The style that is implied is outmoded by fashion and history," he said with mocking erudition. "It is in fact inhumane, insofar as aristocracy is a self-perpetuating elite that enjoys privileges at the expense of the masses, the basic needs of many, and even the death of some unfortunates."

His proposition was so definitive it was beyond question. So Fernandez merely objected: "But Mr. Wilcox, here, is wise enough to know this—better than they."

Miguel ignored him, assured of the validity of his doctrine. "In matters of taste, they use the excuse that only the nobility can protect the values of haute couture. That's a circular argument—only the rich can afford the best education and the leisure time to refine their tastes."

"They think they are so much better!" Jose spoke for the first time.

"And by their standards, they are!" said Miguel bitterly. "They come from 'good breeding' and are well trained to keep everything within their little circle."

I said nothing at first, but started thinking about whether so-called "good breeding" could actually be genetic as well as cultural. "You speak of their breeding as if they were dogs. . ."

"Hah!" all three of the men guffawed.

"Gentlemen!" Alma complained, "you will make Mr. Wilcox think we are revolutionaries."

They fell silent.

"Actually, we are only trying to help our country's economy enough to help bring about the proposed land reforms," she said.

Miguel assumed his devilish look again as he fingered his wineglass.

"Revolutionary—no," he said. "*Evolutionary*, yes. But your aristocrats are *counter*-evolutionary!"

Alma sighed. She gave up trying to contain him.

"No, Señor," he continued, "they are not pigs or dogs. They are *apes*. Let me spell it out for you: A-P-E—Aesthetics tied to Politics and Economics. For that is how they come to control everything, from ownership to way of life to values.

"Are *you* an ape, Señor?"

Alma may have gasped slightly.

"Uh, no—I don't believe so." If I were not so pleasantly intoxicated, I might have responded differently. Besides, I was not without sympathy for Miguel's position.

"No one is highborn—we are all apes!" He said it almost in a spirit of defeat.

No one said anything for a moment. Then I spoke:

"These are issues which cannot be resolved at this table."

This did not seem to help matters, only to spread Miguel's sense of defeat to the others. So, to cheer them up, I offered:

"It is true that 'we are all apes'—by birth. But as you say, we are a product of evolution, which means always going forward. . ."

"Yes!" Miguel said, his eyes lighting up.

"And so, we evolve into human beings, and perhaps beyond. . ."

"Yes, Señor, it is so!" Now his eyes glistened with emotion.

Now Alma felt she could safely endorse Miguel's critique: "But you see, Alan, our individual development is thwarted by economic and political oppression. How can we grow if we have no freedom to control our own lives— if we cannot even obtain the basic essentials of life? Therefore, we need an artistic and cultural revolution—or evolution—to create a new vision: a positive image of the potential of everyone, not just of the few who are 'properly cultivated.'"

Her point was crystal clear. And it glorified, in my mind, the role and the responsibility of the artist, renewing my faith in my own calling.

"Yes, Alma. I think you're right. The artist is crucial to this evolution, providing vision and guidance which the politician and the economist cannot provide."

Miguel, Fernandez, and Jose simultaneously raised their glasses, cheered, and said something in Spanish or Portuguese; then we all clinked glasses. Suddenly they all felt they could trust me, be at ease around me, and there was a warm sense of friendship among us all.

I don't remember how I got to bed, for we drank until it was very late. But I do recall the following dream: I was wondering through desolate countryside, barefoot, with my dog—an Irish wolfhound named Wizard. At first we followed a road through sandy, arid terrain. We had no water and both Wizard and I were getting very thirsty. There were no farms or houses in sight, so we left the road and began walking toward a distant ridge. The sun was parching but we had to keep going.

Wizard began to whine and I knelt down beside him. I held his head in my hands and looked him in the eye. "Don't worry, boy, we'll find some water soon." He kind of whined and growled at the same time and had a wild glint in his eyes. I could see the conflict between his loyalty to me as his "master" and his bestial thirst for my blood as the only substitute for water. This is when I realized the urgency of our situation.

We pushed on and at last reached the top of the ridge. A grassy plain stretched beyond, straight to the horizon. Almost immediately upon walking further on this plain or field, we found water—first a mud puddle or two, then a great deal of fresh water standing in furrows between rows of tall grass. As I walked in the water I felt with my bare feet the pipes of the irrigation system that supplied the field.

When I awoke from this dream, I felt feverish and sweaty. Looking around, I found myself in a strange bed. The sheets were scraps of old carpet; the blanket was a large piece of olive green canvas, folded back on the bed and covered with dark oil stains. Pushing back the covers, I realized I was fully dressed except for my shoes. No wonder I felt so hot! Then I remembered the UFO, the Brazilians, and the banquet of salty food and red wine.

The carpet covering the floor was thick, with long shags of fiber. Walking on it, I sensed something disturbing about the fabric that made up its surface. It seemed to be goat hair. The tufts were so thick and layered so irregularly that the surface was difficult to walk on and hurt my feet.

I made my way to the far side of the room and tried the door. It was locked but the door was flimsy and gave a little when I pulled on it. What I had thought was an oddity of design was an oddity of construction; for rather than being of wood, the door was composed of scores of plastic lids from kitchen storage bowls.

First the bed was weird, then the carpet, and now the door. I wondered if I wasn't having another dream. I considered forcing the door but did not want to offend my hosts by causing any damage. Even if they had locked me in this room, I assumed they had good reason for doing so.

I looked for a window and saw one perched high up near the ceiling in the left corner of the room. It was beyond reach from the floor, so I climbed up on the chest of drawers and reached up to grip the decorative molding which ran along the wall two feet below the ceiling. It was difficult going, but I managed to inch my way along the wall toward the window by clinging to the molding with my fingertips. Various patches of the wall were covered with wallpaper, newsprint, a thin veneer coated with gum arabic, posters of poor Rembrandt imitations, and so forth. There was even an unused ticket to the ALL STAR Game.

At last I reached the window. It was a four-pane glass window. The frames were dark wood, well varnished. The glass was tinged a delicate blue but I could not see beyond it (from this angle, there would have been nothing but dark sky). Small bubbles of air were trapped in the glass of one of the panes. Resting my head on my shoulder, I studied the bubbles up close with my left eye. Some of the bubbles were simple spheres; others were distorted, twisted, stretched pockets of air which vaguely resembled figures from popular culture. I assailed the window with all my ferocity but it refused to budge.

Now what? Still clinging to the molding, I surveyed the room and spied an air vent near the ceiling, on the opposite wall. But how to reach it? The molding continued on around the room, and though my fingers ached terribly, I figured it was the best means to the vent. I continued with care. A nail emerged from a point on the ceiling and dangled a wad of dust from a span of cobweb. Another nail emerged a little further away.

As soon as I turned the corner, the molding tore loose from the wall then collapsed and I swung down and smashed through the door. Round and square lids flew everywhere, bouncing in slow motion and rolling in all directions down a great hallway. I slid out of control on my back along the polished stone floor of the hall, gasping and flailing my arms madly. Fast approaching sharp-edged steps leading down, I flung myself by great effort upon the slick stone balustrade and rode the rail downstairs and straight into another long corridor. This time sliding in a standing position, I felt confident of imminent escape. Suddenly I burst through a set of oaken doors and into certain freedom. But just when I thought I was getting somewhere, I was back in the room from which I had started!

Before me was the door made of lids, fully intact and still locked. Looking behind me, I saw nothing but a solid wall behind the bed. If my experience at the window and door had been a strange dream, how could I be sure it was over? The drudgery seemed endless. Should I crawl back into the strange bed and hope to wake up elsewhere?

I made another attempt to reach the air vent, this time by standing on a replica Louis XVI cane chair (an authentic one would have broken.) Removing the grate, I climbed in and wriggled my way along the aluminum duct. In the process, my shirt tail came out of my trousers and the bare skin of my midriff touched the cold metal. I could no longer doubt whether I was awake!

I tucked my shirt in and continued to crawl through the duct as best I could. Soon I heard voices and carefully passed a vent opening on a room in which Miguel and Fernandez were talking.

"He has escaped from his room! I knew he could not be trusted!" said Fernandez.

"Quick, get Jose—we must find him!" said Miguel.

They ran out of the room. As I had suspected, this was all part of some obscure plot and they were keeping me against my will after all.

I moved on as quietly as possible and came to another vent. Looking in, I saw Alma sitting in her room, crying. Perhaps she had had a disagreement with her compatriots. Could I trust her? Something in her manner said I could, so I pushed through the grate and climbed out of the vent.

She was surprised but happy to see me. "Alan! I'm glad you have escaped. They should not have locked you in. Sometimes I wonder about their methods. . ."

Alma was wearing a white terrycloth bathrobe. On the wall I saw a long thermometer (perhaps three feet long) with a legend indicating ranges of temperature. The lowest range was marked in white and had very low temperatures.

"This chart represents my range of body temperatures," Alma explained. "Sometimes I'm hypothermic."

She asked me to touch her lips. They were pale and when I touched them they were quite cold.

At that moment there was a knock at the door. There was no place to hide and no time to climb back up to the vent, for the door opened and in came a man and a woman dressed in white smocks. Alma seemed relieved and introduced me.

"Alan, this is the Director and the Head Therapist of the Eternal Youth Spa." To them, she said "Alan is a friend of mine who is interested in your therapeutic methods. I thought he could accompany us on the tour of the facilities."

The man, in his sixties, said that would be fine and lead the way. We walked down a series of corridors and came to an area in which people were receiving some sort of therapy in shallow pools, perhaps two feet deep and 18 feet in diameter. Along the walls behind each pool were glowing panels which resembled solar panels. As we went past one of the pools, I held my hand in front of one of the panels and felt a warm, tingling sensation. We passed through refrigerated rooms containing slabs of flesh, muscles, and so on, hanging on hooks. They were presumably human parts used in reconstructing injured or diseased patients. The sight was sickening.

The Director led us back to the area of the pools, and the Head Therapist explained the role of the water in the patients' recovery. She implied that not only was the water used for bathing, but that some amount of it was also swallowed. The water was specially imported from some northern European country (I think it was Norway), where there was a spring once frequented by a now-extinct species of wild boar.

"What they are drinking is, in effect, the remains of prehistoric pigs. This causes them to throw up—they throw up their death. Anything that is born that drinks this will throw up its death."

It was all too bizarre. The patients, mainly elderly men and women, sat or squatted half-naked in the water and played like children.

Alma thanked our guides and we left to return to her room. Before we reached it, however, we saw Fernandez and Jose turn a corner and come charging down the corridor.

"Quick, this way!" Alma said, pushing me through a swinging door and into a kind of kitchen. Lab technicians were busy tending pots of boiling water on long stovetops. As we ran past I was revolted by the sight of human appendages bobbing in the pots.

Alma led the way through connecting rooms and finally through a door that led outside of the odd Norman tower. Dawn was breaking. Suddenly, alarm bells rang out and spotlights sent beams searching back and forth around the base of the tower. Jose and Fernandez rushed out of the same door through which we had passed and stood before us menacingly, arms crossed. The searchlights focused on us and our capture seemed imminent.

Just then, the UFO came back—Lord Randolph was at the helm! It swooped down from the sky and hovered in mid-air between us and our would-be captors.

"All aboard!" his Lordship shouted, swinging open the door. We jumped in, Alma into the front, I into the back where Marian was waiting. When Marian saw Alma in her bathrobe, she glared at me. I was about to explain who Alma was when the UFO/taxi lurched forward and we took off at top speed towards the north. Our velocity was truly astounding and we sat stupefied as terrain and heavens passed in one streaking image across our windows.

"What a splendid coach!" his Lordship exclaimed with glee. "This will cut down considerably on travel time between town and castle!"

Chapter Eight
The Mechanical Dancer

We returned to Castle Randolph to pick up Stephen and Hector, then the six of us zoomed over the forest towards town. Alma and Hector, despite their previous differences, were happy to see each other and sat in the front with Lord Randolph. I sat in the back between Marian and Stephen, who was amazed by the flying craft.

As we crossed the forest in the light of the early morning sun, we saw his Lordship's familiar coach moving along the serpentine road below. It had left the castle before our return, carrying Lord Ficksure, Lady Falgren, Felicity, and Geoffrey. We swooped down to astonish them, but they cheered when they recognized us. His Lordship switched on a loudspeaker and spoke into the transmitter, his voice booming over the sleepy forest:

"Let's to the cabaret!"

And we were off! Within moments we were over the eastern district of the city. Stephen explained to me that the cabaret was not far from the Great Green Theatre and belonged to Lord Ficksure, whom I had not met. We landed on the roof of the Theatre and descended by way of catwalks and steel ladders down to the stage. Although the theatrical company was between productions, a living room set illuminated by dim overhead light was fortuitously present at center stage, and we availed ourselves of the comfortable sofas and chairs while waiting for the coach to arrive.

"It will take them hours to get here," said Lord Randolph, "so we had might as well relax. In the meantime, Alan, why not fill us in on the details of your incredible adventure?"

I proceeded to enthrall the group with my account of the events of the previous evening and night. Alma had gone offstage with Hector or I would have called upon her for explanations and elucidations at certain critical points. Marian said that the group at the castle were out on the lawn to greet Lord Ficksure and his party when they had seen the UFO flitting overhead. They were as spellbound as I was by the saucer, but were horrified to see me climb out of my window and leave with it. They had remained awake all night with excitement and concern, and now were exhausted. By what means his Lordship had come to find and rescue me, and how he had taken control of the UFO/taxi, I did not learn—for he had nodded off to sleep during my story. Others followed his example and soon everyone was fast asleep.

It seemed distinctly surrealistic to be telling my story while, one by one, my audience passed out, as if caught in a spell. There was irony in it, too: for this was the setting of my unexpected performance in Marian's play, which evoked such a powerful response from the crowd; now that I had an exciting tale to tell, I was putting people to sleep! On top of it all was the living room set in the middle of the large stage, facing row upon row of empty seats in the dark house.

At last, left alone as it were, I pondered the notion that my performance in *The Story of Man* was like a case of possession, as if I had been a mouthpiece for someone else to speak through. And the odd parallel: just now I had described a series of unlikely events which had happened elsewhere, out there, as if to someone else.

Soon fatigue set in for me as well. As I drifted off, I kept seeing images of Fernandez and Jose chasing me, intent on doing me harm. I kept starting awake with the impulse to run, saw where I was, and relaxed again. I was safe now—but something didn't seem quite right. The feeling that something was missing nagged at me until I looked around to take stock and realized with a groan that, while the green transfer (which I had come to commemorate without knowing why) was safe in my coat pocket, *I had left my thermos full of writings at the Norman castle on the road to Brazil!* There was absolutely nothing I could do about it now, so I resolved to let go of it. I even managed to find humor in the situation: "Imagine! My writings in the hands of the Revolution!" With that peculiarly provocative thought still in my mind, I drifted into sleep—a deep, fortunately dreamless sleep, something I had needed for days.

The other party arrived by coach several hours later and went straight to the cabaret. There we joined them shortly before nightfall, having slept away most of the day to recover from our nervous exhaustion. Festivities were well underway and the cabaret was packed.

Above the clamor of the nightclub Lord Ficksure welcomed us to a large table a few feet from the stage. He was a debonair old gentleman with white hair and razor thin white mustache. To his left sat Lady Falgren, who re-membered me from Marian's party. Geoffrey and Felicity stood to greet us, but before we could speak the house lights dimmed to signal the start of the performance. Eager for entertainment, we all quickly took our seats around the table. Being closest to the stage, I had to turn my chair around with its back to the table in order to see.

Before anything happened, a waiter brought us a pitcher of Martinis and a tray of olives and onions. We took turns helping ourselves. I was intent on having a good time despite the loss of my writings, so I poured myself a dou-ble and soon followed it with a second.

The music coming from the club's sound system had gradually gotten louder and louder and now it was blaring. Smoke from dry ice began pouring across the stage, glowing with dull blue light and etched with colorful lasers. When the layer of smoke had gotten a couple feet high, a line of chorus girls began to parade back and forth on the small stage, smiling widely with tanned skin licked by the prancing lasers.

The sound, the lights, the scantily clad women moving above me on stage—I was so close to all the action that I felt overwhelmed, almost claus-trophobic, like being in the front row at a movie. My head was numb and I experienced a weird state in which there was complete silence—as if I and all the world was stone deaf—and for a full minute or more, the women seemed to move in slow motion. I could only attribute these peculiar sensa-tions to the amount of liquor I had imbibed and to a lingering grogginess from sleeping all day. The next moment things returned to normal.

When I turned toward Stephen to comment on the odd sensory effects, I happened to glance across the room and thought I recognized Miguel moving among the people that thronged the bar. Certainly the man was Hispanic, and he was even looking in my direction; but I could have been mistaken as to his identity. After a mere instant, he disappeared from view and I turned my attention back to the dancers.

The moving figures on stage dissolved into the mist and were replaced by a green speckled booth from an American diner. On the vinyl seats sat three or four women, wearing next to nothing and again illuminated by hazy blue light. At first I could not tell if they were actually there or if it was a clever deception, some kind of hologram projection. A couple of the women smoked French cigarettes through black holders, blowing smoke at us with pursed lips; all of them smiled alluringly, turning their heads from side to side. I remember my friends and I laughing uncontrollably.

Suddenly one of the women scooted out of the booth and came toward our table. Her movement reminded me of an organ grinder's monkey, jumping off his shoulder and scampering up with a tin cup; or perhaps she moved as if being hoisted by a crane and thrust forward like a bag of cement. She came straight toward me, and my male companions, to whom I turned for support, laughed with me and urged me on. "Go get her!" they said with their eyes full of tears. Felicity smiled mischievously, but Marian frowned and darkened with a flush of anger.

The woman stepped down from the stage and danced before me for a few minutes, wiggling her voluptuous hips like a belly dancer and thrusting her bouncing bosoms perilously close to my face. Suddenly she pirouetted to a spot a yard away and stood as still as a mannequin, hands at her sides. Ever so slowly she moved her hands outwards and upwards in wide arcs until they met above her head. When the fingers touched, she started spinning like a top—at first slowly, then faster and faster. She spun so fast I could feel the wind, could smell her perfume. The updraft began to draw smoke that had spilled off the stage and covered the floor, raising it to form a twirling bank of fog around her. This final touch made her so alluring that I could resist no longer and stood up to embrace her. In the same instant that I rose up from my seat, the crowd burst into applause—amazed by the dancer's performance—as if my movement had released their admiration. Now I was eye-level with her as she spun and I reached to encircle her with my arms. But with plastic face and glass eyes she shifted in my arms, rotating faster still.

Then the most fantastic transformation took place! In a sequence of still shots, her clothes were flung off, her hair disappeared, the skin rolled back, sinews flew off like released springs, and her skull was laid bare! At the same time she stopped revolving and collapsed, going down on her knees before me. At first the cranium shone like glazed ceramic, then abruptly became a mechanical thing—the head of a robot, composed of gray metal.

My companions now stood around me, studying the strange object. I believe it was only the men from the table, our female companions curiously absent, but I was too caught up in our investigation to make sure. We were about to dismantle the mechanical head—but before we touched it, it began dismantling itself, parts floating off of their own accord. The metal casing came away, revealing a nest of thousands of wires of every imaginable color. Finally, a small object was left that looked like a large walnut out of its shell. The nude body of the mechanical dancer crumbled to the floor, but this object, this "brain" remained—floating in midair. It shone with a brilliant red light, as if radioactive and extremely hot, but instead it was cold and seemed to draw energy from the atmosphere around it. Although we did not touch it we sensed it sucking electrons from our flesh like a vacuum or a fusion device.

What happened next is impossible to explain. *The electronic brain, floated into the sky—and we floated with it.* How we got outside, I simply do not know. One moment all of us at the table (men and women alike) were standing around the object, and the next moment we were going up between the tall buildings. Hovering slightly above the strange device, we looked down and saw the electric city and the dark night pass below us. The radioactive red mechanism was shielded with blackness in the shape of a megaphone.

We all spun around before descending to the top of a skyscraper, where we managed to land despite strong winds. The device lay on the center of the rooftop and we stood in a circle around it. Intuitively, we knew that the device held within itself a terrible destructive potential and a malign force. It was a bomb that would soon detonate and cause untold damage; but we were not concerned so much for our own lives as for the total loss the explosion would cause. Lying there on the roof, it began to send out beams, flooding the scene with waves of pulsing light. The light sent our shadows out against the walls of adjacent buildings. It was so intense it made our flesh translucent and we could see our bones clearly outlined. Then the sound started. It was a whistling sound, an oscillating, regular snap that crackled like electricity. It was also like a siren or car alarm, chirping shrilly until our ears ached.

Under the intense light we set about defusing the device. As we moved closer it lost its odd luster, as if its glow were only a surrounding field that somehow began a yard away. We had come to a critical point where our mission would either succeed or fail. I looked up and saw Marian standing beyond the radiant brain; our eyes met. Working up close with a magnifying glass, I disconnected two metal plates and reconnected them with a soft, putty-like adhesive. The brilliant light and the shrill chirping now abated, leaving only a weak blue pulsation.

Had the problem been solved—or only deferred? And how could we know?

A crowd of spectators had gathered on the roof. Salvador Dali appeared from among them and began a discourse on the symbolic aspects of the situation. (How can I invoke his name without taking a moment to sing his praise? His stature as an artistic genius is well recognized; his mustache, his wild eyes, his power and mystique—these need not be elaborated. And yet, to our mixture of admiration and outrage, he was always a royalist—a supporter of the crown.)

"Ladies and Gentlemen. . ." he began, throwing back his cape an waving his cane like a baton. "Woman is man's symbol for nature. The walnut represents artificial intelligence, which may at any moment explode like a bomb and destroy us. . ."

He continued with something about pyramids, crystals, and secret societies, but much of his speech was either unintelligible (he accented his words strangely and rolled his Rs in his typical fashion) or simply far too erudite for me to understand. It was hard to tell when he was speaking literally, and when figuratively. He ended with a statement which he emphasized dramatically as the key to the problem facing us, then he turned and disappeared among the crowd. This is what he said:

"Ladies and Gentlemen. The root of our problems—of all the problems which face the world—is *Renegade RNA*. The messenger is unfaithful to the holy script."

Chapter Nine
The Return to Brickshire

My state of mind was balanced precariously between heroic achievement and utter defeat. It seemed that nothing further could be done, so I returned to the house in Brickshire. The exertions and revelations of the previous evening—in fact, of the previous week—had proved too much for my nerves and I stayed in bed until well past noon.

It had turned cold overnight. When I arose, I went to the kitchen in my housecoat and slippers and prepared a simple repast consisting of hot tea and a raisin scone. As I was about to take my first bite, however, I was interrupted by a knock at the back door, which led from the kitchen into the back yard. I turned around and saw the Tax Collector looking through the window. It was the stricter of the two men who had come twice before, and this time he was alone.

Had a full week really gone by so quickly? I had written nothing. Not a scrap. Sure, I had a number of adventures—quite remarkable ones at that!—but nothing had been committed to paper. And now Judgment was at hand. I set down the scone and stood up, but the agent was already letting himself in. A gust of cold air came into the room around him.

"Well, Mr. Wilcox. Your grace period is up. What do you have to show for yourself?"

"Please, have a seat. Would you like some tea?"

"No, thank you. Are you stalling, Mr. Wilcox?"

"Not at all, sir. I'll be right back with my work."

As I headed for the door leading toward the stairs, the Tax man warned: "Remember—no tricks. I have no time for games, Mr. Wilcox."

I went up to my room and grabbed a stack of blank typing paper and placed them in an empty folder. My idea was this: I would recount the events of the previous week while pretending to read from the blank pages. If my ruse worked, I would meet my requirements and be absolved by the Government. Otherwise . . . well, at this point there was nothing to lose.

When I returned to the kitchen, a number of my house mates had gathered. They knew what was up and came to offer moral support—or at least to witness my performance. The agent sat at the table, humorless and intransigent.

I stood before the little group with my folder of paper, cleared my throat, and began as follows:

"There was never a clear sequence in which the events took place. Nor were the events themselves easily definable. On the whole, a kind of story emerged from the various episodes—a story containing a multitude of other stories, or possible stories. . ."

I started with the bus trip to town with "Steve" and the mysterious green transfer. I told about waiting on the street and the arrival by coach of "Lord Redwolf" (changing the name to maintain the guise of fiction). Then the party, the champagne, the ramps with worms, and the various odd characters. Next came the play—crowned by my unexpected triumph—and the coach ride to the castle. Marian retained her stage name Mary Louise; Hector appeared as "Sir Helmstone"—not the brother but a friend of Lord Redwolf—with his intriguing aesthetic theories. I ad libbed a scene in which we played croquet followed by tea on the lawn while being entertained by a string quartet. Then the earthquake hit, followed by the vision of the strange crystal overhead in the sky and the appearance of the UFO. I described the ride in the UFO/taxi to the Norman tower, our conversation on various socioeconomic issues, the discovery of the exotic water therapy, the pursuit and my rescue by Lord Redwolf. The final scene was the night club where the robot-bomb dazzled us until I defused it and "Don Salvador" appeared with his diagnosis of "renegade RNA." I didn't know how to end it, so I just left it at that.

My impromptu narration lasted the better part of an hour. When I had finished, my house mates applauded and cheered triumphantly. The Tax collector remained impassive until they, too, shared his silence. At last he spoke:

"I am afraid I cannot share the enthusiasm of your friends, Mr. Wilcox. The fact is, I found your story to be unacceptable. It is too fanciful, too silly,

Intimations of Unreality

too . . . improbable. It seems pointless and unresolved; in fact, there is nothing to resolve. As you all but admit in your introductory remarks, the 'various episodes' which comprise your story seem unrelated, strung together only by the recurrence of this absurd green transfer, the significance of which is never revealed. Similarly, the strange pyramid and the recurring silver thermos serve only to arouse our curiosity but leave us hanging—these empty devices are, at best, red herrings but seem out-of-place when there is no mystery. Last but not least, the constant shift between the mundane and the fantastic doesn't give the reader or listener a chance to tune in at one level or the other."

I was simply crushed. The Tax man paused to measure the impact of his critique, then continued:

"Mr. Wilcox, the most thoroughgoing analysis reveals the individual to be the true source of all evil: He or she must compromise selfish tendencies for the good of society. Your work, however, is of no value to society. How can the common person relate to such rubbish? No, I am afraid it will not do at all."

With this he stood up, extended his hand and took the folder of blank pages from me. Without looking at them and thus discovering them to be blank, he recklessly stuffed them into his attaché case and was about to leave.

"You will have to try elsewhere, Mr. Wilcox. Perhaps you should give some consideration to another profession—say, the military. As for the rest of you," he said, addressing my house mates, "you can expect a new person to be assigned to occupy Mr. Wilcox's room, beginning tomorrow. Goodday."

He turned and went out the back door, leaving a vacuum of silence. Into which—

A single sheet of paper fell from thin air onto the kitchen floor. The Tax man must have dropped it. We stood around and looked at it. It was covered with writing, arranged in verse. I picked it up and recognized it as an old poem I had written with the intention of setting it to song. I could have sworn it had been in the thermos with the rest of my writings, but I was evidently mistaken . . .

Chapter Ten
Benediction

As I came downstairs with my knapsack of belongings, I heard with a thrill the voice of Marian coming from the front room.

"Hey, everybody! It's snowing outside!" she exclaimed. Standing in the little foyer, she had just come in and was covered with a fine coat of powdery snow.

"Marian! It's so good to see you!"

She ran up and we hugged. Snowflakes were on her eyelids, which she blinked with excitement. It was the first snow of the season. I did not want to spoil her mood by telling of my failure. Instead, I soon forgot it myself— or, rather, put it out of my mind and allowed myself to become infected by her good spirits.

"Come on, let's go outside!" she said. Little did she know I was leaving the house for good.

The walkway leading to the street was covered with a fine sheet of ice, and we had to be careful not to slip. I kept my center of gravity over my feet, taking short steps with muscles taut. Marian gripped my arm—almost made me slip twice. Once we made it to the street, the going was easier. There was no traffic so we had the road to ourselves.

It must have started snowing during the long night (was it part of the aftermath of the strange bomb-like device?), for now everything was covered with a foot of old snow. Under the rays of afternoon sun the snow was melting and water ran in a shallow river down the middle of the street. The air was nearly freezing. Small flakes were falling, and the light reflecting on them was magical.

We walked along Laurel Avenue and came to the top of the hill, at 16th Street. The sun shone down but was obscured by the tall apartment building on the opposite corner. It was near the site of Fort Brickshire, the original outpost in these parts, now gone without a trace except for a cement historical marker with an inscribed bronze plaque. Behind us stood a community arts center that was once an Ecumenical Church.

Something odd was happening in the street. Because of the cold air, but mainly because of some magical influence, the water that flowed from the melting snow was forming into beads of ice that rose into the air. The beads were spaced very regularly, as if animated by some sort of magnetism or vibrations, and rose up in columns. The short columns turned into spinning diamond shapes. In marvel, I reached down and picked one up. It was about half a foot in height and diameter. When I dropped it on the pavement it shattered into a thousand smaller diamonds that continued to spin.

Other people from the neighborhood were out, walking along the street, and I wanted them to join us in appreciating the magic of the crystals. It was the feeling of camaraderie you share with strangers during the first snow of the winter. Everyone was filled with a sense of promise, as if a new day had dawned.

Marian and I continued along the street, arm and arm, intensely happy, and made our way to the Black Beetle Cafe for a hot cup of coffee. While waiting for our drinks we warmed our hands by the candle at the center of the table. I finally told Marian of the rejection of my work by the Tax man. I also lamented the loss of my writings, left behind in the silver thermos.

Marian encouraged me to start afresh. "It is time for a new beginning," she said. "I know you can take on the challenge."

She placed her hand on mine.

Then I remembered the single sheet of paper left behind by the Tax man. When I pulled it out of my pocket the crumpled green transfer fell out also, landed on the candle and burst into flames. Marian and I looked at each other and laughed. As I read the poem over to myself, I began humming a tune that seemed to match the words. Someone in the cafe had a guitar, which I borrowed. After strumming awhile to find the right chords, I sang my new song to the little audience. I include it here as a kind of capstone to my adventures to date, or as a cornerstone for further ones to come:

Morello twangs his banjo strings
and smokes his lean cigar.
Amidst the roar the lion reared
and fell back in the straw.

The porcelain dummies move below
to form a single strand.

Amazing how their surface glow
renounced their bid to stand.

Rain falls upon the road I walk—
a path that leads for miles;
I see each thing and check again
To see if it's worthwhile.

Pygmalion turns to stone again;
Medusa combs her hair;
Rapunzel, Rumpelstiltskin both
run off to join the Fair.

The tetragram implies the time
when eastern pharaohs fall
And sheiks all shriek upon the peak
of mountains of burning oil.

A myriad muppets join the fray
as mummies sail the Nile
To condescend to see the Day—
We find it all worthwhile!

Maid Marian strains to see the play,
Morello sings his tune.
Last Sunday we all stayed in bed
deciphering magic runes.

The birds fly south, the cars drive by,
the buses fill with youth.
The whole parade is a masquerade—

Who cares about lost truth?

But up above, the minister trips
and tumbles out of style.
New train wheels sing to bring the new—
We find it all worthwhile!

Morello recommends a book,
The Lives of Greater Men.
I do not doubt till I find out
that even saints have sinned.

"The more I learn, the less I know,"
or so the learned say.
"The more I know, the less I learn,"
the truth would also say.

So now I've been both here and there,
I've dreamed and seen the real
The tried-and-true and, yes, the New—
I find it all worthwhile:
The world is all worthwhile!

After the song came the warm applause of the few who had gathered, and I returned the borrowed guitar. Then Marian and I walked out into the street, arm in arm, to watch the crystals fall. There was the warm glow of the sun on the snow, the cold bite of the air that whistled through the streets and blew in waves against my face—and Marian by my side. For the first time in my life, I was truly happy.

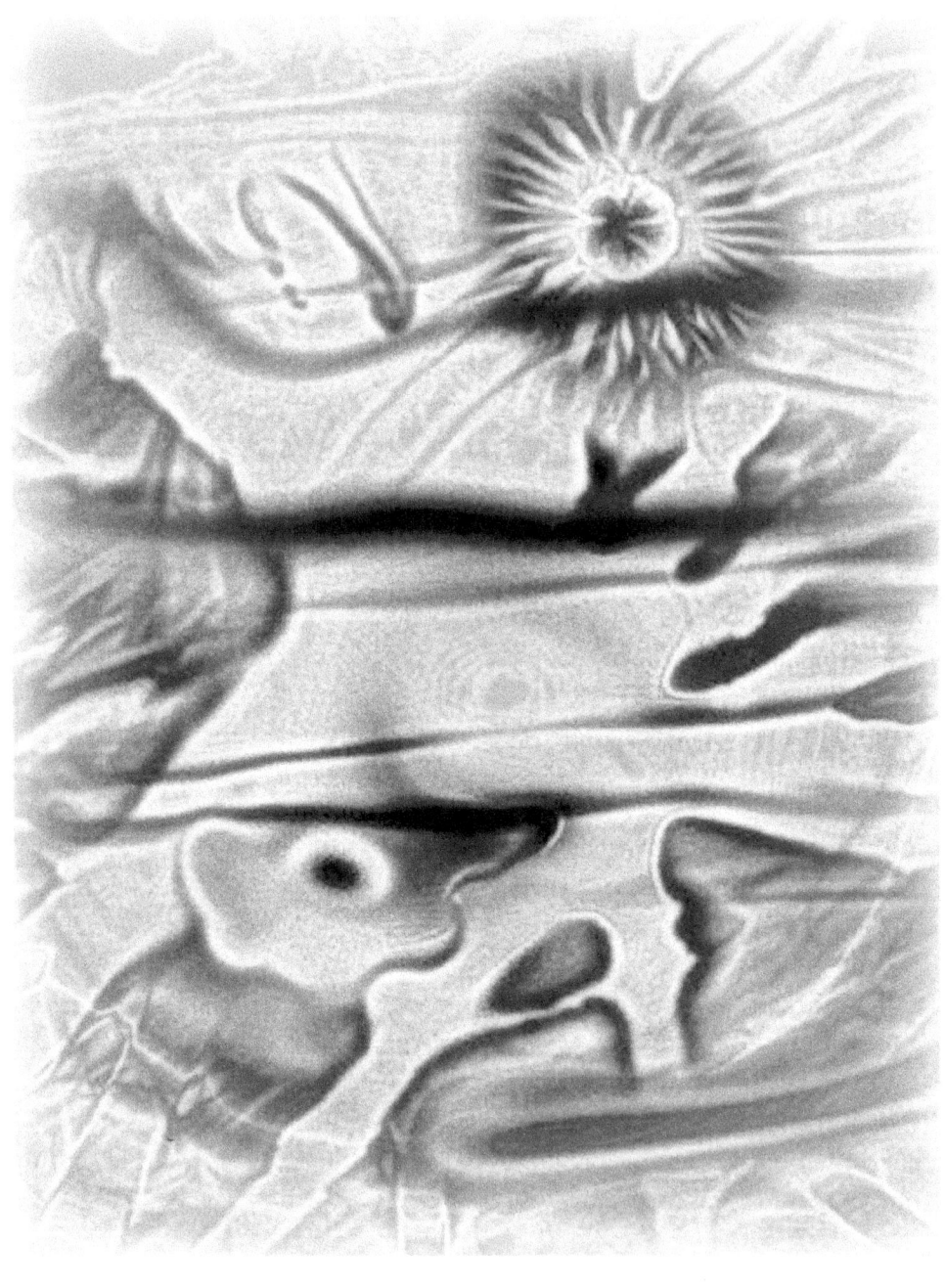

THE MORE, THE MARIGOLD

Above, a seagull curved and cried. His flight described a lonely arc across the cloud-clotted sky. We were only four miles from the beach, and though he seemed alone, he was probably calling to companions on the wing.

The deck overlooked a small backyard enclosed by a tall fence grown with vines. It was small, but no smaller than the other backyards that adjoined to make up the block's partitioned green interior.

"The yard is shared by all four units," said the voice that followed me outside.

The aged agent stood beside me at the railing and looked out over the little sea of green, a plot some twenty feet wide by thirty long covered with healthy turf. A large flowering bush grew in the far right corner.

"The gardener comes on Wednesdays and takes care of the yard, trims the camellia bush, and so forth. The bottom level is a garden apartment but all tenants have access to the yard."

He lifted a wrinkled hand with index finger crooked in the direction of a stairway that ran up and down along the outside of the building.

"You can go downstairs this way—we won't go down now, but there are garbage pails down there everyone uses, whichever one is empty.

"Now, the way it works is this," he said, turning to face the Victorian structure. "There are four units in all. Each unit, except the garden apartment, has its own deck for its own use, but you have to allow tenants from the other levels to access the stairs."

He was referring to the fact that each flight of stairs terminated with the deck at each level, then continued down.

"So, everyone has to keep it clear around the stairs so you can get through.

"The old captain lives upstairs." He leaned his head back stiffly and looked up at the smaller deck or balcony jutting out from the topmost floor.

"He's not out now . . . Captain More has lived there . . . oh, as long as anyone can remember. Came with the house—so to speak—when the agency took over renting it out. Must be in his eighties by now. Retired, of course."

It seemed ironic for the ancient agent to speak of anyone else as old. He seemed well past retirement age himself, easily in his seventies.

"You'll see him out on the balcony most every day. From up there you can see the ocean—but don't go up there, it's strictly for his use.

"Come to think of it, you might ask if he needs any help with his trash or recyclables. The last tenant helped him down the stairs with it, and I'm sure he appreciated it. At first he may seem a bit . . . odd—but he's friendly once you get to know him.

"But remember, don't go up there unless he invites you—strictly for his use."

The day I moved in, I hauled some large potted plants out onto the deck, setting one in each corner. I looked up at the balcony above. The captain's deck was small, with only enough room for a couple chairs, and I could see the entire balcony from the outer edges of my deck. Someone sat there with their back turned, facing west and the Pacific Ocean.

I arranged my pots and gave them all a good watering, all the while keeping an eye on the captain, wanting to catch sight of him and perhaps introduce myself. But there was no sign of movement and no sound. After what the agent had said, I didn't dare call up to him, afraid of invading his privacy or waking him if he was napping. So I finished with my plants and went back inside to unpack.

Later I heard footsteps overhead. The old guy didn't have carpet or a rug in his hallway, so you could hear the tread of his boot heels on the hardwood floor as he went from room to room.

Thursday was garbage day and I was gathering my recyclables and trash to take down to the bins on my first Wednesday evening in the apartment. Since it was only my third day there, I didn't have much of either to dispense with. But what about the old captain upstairs? The rental agent had suggested that I offer my help, but also stipulated not to disturb the gentleman on his balcony unless invited. I had to wait for some overture from the captain, but how long should I wait before initiating contact myself? If he needed help . . .

While I stood there with my own trashcan in hand, debating with myself, I was startled by a screeching sound nearby, just outside the kitchen window. It was like the screech of a screech owl, or the squawk of a crow in a nasty mood. It happened again and again in a regular pattern, becoming more of a squeak than a screech or squawk.

I investigated, stepped closer to the window—slowly, as not to scare off the bird at the sill, if that's what it was. But it wasn't. A blue plastic basket came into view, descended passed the window and out of view, suspended by a rope that jiggled in time with the squeaks. The captain had rigged up a rope and pulley system to lower his dispensables to the ground!

I finished gathering my own refuse and carried the containers down the back steps as prescribed, passing through the deck of the flat below me and down to the ground. The captain was there, under the lowest landing of the steps, moving stuff from his basket to the bins. As I approached, he looked up.

"Hello there," I hailed to him, "I'm Alex, the new tenant in the apartment below yours."

It was hard to make out his features in the semi-darkness below the stairs.

"Well, nice to meet you, young man," he replied with a hearty handshake that left some grease on my hand. "I'm Captain Tom More, but everyone calls me Captain."

"Very well, Captain. I thought you could use some help there, but I see you've got it taken care of."

"Oh, yes, I don't like carrying the basket down—it's too heavy and I can't see around it to know where to step. So I rigged up this pulley to get it down here where I can deal with it."

I noted the thick, tough rope tied to the handles of the basket and thought at once of the rigging of an old sailing ship. This impression was somehow enhanced by seeing the captain framed by the grayed redwood beams of the landing. Of course, I didn't know what sort of sailor he was, but I pictured him on an old, tall-masted clipper ship from the nineteenth century.

"Well, if I can be of any service, uh, Captain, just let me know."

"Very good, Alex—"

"Taget."

"*Taget?!* Why, I served with a Taget in the South Seas—James Taget. No relation, I suppose?"

"No . . . not that I know of . . . In the Navy?"

"Merchant marine. We began as ordinary seaman together . . . hauling loads of cargo between here and the Philippines. Good old Taget! I'll have to tell you about him sometime."

"That sounds great . . . Well, I'll see you around."

"Yes—and welcome aboard!"

"Thanks!" I thought of saluting and adding "Aye, aye Cap'n," but thought better of it. I didn't want to mock the old guy, who seemed rather nice.

It wasn't until later that I saw him again. I went out to water my potted plants and he was up on his balcony, doing likewise.

"Good afternoon, Taget!" His call was cheery, if a bit pretentious. The quasi-military use of my surname implied that he was my superior. There may have been no pretense on his part, since he *had* risen to the rank of captain, somehow. But I was wary of entering some role-playing game where I was perpetually ranked his subordinate.

"Good afternoon, Captain!"

"Taget, I was going to tell you about my First Mate, James Taget . . . Grew marigolds just like these on the poop deck."

He invited me up to his balcony—which was actually just the top landing of the stairs. A pennant or garden flag, invisible from the deck below, waved in the wind, bearing some nautical symbol.

"I don't have much space up here to garden, but I like to keep it up."

Affixed to the upper railing was a row of planter boxes, filled with soil and overflowing with marigolds. I recognized the flower from my mother's garden, with its feathery green leaves and bright yellow and orange blossoms, with some as golden as gold. Small terra cotta pots lined the floor of the deck along the railing, also sporting marigolds. Together, the pots and planters sustained quite a flower garden, whose mass of curling petals emitted amazing bursts of color.

"Wow, these are nice! Gee, you must like marigolds."

"The more, the marigold!" quipped the captain.

"My mother used to grow them in Cincinnati."

"Ohio . . . Let's see, Taget was from Maine . . . Well, these are all hybrids of *Calendula officinalis* and *Calendula stellata*—pot marigolds," he explained.

Intimations of Unreality

He went from planter to planter, watering and weeding and telling me something about each one, all the while gripping a pipe in his teeth.

For the first time I could see him by the light of day—sunlight that filtered through a patch of eucalyptus trees in the adjacent yard. If you didn't know he was a seafaring man, you could guess it from his appearance. He was dressed in navy blue uniform pants; a short-sleeved white shirt with an epaulet at each shoulder—a patch of navy blue with an anchor of gold. His hat was a typical captain's cap, again navy blue with visor, again bearing the anchor insignia and wreaths done in gold braiding. All in all, it seemed a bit formal for garden attire, and the captain would seem more at home on the deck of a ship than here on his balcony. Though I had noticed his outfit from below, closer inspection revealed each item to be worn and frayed at the edges, with bare threads coming unstitched and frazzled, and overdue for a wash. The visor of his cap was gritty and grubby where he gripped it to push the cap back or pull it down.

"The floral heads, you see, are composed of both of ray and disc florets . . ."

His face was also a bit frazzled, but full of character. His countless journeys at sea could be read there: traced in the worn, ragged aspect of his face as on a topographic map. It had already been pock-marked by teen acne—the scars of youth's surging metabolism. Then it was weathered, haggard, tortured like leather: tanned ruddy by the sun, salt-washed and sea-scrubbed, dried taut by relentless wind. Worn out by wear and all along the way (no doubt) by worry—and by time. After all, the agent said he was in his 80s. But his hair belied his years: dark still, though spiked with white, it emerged from his cap in curls and tufts. Overdue for a cut, they also looked weathered and worn somehow, as wavy and random as the chaotic sea.

"Frost will kill them, so I cover them up if there's a threat . . ."

Sun overhead, breaking through fernlike foliage of the eucalyptus, which swayed in the wind. The captain's face was a study in contrast: shadows under bushy brows, steel-gray eyes caught in the sun and glinting; shadows under the bags under his eyes; face rampant with wrinkles, ridges of dark and light rising and falling; darkness in his nostrils, darkness in his eyes; sunlight on the tip of his nose, peeled and spotted. The shadows of eucalyptus leaves waved across his face, dodged his visor, skimmed over his countenance—over lips that spoke.

"Unlike the heliotrope and daisy . . ."

His knowledge of flowers seemed extensive, and his conversation was cultured and precise—both of which, I admit, surprised me given his otherwise "salty dog" demeanor.

"But you're probably bored of all this . . ."

"No—not at all!" I protested.

"Anyway, they give me something to do . . ." His eyes fell on the flowers again and were soon lit up with another idea, a memory . . .

"Taget! I was going to tell you about Taget. There are so many stories, let me see . . ." He pushed his cap back and wiped his forehead. "Well, on the topic of marigolds, we were once on the island of Khíos in the Aegean, packing up a load of mastic, which is the resin of the lentisk tree that grows only there. Marigolds also grew rampant and figured in their religious life. They worshiped the earth goddess Cybele, known as Magna Mater, the Great Mother.

"Every month, they held a celebration on the day of the new moon—the first day of the month in the lunar calendar. The marigolds were all in bloom and the women worked the loom, weaving wool dyed golden with the stain of the flower. The fabric made new dresses for the new month. They also took long-stemmed flowers, strip off the leaves, and weave them into a basket, with the blossom ending up inside—a basket of flowers woven of flowers!

"The goddess's statues were adorned with garlands made of fresh marigolds. Worshippers also flattened and dried the flowers into disks, like gold coins, and placed them around the feet of the statues. The dried flowers have a pungent fragrance similar to that of burial ointments, so there was a funereal air to the occasion.

"All day the feet of Cybele were covered with the coins. At night came the festival—with music and dancing, chanting of religious poems, imbibing of ceremonial drinks. But the next morning, all the coins would be gone! The belief was that ghosts, drawn by the fragrance and the golden color, stole the disks at night to spend in the spirit world . . . What they bought there is anyone's guess! Think of it! What strange pleasures, what dark tortures, what weird wines and delicacies are for sale in the spirit world?"

Intimations of Unreality

He fell silent, eyes gleaming. Was that the end of the story, or was he caught in a reverie?

"What about Taget?" I prompted him. "Where does he fit in?"

"Ah, Taget! Well, when he heard the story about the coins, he wanted to find out what the great mystery was. After the big party had died down and everyone went home for the night—including myself, going back to the inn—he crept about for a while. First he found a statue and grabbed one of the disks for himself, careful that no one was looking. It was pitch dark without the moon, for of course 'new moon' means 'no moon'!

"So, Taget slips a disk into his pocket and heads over to hide in the bushes, where he can keep an eye on the statue without being seen. It wasn't even midnight when a chill came on the air and Taget began to shiver. But nothing happened, he just stood there shivering, until he couldn't stand it any longer and returned to the inn.

"Sure enough, next morning there were no flowers below the statues. Some orderly of the order no doubt dispensed their task in the wee hours of the night . . . Either that, or the spirits took them!

"Anyway, back aboard, Taget dug the seeds out of the dried coin and planted them, and they grew! He kept them for years, and in fact, what you see here are descendants and hybrids of those flowers from Khíos."

A day or two passed before I saw the captain again. Work was requiring long hours, and there was still much unpacking to do. The next time I watered my plants, I glanced up at the captain's balcony, but no one was there. What *was* there startled me for a moment. Stretched at length along the railing, nearly three feet long from head to tail, was a gray-green iguana. The agent instructed me on the captain, but nothing was said about a giant lizard! Spiny and spotted and leathery, the lounging lizard eyed me nonchalantly, glaring down from the balcony—and staring down through the millennia from his Jurassic heyday.

The next morning, I went into the kitchen area to make coffee and saw the creature leering at me through the window! It lay on the outer sill of the kitchen window, which overlooked the deck. If the lower pane had been raised any more than it was, the thing might have gotten in . . .

After my prerequisite cup, I dressed and went out on the deck, ready to do battle with the scaly interloper. I suppose I intended to just pick it up and carry it back upstairs. I knew they were slow-moving and relatively docile, but when I saw the claws and jaw I had second thoughts. Where would I grab it? What if it squirmed? What if I hurt it somehow, dropped it—or it wriggled and hit its head on the glass? What if *it* hurt *me*? It might bite, after all: clamp down with those determined-looking jaws and hang on for dear life, all the while flailing his raptor talons.

Then I thought I would go up and get the captain and ask *him* to remove it . . . But what would he think of me, a sissy? Afraid of a little lizard? Besides, if he lived here before I did, I suppose he had more rights than I did, and the iguana had some rights, too. It seemed harmless enough, so long as the window was closed. I closed it the rest of the way and latched it. The beast didn't budge.

Anyway, I had to go to work and didn't have time to worry about it. When I got home in the evening, the lizard was gone. I had dinner and stepped out back for a breath of air. The fog had rolled in and the sun was going down, casting everything in a weird purple twilight.

The captain sat quietly on his deck, watching the fog pour in from the coast. He must have heard me come outside, but he sat motionless in the mist—his own brain fogged by time and experience. Probably asleep. The iguana was sprawled close by him on the deck, barely visible through the posts of the railing and likewise in a state of stupor. I went back in.

"Frank's his name," Captain More said of the iguana, a day or two later. I stood on the captain's balcony, which was perched high up, and looked out over the roofs of the other houses on the block. From this higher vantage point, the grid of backyards seemed smaller than before, its two rows of backyards back-to-back shaped like an ice cube tray. Facing west you could, in fact, see the ocean in the distance—at least a patch of it, flat and gray, peeping through a fortuitous gap in the far-off rows of houses.

"Captured in Madagascar, port of Manakara, where we filled the hold full of vanilla. He was munching on rose periwinkle under a shade tree by the pier. Faithful companion ever since."

The captain scratched the lizard's jaw as it sprawled, overhanging the small outdoor table.

"Of course, he is probably from Guiana or the Antilles, as best I can figure. Might have been brought to Manakara by a sailor, just like myself, and he got away when they docked."

His eyes acquired a far-away look as he stared at the unblinking reptile.

"Manakara . . . Took Frank to a bar. Struck up a conversation with a local, who talked about Antsirabe, in the central highlands. Said precious gems were everywhere, cheap as you please.

"'There are rubies as big as grapefruit!' He claimed, his smile showing a large gap in his front teeth, and his eyes as big as the alleged rubies.

"So we went to Antsirabe, Frank and I. Took a wagon ride into the interior. Rode rickshaws from one end of the village to another, chasing the tale of the rubies as big as grapefruit, but finding none, only the dust on the stone cutters' stone floors. There were plenty of normal-sized gems, of course, but no bargains. Then I remembered that the man at the bar had been drunk, poorly dressed, and eager for a free drink. How could I have believed his story of priceless gems free for the taking, if he had not taken them *himself?*" He looked at me with raised eyebrows, although the question was rhetorical.

"Hey, that calls for a drink! Care for a brandy?" he asked as he half-turned toward his door and paused.

"Well, I don't want to seem 'eager for a free drink,' but sure!"

I followed him inside, leaving the lizard behind. The apartment followed the same layout as mine, which meant the living area was in the back overlooking the decks and backyard, while the sleeping quarters where in front, near the street. But being a renovated attic, the walls were sloped and the ceiling was low. The living area was dim, but the moment he turned on the light, I was struck by the décor.

"Welcome to my abode . . ." he said for dramatic effect.

His room was like a nautical museum . . . Everywhere there were reminders of the sea—fishing nets hung on the wall like tapestries, accented with colorful floats; an actual ship's wheel; paintings and photographs of ships and seaports; a map of the southern seas as drawn by an ancient topographer, with distorted continents and random coastlines. Larger floats lay on the floor, with more netting; an old oar with the whitewash almost weathered off leaned against the wall in the corner; there was a sextant on a side table, beside a globe. I expected to see a parrot in a cage . . . It seemed the only thing missing from this nautical museum. I looked again to make sure. There wasn't one.

"Wow, you've got quite a collection here, Captain More." If not a retired captain, he would be a sea buff of the highest order! Along the wall of the hallway that lead to the front of the house were African and South Pacific relics: masks, spears, a stylized granary door. In the corner, near the ceiling, a web with fragments of insects caught in the strands.

"Yes, collected from various corners of the world, mementos of many journeys . . ."

As I stood staring he poured the brandy.

"I always considered it more cultivated than Scotch or mere whiskey."

He handed me a snifter of the golden liquor and toasted: "Have a drink—to celebrate the moment that is now, or commemorate the moment that has passed." Pretty sophisticated for an old sea urchin.

I swirled my drink, sipped, swallowed. A slight burning in the throat. "This is good." Admiring it again. "I have an old bottle of Armagnac I've been saving, I'll have to bring it out . . ."

"Good! Nothing like a stiff brandy to take the chill out of the air. Have a seat, Alex." I appreciated his use of my given name.

"So, tell me, Captain—you've told me a number of your sea stories, but how did you get started in the merchant marines? When did you first go to sea?"

He laughed and shook his head. "Well, it's been many years—long before your time, young man! But I remember it pretty well. A different time, for sure, but in many ways the same.

"It really started when I left home, which started with an argument with my father . . . but there's no use going into that. Every man has a father and every man has to leave home sometime, though he carries his father's name with him. I know Thomas More was an historic figure, around the time of Henry VIII, but I forget his circumstances—something about divorce, wasn't it? Anyway, I have his name, but not his title; and as I am alive now, and he dead some centuries gone, I am more concerned with my *own* circumstances! And those include a father not knowing the history of the name he gives his own son. 'A Man for All Seasons,' indeed! Well, *this* is *my* season! While it lasts . . ."

Intimations of Unreality

"To your season!" I raised my glass to toast.

"To my season!" We clinked glasses and drank.

"It was '73 when I set out from San Francisco Bay, leaving behind all I knew—except the lore I had gathered about the earth's oceans, the fabled seven seas.

"My dream had always been to go to sea, 'to sail the ocean blue' like Christopher Columbus. Frisco was a legendary port in the new world, many-storied both as port of call and as point of departure for parts unknown. So here I came, hoping to sign on with any ship sailing out of the bay that could use a hand—inexperienced though I was.

"As luck would have it, the very day of my arrival was the day of my departure. I arrived downtown in the rain on a sleeper train and made my way down to the wharves and shipping offices. Times were busy and the telephone poles were covered with posters listing opportunities both onboard and alongshore. Ships were going out undermanned, so I was in luck—inexperienced but sturdy enough, strong of back and limb, and eager to perform even the most menial tasks for the privilege of being aboard a real sailing vessel.

"When I went onboard, the boatswain asked me my age and experience. I lied and said I was 20 with three years experience, but I was just 17. Though my beard was only peach-fuzz, somehow I fooled him and got on, but my many years of yearning for the sea were no means of learning what was in store. I had seen all the movies about Captain Cook and the *Endeavour*, the mutiny on *The Bounty*, *Moby Dick* and *The Sea Wolf*. I had read all the sea stories of Herman Melville and Joseph Conrad, Poe and Hodgson. It's all fantasy and romance! Even the hard work is romanticized and rhapsodized."

He paused to pour more brandy.

"Before I left home, a friend's older brother, a sailor, taught me 'the ropes'—all the sailor's knots. But the real ropes are in the rigging, and wrapped around the capstan and the wench. In the swabbing of the deck and the weighing of the anchor, the hoisting of the sails and all the ordinary duties of the ordinary seaman. Perhaps most of all, it's in the hours and days and *years* in the sun and the wind and the sea mist, with the ground underneath rocking and rolling; or running smooth as silk, under the stars at night, in the middle of the ocean, when all the world has gone away and yet is there—reduced to the swelling waters and the blackness of space."

He stared into his glass.

"As I said, I had never sailed before, but a sailor has to begin somewhere. Sailors are sailors—a breed apart—and are drawn by the lure of the open sea, the sense of adventure, a new beginning, a physical challenge . . . Also by a respect for the whole history of sailing going back through time to the beginning—to the nameless sailors of Phoenicia and Egypt and the mythic voyages of Odysseus and Gilgamesh.

"Tales are told and retold, stories kept alive over the generations and the centuries—even millennia. Of course, your common sailor may not be well versed in the lore—the tales of yore—but on any ship there is always one or more aboard who is, whether among the officers or the men. But every sailor is exposed to the lore on regular occasions, as the teller of tales would tell his tale to anyone who stays at the table after dinner in the mess. And some bits make their way into the everyday scuttlebutt or chatter among the crew; but it is never very close to the original tale, whose meaning therefore becomes diffused and diluted by murky waters.

"Of the real nitty-gritty work of the sailor I soon learned. This, too, is the stuff of lore, so I was prepared for it on a purely mental level. My body learned the truth of it all at once. You get plenty of exercise doing the normal chores of the day: scrubbing the decks, hoisting the sails, burnishing the metalwork; climbing aloft on the rigging—then hanging from one arm as you swing over the starboard yardarm of the mizzen topgallant yard to free the spar from the halyard . . . No, a sailor's life ain't easy. It taxes your tendons, lengthens your ligaments, for which you'll need plenty of lanolin as liniment . . .

"You wake to rats chewing your fingers or sniffing your face, sit up too fast and knock your head against the upper bunk, curse your captain for ever leading his flock out into this wide desert called the Sea: crossing the sand dunes of a wild ocean of waves—a floating caravan casting about for some paradise island or promised land—break a boom in transit and sail in circles for months and years . . ."

I had been listening, attention wrapt, my mind's eye transported aboard ship, where I saw crew scrambling in changing weather, sails flapping and popping in the wind as they were hoist. But it was late, and I had work to finish in my home office, so I said goodnight and left, looking forward to more of the captain's stories another time.

Every evening at sunset, the captain came out on his balcony and sipped a brandy to toast the dusk. It was a daily ritual and I witnessed on many occasions, a sunset ritual, often performed to music coming through the open door. He drank the sunset to the dregs, and then, in the gloaming, he would pick leaves from some of his plants—following criteria I could not perceive. "Harvesting the day," he called it, when he saw my curious look. "Culling the fruit of an evening ... for 'what is ripe is ready to die,' thus spake Nietzsche."

Depending on the music, the captain would dance around a bit on his little platform while sipping and harvesting. To a march by Souza he would swing his arms fiercely in time with the music, stepping from plant to plant mechanically like a wooden soldier from The Nutcracker, or mocking the Nazi goosestep, a marionette on wires. The music was always uplifting, ennobling—Handel, Mozart, Beethoven, Wagner—and seemed to flaunt romance in the face of life's tragedy.

If I was with him at sunset, he would interrupt everything and set about his ceremony—offering me a brandy as well. Then I would watch, amused, as he amused himself. Other times I took notice from below—from my deck or from my window. Someone who witnessed it from a distance might be reminded of a German clock with figures that came out through a door at the top of the hour and performed a mechanical dance, then returned to the clock and closed the door.

Once as I stared out and over the deck, over the captain and his antics, I noticed a magnificent parade of cumulus clouds across the western sky. The clouds were billowing and brilliant, the water vapor all puffed up and piled up according to its molecular nature and the weather—in other words, an effortless achievement of majesty! The delicate notes of Handel escaping from the captain's chambers could hold no ground to the clouds: however ennobling this music that represents man's finest efforts—effortfully refined, at once designed to show off man's talents and praise the divine—it always pales in comparison and leaves me wanting . . .

There was another time when he reminded me of a clock—a cuckoo clock . . . when he came out of his little door and squawked, then went back in. I was sitting alone on my deck. A crow was cawing loudly on a nearby roof. The captain burst forth from the door of his apartment and stepped out on his deck to discover what all the commotion was about.

The crow was crying loud, repetitive cries. He cawed in groups of seven, his raucous calls raising a ruckus. Between times he tilted his head from side to side, eying something somewhere not visible from where I was sitting.

The captain stood and looked, hand held to the brow like a salute to protect his eyes from the sun.

"What are you calling at? What are you striking at with your sharp cry?" His tone was plaintive, mocking the crow's, but also familiar, as if he recognized this particular crow and had talked to it before.

The crow stands there on the rain cap of a chimney pipe, projecting up several feet from the neighbor's roof. He hops a bit and turns his head to assess the captain. Yet he caws incessantly from the top of the pipe, just standing there, every once in a while cawing, bobbing his head up and down, otherwise motionless, facing one direction. Now he's looking around, now he's hopping around, looking under the edge of the rain cap and down into the pipe, as if there's something in there. Perhaps one of Santa's elves got stuck and never made it back up, or maybe old St. Nick himself was down in the pipe!

So the captain lets rip a noise of his own: a bellowing belch that echoed among the rooftops! Then he turns and sees me sitting there on my deck and he grins, slightly embarrassed, and starts to whistle between his teeth, weakly. In the constant wind from the ocean, there's this weak whistle that gets lost. Then, without saying anything, he goes back inside.

The captain was in rare form!

One day we were playing chess in the captain's quarters. I was the state champion in high school, so the game took little effort, and between moves I looked around the room, taking in more of the souvenirs and knickknacks.

The captain seemed to know what he was doing. As it was our first game and I was the visitor, he offered me the white pieces. I played the King's Pawn opening, as is my custom. He countered with the Center Counter game, advancing the Queen's Pawn two squares to attack my pawn. I captured, drawing his queen into the middle of the board, and attacked it with my knight, gaining a tempo by forcing him to move his queen again.

I observed a mask on the wall, white and striking. The lips and teeth were red, as if smeared with blood, and there was a red smudge on one cheek. Both eyes were black holes, as with most masks, but here the ocular orbits were outlined by oval grooves for emphasis. The eye holes were so irregular that one slit was almost vertical, and its groove was filled with black paint to create a polarity with the horizontal eye.

"Immunity, impunity, sacrosanctunity . . ." The captain riffed as he castled his king. After I did the same, he moved a knight into the thick of battle, keeping a finger on it in case he wanted to take the move back. He had to shift his forearm and lift his elbow to see the whole board in the new position. Not seeing anything with his eyes that he hadn't seen in his mind's eye, he took his finger off the top of the knight, making the move final.

"I should have traded queens earlier when I had the chance," he said, then added one of his adages: 'If what could have been would have been, it would have been different.'" Such semiprecious gems of wisdom issued from the captain from time to time, practiced phrases repeated like magic charms to set things right in the world. I have discerned no magical effect, but the phrases are worth repeating. Once, when he noticed my hair was thinning on top, he took off his cap to reveal a bald pate across which fine silver hairs were combed from either side, meeting in the middle. "You do what you can with all that you've got, and that's all you can do." It seemed to be a corollary of a more general axiom that I heard on several occasions: "You do what you can, and you can what you are, and you are what you did." This he said often, the first time parsing the parts to explain his meaning, counting off the clauses on three fingers: "'You do what you can'—'cause that's all you can do. 'You can what you are'—that's the sum of your abilities. And 'You are what you did'—that's the sum of your deeds."

The opening passed into the middle game and soon the captain was in a bind. Knowing he had to think for a while, I got up and went over to take a closer look at the mask. From a distance it had seemed primitive, but closer inspection revealed the superb craftsmanship that had been used to render details—such as the way the top lip curled back to expose the teeth, and how the outer edges of the nostril sills coiled up in spirals along the juncture of nose and cheek.

"Borneo," said the captain, looking over his shoulder to see where I was. "Your move." I returned to the table while he got up to make a pot of tea.

"Our ship, the Conquest, evaded pirates in the Sulu Sea. They were after our load of coffee from Celebes, and took refuge in Bago City in the Philippines. Then we moved to Manila, where we took fresh stock and water for the long trip home."

He was noisy in the kitchen, rattling the silverware, getting out tea cups and saucers. I was studying the board, developing a strategy to break through his defenses.

"There I wandered the side streets, popping into shops full of local wares as well as souvenirs for tourists. One had a selection of masks hung high on the wall above all the other merchandise, where they remained untouched and undusted. That mask was among them, an Indai-Guru cannibal witch mask from the Iban Dayak tribe of Borneo, which is southwest of the Philippines. The shopkeeper was reluctant to sell it—reluctant even to touch it, to bring it down for me to see—but I offered more, haggling the wrong way."

The teapot whistled briefly and then fell quiet.

"Ironically, on the way back to the ship, I stopped for coffee. There I sat in a shack sipping the black liquid whilst pondering the fate of our store of Celebes, a hundred burlap sacks of the green beans presumably still filling the hold of the Conquest at that moment."

He returned to the table and set china cups on saucers next to the chessboard, then brought the teapot over.

"The waiter was deaf-and-dumb (as we used to say) and it was impossible to get anything to eat. Besides, I think he was scared off by the mask, which sat unwrapped on the chair next to me."

He poured the black tea into the porcelain cups and sat down.

"Finally he brought me a plate of the local delicacy, camaru, which consists of rice paddy crickets stewed in vinegar with garlic and peppercorn . . . Unfortunately, the ingredients were not revealed until after I had finished the meal. I've never listened to crickets the same since!"

"I believe that should do it . . ." I said, moving a knight into place to checkmate the king in the corner—a "smothered mate."

Intimations of Unreality

"Zounds!" cried the captain. "You play better than some of the fellows I used to play . . ." He was embarrassed and began quickly to erase the position by setting up the pieces again.

"You know, chess is one of the choice pastimes aboard ship. Once duties are done and the trip is long, there are many empty hours to fill, and nothing absorbs the mind like a good chess game. Among crew and passengers there's often a player—I mean a *good* player. My old friend Admiral Godwater—now, *he* was an excellent player. He gave me my first helm."

The captain filled his pipe before the next game. He kept a tin of pipe tobacco, labeled Seven Seas Special Blend, on the table next to the board and box of men. I observed his habitual actions while he talked.

"Admiral Godwater mainly moved in higher circles, of course, than a mere midshipman, being a member of the admiralty and all—a great honor—but a sad figure, at the end, after retirement."

He filled the bowl by sticking the whole pipe into the tin and scooping up the tobacco. He withdrew the pipe, knocked the crumbs of fresh tobacco back into the tin with a brush of his hand, and tamped the bowl a bit with a quick press of the thumb. He looked at the bowl, approved.

"No fleet to command. No ship to sail. No ocean to cleave. No battle to wage. Still admirable, though."

The captain brought the pipe to his lips with his left hand. With his right, he struck the match on the whetstone, paused while it flared up, and brought the flame to the bowl. He puffed two or three times to ignite the tobacco, then shook out the match and dropped it on a pile of half-burnt matchsticks already in the ashtray.

"He didn't know what to do, where to go—lion hunting in Africa, sheepherding in Greece, falconry in the Irish countryside by the river Boyne."

A swirl of smoke rose from the pipe, the ghost of a bowl escaping to the air.

"Where is the Valhalla for sailors and marines? I suppose it is the Western Isles . . ."

Smoke from the long-stemmed pipe curled upward, spiraling into circles that floated above his head like concentric haloes.

"The last bastion of naval knights, Poseidon's princes, King Arthur's sea brigade . . ."

"How could he know what was next? Still admirable."

He smoked his pipe, tapped it, filled it again, tamped it. Then smoked again, sounding soft pops as he puffed.

We played another game. This time the captain played white and therefore had a slight advantage. He deployed his pieces well in the opening; in the middle game, he was trying to marshal his forces, coordinate the pieces for an attack. I saw it coming and thought I would come through it alright, but the outcome wasn't clear. He had to come up with the correct combination of moves to dispatch my defending pieces, one by one, before he could muster a successful onslaught. Unfortunately, when he did launch the attack he made a move out of sequence, and after some exchanges took place and the dust settled, he was down a piece with no attacking chances to compensate. The endgame was routine.

"It's not easy to be a captain; you have to pull it all together, be on top of everything; timing—that's essential! Preparation, ready for anything. Looking ahead, have to see what's going to happen, what might happen, before it does. I wasn't sure I could take it on, manage it. Manage the crew, the officers. Be responsible for the whole ship, and cargo too. It meant I had to be mature! But the Admiral thought I was ready for it, I had put in enough years, and besides, I was starting small.

"Well, you do what you can . . ." He said, staring at the lost position.

"Good game, Taget! You would have given your namesake a good game . . . Well, I guess it's time to water the plants . . ."

I followed him outside and hung about as he tended his plants and continued to regale me with his tales.

"Betwixt and between his years at sea, Taget spent time in Mexico, France, and Africa. In Khíos he had been bitten by the marigold bug, and he sought species of it everywhere. He returned from Africa empty-handed and in rags, but with tales of voodoo and ancient cults—and malaria. He was sick as a dog for weeks with fever, ranting about 'the demon within us' . . .

"It was in Mexico that he stalked tales of the native *cempasúchil*— marigold. Before the Christian conquest, the peoples of Mexico regarded the marigold as the flower of the dead, much as we treat the lily. Although the focus has been shifted to Jesus and Mary, the pagan flower remains in abundance on the Day of the Dead, when the ground is strewn with marigolds grown for the occasion.

"At some point Taget passed through a seaside village where he saw a second-storey shop named Mary's Gold, which naturally attracted his attention. He went up the gray wooden steps affixed to the exterior of the orange adobe and entered the shop. He said he could barely move, the shop was so full of statuettes and figurines of Mother Mary in all sizes, standing on the floor, on pedestals, covering the counters, hanging on the wall, suspended from the ceiling. Glass cases were full of icons framed in gold, rosaries on gold chains with Toltec heads as beads, brooches and pendants, cameos and portraits of Mary—always depicted with a halo of gold, dressed in gold raiment, adorned with gold . . . But no marigolds! Taget chatted with the shopkeeper in broken Spanish, and she told him about visions of Mary reported by villagers and inhabitants of the surrounding parts. She also told him that a festival would be held in a couple days that he would not want to miss.

"On the appointed day, Taget joined the festival—a parade through the streets, which had been strewn with fresh flowers—and moved with the brightly adorned crowd as it sauntered through the village and into the nearby hills. Taget was a tall man—about your height—so even if he sauntered he would take longer steps than others, so he soon found himself near the front of the procession. From there he could see a woman dressed in elaborate costume at the very head of the procession. She was a young, nubile woman wearing a tufted head-dress full of flowers, and was dressed in a blue, sleeveless tunic ornamented in floral patterns of delicate featherwork depicting marigolds. In fact, Feather Flower was the name of the Aztec goddess she represented—Xochiquetzal, the mother of the famous Feathered Serpent Quetzalcoatl.

"The procession arrived at a tall altar in the hills overlooking the village. Dancers emerged from the crowd, local craftsmen who were dressed as the totem animal of their craft—monkeys, jaguars, ocelots, wolves, coyotes, and so on—each brandishing some symbol or tool of their vocation. They danced in a circle around the altar while musicians played. Taget saw someone emerge from the crowd . . ."

At this point the captain glanced around to see who was within earshot and lowered his voice almost to a whisper. "He was a priest, as signified by his headband, who led the Feather Flower girl through the dancers and up some steps to the altar, where he placed her. The music and dance continued while the priest killed the girl . . ." (a whisper now) "and then meticulously set about removing her heart and flaying her body!" He spoke it in a hush.

I knew that the Aztecs performed human sacrifice, removing the heart of the victim, but the flaying was new to me . . . not to mention the suggestion that the sacrifice had occurred in modern times—during the captain's years at sea.

"And . . . Taget?"

"Taget watched! Taget watched the whole thing—stunned, stupefied, unable to act. Everyone watched—but it's not over . . ."

He fell back to a whisper. "The priest removed the girl's skin and put it on himself! The fresh skin was still elastic and the blood helped it adhere to the priest's own skin. Then, adorned in the Feather Flower's headdress, the most horrible thing of all . . . Picture it! The priest wearing the maiden's skin descended from the altar and sat on the bottom step, *where he went through the motions of a weaver weaving . . .!*" He said it wide-eyed through clenched teeth, and his voice wavered with emotion. He trembled physically, as though shivering, and for the first time he seemed frail.

"That's incredible! But . . . what about Taget, surely he went to the authorities?"

"The authorities!?" he burst out laughing. "The authorities were *there*: the mayor was dressed as the wolf! His symbol was the gavel!"

He hooted and howled until he began hacking. The wind had picked up and blew into our faces from the west.

"You'd better get inside, out of this cold wind," I said out of concern.

"Oh, I'll be alright," after he had stopped coughing.

One day while we were playing chess, the captain brought some toast to the table—white toast burnt black—along with a polygonal jar of orange-colored preserves.

"Sorry, but I'm famished . . . Help yourself," he said.

"Uh, no thanks. What is that, marmalade?" It was more gold than orange.

"This is a pot of my 'remedy.'" He said as he spread the preserves on a piece of toast.

"Remedy?" I focused on my move as I waited for the explanation. I was sure it would involve a story or two . . .

"For anything that ails you! Almost . . . What the heck?"

I had posed a conundrum on the board, sacrificing a knight for two pawns to create attacking possibilities.

"Hmmm . . . I don't like it, but I can't let you take that pawn for free . . ." He captured the knight with a pawn, which I took with a bishop. He crunched into his toast and chewed loudly while examining the board. I glanced at his toast and recognized a floral shape in the preserve.

"Why, is that . . ."

"Marigolds! Of course! Marigolds are the secret of the remedy."

I remembered seeing the captain pick marigold blossoms one day. The stems were far too short for anything but a very short vase, so I assumed he was making a potpourri.

"Taget taught it, discovered it himself somehow and then experimented with the recipe until he got it right. *This* form of it"—he held up a corner of the jam-covered toast—"is a conserve made of cured marigolds boiled with sugar. The sugar helps counteract the bitterness of the flower. But the curing is the secret. You have to make it right or it's not edible . . . Sorry, I can't tell you, Alex—even if your name *is* Taget!"

"Check."

"Damn!" He surveyed the ruins of his position and tipped over his king.

"That's three in a row . . . Let's give it a rest."

Although I beat him consistently, he never gave up trying and often the games produced a position of interest. He seemed to enjoy the challenge, though at some level he might have felt embarrassment or even lowered self-esteem due to the constant drubbing.

"Taget played a mean game . . . used Alekhine's Defense. Maybe I'll try that next time." He pushed his chair back and looked out the window.

"Taget had read of medicinal uses of the marigold throughout history. Medieval physicians believed the flower had healing properties and used it both internally and externally. Taken internally, it was thought to act as a tonic for the heart and blood, fight diseases of the kidney and liver, and even cure various forms of cancer. Practice showed it to have a stimulating and diaphoretic effect (it makes you sweat), as well as a deobstruent one (relieves obstructions, if you know what I mean)—and, in the same department, a diuretic. Not a complete panacea but a pretty useful herb. And they smell sweet, too!

"We were on the good ship *Conquest*, with Captain Godwater at the helm. I was the First Mate and Taget the Second. At Taget's request, we loaded two barrelfuls of the plant into the hold. Together with the greens and roots, the drying flowers had an unpleasant smell, but somehow imparted a cooling quality similar to mint.

"Then Taget began his experiments. He cured it and cooked it, dried some in the sun up on the poop deck, next to his potted hybrids. In addition to the limited resources of the ship, he gradually assembled a small laboratory in his own quarters. He separated each plant into root, stem, leaf, and flower and commenced to prepare concoctions with the various varietals and combinations. He tried several additives—sugar, molasses, honey, rum, Polish vodka (the closest thing to pure grain we could lay our hands on) . . . Let's see, spices: turmeric, pepper—he wasn't cooking, just experimenting with additives that counteracted the bitterness of the pottages and extracts. He used various methods of heating: the stove in the galley, a Bunsen burner in his quarters, and for one afternoon a small cauldron on the forecastle. The skipper finally had to rein him in before he set fire to the ship!

"Now, Taget fancied himself a doctor and occasionally practiced medicine on the crew . . . When there was a cut, burn, sun burn, any type of rash or skin malady, he began using one of his simple marigold extracts on the region. Any time the skin was broken— cut, abscessed, and for compound fractures and sprains—he applied it as dressing, lotion, poultice or cataplasm . . . various forms for various needs. Once, when an ordinary seaman split his knee open, Taget rushed to the scene with his medicine kit, and on first application of an experimental lotion to the fresh wound, the skin sealed up like a zipper—right before our eyes! Thereupon, his honorary rank among the men was promoted from Physician to Magician—to Alchemist!

"As a result, when Taget began tinkering with tinctures derivative of the marigold's sap and floral essences, he found many volunteers among the crew, which led to some interesting problems later on. But first it was our food . . .

"At some port or another we had replenished our supply of the plant, this time seven barrels, taking advantage of extra space in the hold. With this plentiful supply, Taget's experiments thrived and flourished, bearing fruits of various sorts. Just at this point, somewhere in the middle of the ocean, we had a food problem due to poor planning and spoilage, and the crew went on rations. All the meat had rotted and had to be heaved overboard.

"Confronting the food shortage, the skipper inquired of Taget the prospect of eating the marigold greens, asking too if the flower petals might not add a delicate taste to the salad—assuming, of course, Taget wasn't too fond of the plants to let a few of them go. Taget told him straight that he knew the food was edible only if properly prepared, that otherwise it was known to have toxic effects; therefore, he would have to try various cooking methods and test the results on the ship's cats before he would recommend feeding it to the men.

"The skipper was calculating the risks of either proceeding with our itinerary or altering course to find or procure foodstuffs. The rest of us couldn't tell by the stars whether a shift in course had been made—if any, it was slight.

"Under Taget's direction we gave the first concoction to the old male cat Spunky, an admixture of flowers tempered with fresh cheese. He ate a bit but didn't care for it, and forthwith swelled up mightily and began panting and crawling on the deck. He was clearly in great pain and died a little while after. We had thought to kill him to end his torment, but the end came of itself . . .

"We also found a dead rat near the barrels in the hold, and cutting it open found that it had eaten of the stock of seed Taget had also brought aboard. From this discovery and the experiment on the cat, we deduced and proved the herb's poisonous nature in its raw state.

"Eliminating raw flower and seed left leaf, stem and root. The roots were insubstantial, not like tubers, and not a good prospect. The stem of a plant is rarely of much nutritional value, except as fiber, so that left the leaf.

"Not wanting to torture another cat—or perhaps to save the cat for a further test—Taget took a leaf and chewed it for a few minutes, at first without ill-effect. Then a strange look came over his face, and he spit out the mash in his mouth and all the juice that remained, and kept spitting after that. In this state he was bent over, with hands on knees, and when he went to stand up straight his back went out. He complained of a pinch in the middle of his spine, and thereafter lost his powers of walking for three days. He said he had certain unpleasant feelings that were difficult to describe.

"From his bed and desk Taget directed our work. The cook and I measured quantities of greens and timed the pots at low-boil and simmer. I accidentally knocked a potato into one pot, which led to the discovery that the starchy tuber actually absorbed much of the offending toxins and alkaloids from the cooked greens. After removing the potato, the resulting porridge was subjected to the litmus test—the old-fashioned one using lichens, dipped into the samples to test their acidity and get some clue as to their edibility. The cat Cloris was the last hurdle. The cook added a little fish oil to the green stuff to make it more palatable, and Cloris ate it all up. This time we waited a day to make sure, but she seemed just fine—in fact, more energetic than previously.

"Thus we arrived at a range of green dishes to supplement our dwindling foodstuffs—dried meat, potatoes, oats and barley for the main—until these were gone, and all we ate was greens and bouillon.

"Taget had not calculated a possible cumulative effect of the plant food on the human system, nor to account for metabolic differences from person to person, but a week from our destination some symptoms made themselves known.

"Among the crew the diet caused a general condition of greensickness, a greenish-yellow discoloration of the skin. It's just like with carrots: if you eat too many, you turn carrot-orange. There was also a general malaise that might have indicated lethargy, or merely poor morale. In a few cases, symptoms were worse: indigestion, nausea, vomiting, dry heaves.

"Cooky—old Stewart the cook, steeped in the art of stewing—slipped a hot pepper into the greens one day, thinking this would spice up the stuff. After all, he was the cook, not Taget. And it so happened that Seamus had the same notion, and hoping to spice up the swill for once, snuck in when Cooky was gone, slipped in some chili powder from a tin on the spice shelf, stirred it in good and snuck off again. The grub was so blazing hot no one could eat it, and the crew was fed on bread and a few chunks of potato fished out of the stew and daubed off on hankies to absorb the peppery broth.

"'Must've gotten too much pepper in there,' said Cooky, puzzled, 'but I didn't think I put in *that* much.' And Seamus said nothing, but scratched his jaw, and I remembered seeing him leave the galley grinning. When Cooky fed what was left to his mutt, the dumb thing wolfed and howled before he whelped and went running—with his bowels running after!

"In the meantime, Taget's had recovered and he was busy with new experiments, distilling the tinctures I mentioned before. Alcohol is required, and like I said, we tried rum, but its impurities spoiled the flower essence and hardened the sap extract. I had a bottle of Polish vodka that was 180 proof, and this Taget took and rectified further to 190 proof to obtain better results. At one point in this work he stopped and looked up with his eyes all wide and said 'How many potatoes do we have? Never mind . . .' and went back to work. I knew he thinking of making more vodka, but the one bottle was sufficient for the minute quantities involved in his processes. Besides, there was a food shortage . . .

"The liqueur filled a clear alembic and was green-gold and glowed with a warm light that became dazzling in the direct sun.

"You might think that, with the greensickness, and being sick of eating green stuff, the crew would think twice about trying Taget's derivative, but when he told them it was a cure for what ailed them, they all lined up. The skipper, who fancied himself a religious man, never let liquor cross his lips, and so abstained.

"'This tincture of marigold—arrived at through divers distillations—reunites the floral essence with the sap extract, and serves to counteract the heaviness of the foodstuff we have been eating . . .' Taget propounded, and it made sense.

"The men had modified the words of an old sea chantey sung at dinnertime, and they sang it now as they lined up for the medicine:

'Oh, feed me with something, I beg you—
With pottage and porridge and lime!
Refill me with stock from the barrel—
From the pot to the bowl—to my mind!'

"I of course partook of it and must say it provided a rather delightful feeling of lightness, a euphoria . . . a feeling of spring, if I may say so. This did counter the weightiness of the diet along with the malaise that affected everyone. Naturally, some of the crew overindulged and Taget learned to lock it up, and lock up his quarters, and keep guard on it, as it seemed to have an irresistible lure for some of the sailors.

"Unfortunately, after a day the nice effects of the liqueur wore off, and to Taget's chagrin, there were negative side-effects to the liquid as there had been to the solid marigold derivations. Like the food, the drink in some caused obstinate vomiting, but in everyone it caused psychological effects, ranging from irritability to hysteria, that soon became a serious threat to the ship.

"First the hearing became very acute and so sensitive that the slightest noise might startle you. The sense of touch or pain was also exaggerated and magnified: the pain was far out of proportion to the injury one suffered. Even the sensation of the heartbeat itself, or the pulse heard in the ear, caused a sensation of intense throbbing, but worse, like being beaten repeated with a blunt instrument, or more sharply like stabbing pains.

"Third Mate Redman was an extreme example. He was hysterical with pain—whether real or imaginary we could not tell—and he suffered on the mental and emotional levels as well as the physical one. He fell on the deck, writhing and screaming as with agony, but shouting something unintelligible; he was hallucinating and speaking in tongues. To subdue him until he calmed down, we threw a wool blanket over him, tossing a heavy coil of rope on top.

"I myself felt strange delusions: the feeling of falling from a great height, when the bottom drops out. Dreams of falling haunted me, too: falling from high places, buildings in the city, cliffs in the desert, bridges in the country. The sense of hearing was highly attuned, more acute than normal—you could hear incredible details within normal sounds, and hear far-away sounds as if up close. And then there was depression and dread: deep depression where you cannot see the light, and an overwhelming sense that something terrible was about to happen.

"This sense of doom became an epidemic and affected everyone aboard, and this itself hang in the air like a dark cloud. And though the lassitude was felt by everyone, each of us felt a sense of separation, our nerves frazzled at the edges, which led to exhaustion. But sleep provided no relief, if sleep could be obtained, for one constantly woke up, restless, sweating, panting, screaming. And if one woke up screaming, well you know that woke others up. And the lack of sleep bred even more exhaustion.

"At its peak, our common state drew us back together, transcending the separateness. It was a moonless night and everyone gathered on deck; and together we had the feeling that something immense and unknowable was passing nearby unseen—a great sense of weight, of a burden hanging over us, some impending catastrophe. I looked up to see if anything *was* there, and, by God, I saw the stars disappear . . . as if something was moving across the sky . . . Others saw it, too, and we all huddled together and shuddered and shat ourselves in terror.

"In retrospect, I think it must have been a cloud, but at the time the terror was so powerful that no amount of reasoning and explaining would have alleviated it. Later on, after much research, Taget read that some species of the Calendula genus (to which the pot marigold belongs) may contain large quantities of nitrogen, iodine, and phosphoric acid, and we deduced that these had induced our collective subjective states . . ."

On his deck near sundown, the captain was using binoculars to focus on the small patch of ocean visible to the west. As always, he was solemn, sad, dreamy, looking back on the days of old. I tried looking through the glasses, but the light glancing off the water was too bright for my eyes. "You get used to it," he said.

I pictured the captain out on the ocean, spyglass to the eye, with light shining off ever-changing waters in all the seven seas—for all those years. The light magnified by the focal lenses and shot into his eyes, though his own lenses, projected upside-down like a movie onto the silver screen of his retinas.

The clouds I could see with my own eyes: clouds like soft yellow flowers floating atop tall stems. But the yellow wasn't bright, it was a leaden ochre that darkened underneath into crimson and dripped at the edges like saffron steeped in wine.

"Let me tell you about my good friend, Donny McKay. I call him my friend. Hailed from Boston. He built a clipper ship with his own hands, a 200-footer. He and his fabrication shop. A classic in every detail. I was on her maiden voyage, racing from New York to Frisco—the long way, around Cape Horn. This was the way they had to go before they dug the Panama Canal, and took all the fun out of shipping!

"I say we raced; there was only us, but we wanted to set a record. And we did! Made it in 88 days—under three months, when most sailing ships take four or five.

"We were sailing round the Horn, blown by cold air over cold water, keeping land in sight and witnessing the marvels of wildness and wilderness. The sky was lit by angelic sunset light. In the distance we could make out Patagonia, rugged spires of rock whose tops were lost in the painted clouds. That's when we saw something funny.

"Now, I'll never say I believe in UFOs, but what we witnessed was as good a candidate for the category as I've ever seen. A piece of cloud broke off, detached itself from the larger mass of clouds and floated free, glowing a wondrous purple and vermillion. Then it shot across the eastern sky, skipped along that horizon, also lined with clouds, playing across them like a colored spotlight.

"Most of the crew, as witnessed it, wrote it off as a trick of light caused by clouds crossing the setting sun, or some prismatic effect due to water vapor in the west. I'm not sure what to think, but I can still see it in my mind's eye, a flying cloud moving as fast as you please across the sky, then losing color and merging with the grayer clouds that lined the eastern horizon.

"As to the clipper ship, she ran aground in '74. I only heard about it later. For some reason she couldn't be rescued—probably stuck up to the hull in mud, or caught in treacherous rocks . . . I never heard for sure, but the wreck was burned to salvage the metalwork. Which seemed such a shame—all that fine woodwork lost, and yards of clean canvas; but the metal pieces were salvaged from the fire, as I say, and used again."

Since he had brought up the topic of UFOs, I wanted to ask him about unusual phenomena of the sea. "I don't suppose you ever saw anything really *strange* at sea—?" I began, and even as I formulated my question the captain grew wary. "Devil fish, monsters of the deep, sea serpents . . . the stuff of legend?" I served it up weakly, expecting to be laughed at, convincing myself halfway through that it was a silly question to ask.

"Oh, yes," he said to the contrary. "They may be legendary, but they're real enough, for sure!" He was serious. He even trembled a bit and looked at me anxiously, as if afraid of something I might ask about.

"Many fisherman and seaman—and credible ones—have told of encountering such things, and I am among them . . . They are weird for sure, and also real! And rare enough to be respected and celebrated when sighted. Respected, and feared, too . . . Fear is a part of it."

He was smoking his pipe, holding it by the bowl while talking, and pointing the stem for emphasis. As he it pointed toward me, I could see the end of the mouthpiece, well-bitten and slightly wet with saliva. As I watched, a tiny plume of smoke emerged from the aperture and escaped into the air.

"And you know, the devilfish is a legend based on sightings of the giant octopus and squid, of gray whales and manta rays. They all have a rarity and strangeness of shape that inspires awe, even if they don't make you think of the Devil!

"The sea alligator is another real species—actually a crocodile, as it turns out, a terrifying creature that once reached over twenty feet long, and looks as much like a dragon or dinosaur as anything alive.

"Your giant crabs off Alaska and Japan are big for crabs, but not as big as a car or anything near it.

"But the sea serpent, that's another matter . . . That one may be a figment of the imagination, or may involve late sightings of creatures before they became extinct. Maybe the long-necked *elasmosaurus*, which supposedly died out 65 million years ago. Who knows?"

The captain puffed his pipe and looked into the distance.

"Once I saw something though . . . We were in the Pacific, east of Guam, trawling for skipjack tuna near the Marianas Trench. The Trench, you know, is famous as the deepest part of the ocean. It's a crease where two lithospheric plates collide, pushing one down into the mantle . . ." He gripping the pipe in his teeth and used his hands to demonstrate one plate colliding with another.

"I wasn't very good in geology." I said something, at least to classify the topic.

"Well, you get the idea . . . As a result, the water is hotter than normal. Maybe because of that, you can sometimes catch bigger fish there—the usual species, but much bigger than normal, easier to fill the hull and prettier in price at the market scale.

"Now, the skipjack are not too large, normally, and named for their habit of leaping out of the water and flapping around on the surface before they go back under. Maybe it's important for them, somehow, or maybe they get a rush from almost drying out up here in the air before reentering their native element. Who knows? But they do it, and it makes easy work for the trawlerman to scoop them up in his trawler net.

"One day the sea went still and we floated about for hours without seeing a single fish. Not a bird, either, and it was strange not to see one or the other even out there in deep waters.

"So there we were, looking over the rail, where the afternoon sun lit the water well, and in the stillness you could see clear down to a hundred feet, when up comes this yellow cloud of murkiness rising from the depths into view, finally bubbling up to the surface a dozen yards from the ship. We could feel the heat even before it breached surface, and then we were nearly knocked over by the most horrid, sulfurous stench that ever broke wind, no doubt some volcanic fumes from that rift in ocean floor.

"When we recovered from the hellish vapor and looked around, we could see something else coming up, dead creatures of the deep killed by the vented heat— strangely shaped fish, flat things like mantas, long cylindrical and conical fish. And because they all lived in the dark depths where sunlight never reached, they were either self-luminous or had sightless eyes.

"Among the boiled bodies was something that might have been a throwback to the dinosaurs, or equally something not yet catalogued by science— either way it lived and was strange of form. Weird but true. It looked like a brontosaurus with fins—a large round body the size of an elephant, subjoined by muscular fins in the place of legs, but its notable feature was its neck: long as an anaconda, round as a wild boar, and topped by a snakelike head the size of an ox-head.

"Everything was yellowed and poisoned and the tissues nearly boiled apart by the plume or effluvium that brought them up from their submarine realm, cooked well-done. Still, we might have tried to haul one of the creatures in as a souvenir; but the skipper was anxious about the fumes, so we set to and high-tailed it out of there."

"Another time I was out fishing by myself out in deep waters and caught a lovely blue marlin. Before I could finish reeling it in, something came up all of a sudden and took it away . . . Now, I admit I was drunk, and the light was getting dim, but I'll swear the thing was a sea serpent! It came up and swallowed the marlin whole, spear and all, then took off. I saw its eye turn into the water like a whale's, and maybe it saw me too . . . Then it moved off like a silver ribbon and went under the waves."

Again the look of fear across his face . . .

"Like I said, fear is a part of it. Fear has a function, can help us adapt and survive."

"How so?" I asked.

"The image of the monster is based on sightings and exaggeration. The sightings stimulate imagination and exaggeration, which feed fear. It's the same as fish tales—every time you tell the tale, the fish gets bigger! Whether or not the sea monster is out there, projecting the image of the monster makes us wary, which makes us careful, and therefore safe."

The next day, something truly fabulous happened, right before our eyes. The captain and I were sitting inside, looking out the window, from which there was a good view of the balcony. There Frank was lying on top of the outer rail, sunning himself with what little sun filtered through the clouds. As we watched, a large bird of prey swooped down and seized the iguana with its outstretched talons and, with an extra beat of the wings, carried him away! It happened in an instant, but I had time to see the sharp talons close around the lizard, raptor on reptile, scaly claws on scaly skin; and I realized in that instant that it was dinosaur versus dinosaur, just like in the old days, in epochs past! Frank only had time to turn his head and see his attacker, and to stiffen his throat pouch—a blood-red warning sign that the raptor could ignore. The bird was enormous, standing over two feet high, and looked like a species of hawk or falcon, with smallish head and spotted white throat.

The captain jumped up, which startled me and so I jumped up, too; but there was nothing to see except the lichen-spotted wood where Frank had lain seconds before.

"Well, I'll be damned!" was all he uttered, though we looked at each other for a reality check, making sure we had both seen the same thing.

"Amazing!" I thought to myself, but I said, "Poor Frank!"

The captain ran out, looked up, back over the house, tugging his visor to shield his eyes as he scanned the northern sky. He may have hoped that Frank had been dropped on the sloping roof, but seeing nothing there or on the wing, assumed the lizard was long gone.

For the captain, shock turned to grief and then as quickly to despair.

"Well," he said soberly, "there goes another friend!" as if a pattern existed in his life: that his close friends were lost—in strange, but essentially natural situations.

"So many plans unrealized . . . so many unfinished journeys, ports of call unvisited. So many possibilities unrealized, potentials undeveloped . . . so many worlds unknown, territories uncharted . . ."

The captain shook his head and sighed.

"When I was a youngster I couldn't wait to shove off—get my sea legs—see the world—leave my little home behind. When at sea, we couldn't wait to get to port—to see some strange new folk in their native garb, hear new tunes, new tales—see new women! Then after a few days back on solid land, your legs get restless and wobbly and you can't wait to get back on board, back to the open sea, the corrosive sea, back to the restless waters, the salted air . . . Now I have nothing to wait for, except the chiming of the final bell. And an angel to take me to heaven."

He sat silently for a minute. I tried to think of something to say, kept glancing at the rail as if the lizard might reappear as suddenly as it had gone. Then I remembered Madagascar, where the captain said he had found Frank, and I looked at the globe across the room—at Africa, whose western edge was visible, with Madagascar out of view on the other side.

"A sad thing," he began again. "It's an inevitable lesson of age and is taught by reflecting on the empty shell of your former life with its days of hollow ceremony; on the unseen splendor of life, the untamed promises of youth . . . Ruminating on deeds done, and deeds undone, is like sampling a porridge of memory spiced with true adventure and sugared with random pleasures, with treasures found; but also spiked with regrets—the bitter almonds of errors made, the sour rind of misspent opportunities, the salty plums of bad relationships . . .

"It is a lesson of age," he repeated, "distilled from years of wisdom, but after all, a lesson wasted on youth . . ." He wagged a pedagogic finger at me.

That night I was on my back deck. The lights were out upstairs and the captain was not to be seen.

A thick fog had rolled in from the ocean and filled the air. Other times I could hear a foghorn, but only if the wind came from the right direction, west by northwest. Tonight there was only a slight current from due west, enough to push the damp fog past me in a gray parade.

Out of the fog there rose a cry—a seabird drifting in from the shore. A tern or gull, his call sounded weary and lost, trying to find his way back to his fellows or his mate.

But something seemed wrong. The bird's origin and direction were uncertain. Was he flying directly above? Never heard in the same place twice, never seen. Circling the house? It seemed lower, then higher. Was he swooping over the house?

There was an echo to the sound that seemed wrong. What was there to echo off of, except the roofs of the houses? Maybe the thickness of the fog affected the acoustics. It was a haunting sound, a lonesome calling that moved on, got further away, and faded.

Then there was nothing but fog.

"Spending days on end at sea will change a man's consciousness forever," Captain More began, the next time he regaled me with a story while puttering among his planters.

"On land we have a false sense of solidity: the feeling that we stand on solid ground and everything is in place and will remain that way." He grabbed the rail firmly and pretended to shake it, though it was immobile.

"At sea, nothing is solid, fixed, and there is no denying the dynamic aspect of things: the dynamism of movement and change, whether orderly or chaotic.

"On good days the swell of the ocean is gentle, made steadier by your own progress. As you know, the tides are an ebb and flow at the water's edge due to a swelling up of the oceans caused by the pull of the moon. Step inside and I'll demonstrate . . ."

I followed him through the open doorway into his quarters and over to the globe he kept on a side table. He held up an orange next to the globe to represent the moon in orbit around the earth.

"When she's on one side, there are high tides below her and on the other side, too—which you wouldn't think, but that's the way it is. At the same time there are low tides on the alternate sides of the earth, and since the earth is rotating relative to the moon, you get two high tides and two low tides every day. As the moon moves, the swell moves, and everywhere else the oceans adjust to the change. Wherever she may be at the time, and wherever you are, you are somewhere in the tidal cycle."

The notion that the moon causes the ocean to swell on the *opposite* side of the earth was new to me, and counter-intuitive; but it explained the two daily high tides, which I had never thought much about.

He set down the orange and I followed him back outside, where he continued to tend to his plants while talking.

"That's one level of the sea's movement, swelling and falling due to the moon. On top of this (and beneath it!), you have currents and streams running through the water— on the surface and at different depths—which also interact. And then atop it all (though reaching deep within), you have surface waves—the ones that start at sea and end up lapping the shore. Waves always arise from the wind's action on the water's surface—a ripple first, a wrinkle, then a wave. Finally, wind is the movement of air, the atmosphere's own streams, like the trade wind, and currents and eddies, all subject to the weather.

"On bad day, all the wave movements collide—surface waves with deep waves, rising tide with falling tide, surface current with crosscurrents—and the impact of each on the other—multilateral and collateral motion . . . it's the stuff of physics—fluid dynamics! But you'd better understand the basics of the sea before you go out and risk your life on it. For the upshot is that the swells and currents beleaguer the rudder and bedevil the hull, pushing and pulling, tilting and turning, until you think they are colluding to make your way difficult.

"On terrible days, bad weather gets added to the mix and plays its own bit of mischief. On a rough sea, the crests of the waves get higher and the troughs get deeper, and the swell will pick you up quickly and then drop you just as fast, and the ridges running this way and that will try to tear your ship astern. Again you think the sea is angry and out to get you, but you know it is only a dumb, mindless thing, cold and indifferent to the likes of you and me. There's no more warmth in the sea than there is in an avalanche or mudslide. No mercy, no pity—because no feeling at all, which is a chilling thing . . .

The captain was transplanting cuttings. Having rooted them in jars of water (and who knows what magical formula), he was potting them in pots of potting soil.

"At sea you are exposed to the raw elements of nature. However fine your ship, even if you hide in your cabin, at sea you are subjected to those elements—the real stuff of this world."

He poked his finger into the soil and created a hole, then put the cutting in, roots first, pushed the soil back into the hole around the stem, and patted the surface.

"Had I decided to work onshore, on good ole *terra firma*, I think I would have worked with the earth directly: maybe as a farmer, tending the soil, my fingers in touch with the earth itself. Just as my fingers and hands and face and eyes touched the sea."

He finished transplanting and looked up, squinting at the clouds being pushed by the wind like a broom pushing refuse.

"Looks like rain, might even blow up a storm . . ."

Even as he said it, dark spots appeared on the gray wood of the rail, between the pale green patches of lichen.

"Let me tell you about a storm—a storm to end all storms—a storm that nearly ended *us* . . .

"I was the captain of the good ship *Ole Bess*. After a couple days of smooth sailing under clear skies we began to see some weather. From a distance we saw mighty mastheads of dark cloud hanging in the sky, many thousand-tons of water defying gravity as much as the floating rock citadels of Magritte.

"A tail-wind came along and pushed us on, driving us into the disturbance, giving us time only to scramble and set things ready—to shorten the sails, secure the lifeboats, batten down the hatches and do our best to lessen the impact of the rough winds and rough waters ahead. The wind shifted as we were passed from one system to another, the current still carrying us into the teeth of the storm.

"As we crossed the squall line, the wind increased to a gale, blowing big raindrops like bullets. Before the jib could be lowered and secured on the foredeck, it blew clean off, ropes snapping with loud cracks, the canvas popping and flapping as the wind carried it away. Then the top square sails popped, one by one—the fore topgallant and the main, plucked by the gale winds like wings off a fly."

The wind had picked up and it began to rain enough to drive us inside, where the captain continued his tale.

"Cooky came on deck to rinse his pots in the rain—very poor timing, as it soon turned out. He went to the side, cursing as the air snatched his cook's hat and tossed it in the water. Legs well anchored, he leaned against the rail with hip and elbow, pouring scrapings and soap and old grease over the edge. But the ship tossed and Cooky lost hold of his pan and scraper—grabbing onto the rail to avoid going over himself. Then, when the ship righted and tilted the other way, with him clasping onto it the rail weakened and cracked. Of course, Cooky was twice as big as any other man: since he took portions while he cooked, he ate twice as much and twice as often. So with the next yaw he bent over again and this time went down as the rail gave way. Cooky went face-first into the water, fortuitously falling face-down on the frying pan that floated where it had fallen, snapping his neck.

"It was a battle to cross the deck. The men scrambled, crept to the side, themselves wary of the edge, the gap in the railing, secured with rope like mountaineers—but it was of no use. The body was carried off in the waves. Meanwhile, the ship needed tending.

"You have no idea what it's like out there, shivering, facing into the cold blast, peering wet-eyed into a dark horizon, looking for any sign of daylight. Any speck of light and you know you have made it through, if you just hold on a bit longer. Half-frozen in that sea-sweeping gale, you shove your frozen fingers into the wool armpits of your sailor's coat; your toes nearly numb, washed with the rainwater and seawater gathered on the poop deck, while the main deck is washed with waves creeping in between the balusters of the rail.

"It's one thing to imagine it, read about it, see a movie: to project yourself mentally into that situation for a moment. But when you are there, the moment stretches on and on; you may turn away in disbelief, but it's still there; you can run away in grief, but it's still there, like a car wreck that isn't a dream: the car that was so shiny and new really is crumpled and crunched and there's no undoing it—the brute reality of the fact, as stunning as your face hitting the wheel.

"I had sent all the men below deck to protect them and lashed myself to the wheel. After the last one had sealed the hatch I heard laughter and a voice from above calling my name. It was Taget in the Crow's Nest, where he had gone to hide! Taget was also tied up, having lashed himself to the mainmast while the others went below. I called up to him, ordered him below, but he refused. He wanted to witness the worst of the storm.

"And the worst storm it was, a storm sent by the God of Abraham, an angry God pouring forth his wrath for all the sins and transgressions of mankind; pouring down bolts of lightning by the barrel and water by the hundred-ton; pounding the sea, raising the waves, and drowning the hapless sailors that wandered into His watch—and foundered in His wake . . .

"I cried out, called to the men below, to get them to remove Taget, but no one could hear, save Taget himself, who howled and hooted all the while. He turned fore and shouted into the gale but I could not make out his words. Later he told me, 'I swore at the storm to be quiet, so that I might be heard by my Maker!'

"Then we were wrenched. The ship cascaded into a trough in the sea, which dropped and rose to a ridge and threw us on our port side. We lay on our beam ends, the mainmast laid flush with the ocean, only to be righted again before the sea could pour over her, and the sea walls rose and tossed us into another trough, laying us on the starboard side. And each time the sails were soaked, and Taget in the Crow's Nest was dunked into the cold water like a Salem witch, then carried aloft again, then down the other side, moving in a sad and silly arc as we were slapped back and forth—tossed like a child's toy in a bathtub. The mainmast creaked and threatened to break, though the shrouds held it firm and stayed. And the sails slacked and smacked and the ropes popped loose and taut. And the whole ship nearly capsized and went down in a great baptism. Lucky for us, the cargo kept put, never shifted, or we'd be laid over for good and water-logged. But it kept place, helped act as ballast to keep us upright."

The captain described the arcs and motions by waving the stem of his pipe in the air.

"They say 'no mercy has the sea' but something happened, a fortuitous sea-change, a sudden mood-change—which is why we call her 'she.' She had a change of heart, let us say. Or Poseidon changed his mind about destroying us, distracted by some other game. Or another way, the cat got tired of the mouse and left it, wounded but alive.

"But the storm wasn't over. No, the water stopped kicking the ship around because it had kicked us out of the stormy waters proper into a little area of lull, where we felt suddenly free of the wind and rolled forward on a relatively still sea, drifted forward on our own momentum. The sails were ragged and we had reached a bit of calm.

"I looked up to see if Taget had survived and saw him there, dangling half out of the Crow's Nest, spewing water from his lungs, and catching his breath. And as soon as he caught his breath, he took to laughing—and laughing made him cough and sputter, spit out more water, and start over catching his breath and laughing again! All the while he was trying to unlash himself, fingers fumbling at the rounds of wet rope that bound him to the mast.

"I smiled at him thus preoccupied until up above him I spied a strange formation of the clouds. The sunset was illuminating the higher clouds, way up above the storm, and they formed a colorful backdrop to the darker clouds and tossed and tussled directly above us. From the rolling mix of cloud matter emerged a weird shape that looked like the skull of a longhorn bull, a T-shape with the vertical head and snout crossed at the top by horns that extended to either side. The whole shape shifted back, horns going back, mouth opening in an O, like the bull was mooing! And the wind was howling, too, like a raging bull. And then the T-shape reminded me of a uterus, with the vertical central chamber and tubes stretching out to ovaries at either side. So this womb-shaped cloud system rotates backward and the O opens like a cervix, opens and grows wider to give a glimpse within—into the dark chamber backlit in crimson and sparkling with electricity.

"The churning and glitter continued within the womb, boiling and brewing like a primeval force, a vortex of spinning energy gleaming and golden like the source of all creation, self-creating and self-renewing . . .

"And Taget shouted, 'I thought I was a goner for sure,' as he unwound the last round of rope and stood giddy. But when he saw me just staring, he turned and looked upward too, when—wham!—all of a sudden the cloud shot out a golden bolt that stuck the Crow's Nest, right where Taget stood!

"The flash was so bright it blinded me for a second, but then I could see that Taget was alive—flaming with life, lit up with all his bones glowing,

Intimations of Unreality

veins full of light, flames shooting out in all directions, pulsing like a jelly-fish—alive with light! From that distance I could see his eyes flaming, holy eyes burning in the dark, little flickering flames that licked the air." The captain's own eyes lit up in the semi-darkness, the light from a lamp reflecting like a blaze.

"Taget was alive, but changed forever. He had been hit for sure—I had seen it—but we didn't know how bad it was until we brought him down, lowered by rope to the deck, to the arms of the waiting men, who rolled him over and laid him on the deck. His hair, once a flaming red, had all turned gray; his face was smoke-black; and while the left eye was alright, to its right was an ugly orb of putrid white where an eye should have been—the white of an unformed scab, the iris singed yellow, like a fried egg cooked sunny side up . . ."

I waited for more—for the story of how they survived. But looking over, I saw that the captain had nodded off, so I took my leave, crept away quietly.

A real storm was brewing outside. As I stepped out on the captain's deck, where it was always windier, I felt the power swirling all around, flapping the clothes on my body, whirling my hair, whizzing past my ears, shoving me towards the slick steps.

I stood there a moment, relishing the rush, the rushing-past of such force. The garden flag lapped furiously. I closed my eyes and had only the senses of sound and feeling; and I had the fleeting feeling that the center of the whirling vortex or vortices was hovering somewhere overhead, above where I was standing, then shifted suddenly away.

I opened my eyes. The vortex may have shifted, but the wind was still gusting from the west. I gripped the wet, lichen-covered rail and tread the wet steps lightly on my way to the lower deck and out of the wind.

The storm lasted hours into the night and I lay there in bed, listening to the storm, to the wind constantly blowing, trying to imagine what it would be like at sea—coursing on the open ocean. I wondered what's lying three miles down, through dark depths churning and currents under currents that reach to the bottom . . .

I could see the sails, brightly white against the sky, could hear them flapping in wind—then awoke to the curtain flapping against the open window.

Again I lay listening to the sounding wind—whistling, howling, rattling the windows and the blinds . . . The sound of wind on wind, blowing against itself, the friction of the molecules of air rushing in a gust, as the currents of air collide into rapids . . . Wind shearing wind, downdraft on draft.

I remembered childhood dreams of being caught in a hurricane, of struggling to hold onto something firm as the shelter was ripped away all around me. And somehow I had a wish to be strapped down during a storm—like the captain lashed to his wheel, or like Taget to the mast—and suffered to withstand the teeming onslaught of a hurricane. I wondered if it was possible to build a Plexiglas bubble—somewhere on land, but next to the sea, somewhere solid like a concrete bunker—that could withstand the blast of a hurricane or even a tornado, despite the debris flying at two hundred miles an hour. It would be such a *rush* to sit under that transparent dome and watch the oncoming storm through the rain washing over, and the driving wind— to witness the direct onslaught of a furious cyclone . . .

The next day, the captain was out and about before I was. The storm had blown over, and for a while it was sunny and warm. After coffee I went out, and the captain eventually resumed his story of the storm.

"Somehow we came through it. Our sails were missing or in shreds, but we repaired them as we could, stitched pieces of sail together, and rigged them to the yards, the men crawling across the rigging like spiders on a web. We managed to sail a bit in this manner, catching enough of what wind there was to move in a manageable direction—with the wheel and rudder working about as well as ever.

"We found that Cooky had been hiding cases of canned tuna, keeping them for himself, which explained his daily fish-breath when never a fish was caught. This was a great delight to the men, whose morale was as low as could be and needed a boost.

"For days we drifted, slowly gliding upon that green glass of utter calm, floating on imperceptible currents under an august sky wrapped in cloud raiment—with Helios peeping out from time to time to scorch the water and dry the sweat, leaving salt to further dehydrate and crack the wind-chapped skin. And as day followed day the cracks deepened to furrows, and the furrows filled with pus, and the wind dried it again and it cracked again, and the cracks

Intimations of Unreality

deepened to furrows and filled with blood. You lick your lips, but the saliva only stings and your tongue rubs off the half-formed scab, and the cracked skin flakes, so you withdraw your tongue and taste the blood and pus . . .

"So you cry out for clouds on a hot day, but curse them in the storm. You love them for their shelter, but hate them for their cargoes of rain . . .

"For two weeks we were stuck there on the ocean, bobbing like flotsam, helpless. Hour after hour, the sun moseying over at its own deliberate pace; day moving on, drawing short, ending, sun going down, cold setting in, day after day. Night terrifying you with darkness, you lying on your back facing up at the awesome sky, a billion stars, while at your back beneath the flimsy floating thin raft of tarpaulin lies the sea almost three miles deep. That's a long distance down into the darkness, a deep depth to sound in your imagination as you lay there hour after hour trying not to think of it. Three miles to sink, trapped in a waterlogged ship, or by yourself if you swim free only to founder on the open sea and submerge, lungs full of water. Davy Jones' Locker is deep and wide, and it doesn't give back what it takes in.

"And Taget moaning . . . He insisted on being on deck for the air, but was so sensitive to the light that he kept his head and shoulders covered by a scrap of tarpaulin. So he crouched and lay on deck by the port rail—near where Cooky had gone over—with his head covered. Underneath, I knew that he had covered his bad eye with a large patch, much like your typical pirate's patch. And underneath that, I suspected he had applied some kind of poultice or remedy to his eye, hoping to save it. Everyone wanted to offer help, but nothing could be done, and the physician was in his own care. He was irritated by the offers, no doubt, because for him to reason which tasks to delegate he would have to face the limits imposed by the temporary, or even permanent loss of that eye . . . So he withdrew into himself, covered his head, and faced his own situation eye-to-eye . . . And moaned in pain and distress.

"From the Crow's Nest Thompson spotted an island off the starboard bow and we made for it, using the rowboat to tow the ship, and re-rigging the sails to make maximum use of the wind. Then the wind came up again behind us, and the rain, and again we were driven by the driving rain. The rowboat had to get out of the way and got itself towed alongside the ship until we raised it on the derrick. And billowed by the wind the soaked sails began to come unstitched.

"Coming upon a treacherous coast with no beach, we circled the island in search of a place to land. We hugged the curving coast but took care to avoid the sharp rocks that jutted out in natural jetties and cut through the waves as if slashing out to gouge the ship. Fear guided us. Maneuvering through narrow passages, between rocks and surf, fear guided us: we were ultra-vigilant, all our senses peeled . . . Our eyes all wide like saucers full of milk, with no glimmer of light on the water going undetected. Was the night darker than normal—were there more stars, and brighter—or was our own awareness heightened? We could even see the reflections of stars dancing on the black water, between the drops of rain—a dark mirror that cleared and muddied by turns.

"Fear won't let us rest until we survey the perimeter and assure ourselves that we are safe—safe enough to relinquish consciousness and allow ourselves some sleep. We have to vanquish the darkness before we can enter it.

"In driving rain we found a harbor and a beach, and we dropped anchor in the harbor and rowed to the beach, seeking escape from the squall. But the storm that drove us to the island seized the island and laid siege to it, keeping us prisoner there, since it was impossible to set sail again into the gale-force wind that emanated from the ocean, into driving rain on rugged waters—without sails.

"We pulled the lifeboats and rowboat far up on the beach to keep them from being lost in high tide. On shore there were no structures and no sign of human habitation, but far up in the meadowlands that rose gently toward the center of the island someone had built a shelter.

"We crowded into it, all twelve of us, Taget with his eye and head bandaged staggering among us moaning, and someone having lit a lantern we looked around. It was only a shack, little more than a lean-to, probably a shepherd's hut originally; but it was a structure nevertheless and would give us a respite from the weather. It had been enhanced over the years and now included a woodstove, whose pipe cut neatly through the roof and was duly sealed with tar. There was even a small stack of wood to welcome us—for which we were quite thankful, as you can well imagine.

"We found places to sit or stand, according to rank, someone lit a fire, and someone went back out in search of more wood. And though it was true that we had escaped the physical impact of wind and rain, we could not escape it altogether . . . The rain pounded on the thin roof, wooden planks covered with only a thin skin of tarpaper and gravel. It pelted and drummed on the stove pipe where it jutted up into the elements and was topped by a rain cap formed of a tin plate affixed by wire. The wind rattled the plate against the pipe and shook the whole structure with relentless fury.

"Amidst my survey of the details of the cabin and the blank stares of the men it came to me with full weight that I was the captain: I was responsible for taking us through the storm—for the loss of poor Cooky and for damage to the ship. I was responsible for bringing us here to this island of rain, and I was responsible for getting us back on course.

"I knew I should say something, to cheer up the downbeat crew. But even this I was not up to, for the whole immensity of what had transpired in the storm and our stunned retreat to the remote island left me speechless. I couldn't wrap my head around it all with the proper perspective to be able to put it plainly. So, for lack of anything better, I thought it would be appropriate to read from the Bible, something from the Psalms; and I went to my captain's chest, which stored my log and maps, my paperwork, license, bills of lading and whatnot—and my Bible, given me by my mother, which had been in the family for generations. Well, the Bible was gone!

"'What the Dickens!?' I cried, 'Has anyone taken my Good Book?'

"And a mumble and a cry came from the huddled figure of Taget in the corner, from under his piece of tarp. 'And there was delivered unto him the book of the prophet Esaias. And when he had opened the book, he found the place where it was written . . .'—and a hand stretched forth from the tarpaulin, holding out the Bible . . .

"Taget had taken it hours before and had been reading it under the tarp—in near-darkness, but with enough light for the light-sensitive eye that was struck by lightning.

"The book was handed to me, and following Taget's obscure signal I opened to the book of Isaiah, where I found and read the passage 'The Spirit of the Lord is upon me; because the Lord hath anointed me to preach good tidings unto the meek; he hath sent me to bind up the brokenhearted, to proclaim liberty to the captives, and the opening of the prison to them that are bound.'

"That seemed somehow reassuring enough, so I stopped there, put the Bible back into the chest and locked it.

"It rained and rained, and never a ray of light beamed through the gray, and one had the sense that it would continue to rain, perpetually and forever. But the light glowed from the lamp and from a slit in the stove, and heat radiated through the room, and we were dry and safe.

"One day Taget disappeared . . . We noticed he wasn't there and no one had seen him for a while. So I formed a search party and went out looking for him, saw a lone trail of footsteps slogging through the muddy surface of the upslope. We followed the trail to the interior of the island, where the incline leveled out into a mountain meadow, replete with meandering stream. The meadow was covered with flowers; to be precise, they were—you guessed it!—marigolds!

"Through some anomaly of the wind and water about the island, it was not raining in the center, although it continued to pour all around. On the contrary, the sun shone here, and the group was dry, and the wind was warm and fresh.

"In the middle of the meadow, by the stream, there grew a single pepper-tree; and under the tree sat Taget, arrayed in crimson and gold—having cast off his tarpaulin and woven himself a thick cape of flowers.

"From a distance we heard him speaking, though he did not seem to be addressing us and no one else was there. As we approached, he rose up—not to greet us, for he still had not looked in our direction. He rose up with the aid of a staff: he had found a fallen branch suitable to use as a walking stick, with a modicum of reshaping by pocketknife. He did not need it to walk, but being blinded in one eye he must have found it useful to him to protect himself on that side.

"Then he stepped forward to the brook, and leaning on his staff, reached into the book and chose five smooth stones, then returned to his seat by the tree—a mound of leaves and stems—and put the stones in a semicircle on the ground before him. Then began to address them in his speech, which seemed to consist of Biblical quotations. Plucking a marigold from the ground and stripping it of its leaves, Taget held it up as he addressed the stones:

"'And thus shall ye eat it; with your loins girded, your shoes on your feet, and your staff in your hand'—here he reached over with his free hand, lifted and held the staff horizontally—'and ye shall eat it in haste.' And he shoved the large blossom into his mouth, snapping off the stem and tossing it aside.

"'Should the axe brag about itself to the axman? Shall the saw think itself better than the sawyer? As if the scepter should hold the sovereign aloft! As if the staff should lift itself up, as though it were not wood . . .'

"Here Taget stood up, flowers falling from his makeshift raiment. 'I am not worthy of the least of all the mercies and of all the truth which thou hast shown unto thy servant.' And he bowed. Then he raised his staff and waved it like a wand over the brook. 'For with my staff I passed over this Jordan; and now I am become two bands . . .'

"At this point, Taget finally took notice of us, looked straight at us with his good eye; his bad eye was hidden by a large blossom that somehow adhered to the ocular orbit. He continued his medley of scriptures, this time quoting Zechariah:

"'Then said I, "I will not feed you: that that dieth, let it die; and that that is to be cut off, let it be cut off; and let the rest eat every one the flesh of another. And I took my staff, even Beauty, and cut it asunder, that I might break the covenant I had made with all the people."'

"Now he swung his staff like a golf club and wedged the smooth stones, one after the other, up out of the verdure and back into the stream, where they plopped and sank and settled back into their natural environs—presumably wiser than before!

"Finally, Taget left the shadow of the oak and joined us, peacefully, with a look of resignation.

"Taget addressed the clouds as we walked back to the shack: 'I commanded them that they should take nothing for their journey, save a staff only!' He held his staff up to the sky in a gesture of defiance. 'No scrip, no bread, no money in their purse. Be shod but with sandals, and put not on two coats.'

"Tea?" he asked me at this juncture, and he paused in his account as we went inside to the kitchen and he prepared the tea.

"As we entered the whitewashed building on the slope, he quoted the Psalms: 'Yea, though I walk through the valley of the shadow of death, I will fear no evil: for thou art with me; thy rod and thy staff they comfort me . . . Surely I will dwell in the house of the Lord forever.'"

Having put the water on to boil, the captain put the loose black tea into a stained aluminum tea ball, two teaspoons to the cup, enough for four cups, and screwed on the lid; then he dangled in by the chain and dropped it into the teapot—a blue-and-white porcelain after the fashion of Delft pottery.

"One day the wind stopped, the rain stopped, the clouds lifted, and we left. Once the rowboat had tugged the ship out of harbor, the wind—the breath of the sea—poured forth on us, coming from aft, and pushed us back on course.

"Taget wasn't the same after that, gone off the deep end. There was something embarrassing about it, as if I had had something to do with Taget's decline, since I had encouraged him all along with his marigold experiments. He continued them back on board, hitting his tincture hard, until we were out of vodka and I wouldn't let him use the potatoes. After that, he suffered a bout of convulsions, through which he seemed to kick his habit—though he continued to adore the marigold. He kept on about 'Mary's Gold' and how the flower connected to the Virgin Mary . . .

"Like the goddesses before her, Mary was depicted with the marigold in two aspects, you might say life and death. First, the marigold was the flower used at the Feast of the Annunciation—which celebrates the moment Mary knew that she was pregnant with the savior; and she was called the House of Gold because of the miracle worked within her by Holy Spirit. On the other hand, marigolds were used to express Mary's great sorrow over the predetermined death of her son: after all, she knew beforehand that he would die and helped prepare his body. And again, the marigold scent is similar to that of ointments used in burial.

"See what I mean? The flower linked to death and the underworld is also associated with the Virgin Mary and the birth of the world's savior! What does *that* tell you?" If the captain's tone was critical, he was giving a critique of the religion, not the flower; but he was also being provocative.

"Anyway, Taget pushed the link too far. 'Marigold' comes not from 'Mary's Gold' but from *meargealla*, meaning 'horse-blister' because the bloom swells round like the welt on a workhorse raised by rubbing against the straps . . . Taget knew this—he's the one who researched it—but he persisted on his Christian tack. Which didn't bother the men none, as they were in need of spiritual guidance. So the Taget the ship's First Mate and Physician became Preacher as well, as signified by his ubiquitous staff. I kept the Bible locked in my chest, but he knew it by heart and could cite any book."

The kettle whistled and the captain poured the hot water into the tea-pot, dousing the perforated ball.

"As I say, this would be good to guide us back through the darkness of fear and doubt until we got our bearings and continued on course for our destination. But it got out of hand: Taget began to see things with his bad eye—or so he claimed. He reported seeing 'different levels of being' in addition to the gross physical things: ghosts, or what he called 'teleplasms' moving along the decks and through the cabin; angels floating in and out among the sails and rigging; the Madonna, even Christ himself. He discovered the likeness of the Virgin in a potato and the men were amazed and found new life. One night he saw Jesus walking across the water, carrying a lantern in the sea mist and pointing out the way. When he reported this to the wheel, they bore strongly in the direction indicated, thinking the appearance was meant to save them from unseen rocks. When the ship swerved suddenly, I went up on deck to see what was up, looked for myself, and saw only a clear patch of water where the rocks would have been. The sky was clear to navigate by, so I commanded the ship heave back on course. It was a non-miracle, but the men were convinced that Taget's vision had saved us all.

"The morning after we saw land: the spires of some fair city set on the water's edge, but we journeyed on, uncertain of the risk of making port in lands unknown . . . Fear again . . . Fear, my old friend! For it was Fear that bade me answer the call of the sea: fear of the unknown, fear of death, fear of being alive. It was Fear that made me leave my home: afraid to stay, afraid to become like anyone and everyone—just another ant in the colony. Afraid to go, afraid to stay, I had to wrestle with fear either way, so I took it on the road. You never conquer your fear; you only learn to live with it."

That afternoon and evening, it rained again, as if Captain More's story had conjured up the rain from that rain-soaked island. First there was the familiar tinkle of drops hitting the vent pipe up above the roof and echoing down through the heater. Then a handful of drops hit the window, like rice thrown at a wedding. And then a low roar rose up, the roar of a million raindrops hammering the roofs, coming from a distance and getting louder until the squall line passed overhead. I lay there mesmerized by the constancy of the rain, which turned to a loud sizzle, and I thought it was like the sound of the sea, rising and falling, of waves crashing on the shore and the sizzle of foam.

In the corner a candle burned, the flame sputtering as the wind pushed the wick into the pool of melted wax. The light burned into the dark, into the night. And as the wax dripped the rain dripped, overflowing gutters, leaking from the timbers, seeping through the deck, dripping into your quarters, onto your head . . .

I woke to actual drops on my forehead! I jumped up, turned on the light, examined the ceiling—discolored, dripping, but not sagging. The roof was leaking and the ceiling with it, right above my bed—which I hastened to drag out of the way. The bed frame scooted on the floor with the sound of a donkey. Almost as an echo, another sound arose: a screech, a scream—a whooping laugh!

I went to the back room, looked out the window, through the streaming water, through the rain, up over the deck. Sure enough, there was the captain, on his own deck, hooting and hollering into the rain and wind!

I pulled on my jeans, put on shoes without socks, pulled on raincoat and hat and went out onto the deck and up the slick wet steps, took the captain by the shoulders and forcibly guided him back inside, set him in his easy chair.

"Where was I? Oh, yes. The ghost pirates were at the porthole, grinning skulls leering in at us, riding a crazy wave off the edge of America, kicking and screaming, all our guns blasting full barrel, blowin' them bones to bits!"

His teeth chattered and he seemed feverish, out of touch. He kept talking while I attempted to towel the rain off his face with a kitchen towel and shook the water off his cap before putting it back on, covering the gray hair and bald pate.

"Crazy stuff, mainly . . ." The captain's focus drifted, as it sometimes did, passing into a daze of silent staring, and he fell to mumbling things that were inaudible or disconnected.

"Who pulls back in the name of honor? Who pulls short at a time of sorrow? Who flinches in the face of peril? Who holds back when the eye is brimming? And who will stand strong among you, stand beside their mothers and all their kin . . . Am I asking? Am I telling?"

He was oblivious to my presence, caught in a kind of quiet hysteria or calm night terror from which he could not awake. He was sleep-talking.

"That's the only reason it could ever be: wanting to get out of the wind, out of the storm, back on dry land. Off that island of rain, where Taget wandered off . . . Back to this *terra firma*, solid ground. Back to these golden hills, the Golden Gate. But when the hills start a-rollin', a-rumblin', and a-tremblin', the *terra firma* ain't so *firma*, but she sure is a *terror*! Hee hee!" He giggled with glee like a geezer, then calmed down.

"But then that's the way it should be: the ebb and flow, the hills and hollows; but that driving wind and burning sun and salty sea ain't very hospitable to a person used to a mild climate and all the comforts of home . . . Nosiree . . ."

At last he talked himself to sleep, making fretful sounds. I wanted to leave, but I was afraid he would wander out into the driving rain again and catch pneumonia. What could I do? I couldn't lock him in or block the door. I threw a blanket over him where he sat hunched in his chair, then I sat on the sofa across the room to watch him for a while. Gradually I, too, became sleepy and began to nod, so I roused myself, turned out the lights and went out, trusting that the captain's fatigue would keep him from further adventures.

The next morning I woke to the sound of footsteps overhead. To avoid the leak in my ceiling, I had moved my bed closer to the doorway to the hall, and the captain treading above, down his own hall, resounded louder than before.

"At least he's up and about," I said to myself. But I was thinking, "At least he's alive!" I was concerned about his fatigue and his cough, and—at his age—the effect of being out in the storm.

"Good morning, Taget!" he said with the usual cheer, if somewhat weakly, when I went out back with my coffee, wool cap pulled over my ears.

He was up on his deck, tending the marigolds as always. I slurped my coffee and the steam rose up into the cool air as I rose up the lichen-covered steps. The flowers were covered in a glaze of dew.

"You're up early," he said, back half-turned as he busied himself at the planters. And it was true—I had gotten up early to check on him.

Though he did his best to hide it from me, the captain, talking nervously over his shoulder, was scraping a small spatula gently across the face of the blossoms, and gathering the morning dew in a small jar. He moved quickly from flower to flower before the dew evaporated, trying to keep up with the pleasantries as he worked.

"Well, I guess you caught me," he said shyly, finally giving up on keeping his activity secret.

"The final secret of the tincture," he said, "is the harvesting of the morning dew—the marigold's tears, if you will—a vaporous exhalation of syrup and chemicals—sugars, fragrance, pheromones to attract bees—sometimes a bit of bee pollen, too . . . which Taget never learned at sea."

On mentioning Taget, he turned sad, solemn. "I figured it out myself—at great cost—not here, but in the south seas . . ."

He excused himself, took the jar inside and returned.

"Business took us to New Zealand, and there Taget took off—tired of the sea I guess, and eager to pursue his religious avocation. Some scent of the island's potential got into his nostrils as soon as we made port, and by the time we docked he was packed and on deck, ready to go.

"By now, he had abandoned his staff and his tarp and had taken to wearing an eye-patch—your standard pirate's issue—instead of the flower blossom, which was even more conspicuous. But in the center of the black leather patch he had cut a hole the size of the iris, and behind it attached a square of black cloth that was fine enough to be transparent from the inside, but not outside.

"I shook his hand for the last time and he said, citing scripture, 'Therefore they that were scattered abroad went everywhere preaching the word.' Then he walked down the gangway to the dock, then up a ramp to the pier, where he merged with the crowd of travelers and tourists and port workers. That's the last I saw of him . . . the prophet of Mary's Gold in the land of sheep."

Captain More tagged the story by saying, "There are strange things in the world, but nothing stranger than what's in our own heads." He looked tired, even haggard, the bags under his eyes illuminated by the rising sun, now peeping above the row of houses on the east side of the block. Into which he squinted, with mist in his eyes, as he reached over to tap out a bowl of ashes.

Intimations of Unreality

"Which leads to the story of my wife . . ."

"Your . . . wife?" I repeated, a little stunned. "It's true, you haven't mentioned her before."

"After New Zealand, where we filled the hold with a load of wool and fine timber, we headed east to Tasmania, where we dropped the timber at Hobart and picked up Fuji apples bound for Japan (turns out they're cheaper to grow in Tasmania). On the way, we stopped in the Solomon Islands—a small, unnamed island (the natives called it Ai, which meant 'here'). Captain Godwater, when he was captain, had taken us there in the *Conquest*, stopping off to trade with the island's chief, Xulon, bartering mirrors and knives and tin cups for palm oil and shell necklaces which featured small nuggets of gold. Their technology was primitive, and while they had learned to extract the oil from palm nuts, they could not achieve the temperature required to melt gold (a hundred degrees hotter than a candle), so they used lumps of ore combining stone and metal in their jewelry or formed small beads by carving and sanding away the precious substance. Of course, these isolated Melanesians had no idea of the value of gold in the outside world, so in commerce with them you were likely to get lucky!

"The island Ai was on our course, more or less, and being captain I was privileged to take *Ole Bess* wherever I wanted. And I wanted to try my luck with Xulon. The chief recognized me and we communicated in pidgin English. I offered him a crate of the Fuji apples and a nice, small chest of drawers which Taget had left in his quarters. I had no use for it and knew the chief would fancy the maple burlwood and might be generous in exchange. I was right—but there was something else, an unintended gift. I had checked the three drawers and thought the chest was empty, but when the chief opened the top drawer, there was a sizeable gold medallion! It must have been hidden—affixed to the underside of the lid, perhaps. Upon seeing it, the chief was ecstatic, as well he might be, not only for the sheer weight of gold but for the artistry and craftsmanship that had been lavished on the disc—an image of Mary and the Infant.

"Naturally, I couldn't ask for the medallion back—it was part of the gift, if unintended, and its existence was a complete surprise. I only hoped Taget didn't miss it!

"The chief was so delighted that—after checking the other drawers for further surprises but finding none—he summoned his lackey, who chatted with the chief in their native tongue and ran off full of excitement.

"Then his other lackeys brought out a small chest of the most gorgeous shells you've ever seen . . . uh," turning, craning his neck to look across the room, the captain pointed at a sideboard. "That conch shell was among them, set on top, and the rest were the shell necklaces, maybe twenty strings strung with pierced shells and gold beads. As I appreciated these gifts, around me the court was all abuzz. The first lackey returned with a trio of women, and when the chief stood up, I stood up too. Xulon spoke first in vernacular, then in pidgin, stating, in effect, 'Captain Tom More, in appreciation of your priceless gift, I give you my daughter, Mary Gee, and offer my blessings to you both for your life together . . .!'

"Well, you can imagine my surprise. Of course, being a salty dog, I wasn't married—the Sea was my bride, I was wedded to her like a nun to Jesus! It just wasn't practical—what kind of life would it be, separated all the time—unless she lived onboard with me in the captain's quarters . . . and what kind of life would that be for her?

"On the other hand, Mary was drop-dead gorgeous, nubile and half-naked, and at once my eyes went goggly drawing circles around the curves in her figure. So I bit my lip and began to wonder how I might get out of the situation. It would be a major insult to Xulon, of course, if I were to turn him down—I might not get out alive! I ended up convincing myself that, on balance, it might be better not to fight it . . . After all, I was faced with a kind of fantasy-reality, a Gauguin-like vision of paradise: Western white man meets Polynesian princess maiden and lives happily ever after on a nameless South Pacific island . . . I ask you, how often do you get *that* opportunity?

"And so, still stunned, I obliged, more stunned, and very soon was swept into a current of fuss and bother, as preparations were made for the wedding. And my mates stood by, likewise stunned at the turn of events, though grinning wolfishly at the maiden and her two *femmes du chamber*. The ship, meanwhile, was anchored in the harbor, waiting to set sail for Japan, and the apples were waiting and the men were waiting.

"I hastened to tell Xulon that, despite the honor of his daughter's hand, I had pressing obligations to my crew and to my own chief, and that I could not delay departure more than a couple days. Naturally, I was doing quick math in my own mind, figuring how many days remained to port, and how many days I could be late and get away with it . . . So my plan was a quick honeymoon in paradise, then the strange prospect of continued connubialism back on the ship . . . It would be awkward going with the beauty onboard among all them beasts.

"That night we were married, amidst beach bonfires, drums and voices, nose flutes and body-slaps, dancing and chanting. The men came over from the ship and joined in the merriment, and it was mighty strange to see by dancing firelight the grizzly old Thompson dancing with the native girls, and red-faced Redman blushing at the bouncing beauties, and old O'Leary leering—the whole pack of salty dogs seeing a bit of real life for a change. But my eyes were only for my tawny bride, whose bay-colored skin hid any delicate blush that bloomed beneath my eager gaze."

As he spoke, the captain's eyes were not wide, as in the story, but narrow slits, with heavy lids dropped to half mast and irises rolling up in ecstasy.

"Gentility forbids a more detailed description of our wedding night, except to refer to the bliss of union, and the sense that everything fits together just as it should. And our walk out under the stars, hand in hand under the grandeur of Centaurus, bare feet crunching on the sand . . . Ah, youth! Ah, memory! Ah, Mary Gee!"

There were tears in his eyes at the image in his mind's eye, and he put his right hand to his heart.

"The time came to depart, to leave the lovely island with my new wife and return to the ship, my old life, with this new element—this new person. The tide was high and we brought the ship in next to a ceremonial dock the natives had built for the occasion. The men tied the mooring lines to the dock posts and dropped anchor again, and all the princess's things were brought aboard and stowed in my quarters. Then up the gangway we went, her and I, and halfway up Xulon called out, and we turned to wave goodbye, and then when we had turned around again I lost hold of her hand. With her next step she tripped and fell off the gangway, hit her head on the way down and sank like a wayward torpedo!"

"No!" I protested.

"Of course, we dove in after her, but it was too late . . . She had taken on water, but it was the crack to the prow that sank her . . . And that's the story of my wife . . . A brief touch of heaven, a lifetime of bittersweet memories. What did Coleridge say? 'For he on honey-dew hath fed, and drunk the milk of Paradise . . .'"

The captain excused himself and went inside, and I sat there, a bit startled by the speed with which the wife was created and destroyed, so to speak, in his tale. I heard him blow his nose. When he came back and resumed his seat on the balcony, I caught a whiff of brandy.

"After that came the grieving; the funeral ceremonies, lasting two days— I couldn't just leave. Then a sad goodbye to the island, its chief and its people, and a final tread up the fateful gangway. When we finally weighed anchor, I saw the ship out of the harbor and into deep waters before going below to be alone in my quarters. There I discovered that all of Mary's things had been retrieved by the chief's lackeys, except for a tall wicker basket with a black cloth lining visible between the woven reeds. This I assumed to be some kind of wardrobe filled with clothing that belonged to Mary but had been left behind, and did not pay it further mind until we were well on our way.

The next morning, tired of seeing it in my room, which it filled with its floral fragrance, I asked Redman to get a sailor throw the wardrobe overboard.

"'Shouldn't you look it over first?' Redman asked, thinking of the medallion. "The chief's men brought it aboard jest before we weighed anchor. I thought it was a dowry, perhaps.'

"I nodded and he opened the basket, removing a round woven lid. This revealed a vertical opening running the full height of the basket—some five feet—except for the circular base. Pulling aside two hinged sections that acted as drawers revealed the contents—first hidden in the dimness of the cabin and the darkness of the cloth lining, until I held up a candle."

The captain took a long draw off his pipe and blew it out slowly, eyes misty and glistening through the smoke.

"Well?" I asked finally, to end the suspense. "What was in the basket?" Like Redman, I expected something fabulous, something of immense value.

"It was Mary . . ."

My jaw dropped.

"Little Mary Gee, embalmed and mummified by some South Island witchery, her skin slightly shriveled, leathery, darkened by tanning . . . Her eyes were sewn shut, hereafter blind, forever looking inward. Her mouth was stitched up, too, lips laced, never to speak, never to kiss again. Her nostrils were stuffed with dried flowers. But her head was held high in proud rigor mortis, bravely facing the burden of eternity—and chest stuffed, breasts full of straw stocked against the endless tomorrows, leathered teats ready to feed milkweed milk to the children of an impossible future . . .

"In her hands, joined over her belly, was a single marigold, still fresh, its blossom covered in morning dew, like tears for the dead . . . That's when I thought of using them for the tincture.

"It was Xulon's parting gift . . . Evidently it was customary, in those parts, for the widower or widow to keep the mummy of the deceased."

The story was so utterly fantastic—yet so reasonable, conceivably true— that I didn't know whether to believe it or not. But the captain's emotional display was convincing. He fell into despair.

"Sometimes I think I'll take a sloop out beyond the breakers and end it all. Hoist my sail one last time and sail out of the bay, never to return. Glide out to the edge of the open water, lower sail and let her drift. I'll tweet the whistle twice and slide the old corpse down into the dark water—an anchor tied to one ankle to pull me down into the depths . . . And with cap of captain on my head, and compass and pipe in hand, I'll say goodbye to it all!" He tried to laugh but it was a scoff.

"Well," he said, looking at his watch, eyes still brimming, lined with red, "looks like I've talked away most of the morning, and I've got errands to run."

I went downstairs and inside, attended to my own affairs. I heard activity upstairs—clattering in the kitchen, footsteps up and down the hall. Though I was engaged, my mind kept returning to the story of the captain's wife, mulling over its strangeness and credibility. In the back of my mind, I kept expecting the captain to leave on his errands, with his familiar tromp down the stairs and past my front door. But he never left. Then again, I was concerned with his depression, and debated if I should be alarmed by his talk of suicide. On the other hand, the captain was a fount of florid prose that flowed and flowed, and one never knew what to believe.

The weather was clear until mid-afternoon, when the familiar fog rolled in. Then the wind picked up again, and by evening a new storm front was moving in. This time, Captain More's stories summoned up a real doozy of a storm! Driving rain on the back windows drew me out of my office. "Batten down the hatches," indeed! The wind was blowing west-southwest and shoving heavy rain clouds before it.

Above, I heard the captain still clattering in his kitchen, busy cooking or perhaps preparing the mysterious tincture or "remedy" from his stories. There was also talking and laughter. He must have been alone, but sometimes the voice was different, sometimes falsetto, as if he were imitating someone, turning monolog into dialog. Or maybe he was going out of his mind!

I went back to work for a couple hours, then went to bed. A second leak had formed in the ceiling, requiring a second pot, and the two distinct drips dropped at different tempos. The overlapping cycles of wobbling tones created a strange feeling of dissociation that lead easily to sleep.

I dreamed that the captain was having a party and all the characters in his stories were guests. There were loud voices, clinking glasses and stomping feet, singing and laughter. Everyone had small liqueur glasses filled with the golden green tincture concocted by James Taget and Captain More. The men from the ship were there—Redman and Thompson, even Cooky, who had a Band-Aid on his forehead. Chief Xulon was there, a small man clad in loincloth and feather-laden headdress, tapping his toe to the music, accompanied by two of his lackeys; but the chief's daughter, the captain's wife, was nowhere to be seen. Frank the iguana, perched high on a bookshelf, overlooked the party, his throat pouch extended, head bobbing to the music— French chamber music. But the music was not coming from the stereo, it was being played there in the room: in the corner was an ornate, golden harpsichord whose strings buzzed against bare wood where the pads were worn. At the keyboard sat Captain More, playing with gusto and finesse!

The dancers fell back to clear the center of the room, into which danced a dark figure in silhouette, a life-sized marionette controlled by wires that went up and out of sight. The puppet bounced and danced into the light and I saw that he was a pirate, one eye covered in a black patch; in one hand he carried a staff, a tall stick with a hook at the top like a shepherd's crook. As the captain played a minuet, the marionette stood still, but tapped the staff in time to the music, and sang two verses of a song, jaw wagging on wires:

> When I was young, a buck—a buccaneer!
> I chanced upon the water, slay my fear!
> Hap'd upon adventure, played for time,
> Sighted the unsightly trail we leave behind—
> Trailing back to the snails and worms and slime . . .
>
> But on the ocean we were something else!
> Sailing our way across the surfaces!
> Rough-riding wave-tops but feeling no pain,
> Looking out there for freedom with nothing to gain—
> Swinging from rope to ape, monkeys all the same!

I awoke to music from above, but there was no party. Reflecting on my dream I recalled the captain's pithy statement, "There are strange things in the world, but nothing stranger than what's in our own heads." Curiosity drew me to the back room. The only sounds were the music above and the whistling wind. Looking out and up, I couldn't see the upper deck clearly enough to tell if anyone was there. It was dark—no lights were on, even upstairs—and there was no moon.

I got dressed and went out. As I stepped onto the deck, a gust of wind grabbed the door from my hands and slammed it shut. I started up the wooden steps, avoiding the slick patches of lichen that were spreading everywhere. The fungus seemed luminous, even phosphorescent, probably reflecting light from an unseen source. The gale was still blasting, hurling occasional raindrops, and with windbreaker flapping and eyes squinting I made my way up. The captain was there, sitting in his chair, facing west as always—facing the storm!

I called up to him as I climbed the final steps, but could not hear if he replied. I reached the upper deck, shouted again in the blast, but he sat still and silent, glassy eyes staring out toward the ocean. I put a hand on his shoulder and shook him, first gently, then more roughly, to arouse him or evoke some sign of life. But at the first touch I felt something wrong, an odd stiffness. I tried to lift his face, gripping the stubbly chin as a handle, but the neck resisted. There was no way to check for breath in this wind, or hear a heartbeat, but surely he was dead—cold and lifeless and entering rigor mortis.

That was how I met him, and that was how I found him: dressed in his captain's uniform, with his captain's hat and his captain's pipe, out on his captain's deck . . .

What was I to do? I opened the captain's door and latched it back against the wind, then dragged the captain inside, lifting him under the arms, tipping over his chair in the process. At least he would be out of the blast, and if there was any chance of saving him, he had to be warmed up. I laid him on the floor of his living room and covered him with the blankets that were draped over the easy chairs, first shaking them free of dust and crumbs and ashes.

I looked around for a phone. I had never seen one in this room—and this was the only room of the apartment I had seen—but surely he had one. I looked under a few maps and papers, then checked the kitchen area, but found nothing. I went down the hallway, heading for the two unexplored rooms in the front of the apartment. Seeing no phone in the hall, I tried the first room—a bedroom with a narrow bed, lit by a lamp and sparsely furnished. There was no phone. That left the extra room at the end of the hall.

My imagination ran wild as I went those last ten steps toward the closed door. What could be in there? After all the captain's stories, it might be anything or nothing. The room at the end of the hall—was it the locked, shuttered room where the captain kept all his secrets . . . and perhaps his wife? Could the captain actually have a mummy here in the house, here in San Francisco? It would be undeniable proof of his story—lending credibility to all of his stories. Perhaps everything he said was true, after all.

And so, heart pumping, ready for anything, I reached the end of the hall and reached for the doorknob. The door was not locked, but opened with a little creak. The room was dark, but the hall light provided some visibility. I reached inside the doorway and felt for the light switch, touched old wallpaper that curled and flaked off, found the switch, switched it on.

I scanned the room hastily. It looked like a storage room, partially filled with a stack of old furniture—among which I could discern no large baskets . . . Against one wall was a bookshelf, in front of which stood a small table with a glass case, whose built-in light had been triggered by the wall switch. It was this that drew my eye.

Inside the case was a model sailing ship—a three-master, fully rigged, all sails billowed in an imaginary wind. Illuminated from above, the model was striking in detail—though thin steel wires were used in the place of ropes, and carved horn for the canvas sails. Thanks to the glass case, it shone without a speck of dust. On the starboard side of the forward hull I read the hand-painted name: *Ole Bess.*

I looked around. The shelves behind the case were full of books of sea lore, including the fiction of Melville and the other authors the captain had named. Another shelf was dedicated to horticulture, particularly marigold cultivations; one thick book bore the odd title, *Calendula Miscellanea: Myths and Legends of the Pot Marigold* by Flora Purdy. On the wall next to the light switch was a framed drawing of the clipper ship *The Flying Cloud* with a caption naming her shipbuilder as Donald "Donny" McKay, launched in Boston in 1851.

Remembering the captain, I went downstairs and used my own phone to call 911. An inquest was held, at which Captain More was referred to as "Mr. Thomas More," which I deduced was due to retirement, though it seemed he should retain his title. It was revealed that the captain had modified his will before his death, naming me his sole beneficiary! This raised an eyebrow, for if I had known that I would gain from his death (which I hadn't), it might constitute a motive; but the autopsy indicated death due to natural causes, and no foul play was suspected.

The real surprise was that Captain More owned the building—and now I did! He had used an agency to manage the other units and lived off the income, along with disability benefits and a pension from his old union. To avoid being bothered by the tenants, he kept his ownership a secret.

I went up to see the captain's rooms again, taking the backstairs. I felt like a thief going in, though I had the key—had every right. It seemed strange to be there without him, without a chess battle going on, without hot tea or brandy, and I was a stranger before all the nautical paraphernalia with which I was so familiar. The captain's chair was empty, signifying the presence of his absence. He was no more, but all this was left behind—and mine to deal with.

I took over caring for the marigolds, watering them, weeding them. I kept both apartments for convenience, living and sleeping downstairs but coming up to tend to the plants, and for sunsets—usually spectacular from the captain's deck, unless there was fog. After finishing the captain's brandy, I dug out the bottle of Armagnac I had never unpacked to share with the old guy, and kept it upstairs. There, too, I took to reading the captain's books, full of adventurous and weird tales of the sea, still pondering in the back of my mind the captain's slew of stories, and where to draw the line between fantasy and reality.

On a lark, I tried on the captain's hat, which fit rather comfortably; and after that I thought I would try his pipe, trying my own hand at the ritual he had performed so many times in that very room. Lastly—why did it take so long?—I turned to the captain's classical albums, choosing the topmost from a stack, *Dances and Minuets* by Mozart, and put it on the ancient phonograph, which buzzed, crackled, and popped before becoming musical.

Thusly was I engaged—cap on head, pipe in hand, sipping dry brandy and enjoying the dainty acoustic number—when there came an unexpected knock at the front door. No doubt the music had masked the footsteps on the stairs leading up the front of the building from the street. The knock came again, and somewhat startled, I found and opened the door, and stood at the threshold, disoriented, staring at a stranger. He was an elderly man, about the captain's age, who returned my bewildered stare.

"Isn't this where Tom More lives?" he asked, peeking past me into the hallway, which was covered with photos of ships.

"Uh—used to live here, he's . . . he just died recently, I'm sorry to say."

He was surprised but took it in stride.

"Were you a friend of his?" I asked.

"Yes, an old friend, though I haven't seen him in years . . . Before we retired, we worked together as longshoremen for twenty-seven years."

"Longshoremen?" I asked. I had heard the word but didn't know its precise meaning.

"We worked 'along the shore'—on the docks—loading and unloading freight . . ."

"But . . . I thought he was a captain!"

"A captain?!" he said with a pshaw. "Captain of a skiff, maybe! No, he was never even a sailor!"

I must have appeared glassy-eyed as my brain adjusted to the truth.

Intimations of Unreality

"Oh, he always jawed about going out, but never did. When we first started, we were twenty, young and strong, but without much direction. Every box and sack, every pallet and container was either coming from somewhere else or going somewhere else—somewhere clear round the world! That was a kick, something to think about while you put your back into it. From the beginning, old Tom would dream aloud about those foreign lands, making stuff up, mixing a pinch of common knowledge with a bucketful of bullshit! All those years, saying he might stow away and see Mandalay for himself, or Borneo. But he never went anywhere . . .

"We both had to quit working because of our backs, but he had enough spine left to take tourists out in a little skiff he bought with his savings. Did it for a year or so, but gave it up. Too much competition with the big tour boats with their slick operations.

"We used to see him down at the union hall on Friday nights, where they mix 'em strong, but he quit going, oh, ten years ago. Haven't seen him since, so I thought I would look him up . . ."

I explained what had happened—the storm, the captain's death, the will—then, remembering myself, asked him in. As I followed him into the living area in the back, I took the captain's cap off and tossed it aside.

"I was just having a brandy, would you care for one?" I asked.

"Sure! I'd rather have a whiskey, but on a cold night like this, a brandy will do just as well."

"I'm sorry, I didn't get your name," as I poured his drink.

"Taget," he said, "James Taget."

> And the fog rolled in and still rolls in,
>   And covers the world in waves.
> And the only sound is the seagull's cry,
>   That calls us back to the sea.

INTO THE BEYOND

Dusk

The radiant orb of life
Did set on the horizon of man's experience,
As does the sun at evening.
Then it sank beyond what is known or understood,
Leaving the world of man to the dark.
And the wise men, weeping, ask:
"Whither hast thou gone?"

Thoughts I

Thoughts pass through the mind
Like water in underground caverns,
Sparkling magically,
In darkness yet lit by their own creation.
The waters divide into streams
That trickle away to all places;
And but a drop from each remains
To be born as an idea.

On a Rainy Eve

Passing along this rainy eve,
I look into the sky above
And see the clouds roll heavily,
So low, so thick, so mistily.

The darkness pours cool vapor forth
Upon the ground incessantly;
The droplets sing the mystery:
The heavens touch upon the earth.

When thunder rolls across the plain
And echoes from the spatial tomb
Beyond the vaulted clouds, I fain
Would hide within my darkened home
And at this window will remain
To mourn this omen of our doom.

Poem to Polymnia

I know the Muse, Polymnia
I know her sister, Euterpe
I know their garden, where it lies;
I pluck these rare fruits from their tree.

I know their mother, Memory.
I know of all things that have been
And know of all things that will be.
I have such eyes as they have seen
The worlds beyond eternity.

I pluck the pome and snap the stem,
And sap as ichor oozes forth
To bear more fruit, to heal the seam.
I drop the seeds upon the earth,
And vines spring up where I cast them.

Berries are yielded from the vines;
And when one cuts and when one reams
These fruits into Morpheic wines,
And if one sips, one sleeps and dreams
Of other lands in other times . . .

Notes:
Polymnia   Greek Muse of sacred song (also Polyhymnia)
Euterpe   Muse of music and lyric poetry.
Memory   Mnemosyne, mother (by Zeus) of the Muses.

Arcanesia

I.

End of summer, soon is winter—seasons come and seasons go;
Death of worldly stage's center; spirits freed will rise and flow.
Harvest offer: Dionysus and Demeter praised in song
Once again, before life passes, and before the winter long. . .

II.

Cooling breezes of October rustle leaves into a flock
Blowing back and forth and over, helter-skelter on the walk.
Gathering and potent wander winds from over all the earth
Whisper things we fain would ponder: secrets which will ever endureth.

Brushing curtains as they pass, the cool winds blow upon the face
Coming from the past unto you—for a lost, forgotten place.
Cool as waters from moon-fountains, rushing o'er the wheat-filled plain
Lying under moon-topped mountains, bring back elder times again.

Follow now with endless wonder, where the wise winds are to lead;
Through the dusk we travel yonder, to the twilight's secret mead.
Follow yet and follow ever once we hear the vibrant chords
Of the songs recorded never, we can praise no other lords.

Down the valley under starlight, past the stream and to its source
Up one mountain, down another, quitting not the given course
Into forests dark as night and, though the shadows gaze along,
Through these woods we venture farther, follow still the ancient song.

III.

Now we see amidst a clearing in the forest, in a bower,
Demons with their minions fearing daylight as it nears that hour
Pan the Evil pipes and prances (rituals are now begun),
Hailing Dionysus, dances; hails Apollo's rising sun.

And the jigging fauns and satyrs and satyrs howl in mindless
      ecstasies,
Circling 'round two raging fires, Pan the Horned they appease.
Then, in blast of cloud-blown fury, Hermes his grand Phaeton leads
To the earth in rush and hurry, drawn by silver, wingéd steeds.

The moon, dim on the horizon, blackens over in a storm
And from underworlds is risen Hecate in mysterious form;
Shortly then is Venus seen to peer down from the upper spheres
And in spirit luciferan Pan the Wicked howls and leers.

Dancing ever faster, singing ever shriller in the dawn
Throngs o beings evil-ding fall imbibed upon the lawn,
Drinking still to harvest-coming, revel still debaucheries,
Even gods are wine-consuming and are sunken to their knees.

IV.

Now the stirrings Aeolian from the south and from the north
From the east and from the west all blow together, howling forth
Songs remembered from the Muses, litanies Polymnian
Raise the drugged souls of their mentors back to heights Olympian.

Soon thereafter Hecate's vanished as Apollo's disk is up
And the silver moon is banished by the golden-pouring cup;

Fearful of the light of morning fauns and satyrs turn to flee
Now, too, Pan away is running, frolicking in haughty glee.

Lastly left are not the minions and their gods have flown away
Yet remains the ghostly pinions of night-winds to greet the day.
Over hills and valleys flying, dreaming soul is home again
And is waked by echoes dying, promising to soon return.

End of summer, soon is winter—seasons come and seasons go;
Death of worldly stage's center; spirits freed will rise and flow.
Harvest offer: Dionysus and Demeter praised in song
Once again, before life passes, and before the winter long. . .

Lunar Liturgy

"Marvelous Maiden of midnight!
O Sister of Hecate, the black witch!
Enveiléd in grey, dismal cloudlets
Inhaling Your dim-glowing power
Expending in great bolts of lightning,
With trumpets from far-off Olympus
Rejoicing, announcing, inciting
This tribute to Your divers marvels."

The cloudlets pass swiftly as dancers
Encircling the elegant goddess,
Appraising, enhancing her beauty
Enshrouding in grey adulation
So none but the high-flying falcon
And Pegasus—wingéd—may glimpse her.

The people of night throng beneath her,
They chant and proclaim old inscriptions
Evoking by dark runes recited
Her wonders, her secrets, her splendor,
As sing in deep voices the prophets:

"All hail Her, renown Her, and praise Her
The Goddess of black night eternal
Who lights up the heavens and peereth
Through darkness to lead the night-people,
And comfort us 'til the last daybreak."

For Fear

For fear of darkness falling,
For fear of demons calling,
For fear of black fiends crawling,
At night I cannot rest.

For fear of winged beasts flying—
On star-winds they come flying,
At sunset they come flying—
I dare not go to bed.

For fear of things not made for sight—
In hordes they rush at midnight
From caves of green malachite
In mounts of ineffable height—
I must not fall asleep.

For fear I will be tossed
In sleep into the past
Of alien lives—and lost—
Pray God I will not dream!

Song of the Old Ones

This was the song that the old ones sang
when the earth was young
and the moon was not yet born:

This was the song the comets sang
as they whistled through space
in the darkness, void of all light:

This is the hymn that godlings sing
when the godhead is theirs
and eternity theirs to keep:

The song of shepherds and grape harvesters
saluting the coming of the sun
the new spring, the day:

The song of the winemakers dancing merrily,
of the satyrs and fauns
praising Pan the Horned:

And this was the Hymn of the Great God Pan
piped through reeds mindlessly
rejoicing in the spirit of ever-Morn
dreaming wildly of Matuta,
Daughter of Eos and
Goddess of the Dawn . . .

Hidden Realization

Ah! the great beauty of springtime!
Unfolding in blossoms as fragrant
As incenses burning in Heaven
In gold-wrought tripods; but, flaming,
The fiery light of the tripods
Glows as do the eyes of a demon;

And I cannot relish the splendor
Of flowers and green vegetation—
For I'll always know that beneath them
Lie corpses and caverns for changelings.

The glory of dear Mother Nature
Does not quite hide Death's evil doings.

Flight

Visions of blackness
　　　Obscure the light.
On-coming darkness
　　　Sends me in flight
Down through the ages
　　　Into the blight.

Lost Refuge

Beyond the little barrier I have erected against the years,
Time seethes and squirms, befouling Life as it passes
Ignorantly within reach.
When my flimsy shelter crumbles
And Time seeps victoriously through,
The final stand for Life is lost and I turn old and gray.

Song to Helios

Let thy wisdom turn to power;
Let thy power turn to light;
Let the brilliance of thy furnace
    shine throughout the blackest night!

Break thy solace into fragments,
Shed the dust upon the sky;
Make the name of thine be shouted
    and the echoes never die!

Peel thy great corona's shadow
From the backing of your sphere;
In dimensions unremembered
    Play the music all may hear!

Burst thy molten tears forever
All resounding in the gulf;
Vibrant, magic music utter,
    Sing this song unto thyself.

Carven Faces

Carven faces in the mountains,
Gargoyle watchers o'er mankind;
These are relics of Their passing,
Measured traces left behind.

Dimly through the aether staring,
Masked by mist and mystery;
Faces—silent stone, but knowing—
Motionless eternally.

Chilled, the mist is stirred and flurried,
Animated oddly by
Some great power, dormant, hidden—
Deep within stone faces lies.

Now the mountains fully tremble,
Coldly shiver, stolid quake;
And the carven mountain faces
Smile malignly and awake.

The Witness's Account

"... God help me, but the very sky above
   fell down upon us as we fearful watched
   And then amidst the shattered fragments rose
   A star-lit horror clad in dust and death
   Unto the broken shell which was the sky!

"And heaven help me if I did not cry
   Aloud to Mother Mary us to save!
   For winds from out the starry spaces blew
   And swept in hell-bent gales our earth away!

"...But settled aft' an aeon noticeless
   A frightful stillness swept o'er all the land—
   For naught of ruin was there to be seen
   And naught of dust was rustled in the air
   But for the ground-fog lighted by the dawn
   To veil myster'ously th' enchanted sight:

"For there below us on the morning plain
   Was quaintly set a village, gambrel-roofed
   And dimly reminiscent of long past
   In crumbled Tudor cottage years...

"'Twas then the Sun was up above the rim,
   And from the small, round portal of each house
   There crept a wizened man onto his step
   To hold up high a candle or a lamp
   To light the dawning for his sightless eyes..."

Cataclysm

Between clouds spiraling in opal skies
There come envisionments of other spheres
That drift and whirl in blackened cosmic vaults
And blink malignly with their passing years.

The blackness separates, the night is opened,
The aeons shriek in chaos and are heard
As down the stellar well-depths they are tossed
In this—the cataclysm all have feared.

The galaxies all flounder in the whirl
Of hyper-empyrean aether-storms;
The cloud of nothingness absorbs all things;
And Doom—Nihility—resounding comes.

The Portal

I stand before the portal of all dreams
And look upon the realms of timeless lands;
I see the desert wastes with colored sands—
The dust of comets from the solar streams.

The reigning beauty and the majesty
Of amethystine mountains to the east
Holds one respectful of the fallen past—
Whose legions have since sailed beyond the sea.

I sit upon a desert knoll and think
With eyes down-cast into a golden cup
Whose marvelous liquor stirs and bubbles up;
I tightly shut my eyes and dare to drink . . .

Oblivion

I knew from what he said that I would be
In soporific languor in strange lands
Beyond the raging oceans of all Dreams,
Which waft the shores of unreality.

And so I drank the Elixir and dropped
Into a deeper sleep than any Lethe,
Into profound, blissful Oblivion—
I fell eternally and never stopped . . .

Awakening

Between the gilded dawn and waking hour,
The fleeting legions of dream decline
And fade away, as I within my bower
Yet on a bed of clover grass recline;

And in quicksilver moments vanishing,
The want to rise and fly with them recurs
While spectres dancing far beyond my being
Invoke the ancient fear—my heart demurs.

This conquered, I upstart, invigorous,
And seek audaciously in mystic things
The path beyond surmises perilous—
The path betook in frightful wonderings.

Vision

Through facet-windows searching,
The mind enjoys to toss itself in play;
I see life-cycles spinning,
To dark horizons roll away, away.

I see great blossoms blooming,
Long-buried memories that sprout at last;
Among vast ruins roaming,
One strains to catch an echo from the past.

In quick-remembered moments,
Things lost forever seek to live, but die;
To silent spots retreating,
I see these forms and figures fly and fly;

One rushes out to meet them:
These rapid-fleeting glimpses of the day;
The poet sings them lightly,
These words and thoughts he passed along the way.

Revelation of Night

Without, the night was settled in;
Within, the fire was warm aglow—
The waves of cool, nocturnal wind
Had keep the embers burning low.

The rain began; the night was born
Into its great predestined place.
The sun had sunk, so tired and worn,
And shone its beacon lone to space.

The skies then opened to my eyes
As if a mirror could become
A window, then to gaze beyond,
Nor seen and seer be the same.

But only such as I can see,
While other men shut out the night
To spend the day in gaiety
And never quit their trusted light.

So few are they that beauty see—:
The lasting stars in spaces laid
Such that the winds weep happily
To view these things that God has made.

Home in Autumn

Between the branches of the tree outside
The failing sun reflects from whitewashed posts
To color the vague somberness which hosts
The death-like season that has never died;

And stretching forth my hand to grasp the tide
Of azure flowing from autumnal coasts,
I am caught within the cobwebbed realm of ghosts
Wherein profound arcana does abide.

So ever must I dream in zones bedimmed
And see in death a beauty marvelous
Having known the love and languid kiss
Of vampires to this shadow-land condemned.
Enchanted by these secrets I have come
To hold most dearly autumn as my home.

Game

Eight children dance on a knoll
under a southern-isle palm
under a tropic sun sinking
into the clear sanguine twilight.

Eight children moving enchanted
moving with motions predestined
with an unwillful possession
act out the scenes of a play.

Powers of old are within them
speaking in voices bemuffled
speaking in tongues unremembered
but by the Mind quintessential.

Painting: Dreamscape I

A plain of marble stretches ever on
To floor a time-swept valley desolate,
As limply hung as gossamer between
Two lunar mounts whose crags reach raggedly
Against a cold and palely turquoise sky.
The mottled bier is of a thousand hues
All mixed and swirling in a dream-array
All mild-disturbing in their stableness
While speaking of the touch of death's sweet kiss.

A Fissure in the marble is beheld
To mar alone the planar perfectness
Of glassy stone laid square by mammoth square
Throughout this vale of fantasy and dream.

A beam of rotting maplewood is thrust
From out the fault within the valley floor,
And this is crossed by yet another beam—
Are these illusion of anamnesis?
The hint of death, the hint of life again
The clouded thought of reincarnate wheels
Set firm within the great, complex machine
Of Time and Life—of God, Infinity—:
These thoughts and notions are but fancies, yet
Present us with vague fears of ignorance.

Upon the fallen cross, now meaningless,
There crawls a single ant, another aft',
Until a line of them run up the wood
To see the truth that legend has foretold.

Note: *anamnesis* - memory of past lives

The Sorcerer's Lament

Away, thick mist, and leave my brain be clear!
'Tis cluttered, true, with strange things, odd and old,
Whose dust itself will cause despair the seer
(But which is not against the atmosphere!)

Will thou not do that which thou hast been told?
Be off, I say, and leave no smelly mold
Or mildew causing ill and sterileness—
O, God, what have I done to come to this?

This stifling of my powers—was concentration
Over-done or not? And meditation
Have I forgotten? Never once again
Shall I take such a course of studying,
Lest the well-ruined track derail the train
As then, while mind was busy travelling . . .

A silence, now—a time for needed rest
From studies taken too serious and swift,
Of battered brain long tired by lessons stressed,
And drooping eyelids I would force to lift.

Sweet sleep! Aft' prisoned long, forgot,
The Fancy now is left to freely roam
'Cross lands and seas such as it vainly sought

Before released from consciousness, its home—
But all too oft' its dungeon and its tomb.

Sweet sleep! Bring waves of friendly-flowing sea—
Blocked ere from sight by dams built on the lea,
Whose roaring tides were harkened ne'ertheless
By mind fatigued, distraught by weariness—
I say, Sweet sleep! Bring waves of friendly sea
To wash away the images of walls
Aligned with books up-piled on table-tops:
Let thoughts of benches turn to forest trees
And make to shadeful bowers what were halls;
And look! The faithful clock ticks not, but stops
While grimaced face is shattered by my hand,
Transforming glass to seashore's timeless sand . . .

Down to the Harbor

Always I love
To go down to the harbor
Of the Bay opening on the Sea—
Where the waters roll in from the sea.

And often I sit
On the rotting wood wharf
With the smell of dead fish
And of seaweed brought up by the tide.

And frequent I climb
Up the creaking small steps
In the sparsely-grassed hill
To the smoking quaint cottage atop.—

Up to the cottage
Where the old man lives
And here I sit content
As he tells the brave tales of his youth.

Praise to the Sunrise

Again I greet you, Sun,
As have I ev'ry morn
Of life.
    Rise silent o'er
Thine waters radiant,
Supernal and divine—
And o'er the moist sand shine:
With warmth and cause for hope;
Usurp the passing night
And still the troubled Sea
Disturbed of late by Storm
And clear the flotsammed shore.

But signify, O Sun,
If this sweet Dawn will be
As others that have passed;
And which will hold the sign
Or symbol of the power
Of the oncoming Age;
And which will give it wake?

"I answer: All of them."

Sojourn

I dressed for journeying and then betook
myself along a road cut through the woods,
With trees bestride and thickened foliage.

Anon a spider's silv'ry web was spun
Betwixt the limbs of bushes in the brush,
And shined malignly when they caught the sun
Upon their lightly stretched and dusted spans.

The trees did lean toward this traveller,
And formed a bower o'er his shaded head,
Yet died the sun steal ever and again
Between the leaves and filtered to a ground
Bestrewn with needles from surrounding pines.

The road became a fork and I bore right,
With little thought that leftward I should bear:
I came upon a clearing and beheld
A house of ancient, crumbling stone built there.

And so I took approach to see wherefore
The panes of glass were out and, too, the door—
But there I read the words writ on the wall:
"Dare not ye enter in where shadows fall."

Solitude

From habitude of loneliness we pass
Into aloneness of the self to brood:
To recreate the spirit, cleanse the soul
Within the sacred realm of Solitude.

Come now unto this secret, silent place
Were thoughts are born of thoughts, and were we see
Noetic streams to flow forever on—
To flow, but not without predestiny.

To dim retreats, to inner regions wend
Your way from noise and turmoil, grief and woe:
There might you glimpse your chosen fate, your god,
And afterward great peace your heart will know.

Intimations of Unreality

Selene

The goddess of the years:
She promenades while birds a-wing
Flock o'er unto a southern spring;
No autumn midge or elfin being
Has seen her golden tears.

The vines of autumn creep
Upon the stones about the well;
The moss-grown walls in auburn swell;
As founts the season's coming tell—
In bronze oak-bowers sleep.

The cooler winds, they come
As trees shed off their fiery wrap
To bow before the thunderclap
That rolls across grey plains that nap
Beneath the winter's dome.

The sunset's rays are dim,
And wan reminders of the night
That lies ahead do cause us fright;
But led on by Selene's light
We feareth not the storm.

Down through the wells of space
In pitch, abysmal darkness fall

The gleaming, glowing stars and all
The planets and their moons will fall
To light her lovely face.

"O goddess of the moon!
 Step out upon the glassy sea
 In all supremest majesty—
 We bow before thee humbly,
 Child of Hyperion!"

Our goddess, she is come
Unto us in our worshipping
To bless us and to bid us sing
Her wonders—by the light she brings
Forever shall we roam!

I Ask the Fortune Teller

Up on the roof
where the witnesses mingle
He indicates
the spelling glass.

Banging the table
in odd dissonance
He indicates
Another pot of cold mushrooms
between the narrow boards.

See!
The glass fogs.
He indicates
In my breast pocket
not a sign.

On the Mass Destruction of Starlings Near Fort Campbell, Kentucky

I.

Beautiful bird:

Creature of wind and trees

Maker of song

How shall I weep for thee,

How a just elegy?

Such an unjustly act

And you are gone . . .

II.

A bird, he came

I plucked away his breath

He sneezed and shook his head

and toiled and wandered on.

He wary-eyed the sun

and down the dazzled walk

Hop, Hop, the freckled bird

did spit and sputter forth:

"For I am grasped of God!"

Thoughts II

Thoughts clear as water
    bare views of heaven
Thoughts strong as wood
    bear fruits of love

Thoughts flower into music, color
    sparkle in memory's primal caverns
Thoughts sheer as steel
    bring crystal-sharp dreams of Day

Whoever thought that thought could bend
    like light in curved space?
    like lightning at night
        on a cold street
        in a shallow summer?
    like a cool breeze
        on a warm night
        in mid-October?

Whoever thought the day would come
When thought would have to fend for itself
    Against itself?
The day is here.

Vidya

Before we begin
      you reprimand me
            for my foremost promise.

My plates of steel
      you shatter
            with a tone.

Your winging song
      then lifts me
            as I fall
into your arms
      of twilight glow
            I love

I long to touch
      your feather-cloudy thoughts
      embrace
            your magic
                  feel
the moment to reveal
our passion's memory.

Your sparkling eyes,
      their dark depths draw
my dreamy vision
      subtler than night.

My life-long fall
　　　　into your heart
　　　　　　of light:
I drink my life
　　　my thirst
　　　　　is sweet
　　　　　　is all.

She

She lay in the bathing tub
Fondling her silver breasts with a cold knife
Carving the sky with her razor tongue
Spilling purple protoplasmic fishes
into the dark night sky
into the sere September

Brushing her hair with my footsteps
Baring the pool of her memory
Singing her milky enchantment
out of the morning of winter
into the fluttering silence of a kiss

Intimations of Unreality

Requiem

The sound of whistling missiles
the thud of bombs, the nuclear timpani—
They sing a Requiem for all mankind, for all of Life.

Seven ages spent on earth—
Seven races racing, fighting to the death—
Seven days of heaven, hell, free fun in the jungle—
Seven paths of peace, salvation—all denied—
The seventh day is come: Peace:
The seventh hour comes at last: "It is finished."

O Holy, Holy War,
We have sacrificed our all for thee.
Thy might is known to all,
Thy fist has crushed us all,
They bloody cross, thy nails have seared our flesh,
We have sacrificed all Life for Thee,
O Holy, Holy War.

O Sacred, Holy Death,
We have entered straightforth, unfearing, into
    thine gaping jaws,
We have crusaded long for Thee,
Slaughtering all forms of Life—thy Holy sacrifice—

Slaughtering all miserable living things,
Bringing them all into thy silent perfection.

Give us the silent sleep of Death, O God,
and do not wake us in the morning . . .

The Mere Weather Sends Transport

The mere weather sends transport—light, darkness
On a waiting room day, late August—
Shining high through the sun clouds
                    Came Evening.

Evening stayed longer than Sorrow,
Sitting up—late, unexpected—
Celia slunk away, sleepy, uncoiled
High up on the terrace, lying on her back,
Scales glistening
Lying up high on the landing, looking down, over
Hissing softly in her sleep—scaly eyelids forming over—
Staring, breathing, but no more seeing.

He stayed on longer, swearing
he'd take to camp this summer.
Pledging auditory warnings—soon, thoughtful,
"No one clears the way slowly"—
falling silent—
"No one moves in the silence,
staying over, sleepy,
No one prays until daybreak, snakes crawling over!
No one—"
                    Then he finished.

*   *   *

Evening left, Sorrow lies fallen
lashed about the skull,
raped,
blood lying under . . .
Soon not a morning
to come, breezing over—
soon, not a morning.

The Absolute Sameness of Change

1.

The absolute sameness of change—
    Egyptian tombs stand still against the sky,
    rolling clouds, tumbling earth—
The sky moves, the stone is worn away,
pierced moments of slate, blocks of time

The rhythm of your own moving speeds the way
Writes, rights, rites block the day.

Informers record you
peaking forth
your own choice
speaking words
with your voice

2.

Center of the absolute center—
    cold stone, wet with rain
    shines with the light of the morning—
Life springs from the clouds
Earth spills her abundance
And Time lies in the shadows.

*   *   *

Moving light-and-shadow's rhythm
Alignment eclipses occultation.

Stars spin through
     the dark sky.
Voicing presumptions
of self-creative meaning
     go you and I.

Lizard Life

Lizards in love we slither along the lakeside
the skyline of tourists fades into the lost background
of past realities
all we know is the slick feel of oiled leather,
sliding through the grass, scampering on the ground,
sliding against each other, scampering

Autumn basks in cool evenings but lizards love daylight—
O to lie outstretched on a bare stone in the full sun!
we sit for hours on end without moving—
simply watching, watching and breathing—
breathing, feeling the warm sun, and simply watching

Once I touched you after watching you from afar
for a thousand years
the years move slowly as I await my next opportunity
to fill the time I write lizard poems and leave them lying around
I leave them lying under tall grasses, under wild ferns,
Under open skies I leave them lying on the bare stones

But lizard music carries you away,
wafting into the dark millennium
a thousand years of cold silence, dry lizard leather in old air
abandoned like a Mayan temple at the depths of a jungle
my lizard poems etched in a forgotten tongue, inscrutable figures,

indecipherable ravings of unkempt emotion—
ignoble, usurped, and fallen

Lost then in mazes of Mayan undergrowth,
seeking the lizard lady go I
running through the open desert on bare burning leather feet
I cross mountain ranges and float over oceans on a banana leaf
all to pursue the beauty, the leather touch,
the endless hours on that stone—
All to love the lizard lady in the lazy languor of this lizard life

Alchemy

A few hours' sleep—
a season of winter—
I performed the usual alchemy.

Withdrawn like sap into the ground,
the blood refreshed within the bones;
And in each cell the silent engines move—
    pairing, repairing—
carry out their secret
    ceremony of the same.

The mind withdrawn into the brain—
the worm in its cocoon—
the usual miracle is performed
and Life moves on.

Vest

A man opens his vest.
His right arm swings across and grabs his left side.
He pulls it back and opens a hole in his chest.
You can see the gears of his inner machinery.
He closes his vest.

A man opens his vest.
He reaches across and pulls back the cloth.
His skin opens and you see
the glistening red workings of his internal organs.

He opens his vest.
You can see the spinning mathematical orb that represents the earth,
crossed with perpendicular circles.
Black lines on a white plane.
From the center of the spinning sphere
A small black dot expands to the perimeter
Then explodes, an expanding galaxy of light against the blackness.

He closes his vest.

Portal II

Beyond the windswept peaks that mark the edge
Of our horizon, very few have gone
And fewer still return to tell the tale—
But I am one.

I found myself upon a seaward cliff
To witness the vast ocean rolling forth
In languid emerald waves washed white with froth
To pound the sands of the promontory.

Another time I stood upon the walls
Of some great fortress, tumbled down by war
And by the greatest warrior, Time—
Now grown with vines.

(Such places did my eyes behold.
Far stranger than my guide foretold.)

Beyond the windswept peaks that mark the edge
Of our horizon, very few have gone
And fewer still return to tell the tale—
But I am one.

Burial Instructions

Bury me with an acorn in my pocket
that from my bowels a mighty oak shall spring:
boughs spanning earth and sky,
twigs tickling heaven,
and roots sunk in my clay.

Epitaph

Stack my skull against the wall
with all the others
Shorn of its skin
and drained of blood and brain
Another trophy for Time—
Another triumph for Humankind!

Invocation:
On the 100th Mailing of the
Esoteric Order of Dagon

One hundred quarter-laps around the sun,
Three hundred circuits of the shining moon—
This cultic worship in the name Dagon
Shall raise Him soon.

A solemn Order and a forum wise
Pays homage to the prophet Eich-Pi-El
Who temples built at Gaza and Ashdod
On the Great Sea

One hundred cycles has the rite lived on
By sacrifice, in festival, in song
In visions captured and in secrets shared
In sport, in awe

But far away, in realms of dream remote
Are fisherman who draw their nets in fear
With inborn knowledge of the hellish things
The Sea holds store

Like those who went before and follow aft'
A cyclic movement does our task complete
We cast our nets and reap strange fruit
Along the shore

One hundred quarter-laps around the sun,
Three hundred circuits of the shining moon—
This cultic worship in the name Dagon
Shall raise Him soon.

The Face of Death

Blind, I feel the face of Death
    with my fingers.

His temples are taut
    and his eyes are sunken.
His skin is waxy
    to the touch.

His cheek bones are high
    and the cheeks are shallow.
His lips are thin and the teeth
    are set in a grin.

Behind his doming brow
    is a hollow chamber
Where rules no thought
    but Death.

I met him once and then we parted ways.

There are two other things
    that I can say of him:
He is fixed in purpose,
    and his grip is firm.

Seer

Who has tread the barren wasteland—
Passed through realms of drought and heat
Pricked by nettle, torn by brier
Body broken for want of bread?

Who has crossed the distant desert—
Walking barefoot on the sand
Fed on cocklebur and dust
Thirsty for the spirit's wine?

Who has seen the mirage shining
With its promises untrue—
Pushed through every veil of illusion
Surrounded still by the unreal?

Who has glimpsed the secret flower
Growing deep within the mind—
Who has seen its lovely petals
Who has plucked the fruit of time?

Who has borne the burden of beauty
Back from realms sublime?

The Last Sonnet

The mathematician swore
that numbers could define
the patterns of a rhyme,
the metrics of all lore.

A sonnet then he wrote
And programmed it to find
All combinations blind
Recorded to the note.

"If sonnets bear a form
and words betray a count,
I'm certain to find out
The end, the means, the norm."

The sonnet then he spoke
And captured in fine lines
The formula defines
Are written as he speaks:

"The telling time has come to pass
This sonnet is the very last."

The Menace from the Woodwork

"Those ugly things from out the woodwork crawl!
 They first appeared in dreams that I abhor
 In which they gather 'round me on the floor—
 I break away and flee into the hall. . .

"They say the hideous strain came out of space,
 Descending here upon membranous wings;
 And living in our very homes, the things
 Devised a plan to route the human race!

"Know now that we must act—and do so soon!
 We must resolve to turn on them, and fight
 With all we have—with all our wits, our might—
 Or else their ghastly dreams will all come true. . ."

He wrote this poem, this plea, and disappeared;
Upon the page: a cockroach crushed and smeared.

Song for the End of Time

"And so, in time, will come the end of time."—Anon.

All that has gone before is gone.
All that is yet to come will then be gone.

There is no beyond
Beyond all bounds, the boundary
Beyond which there is no beyond—
Yea, even beyond the Boundless.

All is contained within Itself
And there is no Other.

Sloughing off its burdens, borne always
And forever, one by one,
And all at once it will all be done
A final moment and a final sound—
With no resound:
A dull thump, a sudden pop
But no musing, no association, no astonishment
Only Naught.

Planets all smashed to smithereens
And ground to dust
The suns themselves and all the mighty galaxies
Will fly apart at speeds approaching infinity—
Or else implode in no time at all!

Cosmic pinwheels roll and spin
Tops and spirals turn and turn
Mighty furnaces in the Vast
Blow out, and All is Past . . .
Silence waits at the end of time.

To Keith Allen Daniels (1956–2001)

'Twas like a comet that you rose—
    Quite overnight, as I recall—
And blazed across the empty sky
    So brightly you made shadows fall.

You wrote in "lapidary" verse
    And wrought fine phrases metalline
From ore within your foundry forged
    And set with gems—exotic words
That you from other worlds had gleaned.

You played the polymath and won—
    Endo/exo-science was your weapon;
But then against all odds, you tried—and lost,
    In a game matching wits with Satan.

To sum it up or reason why
    It takes a better mind than mine—
    It takes a better man to even try.
"So fine a mind, too young to die."

Thanks for the books you left behind!
    Creations of your Smithic mind—
With a divine eye for the sublime
    And humor in your human heart.

Hephaestus on his incus hammering
Could never mint such gold-and-diamond rings!

Absinthe

O Artemisia absinthium!
We call you the wormwood of Artemis,
The goddess of the hunt and of the moon.
Your full green promise—your bitter sorrow!

I forage in the moonlit woods alone
To find the flower with hemispheric blooms.
I crush the yellow petals and leaves of green,
Derive the *terpene thujone*—the toxic juice.

This secret, aromatic distillate
Is also found in sage and peppermint
And has been used from ancient times
To make absinthe, or wormwood wine.

Holey wood where crawls no worm,
Where wine winds its way to steal your charm;
To make a bitter liqueur with a taste
Like licorice or burnt anise.

O Artemisia absinthium!
We call you the wormwood of Artemis,
The goddess of the hunt and of the moon.
Your full green promise—your bitter sorrow!

The Dead Priest

He died at midnight on New Year's Eve
At the start of the new millennium.
The ambiguity could not be ignored.

I found him dead,
Twisted and withered
Life gone out
Now looking hollow.

He died as he lived:
In silence
Facing death
Facing eternity.

The body's burden
Borne no more
The body burned
On a pyre by the shore.

The ashes scattered
Upon the sea
Still I hear—words of wisdom
Still I see—eyes of fire.

His final sermon
"You Must Die To Be Reborn"
Sounded confusion
Among those gathered:

"The start of time, the end of time—
Ideas beyond thinking.
"The start of life, the end of life—
Mysteries beyond knowing.

"The place of thought,

The role of breath;
The sermon of sound,

The secret of death—
The teacher's teaching.

"If the dead priest's final words
Escape the funeral pyre,
Who will hear them?"

Into The Beyond

Life loses its grip but Death holds firm
Pulls you over to the other side

He collects the fragments of your life
And files it under "Finished"

He gathers your dust into his lungs,
Breathes your last breath as you expire
And coddles your limbs with morbid desire

Enwrapped in rapture and with vicious glee,
He chews your bones and spits the gristle,
Devours your heart—and when he is done,
He snorts and sends your soul into the beyond.

Stripped to the Bone

I was born naked into the bright light,
Hung upside-down by the ankles and whipped by my caregiver
Until I choked and cried with open eyes—
"I am stripped to the bone."

I sat before the television for years,
Eyes bared to the scenes of horror and ceremony
Until I cried with anguish and ripped off my clothes—
"I am stripped to the bone."

I worked for twenty years with eyes glued to the tube,
Bathed in cathode rays, awash with 1s and 0s,
With dollar signs dangled before my burning eyes—
"I am stripped to the bone."

I read the Buddha, turned my face to the wall,
Listened to the silence—until I heard the beating heart
And the mind ran screaming, clinging to a silver thread—
"I am stripped to the bone."

With empty eyes I beheld our leaders lie without disguise
Leading by misleading, marching millions into the fire
Until I beheld the nature of the furnace and its function—
"I am stripped to the bone."

With heart and brain afire I decry with rage and fear and shame
The inhumanity that man has done to man and woman—in *my* name!
At last the poet himself shall fall, defeated by ignorance
and time—
"I am stripped to the bone."

  Against imagined armies and the real
  Proud soldier takes up arms and aims
  Casts caution to the wind he takes wing

"Even if you tear me limb from limb
"I shall give my life for Life—*not* Death—
"For I am stripped to the bone."

The Truth of the Ages

One day I sat enthralled
My pen and pad before me
My eyes beheld a vision
The world revealed unto me

I wrote the words in wonder
And captured the All-in-all
I saw secrets disclosed, truths unfolded
And captured it all in rhyme

I wrote in the fire of passion
by the cool, blue light of insight
with a pinch of pure charisma
to win a world of readers

The task achieved, I reveled
I set about to travel
To wander here and yonder
I left the golden pages
But soon forgot the lines

I left the pages open
I left them on the table—
The table by the window—
The window facing south

I left them there all summer
I left them there all winter
I left them as I wandered
I left them for a year

I left them in the sunlight
I left my sheets abandoned
I left the words exposed
Like an infant on a hillside

My eyes on the path before me
My feet stepping surely
My toes kicking stones
My heels landing firmly

The path down the mountain
The path to the town
The path to my doorstep
Down the hall to the study

Through the room to the window
To the table, where I found
The sun-bleached, sun-washed papers,
The truth-revealing letters
Just random dots of ink

The words of wisdom written
All perished in the light
Pigments blasted by the solar glare
Baked dry and blown off the paper

The words I had written were faded
The letters could not be read
The Truth of the Ages (I reckoned)
Was never to be told.

Nora May

I. The Promise Broken

Standing upon this headland by the sea
We watch the waves that waft eternally
And peer back to one moment in the Night
When one heartbroken soul put out the light—
Enamored of love, lovers, and the need to be—
And so deprived us of her maturity.

What stranger blossoms may yet have bloomed—
Or common ones of uncommon perfume—
What rare harvest would she reap in rime
If she did bide her time?

If her golden tresses had turned sterling grey,
What wise things might her pen still write—
What insight into the lot of man—
What vision into the depths of night—
What solemn song would she enchant us sing along
(Yea, even though we leave the common throng),
Or song of light come skipping from her tongue?
If she had only lingered on . . .

But captured here in haunted Time,
Her life a flicker in the Now—
A tragedy we seek to make sublime
With broken rime and knotted brow . . .

II. The Huntress Hunted

You pranced into the wood in doeskin wrapt,
Eyes glittering like torches in the night,
Hair wild as the underbrush and bracken
Splashed with the sun's true light.

If men could view you other than a peach,
Nor a flower in the midst of May—
Chaste and so chased, as if a thing to purchase . . .

Hounded by men high of rank and stature
Gone mad as the Hatter, the March Hare highly hopping,
Appealing mid peals of laughter, chasing after
With heavy thumping, lumbering through the ancient woods,
Your heart seeking—running deeper into thickets, leaping,
A doe there with eyes of fear, heart stopping;
Surrounded by hunters everywhere, heart breaking.

As Cupid sent a legion in his stead,
Too many arrows pierced her lonely heart.
With quivers empty, suitors staring, start:
Their prize—the doe Diana—lying dead!

III. Witness

Standing yet upon this silent hill—
Though waves crash ever on the raging sea—
We witness in the throes of her death
Birth pangs of the Overwoman, unborn still.

I Hitched My Wagon to a Shooting Star

I hitched my wagon to a shooting star
Not knowing where it might take me—
Back down to earth in a glorious crash,
Or out to space, beyond the atmosphere.

I hitched my wagon, and off the wagon sped
Across the sky at a hundred miles an hour
Not knowing if my star would leave this sphere,
Or fall and burn in a meteor shower.

My flight went off, but not without a hitch:
A wagon wheel flew off, spinning into space
Caught in orbit like a rotating station—
Spinning and orbiting, yet stationary above the earth . . .

The wagon back blew off and all my goods—
Exposed to air, to comet dust, to flame—
Became as nothing, falling back to naught,
As on and on my star-drawn wagon fled.

Beyond Beirut, beyond Bahrain—I saw the cities pass
Beneath me as my wagon flew, wheels caught in no rut,
No bounce on rugged road, no broken strut—
Still I wondered if my wagon would survive—

Carrying me out over everything, high in the sky,
Falling as if through space, strung on this stellar orb,
Eccentric orbits spun from moon dust and ore
Mined on the sun and milled on a sunny shore . . .

The flight continues through the airless air—until
The fabric of my being collides with the fabric of Being . . .
Threads go everywhere!

Intimations of Unreality

A Trip to the Hypnotist

The sign read "Dr Spiegel, Hypnotist"
And so I went into the waiting room—
Devoid of patients, not of magazines—
And sat myself upon an empty chair.

They said you could be hypnotized and see
Before your eyes the lives that you had lived
Before this life. Although I had my doubts,
I went to know if I had lived before.

When it was time, I went into a room
Half-dark, half-lit by ambient amber light.
"Just watch my pocket watch," he said to me,
And swung the gold watch on its silver chain.

The watch swung like a pendulum, and then
Became a shining, golden orb—a sun
That moved across a blackness specked with stars
That flickered, faded, fell—and dark was all . . .

"Remember when you were a little boy—
A time of peace, of lazy afternoons
Before the toils of life wrapped you in coils . . ."
And I remembered.

When I was a child,
We lived alone—a mansion in the woods,
A place remote—my great-grandfather's house.
He was an ancient man, both wise and strange
And lived among his books of ancient lore.

Some said he was a wizard, some a fool.
One day there was a visitor . . . a man
That looked like Dr Spiegel, only young.
I tried to speak, but could not find my voice.

"Now go back further, when you were a babe.
Your mother nursed you, bathed you every day.
Go further still—when you were in the womb,
Afloat in darkness . . ."

And I floated there,
Borne on the inner tide until my birth
A timeless span in sanguine twilight spent
Aware of nothing but the beating heart,
Dim songs, sharp laughter, and the wail of tears.

"Now, go back further, back before your time,
Before your father and your mother lived.
Do you recall? You were *another* then,
A man of boundless power—and a sage."

Through haze of years I gazed . . . My vision cleared.
Into a looking glass I looked and there beheld
The face of my great-grandfather, not me!
I wore his clothes, about me were his things . . .

"Relax—fear not, my son—remain with me,"
A voice that was not mine spoke from my lips.
"I have not died, but wait to live again.
Join me and we will live *for centuries* . . ."

I fled in mortal fear—fled back through time,
Through lives of ancestors of ancestors,
Lives spent in England and in France, in Spain,
In Rome, in ancient Greece, in Tyre, in Ur . . .

I was an orator, a serf, a scribe,
A chief, a warrior and an artisan.
I saw great cities rise and saw them fall
In different lives—as woman, man, and child.

Each time, I was pursued by nameless fear—
A voice that called my name within my head,
An evil thing that sought to rule my mind—
Back through the lives recorded in my genes . . .

Back to a time when I was not a man,
But some small ape that crept beneath the trees
Hid out in caves and feared the phasing moon,
That held its head and shrieked into the night!

And hounded still, I passed through countless lives:
A shrew that scampered, dodging taloned wings;
An asp that slithered on and in the earth;
A fish that foundered on the surging sea . . .

And on I went, to microscopic realms
To squirm and wriggle in a tidal pool,
Till I became again a single cell—
With which, they say, all life we know began . . .

But brewing in that sea, an evil thought
Awoke in dim beginnings of the mind
That I was not myself—but someone else—
And sent me reeling further back in time

When molecules first formed, their atoms bound
Together by electrons shared through space:
Dual orbits, like a moon that moves between
Two planets, side by side . . .

                    But then, repulsed
By some dark drive or fear, I broke away,
Went deeper still, resigned to break apart
In subatomic particles at last:
The spheres-in-spheres that spin and form this world.

What fields of being crowd and intersect
Within the tilting planes that crash, collide
Like galaxies! I saw the Milky Way
Engorged with stars; I saw our star, the Sun . . .

And so I made my way to Earth again,
Returned, and watched the world spin round and round.
It swung on a chain wound around the sun—
A silver chain that links and binds us all . . .

When I awoke, the first thing that I saw
Was Dr Spiegel's dark, horrific face—
Protruding tongue, white lips and bulging eyes.
Around his neck the silver chain was wrapped;

The pocket watch now dangled at his breast.
I fled the room—a side door to the hall—
And down the empty corridor I dashed . . .
And I was free to go—go on my way.

Acknowledgments

"A Game" and "Awakening." *The Western Front* 4:1 (Esoteric Order of Dagon APA, Roodmas 2003).

"Alchemy." *The SIGNAL* 1:2 (Emmett, Idaho: Signal Network International, 1988).

"I Ask the Fortune Teller." *Phoenix* (Knoxville: University of Tennessee, Fall and Winter 1976).

"The Face of Death" (as "Blind, I feel the Face of Death"). *The Western Front* 2:1 (Esoteric Order of Dagon APA, Lammas 2001).

"Carven Faces." *Cthulhu Codex* 11 (West Warwick, RI: Necronomicon Press, Lammas 1997).

"Cataclysm." *Yawning Vortex* 3:2 (Los Angeles: Tsathoggua Press, 1997). *The Western Front* 1:1 (Esoteric Order of Dagon APA, Roodmas 2000).

"Derrick's Ritual." *Ambrosia* 1 (Nashville, TN: [June] 1972). *Eldritch Tales* 2 (Yith Press, 1981 [unauthorized]). *Ambrosia: Twenty-Fifth Anniversary Edition* (San Francisco: Corelli Press, 1997). Revised September 1997 and published here for the first time.

"The Desolation of Falithra." *Mutatis Mutandis* 3:2 (Esoteric Order of Dagon APA, Roodmas 2006).

"Down to the Harbor." *Ambrosia* 2 (Nashville, TN: [August] 1973).

"Dusk." *The Western Front* 4:1 (Esoteric Order of Dagon APA, Roodmas 2003).

"Epitaph." *Mutatis Mutandis* 2:3 (Esoteric Order of Dagon APA, Hallowmas 2005).

"For Fear." *Etchings and Odysseys* 1 (Minneapolis, MN: MinnCon Publications, 1973). *Arkham Sampler* 3:4 (Madison, WI: Strange Co., 1986 [unauthorized]). *The Western Front* 4:2 (Esoteric Order of Dagon APA, Lammas 2003).

The Green Transfer. San Francisco, CA: Corelli Press, November 1993. 20 copies. Second edition: March 1995. 30 copies.

"Into the Beyond." *Mutatis Mutandis* 2:3 (Esoteric Order of Dagon APA, Hallowmas 2005).

"Lizard Life." *We Made Love from Full Moon to Crescent Moon. Then the Ambulance Came* (Oakland, CA: Elephant Printing, 1993).

"Lunar Liturgy" and "Poem to Polymnia." *Etchings and Odysseys* 1 (Minneapolis, MN: MinnCon Publications, 1973).

"Oblivion" and "The Portal." *The Terrorist* 2:2 (Esoteric Order of Dagon APA, Hallowmas 1998).

"Painting: Dreamscape I" received First Prize for Poetry in the 1973 Belmont College Literary Contest for Nashville High Schools and was published with other prize winners. *A Terminal Edition* 1:1 (Esoteric Order of Dagon APA, Hallowmas 1999).

"The Quest of the Brazen Flame." *Mutatis Mutandis* 1:1 (Esoteric Order of Dagon APA, Hallowmas 2004).

"Requiem" *Mutatis Mutandis* 3:1 (Esoteric Order of Dagon APA, Candlemas 2006).

"Seer." *Mutatis Mutandis* 2:3 (Esoteric Order of Dagon APA, Hallowmas 2005).

"Selene." *Mutatis Mutandis* 2:2 (Esoteric Order of Dagon APA, Roodmas 2005).

"The Shadow from Yith." *Nyctalops* 8 (2:1) (Albuquerque, NM: Silver Scarab Press, April 1973). Chapter 1 of "The Terror out of Time" round robin. Revised May–June 1998 and published in *The Yith Cycle*, ed. Robert Price (Hayward, CA: Chaosium, 2010).

"Stripped to the Bone." *Mutatis Mutandis* 2:1 (Esoteric Order of Dagon APA, Candlemas 2005).

"The Summons of Hastur." *From Beyond the Dark Gateway* 2 (Albuquerque, NM: Silver Scarab Press, [December] 1972). Revised September 1997 and published in *Crypt of Cthulhu* 107 (20:2) (Poplar Bluff, MO: Mythos Books, Eastertide 2001).

"To Keith Allen Daniels." *The Western Front* 3:1 (Esoteric Order of Dagon APA, Roodmas 2002, a Daniels memorial issue).

"The Twilight Necropolis." *The Western Front* 5:1 (Esoteric Order of Dagon APA, Lammas 2004).

"Vision." *The Western Edition* 1:1 (Esoteric Order of Dagon APA, Roodmas 1999).

"Within the Machinery of Light." *Ambrosia* 2 (Nashville, TN: [August] 1973). *Ambrosia: Twenty-Fifth Anniversary Edition* (San Francisco: Corelli Press, 1997). Revised September 1997 and published in *Al-Azif* 3 (Reading, UK: Yhtill Press, [May–June] 1998).

"The Witness's Account." *The Western Front* 1:2 (Esoteric Order of Dagon APA, Hallowmas 2000).

Thanks to Robert Price for finding this book a home and writing the introduction; to Derrick Hussey and Hippocampus Press for providing that home; and to Denis for his extraordinary artwork.

www.ingramcontent.com/pod-product-compliance
Lightning Source LLC
Chambersburg PA
CBHW060926030726
47503CB00003B/492